## THE HOT WAR

# BOMBS AWAY

## Harry Turtledove

DEL REY • NEW YORK

2016 Del Rey Mass Market Edition

Copyright © 2015 by Harry Turtledove
Excerpt from *The Hot War: Fallout* by Harry Turtledove copyright © 2016 by Harry Turtledove

Published in the United States by Del Rey, an imprint of Random House, a division of Penguin Random House LLC, New York.

DEL REY and the HOUSE colophon are registered trademarks of Penguin Random House LLC.

Originally published in hardcover in the United States by Del Rey, an imprint of Random House, a division of Penguin Random House LLC, in 2015.

This book contains an excerpt from the forthcoming book *The Hot War: Fallout* by Harry Turtledove. This excerpt has been set for this edition only and may not reflect the final content of the forthcoming edition.

ISBN 978-0-553-39072-8
ebook ISBN 978-0-553-39071-1

Cover design: David G. Stevenson
Cover illustration based on an image: © Dmitry Ezepov/Shutterstock

Printed in the United States of America

randomhousebooks.com

9 8 7 6

Del Rey mass market edition: July 2016

*This one is for Anne Groell,*
*who helped it over the hump. Thanks!*

# BOMBS AWAY

# 1

SOMEWHERE TO THE SOUTH and east lay Hungnam, the North Korean port on the Sea of Japan. Second Lieutenant Cade Curtis knew that, if he managed to get there, he could hop aboard a ship and live to give the Koreans and the Red Chinese more chances to kill him as the war ground on.

He and the platoon he led stumbled along a dirt track that he thought led in the right direction. He hoped the track led in the right direction, anyhow. The clouds scudding past low overhead were gray-brown and ugly, like the wool from a filthy sheep. With snow and sleet and hail leaking down out of that uncaring sky, he got only glimpses of them, anyhow. Somewhere beyond them shone the sun. He knew that, but he would have had a devil of a time proving it by anything he could see.

Part of him wished it would warm up. Even with a knitted wool cap under his helmet, even with winter boots and long johns and an olive-drab greatcoat, his teeth chattered like castanets. He and everybody he led might freeze to death before they got close to Hungnam.

But if it did warm up—to the point, say, where it started pouring icy rain instead of the frigid witches' brew coming down now—the dirt track would turn to a bottomless river of mud. He'd already seen the kind of mud they had here. It could suck the boots right off your feet. Moving fast in that kind of goop (sometimes, moving at all) was impossible. Tanks and halftracks bogged down. Trucks were even worse off. Men on foot had the best chance, but *best* didn't mean *good*.

Somehow, though, what made Americans sink to midthigh often seemed to trouble the Reds much less. Kim Il-sung's men, and Mao's, carried their weapons and a few magazines of ammo, maybe a knife for eating and for hand-to-hand fighting, and that was about it. They were mostly scrawny little guys, too. They didn't struggle through the mud the way so many overloaded Yankees did.

*I'm no Yankee,* Cade thought. He'd been born in Alabama and lived most of his life in Tennessee. Most of his life . . . all nineteen years. It seemed as full and as rich to him as an octogenarian's. Why not? It was all the life he had. And if he wasn't a Yankee to himself, he sure as the devil was to the enemy prowling somewhere too close.

He wished to God he were back in Tennessee. It was Thursday, 23 November 1950. In the States, it would be Thanksgiving. Turkey with all the trimmings. Friendship. Fireplaces. Here not far from the Yalu River, Cade had damn all to be thankful for.

A dead dogface lay by the side of the track, staring up at the sky with blind eyes. Blood had frozen on his face and on his belly. Maybe, sooner or later, someone would pick him up and bring him along. More likely, nobody would bother.

One of the GIs near the tail of the ragged column had managed to get a Camel going in spite of the horrible weather. He blew out a mixture of fog and tobacco smoke. After inhaling again, he said, "We'll make it back okay to Watchacallit on the coast, right, Lieutenant?"

"Oh, hell, yes, Lefty," Curtis said, hoping he sounded surer than he felt. Lefty was from Akron or Youngstown or Dayton or one of those other places in Ohio where the glow of foundries lit up the clouds from below at night. They weren't great big cities, not next to places like Detroit or Chicago or Cleveland, but people who came out of them had that same kind of up-yours-Mac attitude.

Lefty tossed away the butt. "I ain't had this much joy since we left the fuckin' reservoir, y'know?"

"Not that long ago," Cade said.

"Yeah, well, time flies when you're havin' fun, right?" Lefty fired up another cigarette with his Zippo. A beat slower than he might have, he held out the pack to Curtis. "You want one?"

"No, thanks. Never got the habit," Cade said. Combat turned a lot of guys into smokers. From what they told him, you got a little buzz and a little relaxation. And cigarettes came with your K-rations. They couldn't very well be bad for you, could they? He hadn't found out for himself yet. One of these days, maybe, but not yet.

Off in the distance, American 105s rumbled. With luck, the heavy shells would blow some Reds straight to the devil. Big guns? Armor? Airplanes? In every category like that, UN forces—Americans, mostly—had an enormous edge on the Democratic People's Republic of Korea and the People's Republic of China.

The enemy knew it as well as Cade did. You couldn't very well fight this war without knowing it. So it seemed logical that the side at a disadvantage in weaponry couldn't hope to win, and might as well throw in its hand.

But the Reds came at it from a different angle. The only way for them to put out a fire was by piling bodies on it? Okay, they'd do that. Casualties didn't worry them, any more than casualties had worried Stalin when he took on the Nazis. We need to spend a division to get rid of an American regiment? Fine. Spend it, and make sure the next division's ready to go behind the lines.

North Korean and Red Chinese losses were four, five, six times as many as those of the UN troops they faced. Their generals, and the commissars who told those generals what to do, didn't give a damn. Men were as disposable to them as bullets or boots.

The really scary thing was, they could win that way. The Reds made brave soldiers—often braver than the South Koreans whose fat the United States had pulled off the fire. They swarmed forward against machine guns, against tanks, against damn near anything. From all Cade could gather, worse things would happen to them if they hung back than whatever American shells and bullets dished out.

He and his men trudged through a little village. An old man and a girl of perhaps eight sent them impassive stares. The village looked to have been fought over two or three times in the recent past: likely, once in the American push up to the Yalu and once or twice in the retreat after Chinese troops swarmed over the river and drove the UN forces back.

Cade shook his head. He wished his beard were thicker. It might keep his face warmer, the way it seemed to with some of the older guys. Lice? He'd worry about lice some other time. Or, with DDT ready to kill off the little bastards with one squirt from the spray gun, he might not worry about them at all.

He'd just thought that maybe he'd try a cigarette after all when the Reds hit them from behind. One second, everything was quiet. The next, swarms of men in quilted khaki jackets and caps with earflaps were screaming their heads off and shooting what sounded like a million Russian-model submachine guns. The damn things were good out to only a couple of hundred yards, but inside that range they'd chop you into hamburger.

His own .30-caliber carbine was a piece of junk by comparison. It was an officer's weapon, one that fired a smaller, weaker cartridge than the good old M-1. Like an M-1, it was only semiautomatic; it didn't go full auto. At short range, even M-1s were in deep against submachine guns. The cheap, nasty little things threw lead around as if it were going out of style.

But the platoon had a light machine gun. If the Chinks didn't know it, they were about to get a surprise they wouldn't like. "Johnson! Masters! Set up in this hooch here"—Curtis pointed to a not too battered hut at the south end of the village—"and give those cocksuckers what-for!"

As soon as the LMG started banging away, the Red Chinese screamed on a different note. Cade and the other American soldiers kept plinking away at anything they saw or imagined they saw. The enemy went on pushing, probing. Without the machine gun, the Americans would have died quickly—or slowly, depending.

Cade sent most of his men down the track. If they didn't, or couldn't, get to Hungnam, they were screwed any which way. They'd have to head south through a countryside that was a lot more hostile than anyone could have imagined before things went sour.

To the soldiers at the LMG, Curtis said, "Hang on here as long as you have to."

"How long is that, Lieutenant?" Masters asked.

"Well—as long as you have to," Cade answered. *Till you make them kill you,* he meant, and they knew it. He'd never had to give an order like that before. He hoped to Christ he never would again. With his rear guard set, he went after his retreating men. Behind him, the machine gun barked death at the Chinese.

* * *

Not quite so smoothly as Harry Truman might have liked, the *Independence* touched down at Hickam Field west of Honolulu and taxied to a stop. The DC-6's four big props windmilled down to motionlessness. Truman had traded in FDR's executive airplane, the *Sacred Cow*, for this more modern one in 1947. He'd named it for his own home town. The bald eagle on the nose warned the world of America's strength.

Warm, moist, sweet-smelling air came in when they opened the door. Truman grumbled under his breath just the same. In spite of that fierce-beaked eagle, America wasn't looking any too strong right this minute. The Red Chinese had cut off something like three divisions' worth of troops between the Chosin Reservoir and Hungnam. In spite of air raids and naval gunfire and godawful casualties of their own, the Reds were chewing them up and spitting out the bloody bones.

People were calling it the worst American defeat since the Battling Bastards of Bataan went under in the dark, early days of World War II. It was a hell of a way to go into Christmas, only a week away now. And it was why Truman had come to Hawaii to confer with Douglas MacArthur. In October, MacArthur had flown to Wake Island to assure Truman Red China wouldn't interfere in the Korean War. Which would have been nice if only it had turned out to be true.

And MacArthur had also been the architect of defeat in the Philippines. Yes, he'd had help, but he'd held command there. Truman hadn't been able to stand him since well before that. MacArthur had led the troops who broke up the Bonus Army's Hooverville in Washington when the Depression was at its worst. Didn't a man have to be what they called a good German to go and do something like that?

Truman didn't care for looking up at MacArthur, either. Not looking up to, because he didn't. But looking up at. Truman was an ordinary, stocky five-nine. MacArthur stood at least six even. He seemed taller than that because of his lean build, his ramrod posture, and his high-crowned general's cap. It wasn't quite so raked as the ones the Nazi marshals had worn, but it came close.

Looking out a window in the airliner, Truman watched a Cadillac approach the *Independence*. "Your car is here, sir," an aide said.

"I never would have guessed," the President answered. The aide looked wounded. Somebody—George Kaufman?—had said satire was what closed on Saturday night. Well, sarcasm was what got a politician thrown out on his ear. Truman walked to the doorway, saying, "Sorry, Fred. I've come a long way, and I'm tired. The weather will be nicer outside. Maybe I will, too."

By the look on Fred's face, he didn't believe it. Since Truman didn't, either, he couldn't get on his flunky. The weather *was* nicer. Washington didn't have horrible winters. Honolulu didn't have winter at all. It was in the upper seventies. It never got much hotter. It never got much colder. If this wasn't paradise on earth, what would be?

The limousine took the President to Fort Kamehameha, just south and west of Hickam Field. The fort had guarded the channel that led in to Pearl Harbor. It was obsolete now, of course; the Japs had proved as much at the end of 1941. Being obsolete didn't mean it had got torn down. The military didn't work that way. No, it had gone from fort to office complex.

A spruce young first lieutenant led Truman to the meeting room where MacArthur waited. The five-star general stood and saluted. "Mr. President," he rasped. The air smelled of pipe tobacco.

"At ease," Truman told him. He knew the military ropes. He'd been an artillery captain himself in the First World War. Knowing the ropes didn't mean he felt any great affection for them. "Let's do this without ceremony, as much as we can."

"However you please, sir," MacArthur said.

They did have a big map of Korea, Japan, and Manchuria taped to the conference table. That would help. Truman stabbed a finger at the terrain between the reservoir and the port, the terrain where the American troops were in the meat grinder. "What the devil went wrong here?"

"We got caught by surprise, sir," Douglas MacArthur said. "No one expected the Chinese to swarm into North Korea in such numbers."

"There were intelligence warnings," Truman said. And there had been. MacArthur just chose not to believe them, and made Truman not believe them, either. The general was finishing up his own triumphal campaign. He'd defended the Pusan perimeter, at the southern end of the Korean peninsula. He'd landed at Inchon and got behind the North Koreans. He'd rolled them up from south to north, and he'd been on the verge of rolling them up for good . . . till the Chinese decided they didn't want the USA or an American puppet on their border. MacArthur'd guessed they would sit still for it. Not for the first time, he'd found himself mistaken.

"Intelligence warns of everything under the sun," he said now, with a not so faint sneer. "Most of what it comes up with is moonshine, not worth worrying about."

"This wasn't," Truman said brusquely. MacArthur's craggy features congealed into a scowl. The President went on, "The question now is, what can we do about it?"

"Under the current rules of engagement, sir, we can't do anything about it till too late," MacArthur said. "As long as American bombers aren't allowed to strike on the other side of the Yalu, the Chinese will be able to assemble as they please and bring fresh troops into the fight in North Korea without our disrupting their preparations in any way."

"How much good will bombing north of the river do, though?" Truman asked, holding on to his temper. North of the Yalu sat enormous, hostile Red China. Bomb Red China, and who knew what kind of excuse you were handing Joe Stalin? "Won't they hit our B-29s hard? The Superforts were world-beaters in 1945, but they haven't done so well against North Korean air defenses. The Chinese should be better yet on that score, don't you think?"

"If we use ordinary munitions, we will slow them down to some degree but we won't stop them. You're absolutely right about that, sir." MacArthur sounded amazed the President could be right about anything. That might have been Truman's imagination, but he didn't think so. His Far East commander went on, "But if we drop a few atomic bombs on cities in Manchuria, not only do we destroy their men and rail lines, we also send the message that we are sick and tired of playing around."

"The trouble with that is, if we drop A-bombs on Stalin's friends, what's to keep him from dropping them on ours?" Truman returned.

"My considered opinion, your Excellency, is that he wouldn't have the nerve," Douglas MacArthur said. "He doesn't have that many bombs. He can't—he just dropped his first last year. And he must see we can hurt him far worse than he can hurt us."

"Once the pipeline gets moving, they come pretty fast,

though. And he has a hell of a lot of men and tanks in Eastern Europe, too," the President said. "They could head west on very short notice."

MacArthur shrugged. "We can destroy swarms of them before they get into West Germany. And how sad do you think the French and British will be if we have to use a few bombs on West German territory?"

Harry Truman's chuckle was dry as a martini in the desert. "I'm sure they would wring their hands in dismay." He scratched the side of his jaw, considering. "If we'd been able to get our forces out through Hungnam, I wouldn't think of this for a minute. The atom is a dangerous genie to let out of the lamp—deadly dangerous. But now the Chinese are bragging that they really can do what Kim Il-sung had in mind— they want to drive us into the sea and turn all of Korea into a satellite."

"Yes, sir. That's exactly what they want to do," MacArthur agreed. "We'd betray our loyal allies in the south if we let them get away with it, too. The enemy has the advantage in numbers—China always will. He has the advantage in logistics, too. He's right across the river from the fighting, and we're six thousand miles away. If we insist on fighting a war with our hands tied behind our backs, what can we possibly do but lose?"

"You've got something there." Now it was Truman's turn to sound surprised. He hadn't expected arrogant MacArthur to make such good sense. In other words, he hadn't looked for the general's thoughts to march with his own so well. He'd already ordered the bomb used once, and ended a war with it. How could ordering it into action again be anything but easier?


"Come on, Linda!" Marian Staley called. "Whatever you do, don't dawdle! We've got to go to the cobbler's and then to the supermarket."

"I'm coming, Mommy," the four-year-old answered from her bedroom. "I'm just putting my coat on now."

"Okay," Marian said, knowing it might not be. Four-year-olds could dress themselves, sure, but not always reliably. And Linda didn't have all the buttons on her coat through the buttonholes they were supposed to occupy. Marian didn't fuss about it; she just fixed things. Then she asked, "Have you gone potty?"

Linda's blond curls bobbed up and down as she nodded. Her eyes were hazel like Bill's, not gray. Otherwise, she looked like her mother. "Just a little while ago," she said.

Young children's sense of time being what it was, that might mean anything or nothing. For that matter, it might be a fib. "Well, go one more time," Marian said. "We'll be away from home for a while."

A put-upon secretary might have aimed the look Linda sent her at an obnoxious boss. But Marian's flesh and blood went off to the bathroom, flushed, and came back. Marian didn't think Linda had enough deceit yet to flush when she hadn't done anything. If she was wrong, she'd find out about it.

"It's raining!" Linda started to open her own little Mickey Mouse umbrella.

"Don't do that indoors! It's bad luck!" Marian said. "Wait till we get out on the front porch."

Once they left the house, she opened her own plain navy-blue bumbershoot—much plainer than her daughter's, but able to cover both of them if it had to, and it probably would. It wasn't raining too hard. Everett, Washington, north of Seattle, had the same kind of weather as the bigger city. You could and did get rain any time of year at all, in other words, but it seldom snowed even during winter.

By what Bill's letters said, Korea wasn't like that. It was hot and dusty in the summertime, and impersonated Siberia now. He was copilot on a B-29. From things she read between the lines in his letters and from little snippets on the news, the Reds gave the big bombers a hard time. She just wanted him to finish his hitch and come home safe.

The sun-yellow Studebaker sat in the driveway. "C'mon, sweetie," Marian told Linda. They went to the car together. Marian opened the driver's-side door and held her umbrella while Linda shut hers and slithered across the seat to the passenger side. She sat up straight there. Even though her feet barely got past the front edge of the seat, she looked very grown-up.

Marian got in, too. She laid her purse on the seat between them, set the choke, and started the car. It was a postwar model, with the windshield a single sheet of glass, not two divided and held in place by a strip of chromed metal. She liked that. She liked the automatic transmission, too. She could drive a stick—who couldn't?—but she didn't believe in working any harder than you had to.

Keeping her eye on the rear-view mirror to watch for kids on bikes or silly dogs or grownups who weren't paying attention, she backed out into the street. The cobbler's was only a few blocks away.

The shop window had a shoe and a cobbler's small hammer painted on it, and a legend: FAYVL TABAKMAN—COBBLER. REPAIRS & RESOLING. Under the shoe was another legend in smaller letters from an alphabet Marian couldn't read. She supposed it said the same thing in Yiddish, but it might have been Russian or Armenian or Greek for all she could prove.

Inside, the shop smelled of the cheap cigars Tabakman smoked. One was in his mouth. He was about fifty, skinny, with a graying mustache. He wore a cloth cap and short sleeves. A number was tattooed on his arm. He knew more about horror than most people who lived in America.

What he knew, though, he didn't peddle. He just touched the brim of his old-fashioned cap and said, "Good morning, Mrs. Staley. Hello, little girl." He had an accent, but not a thick one. If he'd learned English since the war, he'd done a bang-up job.

"My name is Linda!" Linda said.

"Hello, Linda," Tabakman said gravely. "I had a little girl about your age."

"You *had* one?" Linda caught the past tense. "What happened? Did you lose her?"

"Yes. I lost her." Behind gold-rimmed glasses, the cobbler's eyes were a million miles and a million years away. With an effort, he came back to the here-and-now. "Both pairs you left are ready to take home, Mrs. Staley. If you want to see them . . ."

"I'm sure they're great," Marian said. He showed them to her anyway. He did fine, neat work; you could hardly see where the half-sole ended and the older leather picked up. Both pairs together came to seventy-five cents. She gave him a dollar and waved away the change.

"You are very kind," he murmured, touching his cap again. "Have a happy New Year, both of you."

Marian only shrugged. She knew the tip wouldn't blot out the memories Linda had stirred up. It was what she could do, though, so she did it.

The wide aisles and abundant food at the supermarket made her smile. Riding in the welded-wire shopping cart made Linda smile. The prices ... The prices made Marian wish she were on a military base. But Bill had been a bookkeeper for Boeing till the new war sucked him back into uniform. They'd bought the house with the idea that they'd keep it for a long time. Trying to do that on military pay wasn't easy, but Marian had made it work so far.

She bought ground chuck instead of ground round, margarine instead of butter, and pot roast instead of steak. If it came to beef hearts and chicken giblets and lots of macaroni and cheese, then it did, that was all. She'd eaten that kind of stuff as a little girl during the Depression. She could do it again if she had to. So far, she hadn't had to.

She splurged a little—a whole nickel—on a Hershey bar for Linda. After a moment fighting temptation, she lost and spent another nickel on one for herself, too. When she spread her bread with something that tasted like motor oil, she could look back on the chocolate and smile.

When they got home, she took Linda inside first with a stern, "Now you stay here till I finish bringing in the groceries, okay?"

"Yes, Mommy," Linda said. If she messed that one up, her Teddy bear spent the night on a high shelf and she had to sleep without it. That had happened only a couple of weeks earlier, so the tragic memory was still fresh.

Marian hated carrying shopping bags in the rain. The miserable things turned to library paste and fell apart as soon as water touched them. Chasing escaped cans down the driveway wasn't her idea of fun.

She got everything into the house. Linda didn't feel the urge to play explorer—maybe the rain outside held her back. Whatever the reason, Marian put the groceries away and then let out the sigh of relief she always saved for when she'd done the things she had to do.

*A cup of Lipton's would be nice now,* she thought. She could watch whatever happened to be on the one channel the new TV in the front room got. As long as she let it grab hold of her eyes, she wouldn't worry—so much—about how Bill was doing over there on the far side of the Pacific.

Before she could even start boiling water, Linda carried in a copy of *Tootle* and said, "Read to me."

Bill always called those the magic words. Whatever he was

doing, he'd stop and read when she asked. He went through books like popcorn himself, and wanted a kid who'd do the same thing. Marian wasn't quite so dedicated, but she was pretty good—not least because she didn't want Linda squealing on her when Bill got home.

"Let me fix some tea first, okay?" she said. "Then I will."

"Okay!" Linda said.


The Ivans were giving the *Wehrmacht* hell on the Eastern Front again. Gustav Hozzel cowered in his trench. He knew too well that that wouldn't save his sorry ass. Three different T-34/85s were bearing down on the weakly held German lines in eastern Poland. An antipanzer round had just hit one of them—and glanced off the monster's cleverly sloped armor.

Lances of fires in the air. Screams as the *Katyushas* rained down on the German earthworks. Sweet suffering Jesus, there'd be nothing left of the company after those fuckers blew.

Screams . . .

Gustav Hozzel's eyes opened wide, wider, widest. All he saw was blackness. He was sure he was dead . . . till he spied a thin strip of moonlight that slid between two misaligned slats on the Venetian blinds covering the bedroom window.

Luisa set a soft hand on his shuddering shoulder. "You did it again, *Liebchen*," his wife said sadly.

"I . . . I guess I did." Gustav's voice was hoarse. When you screamed yourself awake, and your wife with you, no wonder you tried to talk through a raw throat afterwards. Little by little, his heart slowed from its panicked thundering. "I'm sorry," he managed.

"Was it the same dream?" Luisa asked.

"It's always the same dream. The panzers, the rockets . . ." Gustav shuddered. That dream, and the death it held, seemed more real, more true, than his waking life. He'd never told that to his wife. It would only have scared her—and who could blame her for being scared? He took what comfort he could from saying, "It doesn't come as often as it used to. I haven't had it for a couple of months now."

Luisa nodded; Gustav felt the motion rather than seeing it. "That's good," she said. "Please God, in a while years will go by between one time and the next."

"Please God," Gustav agreed. He'd fought the Russians from late 1942 to the end of the war. When the collapse finally came, he'd fled west out of Bohemia and managed to surrender to the Amis. If the Red Army'd grabbed him, he would still be in one of Stalin's prison camps—unless they'd decided a bullet in the back of the neck was easier than dealing with him.

Here he was in Fulda, safe in the American zone even if it did lie close to the part of Germany Russia still held. Except when he shrieked himself awake in the middle of the night, he was an ordinary printer with an ordinary clerk for a wife. Yes, he had a wound badge and a marksman's badge and the ribbon for the Iron Cross Second Class and the medal for the Iron Cross First Class in a drawer under his socks. But he hadn't taken them out and looked at them more than twice in the past five years. And it wasn't as if most other German men in their late twenties and early thirties didn't have their own little collections of medals.

"Do you think you can go back to sleep this time?" Luisa asked.

"I don't know. I'll try. What time is it, anyhow?"

The alarm clock ticking by Luisa's side of the bed had glowing hands. She rolled over to look at it. "Half past two," she said.

*"Der Herr Gott im Himmel!"* To Gustav, that was about the worst time there was. Everything in him was at low ebb—except his fear. He sighed. "The only good news is, I don't remember the last time I had those nightmares twice in one night."

"Fine. So sleep." Luisa's yawn said she intended to try again, too, even if getting jerked awake like that had to be as horrible for her as it was for him.

Sleep Gustav did. The alarm clock woke him at a quarter to seven. It didn't seem nearly so bad—or so loud—as the explosions inside his head. He ate black bread and jam and drank a big cup of coffee almost white with milk. Then he put on a hat and his beat-up tweed jacket and headed for work.

His breath smoked when he left the block of flats. It was cold out there—what else, at the end of the first week of January?—but not a patch on what he'd known in Russia and Poland. And he could come in from this cold whenever he wanted, and no one would shoot him if he did. It was still dark, too—darker than it had been before, in fact, because the moon was down.

Fulda had come to life even in the long winter night. The noises of carpentry rose from the *Dom.* An American air raid had damaged the cathedral six or eight months before the end of the war. The same raid had smashed the square that housed the vegetable market. One day before too long, though, and you'd look things over and have no idea that bombers had ever struck here. So many German cities got hit far harder than Fulda. A town of only 40,000 or so, it couldn't have been an important target. Bit by bit, those ravaged places were getting back on their feet, too.

They were in the zones the Americans and British and even the French held, at any rate. But something like a third of Germany had gone straight from Hitler to Stalin: a bad bargain if ever there was one. Reconstruction on the other side of the Iron Curtain moved slowly when it moved at all. The Russians were more interested in what they could pry out of their new subjects than in giving them a helping hand.

A jeep with two American soldiers in it rolled past Gustav and east toward the border with the Russian zone. The German veteran kept his head down and glanced at it only out of the corner of his eye. He'd fought the Ivans his whole time in the *Wehrmacht,* but that didn't mean he loved the Amis. If they hadn't decided Stalin made a better ally than Hitler did, the world would look different today.

Another jeep passed him a minute or two later. This one sported an American heavy machine gun on a post fixed to the floorboards. Those damn things could kill you out to a couple of kilometers. U.S. fighter planes also carried them. He'd got strafed by an American fighter the day before he surrendered. He didn't remember it fondly, but it hadn't given him wake-up-screaming nightmares.

He opened the door to the print shop. Max Bachman, who owned the place, looked up from some proofs he was reading. "Morning, Gustav. *Was ist los?*"

"Not much." Gustav didn't talk about his nighttime horrors with anyone. He wouldn't have talked about them with Luisa if they hadn't jolted her awake, too. For all he knew, Bachman also had them. He'd been a *Frontschwein* himself. If he did, though, he didn't let on, either. But then Gustav held up a forefinger. "I take that back. Are the Americans jumpy about the border? Two jeeps went by me heading that way."

"I haven't heard anything special, but I wouldn't be surprised if they are," Bachman answered. "If Stalin decides to start something, all the Russian panzers in the world'll charge west through the Fulda Gap."

Gustav grunted and lit a cigarette. With the Deutschmark a going concern, you could smoke your cigarettes again. They weren't currency any more, the way they had been in the first couple of years after the war.

The ritual of tapping the cigarette and striking a match gave him a few seconds to think. Max wasn't wrong. Gustav knew it. The Amis had to know it, too. The broad, flat valley of the river that ran by Fulda was the best panzer country along the Russian zone's western frontier. Once through it, the T-34s—and whatever new models Stalin had up his sleeve—could swarm straight toward the Rhine.

"I wonder whether they'd want us to lend a hand if the Reds do come," Gustav said in musing tones, blowing a smoke ring up at the low ceiling. "Some of us still remember what to do."

"Think so, eh?" Bachman said with a dry chuckle. "Well, maybe we do. And I'll tell you this—they might not have wanted to play with Adolf, but they won't mind the rest of us dying for our country . . . and theirs. When the Russians come, you grab everybody you can." Gustav nodded. Again, his boss wasn't wrong.

KONSTANTIN MOROZOV SLID A ruble across the bar. "Another," he said in Russian.

"*Da,*" the bartender said, and gave him a fresh mug of beer. The man in the apron was a German, but he understood enough Russian to get by. Damn near every Fritz in Meiningen did. With a couple of Soviet tank armies stationed near the border with the American zone, bartenders and shopkeepers and waiters and whores needed to know the occupiers' language if they were going to get money out of them.

For that matter, Morozov could have asked for his refill in German. He'd never be fluent, but he could manage. Unless he had to, though, he preferred not to. He'd been a tankman since 1944. He'd joined the Red Army just before Operation Bagration, the great attack that drove the Nazis out of the Soviet Union. He'd seen what they'd done to the *rodina,* the motherland. And he'd paid them back, with as much interest as he could add, in the grinding drive west that ended in Berlin the following spring. German still felt dirty in his mouth.

He'd been a private starting out, of course, a seventeen-year-old kid slamming shells into the breech of a T-34/85's cannon. New fish always started as loaders; the job didn't take much in the way of brains. If you showed you had something on the ball—and if you lived, naturally—you could go on to bigger and better things.

He'd had four (or was it five?) tanks killed out from under him. A puckered scar on his left calf showed where a German machine-gun bullet bit him when he was bailing out from one of them. Burn scars mostly hidden by the right sleeve of his khaki tunic reminded him he hadn't got out of another soon enough. That had hurt like a mad bastard—and burning human flesh smelled too much like a pork roast forgotten in a hot oven.

But he was still here. That put him ahead of the game right there. So many of the men who'd fought alongside him were dead, some in graves, some not. And the Nazis had murdered civilians for fun, or so it seemed. He'd heard officers arguing about whether the Great Patriotic War cost the USSR twenty or thirty million deaths. Both numbers were too enormous to mean much to him. Twenty or thirty deaths? A tragedy. Multiply by a million? A statistic, nothing more.

He eyed the bartender. The fellow was about thirty-five. He had a scar of his own, on his forehead. Chances were he hadn't picked it up playing tiddlywinks. "What did you do during the war?" Morozov asked him in Russian.

"I'm sorry. I don't understand," the Fritz answered. And maybe that was true, and maybe it was horseshit. Maybe he just didn't want to admit to whatever it was.

Well, too damn bad if he didn't. Konstantin asked the same question in German. If he didn't like the answer he got, he'd knock the bastard into the middle of next week. It was possible for a Red Army senior sergeant to get in trouble for roughing up a German. It was possible, yeah, but it sure wasn't easy.

But the bartender said, "Oh! During the *war*!"—so maybe that was what he hadn't got. "I fought in the Low Countries and France. Then I went to North Africa. I got this there." Konstantin thought he was going to touch that scar, but he did more. He popped his right eye out of its socket. It lay in the palm of his hand—it was glass.

"It's a good match for the one you kept." Morozov meant that. He hadn't noticed it was artificial. It had to be German work. Russian glass eyes looked like, well, glass eyes. The tankman gestured. "Put it back. You aren't so pretty without it."

*"Sie haben Recht,"* the German agreed gravely. Back went the eye. He blinked a couple of times to settle it in place. Now that Konstantin knew, he could tell the eye was false. But he never would have thought so had the Fritz not shown him.

He downed the beer. He'd drunk enough to feel it, not enough to get tipsy. After the daily combat ration of a hundred grams of vodka, beer seemed like water going down the hatch. It did taste nice, though; he had to give it that. Good vodka didn't taste like anything much. Bad vodka reminded him of an accident with a chemistry set.

Drinking beer, you had to work to get smashed. It was easy with vodka. The whole point to drinking vodka was getting smashed. Maybe the point to drinking beer was drinking without getting smashed. If so, it was a point too subtle for Konstantin to fathom.

He drained the mug, tipped the barkeep, and went back to the toilets. They were cleaner than they would have been in a Russian dive, but not a lot cleaner. The ammonia reek of stale piss stung his nose.

After leaving the tavern, he walked back to the tent city outside of town. It was cold. Some snow lay on the ground. He'd known plenty worse, though. The Red Army didn't worry about the weather. Whatever it happened to be, you did what your commanders told you.

Now, instead of loading in a T-34, he commanded a T-54. He wished the Red Army'd had these during the last war. They would have made the Hitlerites roll over onto their backs and show their bellies in jig time. Thick armor, that elegant turtle-shell dome of a turret, a 100mm gun that would have smashed up every Tiger or Panther ever made . . .

Someone waved to him. He came to attention—it was Captain Oleg Gurevich, the company commander. "What do you need, Comrade Captain?" he asked.

"Is your tank ready for action, Sergeant?" Gurevich demanded.

"I serve the Soviet Union, sir!" Morozov said, which was never the wrong answer. "The tank is ready to roll as soon as we climb aboard." That wasn't quite true, but it came close enough. They wouldn't move forward right this minute. Konstantin didn't think they would, anyhow. "But what's gone wrong now?"

"It's the stinking Americans," Gurevich said. He was even younger than Konstantin. He'd come into the Red Army after the war ended. He didn't remember, or care to remember, that the Americans had been allies against Hitler. Konstantin did, though he didn't say so—admitting such things wasn't just dangerous, it was suicidal. The officer went on, "It's looking more and more as though they think they'll have to use atomic weapons to stop the advance of the victorious Chinese People's Liberation Army. In his wisdom, Comrade

Stalin has decided that the Soviet Union will not sit idly by while the imperialists assail a fraternal socialist state."

One of the signs Gurevich was still wet behind the ears was that he could bring out propaganda slogans as if they were part of his ordinary language. He hadn't seen enough of the real world to know that slogans were like the old newspaper you wrapped around *makhorka* to roll yourself a cigarette. They held things together, but they weren't why you smoked. The tobacco was.

"If the Americans use atomic bombs, we will, too?" Morozov asked, a sinking feeling in the pit of his stomach. He didn't know much about them. But from everything he'd heard, the best way to live through one was not to be there when it went off.

"We will take whatever steps the wise Comrade Stalin decides we have to take," Captain Gurevich replied, so he didn't know, either. Chances were no one did, except the longtime leader of the Soviet Union.

Something else occurred to Morozov: "If our tanks head west and go over the border, will the Americans drop one of these bombs on us? Or more than one?" *One will be all it takes,* he thought unhappily.

"We will not go forward alone if we get the order to liberate the American zone," Gurevich said. "The Red Air Force will move with us, and will give us the air support we need."

"I serve the Soviet Union!" Konstantin said once more. That was more polite than *You've got to be out of your goddamn mind, sir,* even if, here, it meant the same thing. By the way Captain Gurevich turned red, he understood the words behind the words. That could be good. Maybe he wasn't a total dope after all.

An Air Force base was like a little bit of the Midwest plopped down in whatever foreign country happened to hold it. First Lieutenant Bill Staley had been born and raised in Nebraska before moving to Washington state. He knew the Midwest when he ran into it, even if he ran into it in South Korea near the port of Pusan.

Scrambled eggs. Fried eggs. Bacon. Coffee with cream and sugar. Hash browns. Toast with butter and jam. Ham sandwiches. Peanut butter and jelly sandwiches. Fried chicken.

Steak. Baked potatoes. Canned string beans. Canned peas. Apple pie. Canned fruit salad.

Movies. Touch football in the snow. If there was barbed wire around the perimeter, if guards with grease guns kept North Korean infiltrators from getting too close, you didn't have to think about that. You also didn't have to remember that your aunt Susie would have hanged herself for shame at the miserable mattresses on the cots in the barracks.

The one un-Midwestern thing about the base that you couldn't ignore was the B-29s. Without them, after all, the base wouldn't have been there to begin with.

They were also too damn big to ignore, sitting there like a herd of four-engined dinosaurs at the end of the snow-dappled runway. The trouble was, they were like dinosaurs in more than just size. In a world of quick, nimble biting mammals, the hulking brutes got more obsolete by the day.

They'd flattened Japan. They'd had the Japs on their knees even before the A-bombs that cooked Hiroshima and Nagasaki ended the Second World War. But what the generals who gave orders in Korea hadn't understood was that Japan was already staggering even before the B-29s zoomed in to finish the job.

Day bombing raids against air defenses that hadn't been smashed? Against guns and planes and radar tougher and more modern than any the Japs had had? Those didn't work so well. The American commanders took longer than they should have to figure that out. A lot of four-engined dinosaurs and a lot of good aircrews got lost teaching them the lesson.

Bill thanked heaven he hadn't gone down in flames or had to hit the silk over North Korea. Night missions gave the Superforts the chance to come back and try again. Even with fighter escorts, though, they were no piece of cake. He assumed Russian pilots flew the enemy's night fighters. The North Koreans were brave, but they didn't have the sophisticated training that kind of mission took.

When the Russians got in trouble, they scooted back across the Yalu into Red China. American planes weren't allowed to follow them. The Russian pilots had a sanctuary on the other side of the river. Chinese troops? Same story.

No wonder they were kicking our tails in North Korea. Letting them have free rein till they crossed the Yalu made no military sense. None. Zero. Zip. You didn't have to be General of the Army Douglas MacArthur to see that. It was as clear as clear could be to First Lieutenant Bill Staley, and to any American private on the ground up there—any the Chinks hadn't killed or captured, anyhow.

So far, Harry Truman had said it made political sense. The President hadn't wanted to get the United States into a big Asian war. Bill Staley could see that, too. The logistics of a war like that would have to get a lot better to reach merely terrible.

But not getting into a big Asian land war didn't mean losing the smaller Asian land war the USA was already in. Or it had damn well better not, anyway. The horrible things the Chinese had done to the American ground forces up near the Yalu—and to the British and other UN troops that fought at their side—made losing the war and the peninsula seem much too possible.

By all the signs, losing the smaller war wasn't going to happen, not if Truman had anything to say about it. Just that morning, a convoy from Pusan had entered the air base. Columns of trucks bringing in food and fuel and ordnance came in all the time. Bill hardly even noticed them.

This one was . . . different. Trucks full of chicken pieces or crates of .50-caliber ammo, tanker trucks full of avgas, were usually escorted by nothing more than halftracks or jeeps. This convoy was only three or four trucks long. It had halftracks riding shotgun fore and aft, sure, and clearing a path through the snow. And it had four top-of-the-line Pershing tanks in front of the trucks and four more behind.

Whatever that convoy was bringing in, the people who'd sent it wanted to keep it safe till it got where it was going. Those people sure as hell knew how to get what they wanted, too.

Bill Staley suspected he knew what the trucks were carrying. He wasn't sure. He could easily have been wrong. He kept telling himself how easily he could be wrong. He hoped like anything he was.

Two days later, Brigadier General Matt Harrison, the base commander, summoned all the B-29 crews to a meeting. Some of the men—even some of the officers who sat in the pilot's and copilot's chairs—wondered out loud what was going on. Maybe they hadn't seen the convoy coming in, though even a dead man should have had trouble missing it. Maybe they just had trouble adding two and two. Bill didn't, and not just because he was a bookkeeper in the civilian world. He was pretty sure he knew why Harrison had called the meeting, no matter how he wished he didn't. Ignorance really would have been bliss.

Harrison was in his late forties. Among the ribbons on his chest was one for the Distinguished Service Cross. The only higher decoration was the Medal of Honor. He'd done something special in the last war.

He whapped the lectern he stood behind with a pointer. It wasn't quite a judge using his gavel, but it came close enough. Harrison drew all eyes to himself.

"Some of you will be wondering what came into the base the other day," he said. "Well, I'll tell you. Our A-bombs now have pits. We can use them. If the President gives the order, we will use them."

A few of the men—the clueless ones—exclaimed in surprise. Bill Staley only sighed and nodded; that was what he'd expected. The pit looked like an hourglass outline in steel. It had radioactives where the sand would have run from one side of the glass to the other. The bombardier manually inserted it into the bulky casing of an atomic bomb while the bomber was on its way to the target. Without it, the bomb wouldn't vaporize a city. With it in place, hell could literally come forth on earth.

"The Chinese and Russians may think they're safe on the other side of the Yalu," Harrison went on. "They have been, but they aren't any more. Or they won't be after the President gives the word. They think they can get away with slaughtering our troops and shooting down our planes and hiding where we won't go after them. We haven't yet, but that doesn't mean we won't or we can't. When the order comes, we'll show them as much." He looked out at the bomber crews. "If anyone has qualms of conscience, he may withdraw now. No black marks will go into his service record if he does, I promise."

That was bullshit. Everyone knew it, promise or no. The Air Force would neither forgive nor forget a withdrawal now. Several flyers left, anyhow, including a pilot and a copilot. Bill Staley sat where he was. The Red Chinese were killing too many of his countrymen. Whatever he could do to stop them, he would. He didn't care what kind of weapon he used. It wasn't as if they were fussy about such things.

By Harrison's scowl, he hadn't expected anyone to walk

out. "All right," he said. "The rest of us will go on. We are going to interdict the Chinese and the Russians at a much deeper level than they're looking for. Once that's done, we'll finish cleaning up the Korean peninsula." He looked out at them again. "Any questions, gentlemen?"

"What happens if Stalin starts using atomic bombs, too, sir?" a major asked.

"He'll be sorry," Harrison replied. The flyers bayed laughter. He went on, "Anything else?" No one spoke. He nodded. "We'll get ready, then."

Boris Gribkov eased the Tu-4's yoke forward. The heavy bomber's nose came down, just a little. *Easy does it,* the pilot thought as he gave the plane a hair less throttle. You couldn't fly this thing with your dick, the way you could—the way you were supposed to—in a fighter. Well, you *could* do that, but you'd splatter the plane, and yourself, all over the countryside if you tried.

The Americans said there were bold pilots and old pilots, but no old bold pilots. Gribkov had no use for the Americans. He wouldn't have been landing his Tu-4 here at Provideniya if he'd liked them. Like them or not, what they said there was true.

And, like them or not, they built some goddamn impressive airplanes. Behind his oxygen mask, Boris' lips skinned back from his teeth in a mirthless grin. He knew exactly how impressive some American planes were. For all practical purposes, he was flying one.

During the USA's war against Japan, several damaged B-29s made emergency landings near Vladivostok. Till the very end, the USSR and Japan stayed neutral; Stalin had plenty on his plate fighting the Nazis. He interned the crews (after a while, he quietly gave them back to the Americans) and kept the bombers.

Russia had nothing like them, which was putting it mildly. Russian World War II heavy bombers were leftovers from the early 1930s, slow and lumbering and useless in modern combat. Stalin ordered exact copies of the B-29. He ordered them and, because his word was law in the Soviet Union, the Tupolev design bureau gave them to him in less than two years.

This machine had Russian engines. It had Russian cannons instead of American heavy machine guns. Everything else came straight from the Superfortress. Gribkov had heard that more than a few Russian engineers, used to the metric system, had driven themselves squirrely learning to work with inches and feet and pounds and ounces.

Lights marked the edge of the snowy runway outside the little town on the edge of the Bering Sea. Gribkov couldn't see the frozen sea. Provideniya sat less than a hundred kilometers south of the Arctic Circle. Winter daylight was brief at best. The sun had set long before, even if it was only late afternoon.

"Cleared to land, Plane Four," the ground-control chief said.

"Message received. Thank you," Gribkov answered. No one mentioned what kind of plane he was flying. Alaska lay just over the horizon. You had to figure the Americans were listening to everything they could pick up. The less they knew, the better for the Soviet Union.

He glanced over to his copilot. Vladimir Zorin nodded back. "All fine here, Comrade Captain," he said, gesturing to his side of the complicated instrument panel.

"Good." Boris lowered the landing gear. The hydraulics worked smoothly. On most Soviet planes, you had to do the job with a hand crank. More could go wrong with this system, but he took advantage of it just the same.

The Tu-4 was the only Soviet bomber with a nosewheel. A few new jet fighters also had them. If you'd started out keeping your nose up and using your tailwheel, the way Gribkov and every pilot trained during the Great Patriotic War had, doing things this way took some getting used to.

There. They were down—more smoothly than he'd expected. He gently tapped the brakes. The Tu-4 needed a lot of room to stop any which way. He didn't want to send it skidding by slowing down too quickly on this slick airstrip.

"Nicely done, Comrade Captain," Zorin said.

*"Spasibo,"* Boris answered. Zorin had landed the Tu-4 himself. He knew it wasn't easy. A compliment from him meant more than one from someone with no understanding of how things worked would have.

A groundcrew man bundled up like an Eskimo waved red and green lanterns to guide the bomber off the runway. Not having his nose elevated because of a tailwheel made seeing where he was going easier. The revetment to which the man led him was made from snow rather than dirt. After he killed the engine, he patted the arm of his leather flying jacket and said, "I'm glad we have this stuff. Usually, we start toasting as soon as we're on the ground, but not today."

"No, not today," Zorin agreed. "What do you suppose it is out there? Twenty below?"

"Something like that." Gribkov tried to turn Celsius to Fahrenheit in his head. With so many funny measurements going into the Tu-4, funny temperatures seemed fitting, too. The only trouble was, he had no idea how to make the conversion.

Alexander Lavrov crawled back from the bombardier's station in the glassed-in nose of the plane. "Welcome to the end of the world," he said as he, the pilot, and the copilot climbed down the ladder and their boots crunched on snow.

"This may not quite be the end of the world, Sasha," Zorin said, "but you can sure see it from here."

"In more ways than one," Boris agreed. They were all silent for a moment after that. None of the B-29s that landed in the USSR had been modified to carry an A-bomb. The Americans had figured out how to do that later. Soviet engineers had had to work out the details for themselves. They'd done it, too.

The rest of the crew also left the plane. Counting the radioman, the navigator, the radar operator, and the gunners, the Tu-4 carried eleven. "Come on, folks," called the ground-crew noncom with the lantern. "Let's get you somewhere a little warmer." He led them toward one of the huts near the runway.

Meanwhile, other soldiers spread white cloth over the bomber to make it hard to spot from the air. Russians had always taken *maskirovka* seriously. What an enemy couldn't see, he couldn't wreck.

That hut wasn't much warmer than the wintry air outside. It was out of the wind, though; that wind seemed to blow, and probably did blow, straight down from the North Pole. A couple of kerosene lamps gave what light there was. Boris wondered whether Provideniya had electricity at all.

But a samovar bubbled in a corner of the room. Once he got outside of some hot sugared tea, the pilot felt better about the world. Some jam-filled blini sat on a table by the samovar. They weren't terrific blini, but they were better than the iron rations the crew had downed on the way east. Gribkov assumed there had to be vodka somewhere on the base; there was vodka somewhere all over the Soviet Union. There wasn't any in that hut.

A middle-aged man came in. He was too heavily decked out in winter gear to let Boris read his rank, but the pilot wasn't surprised when he said, "Welcome, men. I am Colonel Doyarenko. This is my base." He had the accent to go with his Ukrainian name.

"Thank you, Comrade Colonel. This is . . . quite a place, isn't it?" Gribkov did his best to stay polite.

"It's the Soviet Union's asshole, is what it is," Doyarenko answered, which was only too true. He went on, "But it's also about as close to the United States as this country comes. I don't mean Alaska—I mean the *real* United States. We can strike part of it with some hope of coming back to the *rodina* again. From most of our air bases, attack missions are strictly one-way."

Gribkov licked his lips. "I hope it doesn't come to that, sir." He wondered how many crews sent on such a one-way mission actually would drop their bomb at the end of it. He didn't ask the base commandant his opinion. Ask a question like that and the MGB would start asking questions of you. They wouldn't care whether you felt like answering, either.

Colonel Doyarenko shrugged. "I hope it doesn't, too. Only somebody who's never seen a war is stupid enough to want one. But I serve the Soviet Union. If the imperialists strike at our Chinese allies, we have to show them they can't intimidate us. Isn't that right?"

"Yes, Comrade Colonel," Boris said. You might not want a war, but once you were in one you were all in. If Hitler had taught the Russian people anything, he'd taught them that.

*I, a stranger and afraid / In a world I never made.* Cade Curtis was absolutely, one hundred percent certain A. E. Housman had never been on the run from the Red Chinese in wintertime North Korea. Housman, if he remembered straight, had had a comfortable career teaching classics in English universities and writing poetry on the side. No other eleven words, though, could have better summed up how Cade felt now.

He was filthy. He was scrawny. He'd grown a scraggly, rusty beard. He was cold. He wasn't so cold as he might have been, though. He wore a Chinese quilted jacket under his GI parka. He had some excellent felt boots that fit over his American winter footgear. He'd tied more quilting around his trousers. The enemy soldiers who'd furnished those supplies would never need them again.

He'd taken all the food they had, too. He only wished they'd had more. He'd stolen whatever he could find in wrecked villages. But he wasn't the first scavenger who'd gone through them. No place in North Korea had much worth stealing left in it.

He kept working his way south as best he could, moving by night and hiding during the day. For all he could prove, he was the only American left alive and free north of the thirty-eighth parallel. He probably wasn't. Other stubborn, resourceful souls had to be doing the same thing he was, singly and in small groups. But he hadn't seen another white man since the Chinese overran his platoon as they were overrunning the whole overconfident American force up by the Yalu.

He chuckled harshly as he waited in a hillside cave for darkness to fall. No matter how bad things were, you could always imagine them worse. The next white man he saw might speak Russian, not English.

A squad of Chinese soldiers with Soviet submachine guns tramped through the valley below. They weren't hunting him, not in particular. They were just patrolling. With so much snow on the ground, he couldn't help leaving tracks. But those felt boots did more than keep his tootsies from freezing. They made his footprints look the same as the Chinks'. The waffle-sole pattern on his American shoes would have betrayed him in nothing flat.

He had a Soviet submachine gun himself. It was as least as good a weapon as his M-1 carbine, no matter how much uglier it might be. Again, the Chinese who'd lost it wasn't worrying about it any more. Cade could use it without worrying that the unfamiliar report would give him away.

But the submachine gun was for emergencies only. He also had a long bayonet he'd taken from a dead Tommy's Lee-Enfield. It had had blood on it then. He'd blooded it several times since he got it. It made no noise at all. If you were careful, neither did the people you stuck with it.

Cade yawned. He wondered how far south he'd have to get before he found UN troops. If the Chinese and North Koreans had driven their foes back to the Pusan perimeter again and collapsed it this time . . . Well, in that case he was completely screwed, so he saw no point in worrying about it. Instead, he rolled over and fell asleep.

He remembered what a tough time he'd had on maneuvers in basic when he had to curl up on the ground in a sleeping bag. He didn't have that kind of trouble now. He didn't have a sleeping bag, either. Just him and the ground, as if he were a stray dog. He was stray, all right, strayer than dogs ever got. And he fell asleep instantly. He didn't bother turning around three times first.

When he woke, it was so dark he had to look hard to find the mouth of the cave. Stars blazed down from a black, black sky. Something way off to the east was blazing, too. A house? A barn? A tank? He had no way of knowing. He hoped an American air raid had blown a bunch of Red Chinese to hell, but hope was all he could do. The fire didn't matter enough to make him go find what it was about.

His watch's luminous dial told him it was half past ten. The Army timepiece was Zippo-tough. He'd banged it around like nobody's business, but it kept ticking. The moon was getting close to last quarter. It would rise soon. When it did, he'd start moving.

Not many people would be out and about in the dead of night. You had to be crazy to travel then, crazy or desperate. He figured he qualified on both counts.

He scooped up snow and ate a few mouthfuls. Each one turned to a small swallow of cold water. He would have killed for coffee, or even the tea he was more likely to find here.

Maybe he wouldn't have to. If he was where he thought he was, and if he remembered his maps right—two good-sized ifs—there ought to be a village not too far south of here. If it hadn't been too badly picked over, he might find some tea.

He moved slowly, warily, sliding from one moonshadow to the next. Anyone who glimpsed him might have imagined he was an owl gliding from perch to perch. A low rumble made him dive for cover. As it got louder, he realized it had nothing to do with him. It came from the air, not the ground. It was a formation of B-29s, flying north by night to drop some hell on the enemy's heads.

"Luck, guys," he whispered. The sounds of English startled him. He hadn't said anything at all for a few days. Making noise, especially a kind of noise the locals didn't make, had to be the quickest way to get yourself killed.

He found the village about three in the morning. He really was where he thought he was—or this was a different village. Different or not, it was good-sized: on the way to being a town. It wouldn't make townhood now. It must have changed hands three or four times. The buildings were chewed-up ruins. The carcass of a Pershing tank sat in the village square. Open hatches were more likely to mean the Koreans or Chinese had cleaned out the tank than that the crew had pulled off a getaway.

Guessing the houses near the square would have been looted first and hardest, Cade went to the ones on the southern outskirts. Damned if he didn't find some tea. He'd chew it if he couldn't brew it the ordinary way. Hidden under the floor of the house next to the one with the tea in it, he also found a sack of rice cakes, a sack of sun-dried plums, and a jug of kimchi.

He started to leave that behind. The fiery pickled cabbage had such a stink, the enemy wouldn't need a bloodhound to track him if he ate it. But, he decided, so what? What would he smell like? A Korean. They gobbled the shit every chance they got. Most Americans turned up their noses at it. Cade didn't turn up his nose at anything even vaguely foodlike, not any more. He'd eaten slugs and snails. He might have let a cockroach go, but he also might not.

Food in hand, submachine gun slung on his back, he started south out of the village, happier with himself than he'd been in a while. He'd find somewhere to lie up during the day, and then he'd go on. . . .

Someone behind him coughed.

He whirled, knowing it would do no good. The food fell in the snow. The jug of kimchi didn't even break, not that it mattered. Three Koreans or Chinese, widely separated, had the drop on him. He was history, nothing else but.

Understanding he was history, he didn't make a useless grab for his PPSh. He crossed himself instead, and gabbled out a quick *"Ave Maria, gratia plena—"* If you were done in this world, might as well worry about the next.

The Koreans stood as if carved from stone. Then they crossed themselves, too. One of them came out with his own Hail Mary. His Latin sounded odd to Cade, but Cicero wouldn't have followed either one of them. The Koreans ran up and clasped his hands. Little bits of Latin were the only language they had in common with him. They managed to tell him Kim Il-sung persecuted Christians of all creeds even worse than Stalin did. Any Christian they found was a friend of theirs.

Dizzily—but not too dizzily to pick up the victuals he'd dropped—he followed them out of the smashed village and off toward wherever they lived. Till that moment, he'd been fighting a rearguard action against death, slowing it down, holding it off. Now he began to think he really might live after all. Like an orchid pushing up through snow, hope flowered past despair.

**3**

GRUNTING AS HE SHIFTED the weight, Aaron Finch got the washing machine moving on the dolly. "Plenty of room," Jim Summers said between puffs on a Camel. He'd earned the chance to play sidewalk superintendent—he'd just loaded the matching dryer into the back of the Blue Front truck.

"Okay," Aaron said. He grunted again when the washer started up the ramp. He wasn't a big man—five-nine, maybe a hundred fifty pounds. But he had the kind of whipcord strength that came from working with your hands and your back your whole life long. He'd be fifty on his next birthday. He couldn't believe it. His hair was still black, even if it had drawn back at the temples to give him a widow's peak. But his craggy face had the lines and wrinkles you'd expect from anyone who'd spent a lot of time in the sun and the open air. At least he wasn't shivering now, though he wore no jacket over his Blue Front shirt. It was in the mid-seventies in the middle of January. You couldn't beat Southern California for weather, no way, nohow.

The dolly with the washer bumped once more when it bounced down off the wooden ramp and into the bed of the truck. Aaron paused a moment to settle his glasses more firmly on his formidable nose. Without them, he couldn't see more than a foot past its tip.

To his disgust, that had kept him out of the army. He'd tried to volunteer right after Pearl Harbor, but they wouldn't take him. He was too nearsighted and too old (he'd turned forty less than a week before the attack). So he'd joined the merchant marine instead. He'd been on the Murmansk run, in the Mediterranean, and in the South Pacific. He'd done more dangerous things than a lot of soldiers, but he wasn't eligible for any of the postwar benefits. That disgusted him, too.

He wrestled the washer into place by the dryer. It was one of the new, enclosed models. He and his wife still had a wringer machine. One of these days . . . He'd been married three years now. He'd got into middle age as a firm believer in why-buy-a-cow-when-milk-is-cheap. But after the war he'd come down to Glendale to stay with his brother, Marvin, for a while. He'd met Ruth there and fallen, hook, line, and sinker. They'd run off to Vegas to tie the knot. And now they rented a house in Glendale themselves. Leon was eighteen months old, and looked just like his old man.

"You gone to sleep in there?" Jim called.

"Keep your shirt on," Aaron answered without heat. He draped a tarp over the washing machine to keep it from getting dinged and secured the cover with masking tape. He laid the dolly flat and walked down the ramp to the warehouse floor. He lit a cigarette of his own—a Chesterfield. He thought Camels were too harsh, especially when you went through a couple of packs a day the way he did.

Jim Summers got the ramp out of the way. He was a redneck from Arkansas or Alabama or somewhere like that. He had a red face to go with his neck, and an unstylish brown mustache. He was four or five inches taller than Aaron, and outweighed him by sixty or seventy pounds. But he was soft; his belly hung over the belt that held up his dungarees. In a brawl, Aaron figured he could hold his own.

Summers didn't like Negroes, and said so at any excuse or none. He didn't like Jews, either. He knew Herschel Weissman, the guy who ran Blue Front, was Jewish. He bellyached about it every now and then. He had no idea Aaron was. Jim Summers didn't come equipped with a hell of a lot of ideas. Aaron Finch's name didn't look Jewish, even if his face did, so Summers didn't worry about it.

Aaron chuckled as he blew out smoke. His father had turned Fink into its English equivalent when he came to America. His dad's brothers hadn't, so Aaron had Fink cousins. His old man had figured Finch was easier to carry. From some of the things Aaron had seen, his old man had figured pretty straight.

"Where we gotta take these fuckers?" Jim asked.

"Pasadena, I think." Aaron reached for the clipboard with the order form. He nodded. "Pasadena—that's right."

"Not too far," Summers said, and it wasn't. Pasadena lay only a few miles east of the Glendale warehouse. They were two of the older, larger suburbs north of Los Angeles. In sly tones, Jim went on, "If we take it easy, we can stretch the delivery out so as we knock off as soon as we get back from it."

"We'll see." Aaron had grown up believing you always worked as hard as you could: it was the only proper thing to do. How were you going to get ahead if you didn't work hard all the time?

He stepped on the cigarette butt, then climbed into the truck with Summers. He shook his head once or twice. How were you going to get ahead even if you did work hard all the time? He and Jim earned the same pay for doing the same job. Jim was as lazy as he could get away with. If that was fair . . .

Well, a lot of things in life weren't fair. You couldn't bump up against fifty without seeing as much. Some of Aaron's relatives—and some of Ruth's, too—had become Reds, or damn close, anyway, on account of it. Aaron had voted Democratic since the early 1920s, and he was proud of the Teamsters' Union card in his wallet. He left it there, though.

With the world as tense as it was, you could get into big trouble for admitting you liked the Russians. As Jim piloted the truck out of the Blue Front warehouse, Aaron asked him, "Hear any news since this morning?"

"Heard the Sacramento Solons hired Joe Gordon to manage 'em and play second base," Summers answered. "He was goddamn good in the big leagues. I bet he'll tear up the PCL."

"I wouldn't be surprised." Aaron was a fan, too, but he hadn't been looking for baseball news. He tried again: "Anything about what's going on in Korea?"

"Not much. Far as I can make out, the Chinks are still goin' great guns, the fuckin' bastards. We oughta blow 'em into the middle o' next week, teach 'em they gotta be crazy to mess with white men."

"Stalin's a white man," Aaron said dryly, "and he's on their side."

"Screw him, too," Summers said. "He wants to take us on, he'll be sorry."

"No doubt about it," Aaron agreed. "What scares me is how sorry *we'll* end up being. He's got the bomb, too, remember."

Joe Summers offered a suggestion about where Stalin could put the bomb. Aaron thought it was too big around to fit there, even if the boss Red greased it the way Jim said he should. He let the subject drop. You did better talking politics with Jim than you did if you talked with your dog, but not a whole lot.

They drove east on Colorado Boulevard, then south on Hill Street past the California Institute of Technology. Jim Summers' comment on that was, "Buncha Hebes with hair they forgot to comb playin' with slide rules." He wouldn't have known what to do with a slide rule if it slid up and bit him in the leg. Aaron didn't know much himself, but he'd picked up some when he got promoted to acting assistant engineer on one of the Liberty ships he'd crewed.

The house that got the washer and dryer was of white-painted stucco with a red Spanish tile roof. Aaron was smoother than Jim at hooking up the water and gas connections, so he did that. He showed the housewife both machines were in good working order. "You have any trouble, you just call us," he told her. "The number's on the carbon for your form there."

"Thank you very much," she said, and tipped each of them a dollar. Aaron didn't like taking money for doing what he was supposed to do, but Jim pocketed his single with the air of a man who wouldn't have minded a fin. Declining after that would have been awkward, so Aaron kept quiet. One look at the size of the house and at the furniture told him the lady wasn't giving them anything she couldn't afford.

They brought the big blue truck back to the warehouse a few minutes before five-thirty. Herschel Weissman nodded to them and said, "Go on home, boys. I'll clock you out at the bottom of the hour."

"Obliged," Jim told him. And he'd resent being obliged, too. His mental circuits would have trouble with the notion of a Jew being generous, and that would make him angry.

"Thanks, boss," Aaron added. When they were by themselves, they sometimes talked to each other in Yiddish. Aaron would do that with Ruth, too—but, with her as with Weissman, never when anyone who spoke only English was around.

You didn't want to show American Americans you remembered old-country ways at all.

He went out and got into his elderly gray Nash. The rented house on Irving was only a few blocks away. Aaron smiled as he lit another Chesterfield. He wondered what little Leon had been up to today.


Bill Staley parked his behind on a metal folding chair. The seat felt like what it was: steel painted Air Force blue-gray. The chairs must have been ordered by the carload lot, on a contract that put cheapness ahead of everything else—certainly a long way ahead of comfort.

He had the bad feeling he knew what was coming. General Harrison wasn't the sort to call all his aircrews together unless he had some urgent reason to do so. Urgent reasons did keep offering themselves, dammit. The Red Chinese went right on pushing forward. They spent men in gruesome heaps for every mile they advanced. The next sign they gave that that bothered them would be the first.

An American commander who used, and used up, his troops like that would have been court-martialed. He would have won himself a newspaper nickname like "Butcher" before the brass landed on him, too. Bill figured even a Russian general in the last big war would have thought twice before he expended soldiers as if they were cartridges. The Chinese had men to burn, and burned them.

General Harrison thwacked his lectern with a pointer, the way he had to open the last big meeting. "Gentlemen, I have important news," he said as soon as the officers and noncoms quieted. "President Truman has authorized the use of atomic bombs against the Chinese inside China. He has not directly ordered us to use them, but he has given General MacArthur permission to send out such strikes if, in his view, the situation on the ground can be improved in no other way."

Sighs, whistles, and soft hisses floated up from the aircrews. Just like everyone else, Bill Staley knew what that meant. The only word for the present situation on the ground was fubar. The Red Chinese were in Seoul. North Korea's flag flew above the city, or what was left of it, but the men who'd taken it didn't belong to Kim Il-sung. They got their marching orders from Mao Tse-tung.

If they hadn't done such horrible things to the UN forces

after they swarmed across the Yalu . . . If they hadn't, maybe some kind of stalemate would have developed. Stalemate wasn't the smashing victory Douglas MacArthur had looked for, but it beat hell out of the fiasco he'd got.

Bombing on this side of the Yalu hadn't kept the Chinese from flooding down into Korea. No ordinary weapons had. But the United States had extraordinary weapons, and it had decided that repairing things here was important enough to be worth using them.

"So . . . What we wait for now is the command from General MacArthur," Matt Harrison said. "I don't know when that will come, but I don't think we'll have to wait very long."

Bill didn't think they'd have to wait long, either. MacArthur's military reputation had been on a roller-coaster ride the past few months. He'd looked like a genius after the Inchon landing. That had retaken Seoul and forced the North Koreans to pull back out of the south to keep from getting cut off by the forces suddenly in their rear. He'd planned on wiping Kim Il-sung's army—and maybe Kim Il-sung's country—off the map right after that.

But he hadn't planned on the Chinese incursion when the forces he led neared the Yalu. He hadn't planned on it, and he hadn't been able to stop it. Only stragglers had escaped from the army in the north. Resupplying by air just prolonged the agony, as it had for the Germans trapped in Stalingrad. And the German cargo planes hadn't needed to worry about jet fighters tearing into them.

So if he was going to put Humpty-Dumpty together again, he'd have to break some Chinese eggs instead. Which was fine if nobody could retaliate. Japan hadn't been able to when fire fell on Hiroshima and Nagasaki. Mao didn't have any atomic bombs. But Stalin did.

Whether he'd use them or not . . . was something everybody would find out. Maybe the show of force would overawe him. Maybe he would think Mao had gone in over his head and deserved what he got. Or maybe the world would find itself in the middle of a new big war when not all the scabs from the old big war had fallen off the wounds.

Brigadier General Harrison rapped the lectern one more time. "Something else you need to know, gentlemen," he said. "Aerial reconnaissance shows that the Russians are moving fighters and bombers onto airstrips in southeastern

Siberia, and in Manchuria as well. They are getting ready for trouble, and we are the trouble they're getting ready for."

"Great," muttered a man sitting behind Bill Staley. That was about what he was thinking himself. By World War II standards, the B-29 was indeed the Superfortress. But World War II was over, even if its maladies lingered on. It was 1951. The state of the art had advanced.

In 1917, the Sopwith Camel had been a world-beating fighter. Run it up against a Messerschmitt 109 and it wouldn't last long. For that matter, a Messerschmitt's life expectancy against an F-86 would be just as brief.

Bill wished he didn't think that way. A lot of guys simply did what they were told and didn't worry about anything past the mission. His mind jumped here and there, every which way, like a frog on a hot sidewalk.

He wasn't the only one. A flyer stuck up his hand and asked, "Sir, what happens if they try and bomb this air base before we move?"

"Then they involve themselves directly in the fighting and have to take the consequences of that," Harrison replied. Everybody knew most of the enemy MiG-15s that harassed American pilots had Russians in the cockpit. But those were unofficial Russians, as it were. You couldn't stay unofficial when you dropped bombs on somebody's head ... could you? Harrison went on, "We do fly a day-and-night combat air patrol, and we have radar sweeping the sky. We won't make it easy for them."

Something occurred to Bill. He raised his hand. General Harrison aimed the tip of the pointer at him. He said, "Sir, their heavy bombers will be Bulls, right?" *Bull* was the NATO reporting name for the Tu-4. "If they paint some of them to look like B-29s, will our fighter jockeys up there recognize them soon enough to shoot them down?"

The base commander opened his mouth. Then he closed it without saying anything. A few seconds later, he tried again: "That's a ... better question than I wish it were. With luck, IFF will alert us that they're wolves in sheep's clothing. But, if they look like our planes, we may take them at face value." His expression looked like that of a man halfway through eating a lemon. "You've given me something new to lose sleep over. Thanks a bunch."

A major who wore the ribbons for the Distinguished Flying Cross and the Air Medal with two oak-leaf clusters came up to Bill as the gathering broke up. "Good job," he said. "That's exactly the kind of thing the Russians are liable to do. They take camouflage seriously. They don't just play games with it, the way we do half the time."

"You sound like somebody who knows what he's talking about, sir," Bill said.

"Too right, I do. We flew back-and-forth missions a few times, from England to Russia and then the other way. I was on one of them, piloting a B-24. Man, you wouldn't believe what all they'd do to make an airstrip disappear. We didn't fly many of those, though. The Reds were nervous about 'em. Partly for what we'd see of theirs, I guess, and partly because they didn't want their people meeting us. Russians are scared to death of foreigners."

"I bet I would be, too, if I had Germans on my border," Bill said.

"Yeah, they're good neighbors, aren't they?" The major rolled his eyes. "No wonder Stalin wanted satellites between him and the krauts. But now he's got us on his border, and he doesn't go for that, either."

"And we have the bomb," Bill said.

"We sure do. So does Stalin." The major grimaced. "Ain't life grand?"


"Time, gentlemen, please!" Daisy Baxter had run the Owl and Unicorn since her husband's tank stopped a *Panzerfaust* in the closing days of World War II. Tom's picture still hung behind the bar. In it, he looked young and eager and brave, ready to do whatever it took to get rid of the Nazis once and for all. He'd never get any older now.

*And I'll never get any younger,* Daisy thought discontentedly. She'd been only twenty-two when she got the telegram from the Ministry of War. Hard to believe that would be six years ago in a couple of months. Not at all hard to believe she was getting close to thirty. As tired as the pub could make her, some nights she felt close to fifty.

"*Time,* gentlemen!" she said again. Would a male publican have to repeat himself four or five times a week to get noticed or believed? She didn't think so. Tom hadn't needed to, nor had his father before him. But they were gone and she was here, so she did what she needed to do.

Grumbling, her customers drank up, paid up, and filed—

sometimes lurched—out into the chilly night. Most of them wore the RAF's slaty blue or the slightly darker uniforms of the U.S. Air Force. If not for the air base at Sculthorpe, three or four miles west of Fakenham, she didn't think she would have been able to keep the Owl and Unicorn going. Fakenham was only a small town; there weren't many big towns in northern Norfolk. But the men who flew planes for his Majesty and their Yankee counterparts did like to take the edge off whenever they got the chance. The way they drank, they could have kept someone a good deal less thrifty than she was comfortably in the black.

Closing time meant her customers had to go. It didn't mean her day was done—nowhere near. She had to clean off the bar and the tables. She had to empty the ashtrays. Why was it that so many people who drank hard smoked hard, too? She'd never got the habit herself. She thought it was nasty, in fact. Nasty or not, with so many puffing away in there, she might have been smoking a packet a day. And nothing was more disgusting than the stink of stale tobacco ashes.

Once she got rid of those and the rest of the rubbish, she washed and dried the pint mugs and the smaller glasses that held stronger brew. The Americans said a British pint was bigger than one of theirs—not that they complained about the difference when they were pouring down her best bitter. But it bothered her. Shouldn't a measure with the same name on both sides of the Atlantic also be the same size?

She was low on potato crisps. She'd have to get more before she opened tomorrow. Potatoes, thank heaven, weren't rationed. Too many things still were, all these years after the war ended. England might have been one of the winners, but she'd beggared herself in the process. France was better off these days, and France had packed it in straightaway. From things Daisy heard, even the western part of Germany was better off. That seemed bitterly unfair.

Not that she could do anything about it, regardless of whether the damned Germans ate caviar for breakfast and beefsteak for supper every day. By the way the airmen talked, the bloody Germans were liable to get theirs pretty soon.

By the way the airmen talked, the whole world was liable to get its pretty soon. And even a place like Fakenham, far from any big city, could get its along with the rest of the world. The Nazis hadn't bothered it; the only industry in town worth mentioning was printing.

But Fakenham lay much too close to Sculthorpe. Some of the planes that flew out of the base there were B-29s: bombers that could carry a deadly payload all the way to Russia. Daisy had no idea whether the Russians knew that. If they did, though, they would want to find ways to keep it from happening. She was no general, but she could see that.

Daisy yawned. What she couldn't see right this minute was straight. She'd either fall asleep here, next to the gleaming glassware, or she'd go upstairs to the flat over the pub and do it somewhere a little more comfortable. Upstairs won, though the weary trudge felt a lot longer than it really was.

The sun had risen when she sat bolt upright in bed, but it was much too early. "Bloody hell!" she said, even if no one was there to hear her swear. "I forgot to clean the stinking toilets!"

They would be stinking, too. Beer made men piss more and aim less. She didn't think anybody'd puked the night before—no one had complained about it. The job would be bad enough anyhow. She could see why she'd forgotten about it. It was nothing anybody would want to remember.

Which didn't mean she wouldn't have to do it, even before she brewed her first cuppa and grilled a bloater for breakfast. Those were part of today's business. The toilets still belonged to yesterday's, so they came first.

Sighing, she went downstairs and into that dark, smelly little room to do what wanted doing. The toilets were an afterthought in the pub, put in when indoor plumbing came to Fakenham some time late in Queen Victoria's reign. It would have been Tom's granddad or great-granddad who added them, and he cost himself no more space than he could help. When things were busy, as they had been last night, that made crowding and messes worse.

Afterwards, Daisy wished she could scrub her hands with steel wool. Washing them like Lady Macbeth was the next best thing. She did that every night after cleaning the toilets. Because she did, her hands were red and rough all the time in spite of the creams and lotions she rubbed in.

No matter how tired she got, she was still on the chipper side of thirty. She sometimes dreamt that, in spite of rough, red hands, an American pilot would sweep her off her feet and take her back across the Atlantic to Wyoming or Arkansas or Nevada or one of those other states with a romantic-sounding name. She was sure she'd be happier in some town there than she was in out-on-its-feet Fakenham.

The flyers chatted her up. They would have loved to take her to bed for the fun of it. Going to bed with a man *was* fun; she remembered that only too well. You stayed warm afterwards much better than you did with a flannel nightgown and a pile of blankets and a hot-water bottle on your feet.

But if you went to bed with men for the fun of it, word got around. And they said *women* gossiped! Plenty of flyers would want to sleep with that kind of woman. Not a one of them, though, would want to take her back to the United States when his tour here finished.

And so she smiled behind the bar as she worked the tap. She made pleasant conversation. She swatted hands away when she carried pints to tables. If she had to, she spilled things on people too stupid to get the message any other way.

She slept by herself, in a flannel nightgown, under a pile of blankets, with a hot-water bottle on her feet. If, one night or another when she wasn't too exhausted, her hand sometimes slipped under the nightgown and took care of certain needs, she was the only one who knew that. By now, she'd got over feeling guilty about it, or even very embarrassed. It was just something she did. Under the clothes, people were animals. She slept better on nights when she scratched that particular itch.

She did tonight, even though she was tired. But bombers flying low overhead woke her before sunup all the same. When those engines thundered just above the housetops, a body would have had trouble staying dead, much less asleep.

"Daft buggers," Daisy muttered through a yawn. They weren't supposed to land or take off right above Fakenham. The American colonel in charge of the planes at Sculthorpe made noises about how he wanted his men to be good neighbors.

Good neighbors didn't shake people out of bed at whatever heathen hour this was. Of course, good neighbors also didn't fly thousands of miles across the North Sea and Europe to deliver incandescent hell on people they judged to be not such good neighbors. And those not-such-good neighbors didn't pay return visits. Daisy hoped like blazes they didn't, anyhow. She yawned again and tried to go back to sleep.

* * *

Ihor Shevchenko's *valenki* made the snow crunch as he walked across the field. A hooded crow hopping along looking for mice or whatever else it could get cocked its head to one side and studied him, trying to figure out whether he was dangerous. He was a good twenty meters away and not heading straight toward it, so it decided he wasn't.

Which only proved the crow was dumb. When he was a kid, he would have killed it and proudly carried it home for his mother to cook. He'd eaten crow often enough during the famine years, and been glad every time. He'd eaten anything he could get in those days, and thanked the God in Whom he wasn't supposed to believe any more at every swallow.

Stalin had wanted to purge the Ukraine of prosperous peasants, and to collectivize the rest. As usual, Stalin had got what he wanted. If a few million people starved to give it to him, he lost not a minute of sleep over that.

No wonder so many Ukrainians greeted the Germans with bread and salt when they invaded. Ihor had been fifteen then. He hadn't celebrated when Hitler's men drove out Stalin's; he'd already learned wariness. But he hadn't been sorry, either.

Not at first. It didn't take long to see, though, that the Nazis made an even worse set of masters than the commissars. Ihor at fifteen had watched. Ihor at sixteen had slipped away to join one of the partisan bands operating west of Kiev.

There were bands, and then there were bands. Not all the men in the Ukraine thought Hitler was a worse bargain than Stalin. Some wanted to break away from Russia come hell or high water, and tried to use the Germans as their tools, never seeing that the Germans were actually using them. Some saw and didn't care. They could rob and plunder, settle scores and murder Jews, and they were happy enough doing that.

Even now, going on six years after the end of the Great Patriotic War, a few bands who'd followed nationalist Stepan Bandera still skulked across the countryside. Ihor kept his eye out for more than crows. He hadn't seen any Banderists for a while, but you still heard stories.

These days, they had to know there would be no free Ukraine. As soon as the front started moving west again, that had become clear. But they had also known the secret police would kill them, so there wasn't much point to giving up.

When the front came through here at the end of 1943, Ihor stopped being a partisan and joined—or was dragooned into—the Red Army. He ended the war a sergeant, laid up with a leg wound outside of Breslau. They'd done a good job fixing him up. He hardly limped at all.

He counted himself lucky that they'd let him come back to his *kolkhoz* after they mustered him out of the army. Plenty of men paid the price for seeing Europe west of Russia by going into the gulag instead. Maybe he had an innocent face. Maybe the Chekists had already filled their daily quota by the time they got to him. Who the hell knew?

He could have been messing with a tractor engine or putting up barbed-wire fencing or doing any number of other socially useful things. Nobody would use a tractor for six weeks or two months. Fences could wait. Everything on the *kolkhoz* except his and Anya's little garden plot could wait. He didn't see any benefit from most of the work, so he did as little as he could get away with. It wasn't as if he were the only one.

He stumped along. After a while, he lit a *papiros*. His breath didn't smoke much more when he exhaled than it had before. He wasn't going anywhere in particular: just away from the other *kolkhozniks* for a while. Except for his wife, he wouldn't shed a tear if they all went and hanged themselves. Well, it wasn't as if they'd miss him if he lay down in the snow out here and died.

He drew on the *papiros* again. One thing he'd seen in Europe was that most countries' machine-made cigarettes were like roll-your-owns: they were all tobacco. Russians mostly preferred a short stretch at the end of a long, useless paper holder. For the life of him, Ihor couldn't see why.

A distant rumble made his head come up. He might have heard it sooner if he hadn't had the earflaps of his army cap pulled down. When he did notice it, his gut twisted in fear too well remembered. "Fuck me in the mouth if those aren't tank engines," he said, even if no one was anywhere near close enough to hear him.

Those were diesels: Soviet tank engines. The Fritzes' panzers burned gasoline, and sounded different. None of those still in business, but yes, the fear remained. You could still find coal-scuttle helmets around here, and *Gott mit Uns* belt buckles, and cartridges and shell cases. You could find shells that hadn't gone off, too, buried in the ground but working their way up frost by frost. And if you messed with them, you could still blow your stupid head off.

The rumble got louder. Ihor spotted the black exhaust plumes in the distance. Plenty of Red Army tank crews had died because the Germans could do the same thing. The Germans had made better soldiers than his own countrymen. Ihor knew that. But when you took on somebody with three times your manpower and far more resources, *better* didn't mean *good enough.*

Here came the tanks. Some were dark green; others had whitewash slapped on over their paint. All were dusted with snow. They kicked up white clouds as they rattled west. About half were T-34/85s: the workhorses of the last war. The rest were T-54s, with a curved turtleback turret and a bigger, more powerful gun. They all looked as if they were going somewhere important, and wasting no time doing it.

Looks, of course, could be deceiving. The commander in the lead tank rode head and shoulders out of the turret, so he could see more. Good commanders did that even in battle. It was one reason you went through a lot of good tank commanders.

This fellow spied Ihor. His tank swerved toward the *kolkhoznik.* The rest of the big, growling machines followed. Ihor could have done without the honor, not that he had a choice.

"Hey, you!" the tank commander shouted as his machine slowed to a stop. "Yeah, you! Who else would I be talking to?"

Ihor thought about playing dumb. If he answered in broad Ukrainian, he might convince the tank commander he knew no Russian. But the bastard might decide that made him a Banderist and have the gunner give him a machine-gun burst. The risk wasn't worth it. "Waddaya want?" Ihor would never speak *good* Russian, but his stint in the Red Army had sure beaten bad Russian into him.

"Where's the nearest railhead?" the soldier asked. "Fuck my mother if the map I've got is worth shit."

If he'd said *Fuck* your *mother,* Ihor would have sent him in the wrong direction. As things were, he pointed west and said, "That way—four or five kilometers."

"Thanks," the tanker told him. "I didn't want to break

radio silence to ask the brass. They wouldn't like that, know what I mean?"

"Oh, yeah," Ihor said in a way that showed he'd done his bit. Because he'd done the commander a good turn, he asked, "Why are you guys on the move, anyhow?"

"Whole Kiev Military District is on the move," the man answered, not without pride. "The imperialists are stirring up trouble against the peace-loving socialist nations. We've got to be ready to show them they can't get away with that crap, right?"

"Uh, right," Ihor said. No other reply seemed possible.

"So—" With a wave, the tank commander got his monster moving. The rest followed. Ihor coughed. The stinking diesel exhaust was fouler than the cheapest, nastiest *makhorka* you could smoke.

The whole Kiev Military District? That was a couple of Guards Tank Armies, some of the best troops the Soviet Union owned. Ihor's shiver had nothing to do with the snow on the ground.

**4**

*THIS IS THE WAY* *the world ends / Not with a bang but a whimper.* Bill Staley remembered being impressed with "The Hollow Men" when he first ran into it. Amazing that the fellow who wrote black verse like that and "The Waste Land" could also turn out silly poems about cats. There you were, though.

And there T. S. Eliot was, in London. As far as Bill knew, he was alive and well and still writing poetry. *Good for him,* the copilot thought, hurrying toward the big tent where General Harrison was in the habit of addressing his aircrews.

Eliot was alive and well for the moment, anyhow. If he was in London, how long he would stay that way might be anybody's guess. "The Hollow Men" was a hell of a piece of poetry—no two ways about it. But Eliot hadn't got everything in it right. By all the signs, the world was getting ready to go out with a whole bunch of bangs.

Other Air Force men were also heading for the tent. Bill didn't like the looks on their faces. They had the air of people heading for the doctor's office expecting to hear bad news. He wouldn't have been surprised if his own mug bore the same apprehensive expression.

He ducked inside. There was a seat next to Major Hank McCutcheon, who piloted the B-29 where Bill had the right-hand seat. McCutcheon took a Hershey bar out of his pocket and disposed of it in two bites. "The condemned man ate a hearty meal," he said.

"We can do whatever they tell us to do," Bill said, hoping he didn't sound too much like a man whistling past the graveyard.

Maybe he did, because McCutcheon answered, "We can, yeah. But I hope like hell they don't tell us to do it."

"Christ! Who doesn't?" Like a lot of Americans stationed in the Far East, Bill had visited the ruins of Hiroshima. If you flew in a B-29, a plane that might drop an atomic bomb, weren't you obligated to take a look at what you did for a living? Bill thought so. Even after five years, even with the Japs rebuilding across the vast field of rubble, what the bomb had done was enough to scare the crap out of anyone in his right mind. It had finally made Japan realize she was facing something she couldn't fight back against.

Of course, what the Red Chinese were doing farther north on this peninsula was plenty to scare the crap out of anyone in his right mind, too. Damn few soldiers or leathernecks had made it back to Hungnam. The new troops flowing into Korea were trying to keep the enemy from overrunning the peninsula again, not to conquer it up to the Yalu themselves. They weren't having all that much luck. The Reds weren't in artillery range of the air base yet, but it wasn't impossible that they could be one day before too long.

And atomic weapons might not knock Red China out of the war. Stalin had them, too. He could hit Europe with them, and with his own hordes of soldiers. With his knockoff of the B-29, he might reach America, too. Who had the will, the stamina, to go on after catching a few like that on the chin? There was the question, all right.

Instead of a candy bar, Bill pulled a pack of cigarettes from his breast pocket. He'd just got one going when Brigadier General Harrison strode to the lectern. Harrison carried a pointer in his right hand. He walked as stiffly as if he'd shoved another one up his rear. The way his features looked didn't argue against that, either.

He glanced down at his watch. Reflexively, Bill checked his own wrist. It was 1458; things were supposed to start at 1500. People were still coming in. Bill guessed anyone who showed up late for this particular dance would catch several different flavors of hell.

At 1500 on the dot (well, twelve seconds after, by Bill's Elgin), Matt Harrison smacked the lectern with the pointer. "Let's get started," he said. "You may have guessed why I've called you together again. I'm afraid I have to tell you your guesses are likely to be good."

"Aw, hell," Hank McCutcheon whispered. Bill nodded; he couldn't have put that better himself.

To leave no possible room for doubt in anyone's mind, Harrison went on, "I have received orders from General MacArthur, with the approval of President Truman, to initiate the use of atomic bombs against several cities in Manchuria and other areas of northeastern China. We are going to stop Mao from flooding Korea with Red Chinese troops. We will destroy the rail lines they use and the bases and barracks within China where, up until this time, they have been immune from attack. Are there any questions?"

A pilot stuck his hand in the air. Harrison aimed the pointer at him as if it were a rifle. "Sir, what happens if the Russians start throwing A-bombs around, too?"

"That's the sixty-four-dollar question, all right," Brigadier General Harrison said. "The best answer I can give you is, if they want to play the game, they can play the game. And we'll see who stands up from the table when it's over. Does that tell you what you want to know, Miller?"

"Yes, sir," the flyer answered. What else could you say when your CO came out with a question like that?

Bill wondered whether Harrison would give men the chance to decline to fly in a plane loaded with atomic weapons. The general didn't. He assumed that they'd already done whatever talking with their consciences they needed. "I will call pilots up here one by one to give you your targets and the supporting information related to completing your missions. You may open your orders as soon as you return to your seat."

Hank McCutcheon was the fifth man he summoned to the lectern. The major came back with the envelope in his right hand. He didn't touch the seal till his behind was on the folding chair again; he took Harrison literally. When he did open the envelope, Bill saw a name in big black letters: **HARBIN**. Below the name, a note read *This plane will carry the device. Others in the flight will support and decoy.*

Harbin. Bill knew it was a good-sized city in Manchuria. How many tens of thousands of people would he help fry tonight? Better not to think about some things. *This plane will carry the device.* How could you not think about that?

He tried to turn himself into a machine. Along with the other ten men in the crew, he spent the rest of the daylight hours checking out the B-29. The engines ran hot; they always had. If one failed while you were taking off fully loaded, you had to try to put the plane down.

And if that happened, Marian and Linda would collect on his government life insurance. Pilots had done it and walked away, but the odds lay somewhere between bad and worse.

They took off after dark. The Japs hadn't been able to shoot down day-flying B-29s. The North Koreans and their Russian and Chinese pals damn well could. Radar, better guns, more and better planes . . . A MiG-15's big guns could tear a bomber to bits in nothing flat.

Twin Mustang F-82s flew escort for the bombers. The night fighters carried their own radar. They had more range and more speed than almost any other prop jobs. Put one up against a MiG, though, and it was in deep. The guys in those cockpits had to know it. They climbed in and flew, anyhow.

A little flak came up at the planes as they droned north. When they got over North Korea, it grew heavier. B-29s had often bombed Red positions there.

They took a dogleg to the east to skirt MiG Alley. When they crossed the Yalu instead of turning back, the radioman came forward from his position aft of the cockpit and said, "I'm getting all kinds of hysterical traffic in Russian and Chinese. They know something new has been added."

"Understand any?" Bill asked.

"Not a fucking word, sir," Sergeant Hyman Ginsberg answered proudly.

Harbin lay a little more than four hundred miles north of the river: just over an hour's flying time. The Reds had time to scramble only a few planes. Sergeant Ginsberg reported the F-82s clashing with MiG-9s: second-string Russian jets, a lot like the German Me-262 from the end of World War II. Even a second-string jet could shoot down a none-too-new bomber. Bill was glad the Twin Mustangs were on the job.

"Harbin dead ahead," the navigator reported. He had a radar screen to guide them to the target. Hank and Bill had lights on the ground. Harbin wasn't blacked out—the Red Chinese hadn't looked for American visitors. Some flak climbed toward them. They were up past 30,000 feet, but even so . . .

"Let it go!" McCutcheon called to the bomb bay through the intercom. The B-29, suddenly five tons lighter, heeled away in a sharp escape turn to starboard. The bomb was on a parachute, to give them enough time to get away before the pressure-sensitive switch set it off.

When the antiaircraft guns started going off and woke him up, Vasili Yasevich thought it was the knock on the door for which he'd been waiting so long. He'd been a toddler when his father and mother fled from Russia to Harbin after the Whites lost the civil war to the Reds and their foreign backers pulled out.

For a while, Harbin had been as much Russian as Chinese. Cyrillic signs were as common as ideographs. Vasili's father ran a pharmacy. His mother, a talented seamstress, made clothes for her exiled countrywomen. The family got along.

Then the Japanese burst out of Korea. Manchuria, loosely connected to the rest of China, became Manchukuo, a puppet of Japan's. Life grew harder. But Japan and Russia weren't officially at war. The Yaseviches weren't Jews, as many of the exiles in Harbin were. They still managed to get along.

Vasili's father taught him what he needed to know about compounding drugs. He learned fast but, like his mother, he was better with his hands than with his head. Give him a saw, an adze, a chisel, or a hammer and he couldn't be beat. He helped his father now and then, but he made a better carpenter than a druggist, and they both knew it.

All at once, in August 1945, Japan and Russia—Manchukuo and Russia—were at war after all. The Red Army rolled into Harbin. The NKVD rolled in with it. The Soviet secret police had lists of people to execute or to send to the gulag. Instead of going with them, Vasili's father and mother swallowed poison. They knew what to use. They were dead in less than a minute.

The NKVD didn't bother with Vasili. He didn't show up on their lists. Maybe they thought he was born after his folks came to Harbin. Maybe they decided making his parents kill themselves counted for enough to settle their score against the whole family.

He stayed on even after the Chinese Reds took over for their Russian tutors in 1946. He spoke Mandarin as well as he spoke Russian. He knew a couple of trades people needed. Even if he was a round-eye with a pointed nose, the Chinese in Harbin had got used to such folk.

He drifted from one job to another. The Red Army's thunderous occupation of the city had made sure a carpenter wouldn't lack for work. He picked up bricklaying as he helped rebuild what the Russians had knocked down.

One of these days, he supposed, Stalin's flunkies would come back and take him away. Like any other wolves, they didn't give up a trail. In the meantime, he did his best to keep going.

They were finally getting around to repairing the train station at Pingfan, twenty-five or thirty kilometers south of Harbin. It had been big and fancy during the war years—the Japanese had had some kind of secret project going on outside the little town. Vasili didn't know, or want to know, the details. He just hoped he would get back to the city alive. Workers kept coming down with horrible things like cholera or the plague. A couple of them had caught smallpox, too, but he'd been vaccinated against that.

He lay on an old, musty sleeping mat in a barracks hall that couldn't have been much flimsier if it were made of cardboard. You could see stars between the planks that made up the walls. When it rained, it was just as wet inside as out. Dung-burning braziers did little to fight the icy breezes.

And, of course, those ill-fitting planks—Vasili could have done much better if only someone had asked him to—did nothing to hold out the noise of gunfire. Vasili had snorted to see antiaircraft guns poking their snouts to the sky here. No one would want to bomb Pingfan. He didn't think the Americans wanted to bomb Harbin, either. Had they wanted to, wouldn't they have done it by now? The Chinese volunteers had gone into Korea months ago.

Vasili chuckled to himself, the way he always did when he thought of "volunteers." He'd seen how the Japanese got them in Manchukuo. *Volunteer or we'll kill you* worked wonders every time. His father had told stories that showed the Soviets understood the same principle.

So when the guns started going off in the middle of the night, he thought it had to be either a drill or a false alarm. "I hear planes!" another workman shouted in excited Chinese.

"You hear farts inside your stupid head," Vasili muttered, but in Russian. He didn't think any of the other men he was working with knew the language. Anywhere else in China, he would have been sure that was so. Near Harbin, you couldn't be quite certain.

He couldn't be sure the other workman was hearing brain-farts, either. Through the pounding of the guns, he might have heard engines high overhead, too. Maybe they were his imagination. He hoped they were. But he wasn't sure, not any more.

Then he thought the sun had risen. Light—insanely bright light—filled the barracks. He closed his eyes. He jammed his face into the mat as hard as he could. None of that did any good. The light filled him and began to consume him. It was to sunlight as sunlight was to a candle.

Had it lasted longer than a moment, he felt sure he would have cooked the way a sausage did when you skewered it and thrust it into the fire. But, almost as soon as it was born, the impossible light began to fade and to go from white to yellow to orange.

"How can the sun come up in the north?" someone wailed.

"I'm blind!" someone else shouted. He must not have shielded his eyes fast enough.

Vasili hadn't even noticed the light came from the north. He did notice that the blast of wind following the flash also came out of the north. And he noticed it was a hot wind, when the only natural gales from that direction came straight out of Siberia, if not straight off the North Pole. There hadn't been any hot winds near Harbin for months, not from any direction.

The barracks creaked under the blast. The north wall crumpled and fell in on itself. That brought down part of the roof, too. Men shouted and squalled as planks and beams fell on them.

Nothing landed on Vasili, though a good-sized chunk of pine kicked up dust about thirty centimeters from his head. He scrambled out through the new hole in the building—the door seemed unlikely to work. Then he stared at the glowing cloud rising above what had been Harbin.

A Chinese stood beside him, also gaping at the mushroom of dust and who could say what else rising higher into the sky every second. Blood ran down the other man's face from a cut by his eye. He didn't seem to notice. His cheeks were also wet with tears.

"My family," he whispered, more to himself than to Vasili. "Everyone who matters to me lives—lived—back there."

"I'm sorry, pal," Vasili said. He had no one who mattered to him. Not long before he came down to Pingfan, his latest girlfriend had dropped him like a live grenade. If she hadn't, he might have stayed in the city. Then he would have been part of that boiling mushroom cloud himself.

"White men did this." The Chinese stared at him now, not at Harbin. "Round-eyed barbarians did this."

"Americans did it," Vasili said quickly. If he didn't talk fast, he could get lynched here. "I'm a Russian. If anybody can get even with the Americans, it's Russia. The Americans hit China because China couldn't hit back. Russia can." He'd always hated Stalin and the mess the Georgian had made of Russia. Now, for the first time in his life, his heritage turned into something that might save him.

Something went out of the other man's eyes. "Yes. You're right," he said, and Vasili breathed again. "We will be avenged. Or else we will give Russia what America gave us." China couldn't do that. If Russia didn't back her up, though, she was liable to try. That would be unfortunate—for both countries.


Harry Truman strode into the White House press room. Behind his round-lensed glasses, his eyes narrowed against the TV lights' glare. Those hadn't been there when he took over for FDR. You didn't need a girl to slap pancake makeup on you and cluck at how badly you'd shaved before you went on the radio, either.

Like it or not, though—and Truman didn't, not very much—television was the coming thing, and plainly here to stay. If they could, people wanted to see your face when you told them something. He'd be speaking on the radio, too: there was a regular thicket of microphones hooked up to his lectern, each one crowned with a different combination of alphabet soup.

"Here you go, Mr. President." Stephen Early, the press secretary, led Truman to that mike-festooned lectern. Early had done the job for Roosevelt, and had come out of retirement to do it again after Charlie Ross dropped dead the previous December. Truman missed Charlie the way he missed a just-pulled tooth. They'd gone back a long way together; Ross was another Independence man. But no one could say Early didn't know the ropes.

The cameramen nodded to Truman one by one as he took his place. No reporters sat in the chairs in front of the lectern.

He would be issuing a statement this morning, not taking questions. The questions would come later, but later could wait.

Almost in exact unison, red lights came on under the front lenses of all three television cameras. That meant they were sending his picture across the country, and to parts of Canada and Mexico as well.

"Good morning, ladies and gentlemen," Truman said, glancing down at his text. "Last night, the night of January twenty-third local time, to protect United Nations forces battling the unprovoked Red Chinese invasion of the Korean peninsula, U.S. Air Force planes used atomic weapons against several Chinese marshaling points in Manchuria."

He didn't say how many places had been attacked. The Chinks had hacked one of the bomb-carrying B-29s out of the sky before it could deliver its cargo. Truman hoped that atomic bomb was an unusable wreck now, but he didn't know for sure. He also didn't call the targets *cities. Marshaling points* sounded much more military.

"I took this step with great reluctance, but I did take it," Truman went on. "The bombs were delivered at my order, and under my responsibility as commander-in-chief of the armed forces of the United States of America. I regret the urgent military necessity that forced me to this extraordinary step. I regret it, but I did not, I could not, shrink from it. As I have told you before, the buck stops here."

Some people would have set things up so that, if using the atomic bombs turned out not to be such a hot idea, a good chunk of the blame would stick to General MacArthur. Truman was as sure as made no difference that Roosevelt would have played it that way. He admired his predecessor's subtle political skills without wanting to imitate them. He'd got the job done his own way for almost six years now. He wasn't as smooth or slick as FDR, but he coped.

"We have not attacked the territory of the Soviet Union," he said. "We have not, and we will not, provided that it refrain from any provocative response in the wake of our necessary action pertaining to Korea. We were allies against the greatest menace to freedom the world has ever seen. We do not need to fight each other now. With the weapons in our arsenals, that would be the worst tragedy in recorded history."

He wasn't just talking to the American people. Shortwave

radio would carry his words around the world at the speed of light. Joseph Stalin would see them or hear them as soon as they could be translated. Stalin wasn't the cuddly Uncle Joe we'd made him out to be during the war years. He was as ruthless as Hitler, if less rash. If he had any sense, he would know better than to mess with the USA.

If. Truman knew he wasn't the only one going after Stalin's ear now. Mao Tse-tung would be screaming into it right this minute. Mao would have been screaming into it ever since he got word that big chunks of Manchuria had just gone up in smoke. *Well, too goddamn bad for Mao,* Truman thought.

Aloud, he finished the statement: "We do not seek a wider war. All we want to do is restore to Korea its liberty, which came into danger when the North invaded the South without warning. We have a mandate from the United Nations to do exactly that. We serve the cause of freedom and peace, and want nothing more anywhere else in the world. Thank you, and God bless the United States of America."

As he stepped away from the lectern, the lights under the camera's noses went out. "That was a good speech, Mr. President," the press secretary said. "An excellent speech."

"Thanks, Stephen," Truman answered. He couldn't imagine calling the plump, dignified, gray-mustached Stephen Early *Steve.* Charles Ross had been *Charlie* for more years than he could remember. Truman couldn't help adding, "I hope it does what I want it to do."

"Well, that's partly in Stalin's court now, isn't it?" Early said.

"Yes," the President said, not altogether happily. "Now we find out just how good a friend of his Mao Tse-tung is. If Stalin drops bombs on France and England, the NATO treaty says that's the same thing as dropping bombs on us. I don't believe Russia and Red China have the same kind of formal alliance—"

"And Stalin can ignore it if he wants to," the press secretary put in.

"He sure can," Truman agreed. "He has more practice breaking treaties than Babe Ruth did with home-run records. But if he decides he won't break this one . . . Well, we'll do what we have to do, that's all."

"He respects you, sir," Stephen Early said. "He respects the power of the United States."

"Your old boss talked softer to the Russians than I do." If Truman sounded proud of not being soft, well, he was.

"It was wartime," Early replied. "He always worried that, if he got too sticky, Stalin would make a separate peace with Hitler. That would have fouled up the war effort beyond all recognition."

"Would the Russians really have done that?" Truman hadn't paid much attention to the ins and outs of diplomacy till he got tapped for the Vice Presidency and saw Roosevelt wasn't likely to live out his term.

"We heard that Molotov and Ribbentrop did talk after Stalingrad," Early said. "But Hitler wanted to keep a good-sized chunk of Russia, and Stalin insisted on the *status quo ante bellum.* So the war went on another two years."

"Hitler would have done better to take whatever he could get then, the way it turned out." Truman paused to light a cigarette. With a reminiscent chuckle, he went on, "After one of our little wrangles, Molotov told me he'd never had anyone talk to him that way in his whole life."

"He's a difficult man," the veteran press secretary said. "The few times I had anything to do with him, I saw that plainly."

"Somebody should have knocked the applesauce out of him when he was younger. He wouldn't be such a blasted nuisance now if somebody had," Truman said.

"Probably not. But if he wasn't, Stalin would have found some other son of a bitch to fill that slot instead of him," Early said.

Truman laughed. "Boy, have you got that right! If you work for Stalin and you aren't a son of a bitch, you don't last. Even if you *are* a son of a bitch, a lot of the time you don't last. I'm not saying Molotov isn't good at what he does. But, Lord, he's a hard-nosed so-and-so. At the UN, Gromyko is the same way."

"Mister Nyet? Grim Grom?" Early trotted out the Soviet ambassador's nicknames. "Well, you've given him something new to be grim about."

"Good," Truman said. "I'd sooner worry the other guy than let him worry me—every day of the week and twice on Sundays."

* * *

Wilf Davies stuck his head into the Owl and Unicorn and stared in surprise at how empty it was. "Where'd all your Yanks go, Daisy?" he asked.

"Confined to base," she answered morosely from behind the bar. "They're on alert, and my trade's in hospital because of it."

Wilf stepped all the way in. His left hand was a hook; he'd lost the one he was born with on the Somme in 1916. Daisy Baxter had known him like that her whole life. She wouldn't have had any idea what to make of him had he had two ordinary hands. She might not even have recognized him.

"I'll buy me a pint of best bitter," he said.

Daisy made as if to faint. "Catch me! Now I can holiday on the bloomin' Riviera!"

"Well, if you don't want my money, you don't have to take it." Wilf set a shilling and a smaller silver sixpence on the bar. The pint was one and three. When Daisy tried to give him his threepence change, he shook his head and slid the tiny coin back at her with the tip of the hook. A finger couldn't have done it more neatly.

"You're a gent, Wilf," she said.

He snorted. "You need your head candled, to see if you've got any working parts in there. My missus knows better, she does. Daft old bugger, she calls me. Eh, it's not as though she ain't daft herself, mind. Would she have put up with me all these years if she weren't?"

"Not likely," Daisy answered. They smiled at each other. Wilf's father had been the town blacksmith and farrier. Wilf still worked out of the same shop. He styled himself a blacksmith, though. People brought autos and lorries and tractors to Fakenham from as far away as Swaffham and Wells-next-to-the-sea, sometimes even from Norwich, to have him set them right.

He raised the pint in his good right hand. By the smile on his face, he started to give some kind of silly toast. But the smile slipped. What came out of his mouth was a simple, "Here's to peace."

Daisy drew herself half a pint. She lifted her little mug. "I have to drink that with you," she said.

After a long pull at his bitter, Wilf said, "It's a rum old world, ain't it?"

"Too right, it is!" Daisy said.

"Last war not half a dozen years behind us, and here we're

staring another in the face," he said. "So the Yanks are on alert, are they?"

"They are, and the RAF, too," Daisy answered sadly. "So you can see why the snug's not full to the brim."

Wilf drank some more of his pint. "They fly the big bombers out of there," he remarked. "If I was the Russians, that's one of the places I'd want to knock flat, bugger me blind if it ain't."

"Bite your tongue!" Daisy told him. "If they do that, how much'd be left of Fakenham?"

"Probably not a lot, I reckon," he said. "We were lucky the last go-round—not enough here to put the *Luftwaffe*'s wind up. But a bomb with them atom things inside . . ." He shook his head. "I don't know much about that business, or want to. I'm thinking, though, the only question is whether there'd be enough left of us to bury."

"You say the cheeriest things!" Daisy'd got to the bottom of her half-pint. She filled it again.

Wilf's pint was empty, too. He slid it across the bar for his own refill. As Daisy worked the tap, he fished in his pocket for silver. He gave her another one and six, and again returned the change. "Sorry, ducks," he said. "I'd like it better if I was talking moonshine, too. I wish I was. But that's how it looks to me."

Far overhead, a thin banshee whine resounded. That was a jet fighter high, high in the sky. In the last war, England and Russia had fought side by side. As soon as Hitler attacked Stalin, Churchill had declared that any foe of Hitler's was a friend of his. That lasted till Hitler was beaten. No, a few months longer—till atomic fire blossomed over Hiroshima and Nagasaki. Now the plane up there was watching out for enemies who'd been friends not so long before.

"They won't come by day," Wilf Davies predicted. "We'd spot 'em and shoot 'em down. No, they'll sneak across the sea at night, the way the Jerries did after they saw they couldn't knock us flat."

"That's how the Americans did it when they bombed China," Daisy said. "That's what the radio says, any road."

"That's how you've got to go about it nowadays. Even in the last war, didn't the Yanks pay a beastly price for bombing Germany by day?" Wilf said. "And it's worse now. The jets are so much faster than bombers, and that radar or whatever they call it lets you see in the nighttime almost like it's noon."

"You make me want to sleep down in the cellar tonight," Daisy said. "Not that that'd do me half a farthing's worth of good if the bomb came down on Fakenham, would it?"

"You could do worse," Wilf said. "By all I hear, only way to live through one of them bombs is not to be there when it goes off. But if it blows a ways away, the cellar's best chance you've got. Put some blankets on a bench and hope you see tomorrow morning. Pray, if you think it does any good. Me, I gave up on that rot a while ago." He held out the hook. Catching a packet like that could easily put you off prayer for life.

Daisy wondered whether Tom had prayed, there inside his tank. If he had, it hadn't done him any good. And if she prayed and a bomb came down on the little town here, that wouldn't do her any good, either. She'd given up praying, anyhow, when her husband didn't come back from the Continent. She hadn't had much faith in prayer before the black day, and none was left now.

The flash of light and, four or five minutes later, the roar like the end of the world didn't come from Sculthorpe. The runways and Nissen huts lay almost due west of Fakenham. The blast in the middle of the night was south and east of the hamlet.

Still in her nightgown, Daisy ran downstairs and out into the chilly darkness. She knew what a mushroom cloud looked like. Anyone who picked up magazines or watched newsreels at the cinema would. She'd never dreamt she would see one blazing in the night sky—a very black night in more ways than one, this February first—of East Anglia.

"Holy Mary Mother of God!" a neighbor choked out. "That's Norwich, all gone to destruction!"

Sure enough, the direction was right. The bomb wouldn't have come down anywhere else in this part of the country. Norwich was the only real city East Anglia boasted. If you needed a hospital, or treatment fancier than the local quack knew how to give, Norwich was where you went. If you needed to buy an auto, you went to Norwich. If you wanted a dress in last year's style, Norwich was the place to get it. Local shops could be three or four years behind what they were wearing in London right now.

Norwich was . . . gone to destruction. Daisy's Catholic neighbor had got that one spot on. What the countryside would do without the city, Daisy had no idea. She also had no idea whether other bombs were going off farther away than her senses reached, or whether the Russians would come back tomorrow or the next day to visit fire and destruction on Sculthorpe.

Another neighbor said, "This just turned into the exact middle of nowhere."

Plenty of people already thought Fakenham was nowhere. They moved to Norwich or to London to have a better chance of making something of themselves. The ones who'd gone to Norwich made . . . part of that glowing, swelling cloud. Daisy burst into tears.

**5**

"COME ON, YOU SORRY turds! Get moving!" Sergeant Gergely shouted, sounding like any sergeant in the history of the world from the time of Julius Caesar.

Tibor Nagy shrugged without seeming to, trying to make the straps of his pack dig into his shoulders less. It was a losing effort. He'd known ahead of time it would be. He had an easy twenty-five kilos of stuff in there. Of course the straps would dig in.

Along with the rest of the men in his squad, he tramped out to the truck waiting in front of the barracks. Sergeant Gergely kept right on cussing as they climbed in one after another. He was in his thirties, almost twice the age of most of the kids he led. He'd fought for Admiral Horthy in the big war and for the Arrow Cross after the Nazis found out Horthy was trying to escape from the conflict. He'd fought against the Russians in Russia, and he'd defended Budapest against them after the tide turned.

And now here he was, a sergeant in the Hungarian People's Army. He wore a Russian-style helmet instead of the German coal-scuttle model that had kept fragments away from his brain in the last dance. He carried a Russian submachine gun. Well, he might have done that from 1941 to 1945, too. Plenty of Hungarian—and German—soldiers had. The PPD and PPSh weren't pretty, but they were reliable, and they put a lot of lead in the air.

How had Gergely escaped a reeducation camp? The only thing Tibor could think of was that the Russians realized they needed some noncoms who knew what they were doing. It wasn't as if they had men of their own who spoke Magyar.

No doubt both the MGB and the Hungarian secret police were keeping an eye on the sergeant. They hadn't landed on him yet, though.

"A horse's cock up your ass, Szolovits!" the sergeant barked as he got into the truck. "Shove forward! Gimme some room!" He ragged on Szolovits because the tall, skinny soldier was a Jew. He ragged on the other guys because they were soldiers.

Groaning and farting, the truck chugged away from the barracks. It was a beat-up American Studebaker, no doubt sent to the USSR during the big war and used hard from that moment on. The Russians made their own trucks now. Hungary and Poland and Czechoslovakia and Bulgaria and Romania got their hand-me-downs.

Tibor's rifle was a hand-me-down. The varnish on the Mosin-Nagant's chipped, cracked birch stock couldn't hide the bloodstain under it. At least one fellow who'd used the piece hadn't been lucky. But the action worked smoothly. One of the things Sergeant Gergely was good for was making sure his minions kept their weapons clean and knew how to use them. If Tibor started shooting—no, when he started—he had a fair chance of hitting what he aimed at.

*I don't know why the hell I bother.* Gergely's rifle-range snarl dinned in his memory. *If you can't see that taking care of your rifle will help keep you breathing, odds are you're too fucking dumb to deserve to live.*

They rolled on through Pest, then crossed a battered bridge over the Danube into Buda. The two halves were and weren't part of the same city. People from Budapest sneered at all other Magyars as country bumpkins, hardly better than Slovaks. People from Buda felt the same way about their neighbors from Pest. Men from Pest were ready to punch the faggots from Buda in the nose if they said anything like that too loudly.

One of the things that united the two sides of the Danube was the Russian siege they'd gone through at the end of the war. Everyone had endured the suffering of the damned then. The Red Army cleared the Nazis and the Arrow Cross soldiers block by block, house by house, sometimes room by room. The Germans and Magyars gave up at last because they couldn't fight any more. Even after Budapest fell, the Germans mounted two ferocious counterattacks to try to get it back. No wonder both parts of the city were still full of shell-bitten, bullet-pocked ruins.

"Listen to me, you sorry shitheads, so you know what's going on," Sergeant Gergely rasped now. "The Americans dropped atomic bombs on China. To pay them back, the Soviet Union dropped some on France and England and Germany. They've got their whole army moving west now, so naturally we're going to help out our fraternal socialist allies. Right?"

"Right, Sergeant!" Tibor chorused, along with everybody else in the squad. Telling your sergeant he was wrong might not be suicidal, but you weren't likely to be happy after you did it.

Not for the first time, Tibor wondered how Sergeant Gergely came out so naturally with phrases like *fraternal socialist allies.* Had he mouthed Fascist slogans the same way when he wore that other helmet?

It wasn't something a private could come out and ask him. The Hungarian People's Army did its best to pretend its predecessors hadn't fought side by side with Hitler and the Nazis. Its best wasn't perfect, or people like Sergeant Gergely would be dead now. But the amnesia ran pretty deep.

"Sergeant?" That was Szolovits.

"What do you want?" Gergely glowered at him.

"What do we do if the Americans drop an atom bomb on *us*?"

"What the hell do you think we do? We fucking die, that's what. Anybody else got a stupid question?" Gergely said.

The guy next to Gyula nudged him. Gyula Pusztai was as tall as Istvan Szolovits, and at least twice as wide through the shoulders. He was strong as a bull. Unfortunately, he was also about as smart as a bull. "Did the sergeant say we were going off to fight the Americans?" he whispered.

"That's about the size of it," Tibor whispered back. Sergeant Gergely gave them both a fishy stare. Most of the time, you'd catch hell for any unauthorized talk. But they were heading off to war. Chances were the whole Hungarian People's Army was heading off to war, with its rickety trucks and secondhand rifles and men who were still figuring out how to be good Communists.

Gyula might not have been the brightest candle in the chandelier, but he knew what he thought about that. "Christ have mercy!" he yipped, something no good Communist was supposed to say. "They'll slaughter us!" He was too horrified to remember to keep whispering.

Tibor waited for Sergeant Gergely to tear Gyula to pieces, either with his barbed tongue or with his knobby, hairy-backed hands. But the sergeant's face . . . mellowed? Tibor wouldn't have believed his eyes—didn't dare believe them—till Gergely said, "Don't worry about it more than you can help, sonny. I said the same thing when we got on a train to go fight the Russians. I was wet behind the ears then. You go into combat, you grow up in a hurry. And I'm still here, you'll notice."

"Yes, Sergeant." By the way Gyula Pusztai said it, he also wondered why the sergeant wasn't ripping into him.

Gergely made a small production of lighting a cigarette. Then he said, "The sorry bastards who went east in 1942, there aren't a hell of a lot of us left. The Russians *did* slaughter us, in carload lots. And the Americans'll do the same god-damn thing to us this time around. Gives you something to look forward to, you know?"

Gyula had nothing to say to that. What *could* you say? What went through Tibor's head was *That's what we get for being a small country.* The Nazis had aimed Hungary at the Soviet Union and fired it. If the Russians killed Magyars by carload lots, more of Hitler's Germans stayed alive. Not enough more, as it turned out. Now the Communists in Moscow were firing Hungary at the United States. If the Americans killed piles of Hungarians, more Russians might survive.

Enough more? Tibor had trouble believing it. Not that Stalin would care. Like Hitler, Stalin cared less for a life than Sergeant Gergely cared for a smoke. He burned through lives faster than Gergely burned through cigarettes, too.

And if they really started throwing atomic bombs around, lives would go up in smoke faster than ever. How many cities had already got thrown into the incinerator? The front line might wind up the safest place of all.

Marian Staley listened to the news with shock and disbelief that grew every day. When President Truman announced that the United States had used atomic bombs against cities in Manchuria, they were cities she'd never heard of, cities with names the newsman had trouble pronouncing the same way twice, cities—not to put too fine a point on it—full of China-men. As with the Japs in the last war, who could work up any real sympathy for swarms of Chinamen blasted off the face of the earth? Especially when they, or the people who told them what to do, were Reds?

No, her main worry was that Bill was safe. She dreaded every unfamiliar car that stopped near the house. She stared from the front windows till the people who got out of the car proved not to be Air Force officers bringing her the worst news in the world.

But the Red Chinese had friends who'd taught them how to be Communists. And Joseph Stalin couldn't let his friends and allies get bombed that way without doing anything about it, not if he wanted them to go on taking him seriously.

And so, four nights after American B-29s smashed the Manchurian cities, Russian Tu-4s, flying low so radar wouldn't spot them till too late, bombed Aberdeen and Nor-wich, Rouen and Nancy, Bremen and Augsburg. You might not know exactly where in Britain and France and Germany those towns had lain, but you knew where Britain and France and Germany were. They weren't in the back of beyond, the way Manchuria was.

Then Stalin went on Radio Moscow and made what Mar-ian thought was an uncommonly smarmy speech even by the standards of the twentieth century, which had seen more than its share of smarmy political speeches. "The United States has seen fit to use atomic bombs against a fraternal socialist state assisting in a war of national liberation, and to do so without justification or provocation," the Soviet boss said. "This cannot go unpunished. It cannot, and it has not."

In the English version Marian listened to, Stalin contin-ued, "President Truman stressed that the United States did not attack the territory of the peace-loving peasants and workers of the USSR. I take equal pains to stress that the Soviet Union has not attacked the territory of the USA. Nor will we, unless our own territory is attacked. But the United States must understand that our allies are as important to us as its allies are to it. He has struck at our allies' provincial cities; we have done the same against as many of his allies' towns. We have not increased his terror, but we have un-flinchingly met it."

As soon as the speech was over, an American newscaster said, "The North Atlantic Treaty obliges America to consider an attack on its European allies to be an attack on itself. An attack of this scale, coupled with the Russian mobilization in the eastern zone of Germany and in Czechoslovakia, has caused great concern in the White House. President Truman will address the nation tomorrow to discuss the threat of our safety."

"The President will *address* the nation?" Linda asked.

"That's right, honey. It means he'll talk to the country," Marian told her daughter.

"I know our address," Linda said. "You taught it to me in case I ever got lost, but I never did. Can I go on the radio and tell people what it is?"

"It's not quite the same thing," Marian said.

"How come?" Linda wasn't going to let go of it till she got an answer that made sense to her. But how were you supposed to explain war so it made sense to a four-year-old?

For that matter, how were you supposed to explain war so it made sense to anybody? *I'll keep hurting you till you do what I say.* That was what it boiled down to. If she tried to do that to the family across the street to make them quit throwing loud, drunken parties, the police would cart her off to jail. Her angry dreams of burning down their house stayed firmly in her imagination, where they belonged.

But no policeman could stop one country from going after another. For a moment, it had looked as though the United Nations would become that kind of cop. But the only reason the UN backed America's move against the North Koreans was that Russia was boycotting the proceedings.

If the international organization had taken control of all the A-bombs after World War II ended, and if no country had been able to make them on its own after that . . . Had that happened, policemen might be able to keep unruly countries in line. But it hadn't. The USA had the bomb. So did the Russians, now. That made them both like the Mafia in Chicago in the Twenties, only more so. They could do what they aimed to do, not what anybody else told them to do.

And so . . . war.

"When's Daddy coming home?" Linda asked, maybe out of the blue, maybe not.

"I don't know exactly," Marian answered. "When he can. When they let him. When the war's over." Those were all possibly true. Another possibly true response was *Never.* Marian refused to dwell on that one now. It was for when a branch scraping on the roof woke her at three in the morning and she couldn't go back to sleep.

"I wish he would," Linda said.

"Me, too," her mother said. Bill had been gone for most of a year now. That felt like a long time to Marian. It had to be an eternity for Linda. She wasn't the same person now as she had been then. She'd learned the alphabet. She could sound out words on her blocks and on pages in her books. More seemed to be going on inside her every single day.

She changed. She grew. Bill, meanwhile, stayed what he'd been for her ever since he went back on duty: pictures on the wall and on the dresser in the big bedroom. He was still somebody she remembered and loved, but out of the ever more distant past.

Marian bit down on the inside of her lower lip. Sometimes Bill seemed that way to her, too. Oh, she got letters from him. She wrote to him, too. How could you pour out your heart, though, when you knew a smirking censor stood between you and the one you loved?

For that matter, how could you pour out your heart on paper any which way? Marian always felt like a fool when she tried to set down what was going on in her heart. Writing wasn't made to do things like that, not unless you were Shakespeare or somebody. So it seemed to her, anyway. She could write about how a pot roast had turned out or how a hinge on the closet door needed fixing. She could even write about funny things Linda said. Love letters? When they were together, she could tell Bill she loved him. She did tell him so, all the time.

On paper, though, it was different. The words looked stupid. They sounded stupid, too. Bill had to feel the same way. His letters were full of stories about baseball games between bomber crews and about who was on the latest USO tour. He'd write *Miss you. Love you* . . . and that would be that. Marian believed he did miss her and love her. She would have liked to read it in a way that made her feel it as well as see it on the page, though.

She would have liked that, but she didn't expect to get it. She'd married a flyer, not a writer. A cousin of hers had married a writer. He drank. He didn't make much money. He chased other women. And he was a cold fish in person no matter what kind of pretty words he could put down on paper.

"Do you remember the air-raid alerts Seattle and other

West Coast towns went through in the early days of the Second World War?" the radio announcer asked rhetorically. "We didn't know what Japan could do, and we didn't want to take any chances. Well, civil-defense officials say those days are back again. We will be testing our defense tomorrow at ten A.M. Don't be alarmed when the sirens go off. It's not the Russians. It's only a test. No one expects that the Russians can really get here. We just want to stay on the safe side."

Marian did remember those dark days after Pearl Harbor. She didn't want to think days like those could come again. But she knew that not wanting to think it didn't mean it couldn't happen. *Air-raid alert. Ten tomorrow morning.*

"Come on! Come on! Come on!" Captain Oleg Gurevich yelled over the rumble of a company's worth of big diesel engines. "Are we ready to move? We'd fucking well better be ready to move!"

Konstantin Morozov waved from the turret of his tank to show it could roll whenever the captain ordered. Night was falling on the Red Army encampment near Meiningen. The tanks would move up to the border between the Russian zone in Germany and the American under cover of darkness. By the time the sun rose tomorrow, from the air it would look as if these tanks, and the rest at this enormous base, hadn't gone anywhere.

And, by the time the sun rose tomorrow, the tanks that had moved up to the border would be under netting and branches and dead grass that made them effectively invisible from the air. The Red Army took *maskirovka* seriously. What the enemy couldn't see, he'd have a harder time wrecking.

During the last war, the Germans had been pretty good at camouflage. But pretty good, against Russians, amounted to pretty bad. From what Morozov had seen of the way the Americans did business, they just didn't give a damn about concealment. They thought of war as a boxing match. You got into the ring with the other guy and you slugged away till he fell over or you did.

Of course, when you started slugging with atom bombs, you had reason to believe the other guy would be the one who fell. Morozov's belly knotted. He didn't want to die like that. But he didn't see what he could do about it. He might live through another war. If he tried to desert, the MGB absolutely, positively *would* give him a 9mm bullet in the back of the head.

"Let's go!" Captain Gurevich shouted, and waved toward the west. "*Urra!* for the Red Army! *Urra!* for the Soviet Union!"

Coughing, Sergeant Morozov ducked down into his turret and slammed the cupola hatch shut. The diesel stink was just as thick in here as it had been outside. What kind of *maskirovka* could you use to hide the smell and the smoke? He imagined fresh-air generators sucking up exhaust and spitting out clean, fragrant, transparent gases. Being only a tank commander, though, he couldn't imagine how to make those generators.

"Put it in gear, Misha!" he called to the driver through the speaking tube. "We're going forward." The T-54 had an intercom system connecting the three men in the turret and the driver farther forward. The tank had the intercom, but Konstantin didn't trust it. Electrical systems could fail when you needed them most, but what could go wrong with a brass tube?

"Going forward, Comrade Sergeant," Mikhail Kasyanov answered. Like the gunner and the loader, he was too young to have fought in the Great Patriotic War. Morozov was the only one here who knew what battle was like. He had the bad feeling the others would find out pretty damn quick, though.

The growl from the engine compartment got louder as the T-54 began to move. How much noise did all these tanks make as they advanced? What kind of *maskirovka* could you use to muffle it or drown it out? As with the black, stinking exhaust, Konstantin could see something would be useful, but didn't know enough to work out what it might be.

He peered out through the periscopes set into the cupola. Not much to see: a tank ahead, another behind. He swore under his breath. He'd be breathing those stinking fumes till they got where they were going.

His station was on the right side of the turret. The gunner's seat was a little lower, to the left of the cannon's breech. The loader's was farther back and farther down still. It was crowded in there, especially with the T-54's low, rounded turret, made to deflect shells coming from any direction. The ideal tankman for one of these beasts should have been no more than 170 centimeters tall. Konstantin was a little too big, and had to be extra careful when he moved around. So did Pavel Gryzlov, the gunner. Mogamed Safarli, the loader, was about the right size.

There'd been only a commander and a loader in the original T-34's turret. The commander aimed and fired the cannon along with everything else he had to take care of. The Nazis, who'd separated commander and gunner from the start, could shoot rings around those T-34s, even if the tanks themselves outdid anything Germany made.

When the Red Army upgunned the T-34 from 76 to 85 millimeters, the engineers stole a page from the Hitlerites' book. The new, bigger turret held three men. It also had a cupola for the commander to use. All Soviet tanks from then on kept that same system.

One difference between the T-54 and its ancestors was that Misha had no company up front. The T-34 carried a bow machine gun as well as one coaxial with the main armament. T-54s got along with just the coaxial machine gun. You could fill that many more tanks with four-man crews than if they took five.

After a while, Konstantin opened the hatch atop the cupola and stood up to look around. You could see so much more if you did that than if you stuck with the periscopes. Of course, you also made a far juicier target. Sometimes you had to do it, though, even in combat, if you were going to get the most out of your tank.

Now all he got was a smelly breeze in the face. The noise was far louder than it had been with the tank buttoned up. They wouldn't just hear it on the far side of the border. They'd hear it on the far side of the Rhine.

He worried about that, which was the only thing he could do about it. What were the Americans up to, there on the other side of the plowed ground and barbed wire and tank traps that marked the frontier between the two main conquerors of the Third *Reich*? How ready were they?

Tank against tank, man against man, Konstantin was ready to fight them. He wasn't eager—few people who have seen once what war is like are eager to see it again. And anyone who has seen it once knows that anything that can happen can happen to him. Anything, no matter how horrible. So no, Morozov wasn't eager. Willing, yes.

He thought the Red Army could overrun the rest of Germany and stand on the Rhine in a matter of days. It could . . . unless the Americans started dropping those atomic bombs.

Not all the steel in the T-54's hull and turret would save him from one of those.

Something pale ghosted by the tank on silent wings, close enough to make Konstantin jump. Then he realized it was only a barn owl. He wondered why it would fly so near the noise and the smells of a tank column on the move. Then he wondered how many mice and rats and rabbits the tanks were scaring out of their nests. Maybe the owl knew what it was doing after all.

Foot soldiers waved the tanks of Captain Gurevich's company into position just out of sight of the frontier. More foot soldiers draped them with netting covered with grass and with white cloth to create from above the impression of snowy ground. Things probably wouldn't look the same as they had before the tanks got here, but they wouldn't look so very different, either.

Konstantin got out of his T-54 after it went under the camouflage. He carefully checked the ground on which the machine sat. It was hard and firm—indeed, frozen here and there. The tank wouldn't sink in very far. The crew could sleep under it. They'd be almost as safe as if they'd stayed inside, and much more comfortable.

"It's cold out here," Mogamed Safarli whined.

"You've got your greatcoat and a blanket. What else do you want?" Morozov said. To a Russian, the kind of cold you got in Germany, even at the start of February, wasn't worth getting excited about. But Safarli was a blackass from Azerbaijan or one of those other places that didn't know what winter was all about.

They ate. They smoked. They drank a little vodka. They talked in low voices. Then they wrapped themselves up and slept. The Red Army taught everybody—even blackasses—to get through a really cold night with nothing but a greatcoat. It wasn't all that cold tonight. And they had blankets along with their coats. Nothing to it.

Nothing to it tonight. Tomorrow . . . Tomorrow was liable to be a different story.

Max Bachman nodded when Gustav Hozzel walked into the print shop. "Morning," he said.

"Morning," Gustav said. He glanced toward the east. Any German who'd served on the Russian front had developed that kind of anxious, wary glance. When you looked east like that, you wondered what would be coming your way in the next few minutes or the next few days. Whatever it was, it wouldn't be anything you wanted.

His boss grunted. He'd served on the Eastern Front, too. Most German men their age had. Some lucky guys had just fought in Italy or France. A few even luckier ones had sat out the war on garrison duty in places like Norway or Crete. But the Russians had been the big show—too big a show, as things turned out.

"Remember how you asked whether the Amis would want a hand against Stalin if things heated up?" Bachman asked.

*"Ja."* Gustav lit a cigarette. Yes, he still felt rich every time he did it, as if he were smoking hundred-dollar bills like a fat cat in a cartoon. Silly, but there you were. After blowing a ragged smoke ring, he went on, "They won't get much hotter than they did in Augsburg."

"Or Bremen, or the other places the Russians fried," Bachman agreed. But Augsburg was the closest one, less than two hundred kilometers away. Some people in Fulda who were out in the middle of the night claimed to have seen a flash on the southern horizon when the city that had stood there since the days of its namesake, the Roman Emperor Augustus, abruptly ceased to be. Were they lying? How big did an explosion have to be for you to see it from so far away? Big— that was the only answer Gustav could come up with.

"So what about the Americans?" Gustav asked. If the Russians felt like it, they could drop one of those bombs on Fulda, too. What would hold them back? Needing to go through here was the only thing he could think of. They might not be able to do that if the place glowed in the dark.

"Well, you know how we print things for the town and for the *Burgomeister,*" Bachman said. Gustav nodded. Willi Stoiber was a fat blowhard, which made him ideal to run the city. How he'd got through the denazification trials, Gustav couldn't guess, but he had. Max Bachman continued, "So he likes to run his mouth. The Americans are talking about setting up what they want to call a national emergency militia."

"Is that anything like an army?" Gustav's voice was dry.

"Of course not. We're Germans. We don't deserve an army. Besides, it has a different name." Bachman was as cynical as he was.

Gustav remembered his nightmares, something he usually

tried not to do while he was awake. "Haven't we paid our dues?" he said. "I fought the Ivans as much as I ever wanted to, thanks. If the Amis are so hot to have a go, let them take their crack at it this time. They didn't want to when we could have done it together before, so to hell with them." He made as if to spit on the floor, but didn't.

His boss clicked his tongue between his teeth. "Only one thing wrong with that."

"What?" Gustav Hozzel didn't see anything wrong with it.

"If the Americans fight the Russians here and they lose, they won't have commissars telling them what to do and spying on them from now till the end of time. We will, worse luck," Bachman said.

"Oh." In spite of himself, Gustav grimaced. "Well, when you're right, you're right, dammit."

Plenty of people had fled from the Russian zone to freer lands farther west. The tales they told would curl anyone's hair. More than a few of them lived in Fulda now. And, among those refugees, chances were that some played a double game. Cursing Stalin's name at the top of your lungs didn't necessarily mean you weren't also whispering things in the MGB's ear.

But those horror stories rang true to Gustav. Counterattacks that briefly won back some ground showed what the Russians did when they took over German soil. They didn't play the game by the rules; as far as they were concerned, the game had no rules. Of course, the *Wehrmacht* and the SS hadn't had clean hands when they were going forward, either. On the Eastern Front, no one's hands were clean.

Noise outside the print shop distracted him from his gloomy memories, but not from his gloom. That noise was of big, snorting engines and of caterpillar tracks grinding on asphalt and cobblestones. American panzers and self-propelled guns had smoother lines than the slab-sided vehicles the *Wehrmacht* used, but they sounded pretty much the same.

"Are you going to sign up for this emergency militia, Max?" Gustav loaded the name with a certain sour relish.

"Probably. My guess is it's already too late, though. With the bombs dropping, they won't have time to get us shaken out into units and give us uniforms and weapons. Too bad. I wouldn't mind getting myself an M-1. That's a pretty good rifle."

"My old Mauser carbine would do fine," Gustav said. "Getting ammo for it might be tricky, though." The standard German caliber had been 7.92mm. Some of that was bound to be floating around, but Gustav didn't know where to lay his hands on it. He hadn't worried about it from the time he surrendered till this new trouble blew up.

The Americans used what they called .30-caliber rounds, which were 7.62mm to the rest of the world. They did a perfectly respectable job of killing people, and they were easy to get hold of.

Max said, "Shall we do some work?"

"Why not?" Gustav answered. "That way, Saint Peter can see we were busy until the bomb blew us to smoke."

His boss smiled a twisted smile. Gustav had seen that expression before, on the faces of *Landsers* trying to show they weren't scared when a swarm of drunken Russians were howling and screaming and getting ready to roll over their trenches. The Ivans often acted as if they didn't care whether they lived or died. Considering the kind of country they had to live in, who could blame them?

Even getting through the day wasn't easy. Max kept the radio running, which he didn't do most of the time. A newsman said that Stalin said he had as much right to blow up those European cities as Truman did to blow up Chinese cities. He might even have been right, not that that did the people in those cities any good. The dead had to number in the hundreds of thousands.

"The guy on the news is going on like that's a big number," Gustav said after music replaced word of the latest disasters. "For Stalin, it's nothing but pocket change."

"Maybe the asshole didn't fight on the *Ostfront*," Max answered. "Or maybe he wants people to think he didn't."

The first thing Luisa asked Gustav when they both got home was, "Will it start for real?"

He sent that hooded look toward the east again. Then he sighed. "Probably," he said. "Well, we had five or six good years, anyhow. What's for supper?"

She took a pot out of the oven. It had simmered in there all day, since she went off to her own job. Savory steam rose when she took off the lid. Turnips, cabbage, a cheap cut of pork to add some body and some flavor, dill, caraway seeds . . .

Gustav opened a couple of bottles of Black Hen from the

local brewery. The malty beer would go well with what his wife had made. They clinked glasses after he poured. Everything tasted especially good to him. He was about halfway through the meal when he realized what that meant. He was savoring flavors more than usual because part of him believed this might be the last time he ever got the chance to do it.

Not too much later, he took Luisa to bed. She squeaked, but only a little. Again, it seemed extra good to Gustav. He hadn't been able to do this before a Russian attack in the last war. Now he could, so he made the most of it.

# 6

WHEN CADE CURTIS WOKE up in the drafty little shed, two bowls were waiting for him. One held rice, the other kimchi. Neither was big. He thought it was a miracle these people gave him anything at all. They had so little themselves. Why would they spare some for a foreigner, a stranger, passing through?

Why? Because they were Christians, and took the name and the duties that went with it seriously. That was the only answer that occurred to Cade. It was also one that shamed him. Almost all the people back in the States called themselves Christians of one flavor or another. Damn few lived up to the label, though.

Things here in Korea were different. Christians, Catholic or Protestant, were a small minority. Folks from one denomination didn't sneer at those who belonged to another. They presented a united front against their persecutors. In Kim Il-sung's regime, that meant against just about everybody. Things were easier in the south, but only relatively.

Cade grabbed the chopsticks laid across the bowl of rice. He wasn't so smooth with them as the natives were, but he managed. You got better at everything with practice. He gulped the rice and the fiery pickled cabbage. He'd dropped a lot of weight since getting cut off, but he didn't care. He was getting close to the American lines. Fried chicken and bacon and apple pie and scrambled eggs and hash browns lay around the corner. He'd plump up just fine.

The sun had gone down. Moonlight slipped between the battered planks of the shed wall and painted thin, pale zebra stripes across the dirt floor. The village, like most Korean villages after sunset, was quiet as the tomb. No electricity, no kerosene for lamps. People had candles and oil lamps, but didn't like to use them. Whatever oil and tallow you burned, you couldn't eat later if you got hungry enough.

A dog howled, off in the hills. Some people hereabouts had kept dogs as pets before the war. Now dogs that hung around people turned into meat. A couple of villages back, somebody'd fried a little bit of dog flesh for him, stirred together with rice. It tasted wonderful; it was the first meat he'd had in a long time. Whether he'd like it so well if he were less hungry . . . was a question for another day.

Farther away, still several days' travel to the south, artillery rumbled on the edge of hearing. Getting through the lines would be the tricky part. Cade didn't aim to worry about how he'd do it till he had to try. After getting cut off, he hadn't really believed he would come close enough to the front in the south to need to worry about it.

He'd slept through the day, his felt hat doing duty for a pillow. Only that bare ground under him? He didn't care, not even a little bit. He figured he could have slept on a swami's bed of nails. Now it was nighttime, so, like a cat or a rat or a bat, he was awake.

Soft footfalls outside the shed said a couple of Koreans were awake, too. Silently, he took hold of the PPSh. He didn't *think* anything here had gone wrong. If he turned out to be mistaken, though, a blaze of glory seemed preferable to letting Kim's or Mao's soldiers take him. Especially Mao's. They'd be even less happy with Americans now than they had been before fire fell on Manchuria.

Low-voiced mutters in Korean outside the door. Cade wouldn't have been able to follow even if he'd heard them clearly. He'd picked up only a handful of words from the local language.

The door opened. A man stuck his head inside. *"Ave,"* he whispered, and then, *"Veni."*

*"Sic."* Cade didn't have a whole lot of Latin, either. But what he did have was worth its weight in gold for talking with Catholic Koreans. When Protestants helped him on his way south, he was reduced to sign language.

He scrambled to his feet. His knees and something in the small of his back crackled as he did. He had to duck to get through the doorway. He also had to lift his feet: like the

Chinese, the Koreans put a plank across the bottom, maybe to help keep out chilly drafts.

One of the Koreans outside cradled a PPD, the PPSh's older cousin. The other man had a shotgun that looked only a short step up from a blunderbuss. Well, if they got into a fight, it would be at close quarters. If they got into a fight, they would also die.

The guy with the PPD gestured toward the south. *"Vade mecum,"* he said.

*"Sic,"* Cade repeated. What else would he do *but* go with the Koreans?

They wore felt boots like his, possibly stolen from dead Red Chinese soldiers. Cade did wonder how much damage the atom bombs had done to the Chinese logistics system. Not enough to make the Chinks already in Korea quit fighting. Not yet, anyhow. They were like the Russians—they were expected to live off the countryside. All they really needed was ammunition.

Those felt boots were quieter than ordinary footgear would have been. Cade was at least a head taller than one of his guides, but the other was about his own six-one. Some of the Koreans ran surprisingly tall. Some of them could grow surprisingly thick beards for Orientals, too. Not a one, though, came equipped with a long, pointed nose or round blue eyes.

A plane buzzed by overhead. *Buzzed* was the word, all right. The Chinese flew Po-2 biplanes, ancient Russian wood-and-cloth trainers pressed into service as night harassment aircraft. They fired machine guns and dropped little bombs and got the hell out of Dodge before anyone could do anything about it. *Bedcheck Charlie,* GIs called them. The Russians had used them the same way against the krauts, sometimes with woman pilots.

This Po-2 wasn't much above treetop height. Cade could feel the wind of its passage as it flew by. And the pilot must have spotted his guides and him walking along in the moonlight, because he swung the little plane around for another look at them.

But how much could he really see, no matter how hard he tried? Cade and one of the Koreans were big men, but what did that prove? In moonlight, would the SOB up there be able to tell Curtis was white? Cade didn't believe it. He held his PPSh up in his left hand to show it to the flyer and waved his right hand as if to someone he knew was a friend.

And damned if the pilot didn't waggle his wings in a friendly greeting of his own and fly away. Once he was gone, both Koreans whooped and hollered and thumped Cade on the back. The words were just gibberish to him. He was glad he had on the parka and the quilted jacket underneath it. Chances were they saved him some bruises.

*"Vir sapiens!"* said the one who knew some Latin.

*"Homo sapiens. Homo sapiens ego sum."* Cade thought it was funny. He knew what the scientific name for human beings was.

Since his guide didn't, the Korean didn't get the joke. Pointing at Cade, he said, *"Vir es." You are a man.*

*"Sic. Vir sum. Et homo sum." Yes. I am a man. And I am a human being. Vir* and *homo* both meant *man,* but they didn't mean the same thing. In English, *man* did duty for most of the meanings of both Latin words.

Cade didn't think he could explain any of that to the Korean in Latin. His wasn't up to it, and neither was his guide's. He turned out not to have to. The Korean kind of shrugged, as if to say he wasn't even going to try to understand this inscrutable Occidental. He pointed south and started walking again. Cade and the fellow with the almost-blunderbuss followed.

A quarter of a mile outside the next village, someone called softly from the cover of some pines. Both Koreans answered. They went back and forth for a little while. The one who knew Latin pointed to the pines and said, *"Vade cum."* That just meant *Go with.* Maybe he'd forgotten the word for *him.*

It did get the message across. Approaching the trees, Cade said, *"Ave."*

The greeting fell on uncomprehending ears. A man with a rifle came out and spoke in Korean. Cade sighed. He spread his hands to show he didn't get it. The local sighed, too. He gestured toward the collection of beat-up houses and outbuildings. With a nod, Cade went that way.

He got hidden in a privy. It wasn't the first time on his way south. Nobody had used this one for a while, but it was still fragrant. He muttered, but not for long. Pretty soon, his nose noticed the stink much less. He curled up and got ready to sleep through the dangerous daylight hours.

\* \* \*

"Pechenga." Harry Truman spat out the unfamiliar name as if it were the filthiest word in the world.

"That's right, Mr. President." George Marshall nodded. Truman thought the Secretary of Defense was almost as much a Great Stone Face as Andrei Gromyko. Dorothy Parker had famously said that some actress ran the gamut of emotions from A to B. Truman hadn't seen that actress perform. But by comparison to her, Marshall got stuck halfway between A and B.

"Pechenga!" Truman said it again, even more disgustedly this time. "It sounds like the noise a pinball machine makes."

"Yes, Mr. President." Marshall sounded resigned. He was an extraordinarily able man. As Secretary of State, he'd developed the Plan that bore his name and helped keep Western Europe's ravaged postwar economies from collapsing. Before that, he'd been a five-star general and Army Chief of Staff under FDR.

Truman wondered whether Marshall compared him to Roosevelt. No, on second thought, Truman didn't wonder any such thing. He knew damn well Marshall compared him to Roosevelt. The man would have been even less human than he was if he didn't. What Truman really wondered was what Marshall thought, comparing him to his illustrious predecessor.

He didn't ask. He would never ask. He would go on the rack and let a torturer tear out his fingernails before he asked. But he wondered. *He* would have been less human than he was if he didn't.

"Pechenga." Now Marshall said it. His index finger pinned it down on a large-scale map of Europe, as if he were an entomologist mounting a butterfly on a collecting board. "Formerly Petsamo in Finland, till the Russians took it away when they knocked the Finns out of the war. A little more than fifty miles west of Murmansk. About as far northwest as you can go and stay in the USSR."

"And where the goddamn Russians took off from when their bombers blasted Britain and France," Truman ground out.

"And Germany," Marshall reminded him.

"And Germany," Truman agreed sourly. "But the Prime Minister is screaming in my ear, and so is the President of the Fourth Republic. The Germans aren't part of the NATO treaty. I have an easier time ignoring them than I do with the English and French."

"The treaty does say that an attack against one signatory is the same as an attack against all signatories." Marshall knew what it said. It had been negotiated while he was Secretary of State, even if the dickering wasn't done till Dean Acheson took over for him at the start of Truman's full term, the one he'd won himself.

"I know. I know. I know," Truman said. "And if I didn't know, they're reminding me—at the top of their lungs. And so I am going to have to do something to Russia. If I don't, the treaty is dead in the water, and I can have the joy of watching all the countries in Western Europe line up to hop into bed with Joe Stalin."

The slightest twitch of one eyebrow on George Marshall's craggy face said Franklin D. Roosevelt wouldn't have talked about countries hopping into bed with other countries. FDR would have found some properly diplomatic way to say the same thing. Well, good for FDR. Truman called them as he saw them, and worried about diplomacy later.

After pulling his features back to expressionlessness, Marshall said, "I'm afraid that's much too likely, sir. With the Communists already so strong in France and Italy—"

"I know," Truman said one more time. "And so I was thinking of striking this Pechenga place. It's where the Russian bombers came from, so it naturally draws our notice. We can drop a bomb there if we want to, blow up the air base, look heroic to our allies, and not endanger even Murmansk, let alone any of the really big Russian cities."

"I don't know if it's enough to make England and France happy, and I don't know that Stalin won't feel obliged to retaliate against an American target, or more than one American target," Marshall replied, plainly picking his words with care. "I also don't know that he won't order his armies forward—they're at the border and ready to move, remember."

"I do remember." Truman scowled. "Dammit, George, all my other choices look worse. If I do nothing—we just talked about what will happen then. And if I bomb Russia back to the Stone Age, I know the free half of Europe will get badly hurt, too. We won't get off scot-free ourselves, either. I don't believe Stalin can do unto us as we can do unto him, but I don't believe we'll stop everything he throws our way, either.

If you can tell me I'm wrong and make me believe you, I'll give you a great big kiss."

"Is that a promise or a threat, Mr. President?" Marshall asked, deadpan. Truman guffawed, more from surprise than at the quality of the crack. The Secretary of Defense owned a sense of humor after all!

"Never mind what it is," Truman said. "The way it looks to me is, we have three choices: no response, limited response, and all-out response. If the limited response doesn't seem the best of the three, you'd better tell me right now."

Marshall inhaled, then blew out the breath without saying anything. After inhaling again, he said, "When you put it that way, sir, I must agree with you. Whether Stalin will recognize the limited nature of the reply, though, or whether our friends will find it *too* limited . . ." He shrugged.

"God knows what will happen before it does. He's the only One Who can pull that off," Truman said. "The rest of us, we have to try something and then see what happens. This isn't a good choice, but it's the best one we have now. Since we do agree on that, let's get rolling."

"I was thinking some of the planes should fly out of England and others out of France, sir," Marshall said. "It seems fitting."

"It does, yes." Truman paused a moment. "Not out of Germany?"

"What do you think, sir?"

The President answered his own question: "No, not out of Germany. Okay, get things started. You will know the orders to issue." If anyone in the whole world knew more than George Marshall about how American armed forces around the world worked, Truman had no idea who it might be.

"I'll send them out right away." Marshall hesitated, then said, "It might have been better to accept the loss of our forces in North Korea, then bring in enough reinforcements to stabilize the situation. The choice we're facing now wouldn't seem so . . . stark."

"If I'd let the Red Chinese get away with slaughtering them all, McCarthy and Taft and the rest of the Republicans would have crucified me, and who could blame them?" Truman said. "Don't get me wrong. You have a point, and a good one. All I can tell you is, it seemed like a good idea at the time. You didn't say no then, not that I recall."

"No, I didn't," the Secretary of Defense agreed. "Now

we've got a tiger by the ears, though, and we'd better hang on tight or it will swallow us."

"We'll need to put Alaska on highest alert," Truman said. "If Stalin does decide to play tit for tat, that's a likely place for him to do it. Plenty of space, not many people—it's a lot like Pechenga. If we can keep the Russians from getting through, that's a feather in our cap."

"Good point. I think we're already at the maximum there, but I will make sure," Marshall said. "Is there anything else, sir?"

"Not off the top of my head. I'll phone you if I think of something," the President said.

The Secretary of Defense nodded, dipped his head once more in lieu of saluting, and strode out of the White House conference room.

"Pechenga." Truman still made the name sound like an obscenity. He scowled at the map. An eye for an eye and a tooth for a tooth? Not a big enough eye or tooth to make the Europeans happy. Well, wasn't diplomacy the art of leaving everyone dissatisfied? *If it is, I win artist of the year,* Truman thought.

Leon carried a blue book up to Aaron Finch. He climbed into his father's lap in a rocking chair and said, "Read!" He was only a little more than a year and a half old. He didn't say a whole lot of words yet. He had that one, though. And he always seemed sure of what he wanted—in which he took after Aaron.

"Okay, kiddo." Aaron tousled Leon's curly hair. Leon indignantly shook his head. He didn't like that for beans. He never had. Aaron did it, anyhow. He thought those curls were funny as hell. Leon got them from Ruth. Aaron's hair was straight. His son looked like him most ways, but not there.

He lit another cigarette. He wasn't a chain smoker to the point of having two going at once, but he burned through a couple of packs a day. Leon put up with the wait as well as a toddler could: which is to say, not very well. "Read, Daddy!" he barked, like a squeaky top sergeant.

Aaron started reading about Peter Rabbit and Grandfather Frog and the Merry Little Breezes and Bowser the Hound and the rest of the edge-of-the-woods world Thornton Burgess had made. He thought the tales were tedious. They repeated themselves a lot. They'd originally run as newspaper serials, which made recapping every so often a must. Burgess hadn't bothered cleaning them up when he turned them into books.

Leon didn't care. Little kids liked hearing things over and over. Aaron wasn't always sure how much of the stories his son got. But whether Leon got everything or not, he liked sitting in his daddy's lap and listening. That was plenty to keep Aaron going.

When Lightfoot the Deer made an appearance, Aaron asked, "Do you know what antlers are, Leon?"

His son didn't say a lot, no. But Leon was nobody's dope. Far more words and ideas lodged in his brain than came out of his mouth. He stuck his thumbs above his eyes and spread his hands wide. Sure as hell, he knew what antlers were.

"That's right," Aaron said, and, "That's good." Aaron went on, "Deer have antlers. They're kind of like horns, except they fall off every year, so the deer have to grow new ones. Horns stay on all the time."

Leon nodded. Maybe it was going in one ear and out the other, but maybe not, too. Yeah, the kid was smart. Some of that was good—it helped you get along. Too much was liable to turn you into a white crow. No need to worry about that for a while, though.

The water in the kitchen stopped running. Ruth walked into the living room. She was smoking a cigarette, too. She didn't puff away all the time like Aaron, but she smoked.

Leon lit up like a lightbulb. "Mommy!" he exclaimed, as if he hadn't seen her for ten years, not ten minutes.

"How many other kids who still make messes in their diapers know what antlers are?" Aaron asked proudly.

"Does he?" Ruth said.

"Show Mommy," Aaron told Leon. "Show her what antlers are." Damned if the kid didn't do his thumbs-to-the-forehead-with-fingers-spread gesture again.

Ruth laughed. "He does know! What a smart thing you are, Leon!"

Leon poked at the book. "Read!" So Aaron read. Pretty soon, Leon started rubbing his eyes. Aaron checked his diaper. Leon was dry. As far as Aaron was concerned, that also made the little boy pretty darn clever. Aaron started rocking a little more.

In spite of himself, Leon's eyes sagged shut. Aaron kept

reading a little longer. If he quit too soon, sometimes Leon wouldn't be quite out. He'd wake up again at the sudden silence, and be cranky and hard to settle. But when Aaron stood up with his son in the crook of his arm, Leon didn't stir. Aaron carried him into the bedroom and set him in his crib. Getting the baby down was another danger spot. Leon muttered something, but he went on sleeping.

Aaron walked out to the living room. "Hi, babe!" he said. "Nobody here but us chickens."

"Cluck! Cluck! Cluck!" Ruth said. The Armenian family two doors down raised chickens and ducks in their back yard. Ruth bought eggs from them, eggs that were better and cheaper than you could get at the grocery store.

Aaron sank down into the rocker again and lit a fresh Chesterfield. He could yawn and smoke at the same time—he kept the cigarette in one corner of his mouth while the rest opened wide. "Only trouble is, I'm worn out, too," he said. "I'll be ready for bed in an hour or two."

"I know what you mean," his wife said. And he had no doubt that she did. He moved washers and driers and TVs and iceboxes all day long. She chased after Leon and kept him from smashing his head or swallowing a match or doing any of the other stupid things children did.

Ruth had an Agatha Christie on the table next to her chair. A couple of issues of *Popular Mechanics* sat on the one beside Aaron's rocker. He was a dedicated tinkerer, and used ideas from the magazine every chance he got.

But he didn't feel like reading now. Tired as he was, he didn't have the brainpower to concentrate. He turned on the TV instead. It was a big Packard Bell console: an Early American TV set, if something so modern could also be Early American. Television was even better than radio for giving you something to do when you didn't feel like thinking.

The tubes took a minute or so to warm up and show him a picture. He turned the channel-changing dial to see what all was on. Los Angeles had seven stations, as many as anywhere in the country and far more than most places. He found a fight on Channel Five and went back to the chair to watch.

He did so with a critical eye. He hadn't been a bad man with his fists in his own younger days. In bar brawls, some people dove under the table, while others grabbed a beer bottle and waited to see what happened next. He'd always been a bottle grabber himself.

One of these palookas—middleweights—hit harder. The other was a better boxer. Neither, on his best day, would make Sugar Ray Robinson break a sweat. The boxer was plainly ahead on points halfway through the ninth round. Then the other guy, even though his face looked like steak tartare, landed a left hook square on the button. The boxer slumped to the canvas as if his legs had turned to Jell-O. The bow-tied referee counted him out. He didn't come close to standing again. In the neutral corner, the slugger raised his gloves in beat-up triumph. He looked about ready to fall over, too.

Commercials followed. Because the fight hadn't gone the distance, there were a lot of them. The station had to fill time till the news came on at the top of the hour. Aaron did reach for a *Popular Mechanics* then. He found TV commercials even more annoying than the ones on the radio.

"This is Stan Chambers, reporting on Wednesday, February the seventh," the young reporter behind the desk said when the news started. "Our growing conflict with Russia has taken a dangerous new step. You will recall that, three days ago, American bombers vaporized Pechenga, the northern air base from which Red planes smashed the cities of our European allies. Within the past half hour, we have received word that Elmendorf Air Force Base, outside of Anchorage, Alaska, has vanished in what is being described as a quote tremendous explosion unquote. Radio Moscow, in an English-language broadcast, calls this quote justified retaliation unquote. There is no comment yet from the President or the Defense Department."

"Jesus!" Aaron said. After a moment, he added, *"Gevalt!"*

*"Vey iz'mir!"* Ruth agreed. They'd both picked up Yiddish from their immigrant parents. They found themselves using it more these days than they had for a while, to keep Leon from knowing what they were talking about.

As Stan Chambers went on with the news, Aaron thought about the prize fight he'd just watched. If America and Russia kept slugging each other like this, would either one still be standing at the final bell?

\* \* \*

Boris Gribkov wished he could get drunk. That was what Red Air Force pilots commonly did when they weren't flying and were stuck at a base someplace in the middle of nowhere. Provideniya wasn't just the middle of nowhere. If nowhere ever needed an enema, Provideniya was where they'd plug it in.

Provideniya was so far from somewhere, from anywhere, it didn't even have a brothel. Whores gave pilots something to do when they weren't pouring down vodka, anyhow.

But alcohol—any alcohol, even beer—was off-limits for flight crews for the duration of the emergency. Tu-4s carried atomic bombs. They had to be ready to fly at a moment's notice. Outrage by outrage, the fight the Americans had called the Cold War was heating up.

The base commandant made sure he got the point across. After summoning all his aircrews, Colonel Doyarenko said, "No booze. Fuck your mothers, you cocksuckers, do you hear me? *No booze!* None. Not a fucking drop. You know what will happen if you screw it up? You'll go to Kolyma, that's what. You think you're far north now, assholes? There, you won't see the sun for six weeks at a time. You'll mine coal and dig for gold when it's fifty below. You'll find frogs and salamanders frozen in the ice for a thousand years and you'll eat 'em raw, on account of they'll taste like caviar next to what the camps usually feed *zeks*. No . . . goddamn . . . booze!"

Somebody didn't listen. Put a bunch of people together and there's always somebody who doesn't get the message. One aircrew quite suddenly vanished from Provideniya. Boris didn't *know* the MGB had hauled them off to the wrong side of the Arctic Circle. He didn't *know* they were slamming picks into the permafrost and hoping for frozen salamanders.

No, he didn't *know* any of those things. All he *knew* was, they were gone. An Li-2—which was almost as close a copy of the American DC-3 as the Tu-4 was of the B-29 (though the transport, unlike the bomber, was licensed)—flew in a new crew for the plane that found itself without one. Life went on.

Oh, he knew one other thing. No matter how bored he got here at Provideniya, he wouldn't drink. Kolyma was a name Russian mothers whispered to scare kids who wouldn't behave. It was the worst place in the world. A snootful of vodka wasn't worth the risk of going there.

He read books. He played cards. He played chess. He watched the Northern Lights. When he got five minutes by himself, he jacked off. And he waited for the order to fly his Tu-4 against the Americans. He didn't think he would come back. If they sent him against the U.S. proper, he didn't see how he *could* come back. Well, if you were going to go out with a bang . . .

None of the planes from Provideniya had flown against the U.S. Air Force base in Alaska. That perplexed him enough to talk to the commandant: "Comrade Colonel, what are we doing here? Are we decoys, lined up like wooden ducks on a pond so the imperialists can waste weapons on us?"

"Don't believe it, not even for a minute," Doyarenko answered. "When the time comes, we will hit them, and we'll hurt them when we do it, too."

*Unless they wipe us off the map first.* But Gribkov didn't say it. You didn't want to borrow too much trouble. He did ask, "Well, sir, since we were closest to this Elmendorf place, why didn't we fly against it?"

"Because we're also closest to the American radars at Nome and on St. Lawrence Island," Colonel Doyarenko answered. "They would have spotted us taking off, and the enemy would have been alert and ready for us. When the gloves come all the way off, if they do, we'll have fighter-bombers pound those radar stations to blind the enemy. Then we can do what we need to do."

"Ah, I see," Gribkov said. "Where did the planes that hit Alaska come from, then?"

Doyarenko sent him a hooded look. That wasn't anything he needed to know, even if he might want to. Then the colonel shrugged. "Well, what difference does it make? It's not as if the Americans don't already know we also have planes up on Vrangel Island."

"Ah," Boris Gribkov repeated. The island lay north of the Siberian mainland, between the parts of the Arctic Ocean the maps called the East Siberian Sea and the Chukchi Sea. There wasn't even a gulag on it, which said something, though Boris wasn't sure what. He hadn't known the USSR flew bombers off of it, but he wasn't astonished to learn as much. It was within range of Alaska, certainly, yet even more isolated and able to hold secrets than Provideniya.

The colonel went on, "I've heard the Tu-4s that hit the American air base flew over the ocean, no higher than a cat's testicle above the waves. If you're going to beat radar, that's how you do it."

"I serve the Soviet Union!" Gribkov said, which meant he'd do it that way if and when the bell tolled for him.

But Doyarenko hadn't finished. "I've also heard— unofficially—that our Tu-4s were painted in U.S. Air Force colors." He steepled his fingertips. "They do look quite a bit like the American B-29s."

Gribkov couldn't help snorting, but he managed not to guffaw. The Tu-4 was as close to a copy of the B-29 as Soviet factories could make. There was a story that, because the interior paint jobs on two of the interned B-29s that formed the Soviet plane's pattern differed, Tupolev asked Beria to ask Stalin which scheme to use. The aircraft designer didn't dare choose on his own. The way Stalin chuckled when he heard the question told Beria the answer.

That was what Boris had heard, anyhow. Was the story true? He had no idea. He'd never met either Stalin or Beria, and didn't want to. But that the story could be told as if true spoke volumes about how closely the Tu-4 resembled its American inspiration.

Something else occurred to Gribkov. "Isn't it against the laws of war to fly a plane under false colors, sir?" he asked.

"Officially, yes," Colonel Doyarenko answered, which told Boris everything he needed to know. Doyarenko went on, "But what's the worst thing the imperialists can do to a plane like that? Shoot it down and kill everybody on it. And what's the worst thing they can do to a plane plastered with red stars and with *For Stalin!* painted on the fuselage? Shoot it down and kill everybody in it, *da?*"

"*Da,*" Gribkov agreed. "Comrade Colonel, what if a Tu-4 plastered with red stars and with *For Stalin!* painted on the fuselage turns out to be a B-29 in disguise, though?"

Doyarenko opened his mouth. Then he closed it without saying anything. When he did speak, it was in musing tones: "If we can think of it, the Americans can, too. I'll talk with Colonel Fursenko, the air-defense commander. The MiGs will have to be extra alert."

"Yes, sir," Boris said, his own voice not altogether free from resignation or worry. Extra-alert MiG pilots were liable to shoot down Tu-4s to make sure they didn't let a B-29 sneak through. That might even serve the cause of the *ro-*

*dina.* Whether it served the motherland or not, though, it wouldn't do a Tu-4's eleven-man crew any good.

No B-29s struck Provideniya. It was well below freezing, with snow flurries every other day or so. That didn't keep groundcrew men from getting rid of the Soviet markings on the Tu-4s hiding at the airstrip here and turning them into bombers that looked even more like B-29s than they had already.

When Gribkov asked a sergeant about it, the man replied, "Sir, your eyes must be playing tricks on you. This isn't happening at all." He laid a paint-stained finger by the side of his nose and winked.

"No, eh?" Boris said.

"No, sir." By the way the sergeant sounded, butter wouldn't have melted in his mouth.

"All right." Gribkov wondered if it was. But Colonel Doyarenko had to be right about one thing. Either way, the worst the Americans could do was kill him.

**7**

YOU GOT USED TO things. Vasili Yasevich supposed that was how people kept fighting wars. The horror built up to a certain level, and after that it wasn't horror any more. It was just something you dealt with every day, the way people who made shoes dealt with the smell of leather.

Going through the wreckage of what had been Harbin was like that. Vasili did wonder how radioactive he was getting and what that was doing to his health now and in the future. Wondering was all he could do about it. If he tried to escape, Chinese secret police or soldiers who were just as radioactive as he was and didn't seem to wonder about it a bit would have shot him. So he stayed there and he worked.

The bomb had gone off near the center of town. Ever since the early days of the twentieth century, Russians in Harbin had built substantial churches and offices and blocks of flats in that part of the city, so that central Harbin had been a reminder of what a prerevolutionary Russian city was like.

No more. Those buildings were sturdier than the Chinese-style ones surrounding them. They weren't sturdy enough to survive having a small sun suddenly kindled not far above them. Some of the brick and stone had melted to something very much like glass. Steel and copper had puddled and flowed like water.

And people . . . Those substantial Russian buildings had substantial Russian sidewalks in front of them. Here and there on the scorched sidewalks, and on walls that hadn't quite melted and hadn't quite come down, Vasili saw what looked like the silhouettes of men and women. He didn't need long to realize that was exactly what they were. The atom bomb's flash had printed people's shadows on those sidewalks and walls. Then, a split second later, it seared the people who cast them to hot gas. The shadowprints were all that remained to show they had ever lived.

That was bad. Finding charred, shrunken corpses inside ruins a little farther away from where the bomb went off was worse. You stuffed those into burlap bags and carted them away. With water and fat boiled off, with even bones burnt fragile, you could fit several into one sack. You could, and Vasili did, over and over again.

After the first few days, he wasn't dealing with the wounded and dying any more. The dying had mostly become the dead. He saw burns worse than anything he'd ever imagined, burns that put him in mind of roast meat forgotten on its spit over the fire. Roast meat, though, didn't moan and shriek and beg for someone to put it out of its anguish. He took care of that a couple of times, with the knife he wore on his belt. He had dreadful dreams about the things he saw, but not about helping people die. As best he could tell, he was doing them a favor.

Some of the dying on the edge of the blast area escaped that torment to fall victim to a different one. Their hair fell out. They grew nauseated. They pissed blood. It dripped from their rectums, and sometimes from their eyes and even from the beds of their nails. When they vomited, the black, curded crud they heaved up showed they were bleeding inside, too.

Nobody could do anything for them except give them opium so they hurt a little less. The Chinese doctors called it radiation sickness. Some of the people with it lived: the ones who bled least or not at all. But the doctors admitted they didn't have much to do with that. The only thing that mattered was how big a dose the sufferers got to begin with.

Every evening, when Vasili and the other men and women trying to clean up after the atomic bomb came out of the blast zone, secret policemen searched them. It would have been contrary to human nature not to plunder what the dead needed and protected no more.

But the secret police were as desperately overworked as everyone else near Harbin and the other shattered Manchurian cities. They didn't find everything the laborers secreted on their persons. And even the secret police were human beings. Some of them would take a cut of what they did find and let the laborers keep the rest. If they confiscated it all, the laborers might stop plundering. Then they wouldn't get anything.

"What have you got today, round-eye?" a tough-looking Chinese policeman with a PPD asked.

"Here's your squeeze, pal." Vasili handed him a jade bracelet and some heavy gold earrings set with pearls and rubies. He spoke the same rough northeastern dialect of Mandarin as his watcher, and spoke it about as well. The older he got, the more he used it. The way things looked, his Russian would be the language that got rusty.

"Let me check these." The secret policeman took off a mitten and hefted the earrings. A smile spread across his broad, flat face. "That's gold, sure as the demons! Go on through."

"Thanks. I'm not dumb enough to try to trick you," Vasili said. He made as if to shrug off his quilted jacket. "You want to frisk me?"

"No. Just get out of here." The Chinese gestured with the barrel of the submachine gun.

Vasili got. The secret policeman turned to see what he could extract from the next laborer in line. Vasili walked slowly, as if he were very tired and his feet hurt. He was very tired, and his feet did hurt. One reason they hurt was that he was walking on gold coins he'd stashed under the soles of his feet.

The coins were English sovereigns. Most of them bore Victoria's jowly profile; a few carried her son Edward's bearded visage. He couldn't remember the last time he'd seen any: probably before the Sino-Japanese conflict joined the wider river of World War II. His father had used sovereigns, or maybe gold rubles, to get out of Russia, and to do things he needed to take care of after that.

Even in Mao's aggressively Communist China, gold was bound to have its place. Gold always had a place. Vasili's father'd said so more than once, and Vasili didn't think his old man was wrong. Neither had the people who'd stashed away these coins. But, while gold could do all kinds of things, it couldn't stop an atom bomb. Those people didn't need their sovereigns any more. Vasili was sure he'd be able to use them, even if he didn't know how just yet.

Next stop after the secret-police check was the feeding station. He got a small bowl of rice with a few vegetables on top. No soy sauce—nothing to flavor the mess. Another bowl of the same, or sometimes noodles or a roll, was breakfast. That was it. Along with cash and jewelry, the laborers took whatever canned goods they came across.

"You didn't fill this bowl as full as the one I got yesterday!" groused the man in front of Vasili. Vasili never complained. Getting along in a country where hardly anybody looked like you was hard enough without doing anything to make it harder.

"You're right. It isn't," the guy on the other side of the kettle answered. "Not as much came in today. With the railroads all smashed up the way they are, it's heaven's own miracle we're getting anything."

"But I do hard work every day," the laborer said. "How can I keep it up if I'm hungry all the time?"

"Plenty of people hungrier than you." The server jerked a thumb in the direction the line was moving. "Get out of here, you greedy turtle. You're holding up the works." Glaring, the man walked on. Vasili came up and held out his bowl. Glaring, the fellow with the ladle said, "You going to give me a hard time, too?"

"No, not me." Vasili definitely knew better than to piss off anybody who worked in the kitchens. Plenty of people around Harbin *were* hungrier than the laborers. The government was trying to keep them from starving to death. It didn't worry about anything past that, not yet.

But men and women who handled food never starved. If that wasn't a law of nature, it should have been. This guy wasn't fat, but he sure wasn't starving. If you annoyed these people, they'd find ways to make you sorry. "Well, here, then," the server said. He gave Vasili a little more than the other fellow'd got.

"Thanks!" Vasili sounded as if he meant it. A little grease on the axle helped the wheels go round.


Ihor Shevchenko ate pickles and drank vodka. Pickles, salt fish, meat dumplings . . . Those were the kind of *zakuski* that gave the booze some style. He wasn't smashed yet, but he was getting there.

He raised his glass. "Here's to good old antifreeze!" he said, and knocked back the snort at a gulp. The vodka was icy cold, which made it burn less on its way down the hatch.

"To antifreeze!" echoed the *kolkhozniks* drinking with

him. They downed their toasts, too. His wife giggled. Anya was a little bitty thing. She didn't need to drink much to get plastered.

The next guy who stood up was missing half his left hand. One look at Volodymyr's face, though, would have told you he was a veteran. You didn't need to see the mutilation to know. "To our glorious leader, Joseph Stalin, and to victory!"

"To Stalin! To victory!" everyone chorused, louder than people had toasted antifreeze. You had to show your enthusiasm for the glorious leader. Someone would notice and rat on you if you didn't. Bad things were liable to follow soon after that.

Before too long, the snow would melt. The land would turn to soup for a while. Then it would be time to plow and plant. There'd be more work to do, even if no one would do it with any marked enthusiasm. There wouldn't be so many chances for a bunch of people to get together and get drunk. (It was a Soviet collective farm. There would always be some.)

Ihor eyed Anya. Maybe later on he could get her off by herself, and then. . . . Or maybe, by the time they got done here, he'd be so fried he couldn't get it up with a crane. He wasn't going to worry about it now. He wasn't worrying about anything now.

Pyotr stood up, glass clutched in his meaty fist. He was a Russian, but people on the *kolkhoz* mostly didn't hold it against him. "Here's to the soldier's hundred grams!" he said loudly, gulping the toast.

Everyone whooped and cheered at that one, especially the men who'd fought in the war, which was almost all of them. They'd gladly gulped their hundred grams every day then. You needed something to numb you and make you not think so much before you rushed the Germans' trenches. After a while, there weren't enough Germans left to stop the Red Army, but the Hitlerites always made their khaki-clad foes pay a hefty butcher's bill.

Was the Red Army still feeding soldiers the daily dose? The Americans wouldn't be much fun without it, would they? You could toast victory all you wanted, but they'd dropped an atomic bomb inside Soviet territory. Yes, the radio said the USSR had retaliated, but even so. . . .

What would the Hitlerites have done if they'd had atomic

bombs? Ihor didn't need to think about that one much; the question answered itself. The Germans would have dropped as many of them as they could on the Soviet Union. Hitler didn't just want the Russians and Ukrainians and Byelorussians and Poles conquered and subdued. He wanted them exterminated. He hadn't had the tools for the job. They were here now.

"To smashing all of Germany!" the next man up said, and drank the toast. Ihor followed suit. It matched his mood and his worries. It also gave him the license to numb himself up some more.

Olga Marchenkova—Volodymyr's wife—turned on the radio. After a couple of minutes of music, a familiar voice said, "Attention, Moscow is speaking." Yuri Levitan had broadcast the news from Moscow all through the war. He was still doing it, even though he was a Jew, and Stalin had cooled on them in recent years. Levitan went on, "Here is the latest from around the world on Friday, February 15, 1951."

The more sober *kolkhozniks* started shushing their drunk comrades, some of whom were singing and shouting and carrying on. When the news was over, they could start making a racket again. Now? No. The news suddenly mattered once more, mattered the way it had when Moscow teetered on the brink of falling to the Nazis. Listening to Yuri Levitan then had been a capital crime—the Ukraine already lay under the Germans' harsh yoke. People did it, anyhow. Some died for doing it.

"I regret I must inform you that the forces of imperialist aggression have struck new and harsh blows against the European states helping the Soviet Union to advance the socialist vanguard of humanity," Levitan said in somber tones. "The United States uses as a pretext for its murderous onslaught the Soviet Union's destruction of Elmendorf Air Force Base in Alaska. They choose to forget that the cleansing of Elmendorf came in direct response to their unprovoked attack against the harmless village of Pechenga."

*Why would the Americans drop an atom bomb on a harmless village?* Ihor wondered. Even with vodka fuddling him, he could see that that didn't add up. But it was one of those questions you thought of without asking. You did if you aimed to stay out of the gulags, anyhow.

"American atomic bombs have leveled Zywiec in Poland, Szekesfehervar in Hungary, and Ceske Budejovice in Czechoslovakia," Levitan continued gravely. He was a professional; he didn't stumble over any of the difficult names. "The United States claims these cities were chosen because they are transport hubs through which Soviet troops and those of the fraternal socialist people's republics flow westward toward the frontier between the socialist world and its reactionary opponents. Simple blood lust seems the more likely explanation."

When Ihor was a little boy, his parents would sometimes cross themselves on hearing grim news. It was a dangerous habit in the God-fighting USSR. They trained themselves out of it, and trained Ihor out of it, too. He couldn't remember the last time he'd slipped. But his hand started to move that way now.

Some of the soldiers from the Kiev Military District, the men he'd talked to not so long ago, probably would have gone through one of those towns or another. If not for his own lamed leg, he might have been summoned back into the Red Army himself. In that case, *he* might have gone through one of those towns. And if he had . . . what? Chances were, little pieces of him would be making a Geiger counter chatter right now.

He reached for a vodka bottle and swigged. No one had proposed a toast, but he didn't care. He wanted not to think about that kind of fire blossoming above his head. If he'd had a bottle of ether and a rag, he would have used them instead of the hooch. When you thought of permanent oblivion, temporary oblivion was the only foxhole you had.

He expected Yuri Levitan to go on talking about the American atrocities. Instead, the suave newsreader told of Stakhanovite shock workers in Voroshilovgrad who produced twice as much aluminum as their quota required. "Even then, they refused to leave their posts," Levitan said. "They insisted on doing everything in their power to aid the revolutionary proletariat on the march and on dedicating themselves to glorifying our beloved Comrade Stalin."

That was laying it on with a trowel. With a shovel, even. Or Ihor thought so. And, despite Volodymyr's toast, Stalin wasn't widely beloved, not in the Ukraine. Too many people here had died. He was respected. Anyone who'd beaten Hitler had to be respected. Besides, Hitler had proved himself what seemed to be impossible: an even worse bargain than the Soviet leader. And Stalin was feared. People feared him the way chickens feared the chopping block, and for the same reason. But beloved? No.

All the same, at least half the *kolkhozniks* in the common room were nodding at Levitan's words. Maybe they wanted to be seen agreeing with what he said. Maybe they were just patriots. Love of country was the biggest part of why people didn't abandon Stalin in the Great Patriotic War's blackest days.

Whatever their reasons, they *were* nodding. And Ihor decided he had better nod, too. You didn't want to stick out from what everyone else was doing, no matter what that happened to be. If you stuck out, you got noticed. And if you got noticed, you commonly regretted it.

One of the guys in Tibor Nagy's squad came from Szekes-fehervar. He was as sure as made no difference that the American atom bomb had incinerated his whole family. Part of the time, he didn't want to do anything but roll himself in his blanket and weep and wail. The rest, he wanted to grab his rifle, charge across the border between the Russian and American zones in Germany, and kill all the Yankees on the far side singlehanded.

Right now, Tibor had drawn the short straw in talking him out of taking warfare into his own hands. "You can't, Ferenc. You just can't, no matter how much you wish you could," he said, as reasonably as possible. "Come on—don't be stupid. Give me your piece."

Ferenc clung to the rifle the way a little kid would cling to a velveteen rabbit. "Won't," he said, as if he were about to stick a thumb in his mouth.

Tibor wouldn't have minded if he did—it might have calmed him down. "Hand it over, dammit." He let his patience show. "I know what happened. I'm sorry about what happened. But you can't go shooting up the countryside on account of that."

"Why not? The Americans did." Ferenc just wanted to hit back.

"But they're a country. You're just one fellow. You aren't even a general or anything. You're just a fucking private like me. You'd get yourself killed for nothing. And if anybody you're related to is still alive, they'd roast 'em over a slow fire to pay you back for going off the rails."

Ferenc's eyes filled with tears. "It isn't fair," he whimpered. "It isn't right."

That was undoubtedly true. What it had to do with the price of beer was liable to be a different story, though. As far as Tibor could see, very little that had happened since he and Ferenc were born was either fair or right. Fair and right were for big countries, like Russia and America. Germany had been big enough to make Hungary dance to its tune—but, as things turned out, not big enough to keep playing it. Otherwise, the Germans wouldn't have rival foreign armies stationed on their soil.

And if Ferenc was getting weepy . . . Tibor reached out and grabbed his squadmate's Mosin-Nagant. "There you go, pal," he said. "Just take it easy for a while. Sooner or later, things'll look better."

"Later," Ferenc said, in tones that might have come from the Mask of Tragedy brought to life.

Tibor didn't care, or not very much. He had the rifle. That was what counted. Unless the Russian generals masterminding this operation sent their Hungarian allies over the border in the next couple of hours, Ferenc didn't need it. He'd be as soppy as that "Gloomy Sunday" song for a while. The other soldiers just had to make sure he didn't hang himself or do anything else stupid that he couldn't take back.

Sergeant Gergely noticed Tibor carrying the rifle. "That's not yours," the noncom barked. He might be—he was—a son of a bitch, but he was one goddamn observant son of a bitch.

"No, Sergeant." Tibor agreed to what he couldn't very well deny. "It's Ferenc's. He was talking about going after the Americans again."

"I wouldn't mind if they shot him. It would serve him right." The milk of human kindness was sour cream in Gergely. Shaking his head, he went on, "But he can't go starting a war all by himself, can he? And Schmalkalden is close enough to the border to give him a chance of doing it."

He pronounced the name of the German town perfectly. Tibor would have, too; they both spoke German well, even if they didn't always want their allies to know it. Hardly anyone in the world but Hungarians knew Magyar. German was Hungary's window to what the rest of Europe was saying, and had been for as long as Hungary had been joined to Austria at the hip.

"Well, he won't now, not till he gets the rifle back," Tibor said.

"You do a good job of handling him," Gergely said. Tibor gaped; the noncom wasn't in the habit of doling out praise. Gergely went on, "Well, you do. I've noticed. You know who else does?"

"No, Sergeant." Tibor wasn't used to the older man in a talkative mood. It unnerved him.

"Szolovits," Gergely said. "Yeah, the sheeny. Ain't that a kick in the nuts?" A twisted smile on his face, Gergely bobbed his head and went about his business, almost as if he thought he'd been talking with a fellow human being.

After a little thought, Tibor was less surprised than the sergeant that Istvan Szolovits might have a better idea than most about what Ferenc was going through right now. When the Nazis overthrew Admiral Horthy and used the Arrow Cross as their puppets, lots of Jews had headed for death camps.

That didn't happen till 1944, late in the war. More Jews survived in Hungary than in countries where the SS had got to run wild sooner. Even so, how many relatives had Szolovits lost? Chances were he understood Ferenc's misery better than most of the other soldiers.

The company got a night's pass. They piled into a couple of ancient buses and went into Schmalkalden to see if German beer was as good as people said. The town had been bombed in the last war, but there weren't a whole lot of towns between the Atlantic and Moscow that hadn't been. It was shabby but orderly. The civilians on the street wore clothes that were mostly old, but well-tended. Tibor hardly noticed that; it was the same as he was used to at home.

*"Bier, bitte,"* he told the barkeep as soon as he found a tavern (it didn't take long).

"Here you go." The man gave him a curious look as he served him. "You're not Russian, are you?"

"No, I'm Hungarian," Tibor answered. "How did you know?" His German would have an accent different from a Russian's. His uniform was of a greener khaki than the Red Army used, and of what he thought was a smarter cut.

But the bartender told him, "You said *please.* Next Ivan who does that in here will be the first. And because you did, that one's on me."

*"Danke schön!"* Tibor exclaimed. He sipped. It wasn't

great beer, but it was pretty good. That it was free made it taste even better.

"You didn't fight in the last war, did you?" The German shook his head as he answered his own question: "Nah. Of course you didn't. You're too young—you're just a kid."

Since Tibor *was* just a kid, he couldn't even resent that. He said, "My sergeant did."

"That a fact?" The bartender paused to light a cigarette. By his harsh, rasping chuckle, he went through a lot of them. After blowing out smoke, he continued, "So he's one of those sock people, is he? Hell of a lot of 'em around these days."

"Sock people?" Tibor echoed. He wasn't sure he'd heard straight. If he had, he feared he'd tripped over an idiom he didn't understand.

But the bartender nodded. "*Sockeleute, ja.* You know the kind I mean. I call 'em that 'cause they fit on either foot just as easy."

"Oh!" Tibor giggled like a girl when he got it. He wondered what Sergeant Gergely would have to say if he came out with that. Something interesting and memorable, he had no doubt. He might try it—on a day when he was feeling more suicidal than poor Ferenc did right now. Taking his courage in both hands, he asked, "Did you fight in the last war?"

The bartender looked about forty-five, not that Tibor was any too good at guessing ages. But every German too young to wear a long white beard was likely to have carried a Mauser or a Schmeisser at some time between 1939 and 1945.

"*Ach,* you bet I did, sonny," the man answered. "You can't see, but my left leg is gone a little below the knee. I get around all right, even if I'm not what you'd call quick any more. Shell fragment nailed me when we were pulling back from Kiev at the end of 1943. And after I was on my feet— well, my foot—again, I got to sell drinks to the Russians who blew me up. Life is full of shit sometimes, you know? But what are you gonna do?"

"What is there except the best you can?" Tibor said. His own country lay under Stalin's heavy thumb. It had lost a city, lost it utterly and forever, because it did. Here he was in Germany, about to go to war for Stalin's cause, which mattered not at all to him. Doing the best he could, he finished his beer and slid the seidel across the bar for a refill.

* * *

Days were starting to get longer now. The sun went to bed later and got up earlier at the end of a week than it had at the beginning. But night still stretched plenty far enough for the Red Army tankmen to peel the camouflage netting off their machines, to make sure they had plenty of fuel, and to do all the checks they could in the dark.

Konstantin Morozov didn't know what would happen to a soldier who flipped the switch on a flashlight or even struck a match to get some extra light by which to examine something. The Chekists wouldn't shoot the poor imbecile. That would be too merciful. No, they'd take him away to dispose of him at their leisure. Better the attack should go in short one tank than that a fool or a traitor should give everything away.

He hadn't slept all night. Little white tablets made sure he wouldn't. He still had most of them left. He didn't expect to sleep for the next couple of days. His heart thumped in his chest. His eyes opened very wide. Every time he blinked, his eyelids reminded him how dry and sandy they were. The pep pills were on the job, all right.

He checked his watch again. It was 0454. The last time he'd looked down at his left wrist, it had been 0451; the time before that, 0447. He expected to check a couple of more times in the next six minutes.

"You're ready to go, right, Misha?" he demanded of Mikhail Kasyanov.

"*Da,* Comrade Sergeant!" The driver sounded absurdly confident. Only somebody who had no idea what war was all about could seem so relaxed at a time like this. Kasyanov figured it would be a walkover. He couldn't imagine anything going wrong.

Konstantin Morozov, unfortunately, could. At the end of the Great Patriotic War, the Red Army had massively outnumbered its Hitlerite foes. It had tanks and planes and men and fuel and ammo falling out of its asshole. And attacks *still* got screwed up. The Germans would fall back a couple of kilometers so artillery barrages fell on empty ground. Then they'd hit you when you came forward expecting them to be knocked flat. Or they'd open up a lane in their defenses to invite you through, then jump you from the flanks and rip up your striking column. They had more tricks than a trained circus dog.

If Misha thought the Americans didn't and wouldn't, he was using his dick instead of his brain. Well, he'd have sense knocked into him soon enough. 0457 now. Beside Konstantin, Pavel Gryzlov was a wide-shouldered shadow. Lower and farther back, Mogamed Safarli hardly seemed there at all.

0459. Any second now, unless his watch ran fast. Any second, any second, any . . .

0500. Nothing happened. "*Yob tvoyu mat',* you stupid watch," Morozov snarled. He stared at the luminous tip of the second hand crawling around the dial.

Ten seconds past 0500. Still nothing. Fifteen seconds past 0500. *Still* nothing. He wanted to smash the watch against the breech of the 100mm gun. That would teach the cheap, worthless thing a lesson.

Seventeen seconds past 0500 . . . and the world exploded. It might not have been as loud as the roar of an atomic bomb, but it was the loudest thing Konstantin had ever heard. He'd been there when the final assault on the Seelow Heights kicked off, just east of Berlin. That had been so loud, it beggared words like thunderous. This, he thought, outdid it.

He had no idea how many *Katyusha* batteries and big guns the Red Army had right here. He had no idea how many covered the whole length of what the imperialists called the Iron Curtain. *Lots* was a pretty fair guess for the first of those, *lots and lots* for the second. Even with the tank buttoned up, the noise was a palpable blow against the ears.

Konstantin had to remind himself to shout, "Gun it, Misha!" over or through the impossible din. Either Kasyanov heard him or he remembered they were supposed to get moving as soon as the bombardment started. They were at the very tip of the point of the Soviet spear.

Rockets and shells were still flying west as fast as the crews who served the weapons could send them. The artillerymen had to be as happy as clams right now. They were laying Germany waste, always the dream of any Red Army soldier. The T-54 began to vibrate: the motor was running. Normally, it made a considerable racket. Now, the cannons and the rocket launchers ensured that Morozov knew he was going only through the seat of his coveralls.

The tank clattered west, along with the rest of the machines from Captain Gurevich's company, the rest of the machines from the regiment, the rest of the machines from the Guards Tank Army . . . the rest of the machines from whatever large fraction of the Red Army Stalin had committed to the attack against Western Europe.

"Next stop, the Rhine!" Morozov whooped. That wasn't literally true, but it was the operational goal of this enormous onslaught. Once they'd cleared out the western zones of Germany, they would decide whether the Low Countries and France deserved a dose of the same medicine.

Hitler'd given it to them. And Hitler's forces, not quite eleven years ago, had been nothing, nothing at all, next to the swarm of steel and soldiers roaring west now. The defenders might be more ready to do their jobs than they had been in 1940, but Konstantin didn't dwell on that. *Forward!* was all he cared about.

*Go as fast as you can and blow up anything in your way.* That was what the attack orders amounted to. Bogging down was the worst thing that could happen. The Germans had in 1941, when mud and then snow made them fight in ways they hadn't planned for. It ended up costing them victory.

There were worse dangers now to bogging down and bunching up than there had been during the last war. If you concentrated like that, you gave the enemy a perfect chance to drop an atom bomb on your head. That would slow up your advance like nobody's business.

Captain Gurevich had said the Americans wouldn't do that to territory they were supposed to be defending. No: he'd said he *hoped* they wouldn't do that to such territory. Konstantin hoped the same thing. Oh, did he ever! After all, he was betting his life on that hope.

Misha steered the tank around the burning carcass of one that had stopped something. It happened, however much you wished it wouldn't. Not even the most overwhelming barrages knocked down all the enemy's defenses and gave you a walkover. Konstantin had seen that too many times against the Fritzes. Defenders were like cockroaches; you couldn't kill them all.

A lance of flame brewed up another Soviet tank. Konstantin nudged Pavel Gryzlov as he traversed the turret with his other hand. "Give them a burst of machine-gun fire there," he told the gunner. "That's a goddamn bazooka team."

"I'll do it," Gryzlov answered, and he did. Brass cartridge

cases clattered down onto the floor of the fighting compartment. "We're over the frontier, then, Comrade Sergeant?"

"We must be," Morozov said. "It'll get light pretty soon. Then we'll be able to see what we're doing."

Before long, enough fires were blazing so he didn't need to wait for sunrise to have a pretty fair notion of what was going on. A lot of those fires came from smashed T-54s, T-34/85s, and heavy Stalin breakthrough tanks. The Soviet theory was that you couldn't make an omelet without breaking eggs. Tanks were as disposable as machine-gun rounds. So were tank crews, something Konstantin didn't like to think about.

But enemy tanks blazed, too. The American machines were taller than their squat Soviet counterparts. Their armor wasn't so well sloped, either. As the Nazis did before them, though, they had excellent fire control. They scored hits from ranges a T-54 was unlikely to match. Only one thing to do about it: get in close and slug. Along with the rest of the Red Army, Morozov's tank did it.

# 8

FOR ONCE, GUSTAV HOZZEL was sleeping like a rock. Nothing bothered him—not lumps in the mattress, and not nightmares going back to his days on the Eastern Front. He simply lay there, forgetting the world and by the world forgot.

At five o'clock in the morning, the world remembered him—and everybody else anywhere close to the border between the western and eastern parts of Germany. For a few confused seconds, he thought a thunderstorm was hitting Fulda. But no rain drummed on the roof, and all the noise came out of the east.

Beside him in the warm, soft bed, Luisa sleepily said, "Gustav? What's going on?"

"The Russians are coming." His own voice sounded like the tolling of an iron bell. "You'd better get down to the cellar, dear."

"What? They're kilometers away from here. Even if those are guns, nothing's going to happen here for a while." His wife had woken up enough to think straight, anyhow.

Straight, maybe, but not straight enough. "The shells can't get us yet, no," Gustav answered. "And the Amis will fight hard to keep the Russians from breaking through here. This is one of the key places where they stand a chance of doing that. But the bombers should be here any minute."

"Bombers?" Luisa started to scramble to her feet. "You don't mean dropping one of those atomic things, do you?"

"No, or I don't think so," Gustav answered. "They want to go through Fulda, not make it so nobody can. But that doesn't mean they won't shoot up the place or drop regular explosives on it. So get moving!" He smacked her on the backside, hard enough to make her jump and yip. The noise sounded like a rifle crack—if you'd never heard a rifle crack.

For a wonder, Luisa didn't argue with him. She just threw her hands in the air and hurried downstairs. Gustav put on dungarees, a sturdy wool shirt with lots of pockets, and the stoutest shoes he owned. They weren't marching boots— no hobnails in the soles or anything—but they would have to do.

He started down the stairs himself. He hadn't got to the ground floor before American antiaircraft guns started their percussive hammering. Through the quick-firing guns' racket, he heard a rising roar of aircraft engines. Sure as the devil, the Russians were coming to town.

A split second later, he recognized which aircraft engines those were. They were Il-2s or, more likely, Il-10s: Shturmoviks. Just the sound made his balls want to crawl up into his belly. The attack planes' Russian designers called them Flying Tanks. Fearful *Landsers* tagged them with names like the Meatgrinder and the Black Death. The Shturmovik was heavily armored and carried much too much forward-facing firepower. Though it wasn't very maneuverable, all that steel plating made it a bitch and a half to shoot down.

Explosions rocked the outskirts of Fulda, marching closer and closer. Shturmoviks carried bombs, too. They'd zoom in just above the treetops or roofs, shoot and bomb everything in sight, and get the hell out.

Cannon rattled in the air. More bombs burst. The upstairs windows shattered. A noise like a car hitting a wall and a cloud of plaster dust pouring down the stairs after Gustav said a round from one of those airplanes had ventilated the bedroom.

"Go on!" he shouted at Luisa, who still hesitated near the top of the cellar stairs. "You want the next one to tear through you?"

"What are you going to do?" she asked—he showed no signs of taking shelter with her.

"Whatever the Americans let me. Whatever I can," he answered with a shrug. "Remember, sweetheart, I know how to play this game. I had to quit in 1945, but it looks like things have started up again."

"They'll kill you!" Luisa said.

Gustav shrugged again. "If they do break through here,

we'll have to live under them. That's not living. You don't believe me, ask the Poles or the Czechs or the Hungarians. Ask the Germans in their zone. Now go on down there. Stay safe. I love you." He hurried out the front door, not looking back to see whether she did what he told her to.

Out in the street, the air smelled of more plaster dust, of woodsmoke, and of high explosives. It also smelled of shit, and of the sour sweat of human fear. Gustav nodded to himself. It smelled like a battlefield, all right.

Another Shturmovik buzzed past, guns blazing. Gustav threw himself down behind a chimney that hadn't been lying in the middle of the alley half an hour earlier. A bullet spanged off the bricks, struck sparks, and whined away. He laughed as he picked himself up again. Damned if his reflexes didn't still work.

American jeeps and halftracks added the familiar note of exhaust fumes to the symphony of stinks. They were heading east, toward the fighting, not bugging out. That was good. Gustav supposed it was, anyhow. At least they meant what they said about keeping this part of Germany out of Soviet hands.

Gustav didn't speak more than fragments of English. He'd picked up some Russian during the war—no, during the last war—but didn't think that would do him any good. In fact, it seemed more likely to get him shot.

He went looking for Max Bachman. Max could palaver with the Amis for both of them. And he found his boss and friend sooner than he'd expected. The printer was heading toward his house.

"Here we go." Max sounded surprisingly chipper. "Takes me back, it does, to hear the Iron Gustavs buzzing in."

That was another German nickname for Shturmoviks. Gustav had got into a brawl about it when a *Dummkopf* in his section tried to pin it on him. From Max, he didn't mind hearing it. And he felt surprisingly chipper himself. "Same here," he agreed. "Come on. Let's see if the Americans will give us guns for that militia thing."

"Guns and uniforms." Max wore the same kind of clothes Gustav did. "If the Russians catch us armed and we're dressed like this—" He made a death-rattle noise. Of course, the Ivans might do in prisoners even in uniform. It was one of the things that happened. Gustav knew it had happened a

good bit in the *Wehrmacht*. They played for keeps in the east.
And what the *Waffen*-SS had done . . .

Battle brought new noises now. Jet fighters bansheed overhead. Some, with the American white star, went after the
Shturmoviks. Others, with the Soviet red star, did their best
to keep the Americans off the attack planes. The American
and Russian jets tangled with one another, too. Gustav
pumped a fist when a MiG fell out of the sky trailing smoke
and with a big chunk of one wing bitten out. The crash had a
dreadfully final sound. A plume of fire and greasy black
smoke marked the fighter pilot's pyre.

"Hey! You Yanks!" Max shouted to a couple of Americans
going by in a jeep.

He made them stop, anyway. One of them said something
to him. He answered in English. He sounded fluent to Gustav, but what did Gustav know? Max and the Ami went back
and forth. Then the guy driving the jeep put it in gear and
roared away.

"What did he say?" Gustav asked.

"They're passing out rifles and jackets with armbands and
helmets over by the *Rathaus*," Max told him. "We have to
promise to give the stuff back when the emergency's over.
They'll use us, but they still don't trust us very far."

"I don't care," Gustav said. "No matter how bad the Americans are, Stalin will be worse." Max nodded. They hurried
over to the town hall.

Pom-pom guns in the square did their best to hold maraud-
ing Shturmoviks at bay. The rifles a grizzled American sergeant doled out were bolt-action Springfields, not the
semiautomatic M-1s his countrymen carried. Gustav didn't
fuss. They were close cousins to the Mauser he'd lugged for
so long. The jackets stank of mothballs. They'd probably
been in storage somewhere since 1945. Again, so what? The
band on the left sleeve read *German Emergency Volunteer.*
*Volkssturm* men had worn such armbands the last time
around. Sometimes they helped, sometimes not. The helmet
was an American pot with a separate fiber liner, not a German coal-scuttle. Gustav didn't think it covered enough of
his noodle, but, like the rifle, it was better than nothing.

And he was soldiering again. All he needed was a tinfoil
tube of liver paste to convince him he'd never been a civilian,
not even for a minute.

\* \* \*

"Walk!" the MGB man barked, the snap of accustomed command in his voice.

"*Tak.* I'm walking, Comrade, I'm walking." Ihor Shevchenko took a calculated risk when he said *yes* in Ukrainian rather than using the Russian *da*. He spoke Russian fine. But he wanted the Chekist to think of him as a dim country bumpkin. And if he exaggerated his limp ... Well, his mother hadn't raised him to be a fool.

Maybe he laid the limp on too thick. "Come over here!" the MGB man ordered. "Let's have a look at that leg, dammit."

"*Tak,*" Ihor repeated. He remembered not to lose the limp as he walked over to the unwelcome visitor to the *kolkhoz*.

When he pulled up his trouser leg, the MGB man's face changed a little. It was an ugly wound, with a scar like a crab's spread claws and with a good-sized cavity in the muscle where the surgeon had taken out flesh so it wouldn't rot and poison him. "Put yourself in order," the fellow said grudgingly. "You really did stop something there, didn't you?"

"Afraid I did." Ihor wanted to ask him, *And what did* you *do in the Great Patriotic War, pussy?* Odds were the bastard had spent his time in a heated office a thousand kilometers from the front. His only worry would have been whether he could scare the pretty file clerk into sucking him off. But you couldn't remind him of that, or he'd make you sorry. He had as many ways as beer had bubbles.

"All right," he said now, and made a tickmark on a sheet of paper in his clipboard. "We'll leave you here, then. I don't think that leg will let you go back into the infantry."

"I serve the Soviet Union, Comrade!" That one never let you down. Here, it meant *Whatever you say is fine with me.* Ihor was lying through his teeth, of course. Had the Chekist tried to recall him, he would have done his level best to arrange an accident for the man before they left the collective farm.

As things were, the son of a bitch was taking four men from the *kolkhoz*. Radio Moscow bragged about Soviet victory after Soviet victory, but how many men were going into the sausage machine to win those victories (if they were victories)? Enough so the Red Army needed more bodies. That was as much as Ihor could say.

Would the authorities adjust the collective farm's production norms to take into account the workers it suddenly didn't have? That was so funny, Ihor almost burst out laughing. They would pretend it had as many workers as ever. After all, they had their larger, oblast-wide production norms to consider.

The chances that the *kolkhoz*'s crops would be as large with fewer people to tend them were slim and none. The chances that anyone would get in trouble for failing to meet production norms, though, were also slim and none. Somehow or other, the norms would be met . . . on paper, anyway. If the actual grain brought in from the actual fields didn't quite match what got set down on paper, well, what could you expect in a world full of unreliable human beings?

On paper, the USSR set production records every year. People in the actual world went hungry? Chances were they were socially unreliable elements. How could you get excited about riffraff like that? No one had got excited when Stalin starved the Ukraine into submission. Ihor knew that only too well. No one had cared at all, no one except the Ukrainians. And they were too busy starving to give the matter their full attention.

"Volodymyr was a good fellow," Anya whispered when she and Ihor were in bed together—one of the few places they could talk without much risk of being spied upon.

"They were all good fellows," he whispered back. "We won't be the same without them. You know it. I know it. Everybody knows it. Even the pricks in the MGB know it."

"The pricks in the MGB don't know anything," his wife said.

He shook his head, there in the darkness. She'd feel the motion even if she couldn't see it. "They know. Oh, they know, all right. You bet they know. Those sons of bitches know damn near everything. Knowing isn't the trouble. The trouble is, they don't care."

"That's worse," Anya said, still in a voice no one farther than thirty centimeters from her head could have heard.

"I guess it is. But what can anybody do about it? Not a stinking thing." Ihor was no louder. You learned the tricks that kept you alive when you were small, and you got better and better at using them as time went by. He continued,

"Why, darling, the MGB even knows if I do this." He slid a hand under her flannel nightgown.

Her squeak was a little louder than the whispers she'd been using, but not a lot louder. She didn't slap the hand away, either. She turned toward him instead. After all, he was still there to be turned toward. There were MGB men and MGB men. A really nasty one, or one who didn't think he could make his own quota any other way, would have hauled him back into the army in spite of his wound. Unless he could have come up with one of those convenient "accidents" for the Chekist, he would have had to go, too. His other choices would have been worse.

So he fell asleep happy, and he woke up the next morning pretty happy, too. By the way Anya had snuggled up against him, she was also happy. That was good. If you weren't happy with the person you'd married, you'd married the wrong person. And you would start looking for fun somewhere else, which meant you weren't likely to stay married.

He stayed happy halfway through his first glass of sugared breakfast tea from the communal samovar. Then someone turned on the radio, just in time to catch Yuri Levitan going, "Attention, Moscow is speaking." He was on in the morning. He was on at night. Did he ever sleep? Ihor would have wondered whether every male broadcaster on Radio Moscow called himself Yuri Levitan, only the man's voice was so distinctive, it could have come from but one throat.

"What's gone wrong in the world now?" Ihor said. He assumed something must have. What else was the news but stories about things that had gone wrong somewhere in the world?

After further reports about Soviet triumphs ever deeper in Germany, Levitan went on in grave tones: "In their frantic and futile efforts to interfere with the inexorable advance of the ever-victorious Red Army and its socialist allies, imperialist forces have struck again at the homelands of the workers and peasants' vanguards on the march. American bombers with ordinary explosives hit Warsaw and Krakow, Prague and Bratislava, and Budapest last night, the evening of the twenty-fourth."

He paused. An ordinary human being would have taken a sip of water or tea or vodka, or a drag from his cigarette. Machinelike Yuri Levitan was probably having his neck oiled or something. When he spoke again, he sounded more somber yet: "And the imperialists also struck at the heartland of the proletarian revolution. American conventional bombs fell on hero city Leningrad, on Minsk in the Byelorussian SSR, on Rovno in the Ukrainian SSR, and on Vladivostok in the Soviet Far East."

Another pause from the broadcaster. Ihor listened for the squeak of the oilcan, but didn't hear it. "Civilian casualties from these terror bombings have been heavy," Levitan said when he resumed. "They include innocent children playing in a park in Leningrad. Comrade Stalin has vowed that re-payment will be heavy."

What were innocent children doing, playing in a park in the middle of a nighttime air raid? You could ask yourself questions like that. If you asked them of anyone else, you put yourself in deadly danger. Ihor knew better. He knew better even than to look as if such questions might occur to him. That was dangerous, too. *Me? Just a dumb Ukrainian peasant, that's all.* There lay safety.

*Maskirovka.* It was all *maskirovka.* He drank more tea.


Tibor Nagy hadn't hated Americans. He hadn't hated Germans, either. He'd been a kid when they fought in Hungary. They were ragged and weary and knew they were losing, but when they had any food to spare they shared it. He'd seen Russians as the enemy—till he found that their soldiers didn't act much different from anybody else. People were people, he'd decided. Not profound, maybe, but it suited him.

By the time he got drafted, Hungary had been transformed into the Hungarian People's Republic. He wasn't thrilled about that, but what could you do? If you complained, you could find out all about the MGB and its Hungarian counterparts—that was what. Better to nod when anybody praised Joseph Stalin (whose name was always spelled *Szta-lin* in Magyar, to make it sound right), and to try to get on with the rest of your life.

After he got drafted, political officers talked his ear off, and the ears of all the other conscripts. They shouted that the Germans had been Fascists, which they had. They shouted that Hungary's Arrow Cross regime had been Fascists, which they had. They insisted that Admiral Horthy had been a Fascist. Nobody was dumb enough to stand up and tell them they were full of it.

Americans, as far as the political indoctrinators were concerned, weren't quite Fascists. But they were imperialists and reactionaries and class enemies. They were capitalist oppressors of the proletariat, too. So were the English.

Maybe they were. Maybe they weren't. Again, telling the political officers it was all a pack of rubbish was a long walk off a short pier. You nodded. You gave back the slogans. You tried to go along. You figured being a soldier couldn't last forever, no matter how much it seemed to while you did it.

Then the war broke out. The Russians didn't trust the Hungarians—or think they were strong enough—to break through the enemy defenses. But, no matter how many Russians there were, there weren't enough to do all the fighting they needed to do and to hold down the land they'd overrun.

They figured the Hungarians were good enough for that. And so Tibor and his company found themselves occupying Schweinfurt while the Russians tried to break through at Fulda, farther north and west.

They made ball-bearings in Schweinfurt. Because they did, the Americans had bombed the hell out of the town in the big war. No doubt Stalin had cheered them on when they did, too. Now the Red Army's planes and tanks had flattened a lot of what the Germans worked so hard to rebuild during the war and after it.

"No fraternizing with the locals!" Sergeant Gergely shouted, again and again. "You can't trust them. Anything you say to them is liable to go straight to the enemy's ears. Or some of the bastards who learned their trade with the Nazis may try and blow your head off."

*Bastards like you?* Tibor wondered, but that was one more thing you didn't say.

They'd already had trouble with sniping. Some of the Germans wore almost-uniforms and armbands that proclaimed them part of the emergency militia. Orders were not to kill those guys out of hand, but to capture them if possible and hand them over to the Red Army. What the Russians would end up doing with them or to them . . . was anybody's guess.

Other Germans just had rifles or pistols or grenades and a sense of determination. Somebody would toss a grenade at a truck or shoot from a third-floor window or from behind a burnt-out auto. The Magyars took casualties, and couldn't always catch the sons of bitches who caused them.

Hungarian authorities dealt with that problem the same way the Germans had in two world wars before them. They seized and shot large numbers of hostages. Tibor hated firing-squad duty. You couldn't shoot to miss, though. You'd land in worse trouble if you did.

To his surprise, Istvan Szolovits hated it even worse than he did. "They're Germans," Tibor said to him after an execution. "Don't you want to get even with them for what they did to your people?"

"I don't want to kill people up against a post," the Jew answered. "The SS did shit like that. And I don't know that the people we're shooting did anything to anybody during the war. If I have to fight, I want to *fight,* where the other guys have guns, too. Killing blindfolded people with their hands tied isn't war. It's murder."

"You might as well be a fighter pilot, huh?" Tibor said.

"That would be funny, except it isn't funny," Szolovits said.

His syntax might be twisted, but Tibor knew what he meant. American fighters—jets and prop jobs—often flew low over Schweinfurt on their way to shoot up Red Army units on the move inside the Russian zone of Germany. If they saw a truck column or a few tanks or even some soldiers bunched together, they would open up with their machine guns or fire some of the rockets they carried under their wings.

You couldn't shoot them down, not if you were a rifleman on the ground. You could fire a few rounds at them, but they went by too fast for you to lead them the way you needed to. The slam of your piece against your shoulder might make you feel better, but you had to understand you were only wasting ammunition.

What happened when a rocket hit a truck, on the other hand . . . Tibor dragged a burning man out of the wreckage. The soldier's clothes weren't on fire. He was. Tibor rolled on top of him, careless that his own uniform and flesh were getting singed. Then two men rushed up with a big pail of water and dumped it over both of them.

They took the badly burned soldier away. Tibor got some ointment to smear on his scorches. He also got, for the first time ever, Sergeant Gergely's genuine respect. "Good job, kid," the veteran said. "Not everybody'd lay his balls on the line for his buddy."

"He's not my buddy," Tibor said; his own burns were starting to sting in spite of the ointment. "I don't even know who he is. And I didn't think about taking chances. I just ran over and grabbed him. If I'd taken the time to think, I bet I would've stood there with my thumb up my ass."

"That's how it works most of the time," Gergely told him. "But how you did it doesn't matter. What matters is, you did it. Next time we've got a slot for a lance-corporal, now I know who to fill it with."

Tibor cared about becoming a lance-corporal no more than he cared about being elected Pope. But Sergeant Gergely's good opinion of him meant something—meant quite a bit, in fact. It hadn't while the army was on a peacetime footing. Then he'd wanted to stay out of trouble and to keep the sergeant out of his hair. Past that, Gergely could have gone and hanged himself for all Tibor cared. Tibor might have hoisted one if he had, to tell the truth.

War was different, though. War was different all kinds of ways. You found out why they drilled so many things into you in peacetime training. It wasn't only to kill time or to wear you out. When the bullets and rockets and shells started flying, you needed to obey orders without wasting an instant. You needed to know how to dig a foxhole and how to keep your rifle clean. And you needed to know when to hit the dirt a split second before you had any conscious reason to.

Even second-line soldiering, which was all the Red Army demanded from its none too eager Hungarian, Polish, and Czechoslovakian allies, taught you those things in a hurry. And, though Tibor wouldn't have been in Schweinfurt if not for the Russians, they weren't trying to kill him here.

The Americans were. He might not have hated them before he started trying to hold down the city. When they did things like blowing up that truck, though, whatever kindness he'd felt toward them melted away as if it were snow in a hot oven.

A hot oven . . . The sight of burning flesh was horrible. The smell was even worse. His stomach wanted to turn over. He sternly told it it would do no such thing. To his relief, it decided to listen to him.

American bombers came over that night. They pounded Schweinfurt as if it were the Second World War all over again. "Why don't they hit the Russians?" Szolovits complained from his foxhole near Tibor's. "We didn't do anything to them."

"We're here," Sergeant Gergely said flatly, and that did seem to be as much answer as anyone needed.

*We're here,* Cade Curtis thought. The Korean with him punched him softly on the shoulder to wish him luck, the way an American might have. The man whispered something in his own language, touched him again, and slipped away to the north in the darkness, back toward his own village.

*He's gone about as far as he can go.* Cade's mind played with the song from *Oklahoma!* He hadn't gone as far as he had to go himself. The lines the Red Chinese and North Koreans held lay just ahead, between him and the American trenches he needed to reach.

Here and there, he could see faint red glows among the Communist positions. Some of those, the ones that brightened and faded, would be cigarettes. Others were more constant. If you put kerosene or fat in the bottom of a can and added a wick, you had a lamp or even a puny stove. The soldiers wouldn't need to be so careful about hiding the lights from behind as they were from ahead.

Not much shooting was going on. For one thing, it was 0130. Men on both sides would be at the low ebb of energy and alertness. For another, the Korean War had turned into a backwater fight. It had dominated the world's attention all through its first six months. But then the atom bombs started falling. The big brawl broke out in Europe. And with that donnybrook in full swing—which was about as much as Cade knew about it—the Americans, if not the Chinese, wouldn't worry so much about things here.

If Cade was ever going to do this, he had to go forward. He walked straight down the muddy dirt track that led to the front here. He'd given the U.S. Army parka to his Korean buddies. He'd hacked off his beard. In quilted jacket and fur hat, with a Russian submachine gun in his hands, he looked like somebody who belonged here till you got close enough to see his nose. He hoped like hell nobody would.

If the Reds caught him, they could shoot him for wearing their clothes. Of course, if they caught him, they could shoot him for the fun of it. They probably would, too.

He didn't worry about it. Whatever happened would happen, that was all. He'd been on the run ever since things went sour south of the Chosin Reservoir. He wondered how many other dogfaces had managed to get away. Not a lot. He was sure of that.

When he started getting close to those red glows, he stepped off the path and began to crawl. Some snow still lay on the ground. He wondered whether Korea was ever free of it. He knew which way he'd bet.

Here and there, snores rose from foxholes. Cade was glad to hear them; they kept him from making what would be his last dumb mistake. A couple of men talked quietly in sing-song Chinese. Now he could tell the difference between that language and Korean from only a handful of syllables. He sure hadn't been able to when the fighting here started. He still didn't speak more than a few words of either tongue. Even that little was more than he'd looked for.

The front here wasn't multiple rows of trenches on both sides, the way it had been in France during World War I. Cade gathered it was like that on some stretches of the line. His guide had brought him here because things were looser in these parts.

Somebody called out something. A challenge? Whatever it was, Cade froze—not hard to do in this weather. The Red Chinese soldier called out again. This time, Cade heard, or thought he heard, a questioning note in the man's voice.

Nobody fired off a flare to light up the landscape. Nobody started spraying bullets around as if from a garden hose. After fifteen motionless minutes, Cade slithered forward once more. His thumb hit a pebble. It clicked when it caromed off a bigger rock. He froze again.

Then, to his vast relief, a dog started barking not far away. The beast probably stayed near the soldiers to eat whatever they threw away. It took its chances, though. It would have been safer with the Americans. With these guys, it could end up simmering over one of those makeshift stoves.

But if they went after the dog, they wouldn't stumble over him . . . unless they found him by accident while they were hunting it. *Bite your tongue,* he thought. He did. It hurt. He was still alive, then. He wanted to stay that way.

On he crawled. His hand hit a metal post. Both sides used them to anchor their belts of barbed wire. He had a wire cutter. He got to work with it. The strands parted with twangs he would have thought you could hear in Guam, if not in Hono-lulu. No flares hissed out over no-man's-land, though. No machine guns started chattering, either.

A barb on the wire skewered his finger. He howled and swore—inside his own mind. The stuff was bound to be filthy and rusty. His last tetanus shot, just before he went into action, had left him miserable and feverish for a couple of days. Now he was damn glad that bored army doc had stuck him.

Crawl. Snip. Crawl. Snip. Crawl. Freeze. What was that? Oh—they *were* going after the dog. Crawl. Snip. Crawl.

Suddenly, no more wire to snip. He'd made it through the Reds' belt. If he kept going, he'd find the American entangle-ments pretty soon. How jumpy were the GIs on the far side? Would they open up with everything they had when they heard him coming?

He dreaded that more than anything else. He'd made it all this way, dodged the enemy's hunters down most of the pen-insula. Now, at last, he could see rescue, see safety. How cruel would the irony be if his own side ventilated him, thinking him a Red?

He discovered the American wire with his forehead. The blood trickling down his cheek was warm. He hoped the gash wouldn't leave a nasty scar. Your face usually healed up pretty well, but usually wasn't always.

Crawl. Snip. Crawl. Snip. He moved as quietly as he could. He heard low voices ahead of him. They were speaking En-glish. Not Chinese, not Korean, not even mangled Latin. English!

He cut one more strand and crawled forward again. He didn't come up against any more wire. He was through! Nothing at all stood between him and his own countrymen—except their fear when they finally heard him coming. *The only thing we have to fear is fear itself.* That had been FDR, back when Cade was a baby. He'd been way too little to re-member it himself, but it was the kind of thing you heard all the time.

"Hey!" he called. Why not? The Reds were several hun-dred yards behind him. "Don't shoot! I'm an American!" Sweet Jesus! English felt strange in his own mouth, it had been so long since he'd used it.

Sudden silence slammed down ahead, silence mixed with scrambling noises. No, they'd had no idea he was out here. If he'd been a Chinese raiding party, a lot of these guys would be talking to their undertaker.

Somebody chambered a round. The sharp *snick!* was much too audible. Then somebody else did. "Don't shoot!" Cade repeated, more urgently than before. "Honest to God, I'm an American."

Through the silence, someone called, "Okay, asshole, who played in the Series last year?"

They'd asked the same kind of question to trip up English-speaking Japs in the last war. Cade thanked heaven he was a fan. "Yanks and Phillies," he answered. "Yankees swept."

After a pause, that same voice said, "Okay. Come on. We won't plug you till you get here, anyway."

Cade came. He remembered to leave his Russian sub-machine gun behind. It wouldn't create the impression he wanted. He tumbled into a foxhole. A GI lit him up with a flicked Zippo. The flame was dazzling.

"Fuck me," the dogface said. "He *is* an American—I think. Scrawny SOB, whatever he is." The casual scorn was the most wonderful thing Cade had ever heard.

# 9

A BUS RAN FROM Fakenham to Norwich. It was about twenty-seven miles from the small town to the city. The bus always stopped in Bawdeswell, halfway between. Every once in a while, it would stop without intending to. All the buses on the route dated from the 1930s, and they'd all seen hard service since the day they were built. No wonder they broke down from time to time. The wonder was that they didn't do it more.

To Daisy Baxter, Norwich had always been *the* city. It was the one she could easily get to. It was her window on a wider, brighter, more cosmopolitan life than the one she lived in her hamlet near the sea.

Or rather, it had been. These days, Norwich was a synonym for hell on earth, in the most literal sense of the words. No one knew how many had died there, not to the closest ten thousand. No one knew how many were hurt: burned by fire from the skies, poisoned by radiation, or simply crushed or mangled as they would have been in an ordinary explosion. The word the BBC most often used about the devastation was *unimaginable*.

Daisy didn't want to imagine it. She wanted to see for herself what the Russians had visited on Norwich. She wanted to see what the enormous American bombers at Sculthorpe might visit on Russia. It was morbid curiosity. She understood that.

She also understood seeing any more than they showed in the newspaper pictures wouldn't be easy. Never mind that she'd lose business, because she was sure getting there and back would take all day. She was willing to sacrifice the day's trade. An atom bomb didn't go off in your neighborhood every day—and a bloody good thing it didn't, too.

But she feared she might not be able to see what she wanted to see any which way. The Army and Scotland Yard had thrown a cordon around Norwich. That was partly to help them deal with the devastation in the sealed-off area. And it was partly to keep away would-be sightseers like Daisy.

Since the bomb fell, the bus ran only half as often. No wonder: now the route ended at Bawdeswell. Far fewer people cared about going there than had wanted or needed to go to Norwich. Bawdeswell had nothing you couldn't find in any other hamlet. And, no doubt, the road from Bawdeswell to Norwich would be blocked.

But there was more than one way to kill a cat. Instead of climbing on the bus, Daisy got on her bicycle and pedaled out of Fakenham early in the morning. It was chilly but not freezing, and drizzling but not really raining. If she waited for better weather, she might still be waiting months from now. Some of the grass was greening up. Spring still lay three weeks ahead, but you could tell it was coming.

Before long, she left the main road. A spiderweb of lesser ways still bound the countryside together. She went down one-lane paved roads that saw an auto or two a week, down graveled tracks, and down dirt paths that might have been shaped by flocks of sheep when the Romans still ruled Britain.

A carrion crow scolded her from an oak still bare-branched. "Hush, you," she told it. "Haven't you had your fill of dead meat and then some farther east?" Instead of answering, the big-beaked black bird took wing.

Hamlets that made Bawdeswell seem like London by comparison dotted the countryside: places with names like Stibbard and Themelthorpe and Salle. Salle was as close to Norwich as Bawdeswell was. She didn't see any soldiers when she rode past it.

A rabbit darted across the road. A split second later, so did a fox, red as a flame. The rabbit dove into some bushes. The fox went right after it. Daisy didn't wait to see whether the fox came out with its jaws clamped on the rabbit.

When she got within eight or nine miles of Norwich, she saw that the farmhouses she rode past stood empty. The bomb couldn't have killed from so far away . . . could it? She hoped it was only—only!—that the soldiers and police had made everyone so close to the blast evacuate. But the breeze blew from the east, and it carried an odor—a faint odor, but unmistakable—of meat left out too long.

A black-and-white cat trotted toward her when she stopped to look at one of the abandoned houses. It meowed and flopped down and rolled over and did everything but hold up a PLEASE TAKE ME WITH YOU! sign. It didn't know anything about bombs or why its people had gone away. Tears stung at her eyes as she started riding again.

She hadn't got too much farther before she started seeing damage: broken windows, things knocked helter-skelter, scorched paint on the Norwich-facing sides of buildings, cattle and sheep dead and bloated in the fields. Then she came round a corner—and there were two soldiers getting out of an American-made jeep.

Whether she was more startled or they were wasn't easy to guess. One of them started to point his Sten gun at her, then decided she wasn't dangerous and lowered it. "What are you doing here?" he growled. By his accent, he was a Geordie, from Sunderland or Newcastle or one of the smaller towns up in the northeast.

"I'm out for a ride, of course," she said, which was true enough but didn't say how far she'd come.

The other soldier had a captain's pips on his shoulder straps. "They're supposed to have cleared everybody out of this part of the country," he said.

"Nobody told me to leave," Daisy said. That was also true, although, again, it didn't address why.

"Well, ma'am, I'm telling you right now," the captain said. That *ma'am* put Daisy's back up. She couldn't have been more than three or four years older than the officer. Uncaring, he went on, "You need to get back beyond Bawdeswell. If I tell you to go there, will you?"

"Of course." Daisy lied through her teeth then.

"Hmm." The pause for thought meant the captain knew she was lying. *Damn!* she thought. He turned to the soldier with the submachine gun. "Simpkins!"

"Sir!"

"Why don't you throw the lady's bicycle in the back of the jeep and take her over to Bawdeswell? I can poke about here till you get back."

"Yes, sir!" Simpkins replied. When an officer said *Why*

*don't you . . . ?,* he was giving an order. He was just being polite about it. Simpkins nodded to Daisy. "Come along with me, then."

She did, however little she wanted to. After she got off the bicycle, the soldier lifted it into the jeep with effortless strength. Then he gestured invitingly for her to climb aboard. That was when she really noticed the passenger's seat was on the right side. "It's got left-hand drive," she said in surprise.

"Aye, it does," the Geordie answered. "The Yanks build 'em that way, on account of they drive on t'wrong side o' t'road."

"How do you like it?" Daisy asked.

Simpkins shrugged broad shoulders. "Took a bit o' gettin' used to—you see things from funny angles. But it's all right now." As if to prove as much, he put the jeep in gear and made for the main road from Norwich to Bawdeswell.

As he turned on to that wider—not wide, but wider—road, Daisy asked, "How close have you gone to the center of Norwich? How bad are things there?"

"Not good, and that's for certain." With his accent, the last word came out *sartin.* Shaking his head, he went on, "Some o' the ground right under where it blew, it's all fused to glass, like. Not much left in the way o' buildin's. A few, you can see where they used to be and even some o' what they used to be, but most of 'em's just . . . gone. *Kaput.* You know what *kaput* is?"

"Oh, yes," Daisy answered. "My husband was a tankman. He picked that up from Jerry prisoners."

"Was?" Simpkins heard the past tense.

"Was," Daisy repeated. "Not long before the war ended, his tank got hit, and that—was the end of that, I'm afraid."

"I'm sorry," the soldier said. "A cousin o' mine, he didn't come home, neither. I wasn't old enough to take the King's shilling, or it could've been me. If your luck's out, it's out, that's all."

"Too right, it is," Daisy said bleakly. They didn't say much more till he stopped the jeep in Bawdeswell. He gave her the bicycle. She got on and started back to Fakenham. It was well past noon by then. B-29s rumbled by low overhead, eastbound out of Sculthorpe. Daisy wondered where they'd be by the time darkness fell.

\* \* \*

Harry Truman studied the situation map thumbtacked to a bulletin board in a White House conference room. Red pins in western Germany, in Austria, and in northeastern Italy made the map look as if it had come down with a bad case of the measles. The more he looked, the worse things seemed.

"This is terrible!" he exclaimed. "Terrible!"

"I'm afraid you're right, sir." George Marshall nodded gravely.

"They keep coming forward," Truman said. "We knock out the first wave of tanks and drunken infantrymen. They send in another one, just as strong and just as ferocious. We knock that out, too. Then they send in the third wave, and it rolls over whatever we have left after we took out the first two."

"It's standard operating procedure for the Russians, Mr. President," the Secretary of Defense said. "The Germans found out all about it. One of their generals said, 'A German soldier is worth two or three Russians—but there's always a fourth one.'"

"There sure as hell is." Truman scowled at the map. "What are we going to do? The way it looks to me is, we don't have enough men to stop them, not even with England and France doing their best to help."

"It looks the same way to me," Marshall said.

"We can't let them gobble up our piece of Germany. They won't stop there, either. They'll take the Low Countries, too. And they may take France. What have we got then? Europe Red all the way to the Atlantic. That isn't a disaster, George. That's a catastrophe!"

"There are things we can do about it," Marshall reminded him.

"Atom bombs. It comes down to more goddamn atom bombs." Truman did some more scowling. "You were right— I made a mistake when I authorized using them in Manchuria. And the whole world is paying because I did."

He might have found a way to blame the decision on Douglas MacArthur. MacArthur had agreed with it, certainly. He'd thought it would help his troops in North Korea. It probably had. The Red Chinese were having trouble bringing men and supplies into Korea. Aerial reconnaissance and intercepted radio transmissions proved as much.

But MacArthur and Truman had both miscalculated— guessed wrong, if you wanted to get right down to it—about how Stalin would react. And, in the end, the responsibility lay with the President. It always did. If you took the responsibility, you also had to shoulder the blame. The buck really did stop here.

"No point dwelling on what might have been. We've got to deal with the world as it is," Marshall said. "And the world as it is has too many Russians in it, and they're too far west."

"I just got a cable from Adenauer in Bonn," Truman said. "From Adenauer in a bomb shelter in Bonn, which he took pains to point out." The President made a sour face. Konrad Adenauer was a confirmed anti-Nazi, which had made him a good man to lead the new, hopeful Federal Republic of Germany. But he was also stiff-necked and sanctimonious.

"And what did he say from his bomb shelter in Bonn?" Marshall rolled his eyes. When he was Secretary of Defense, he'd also had to deal with the German politico. His expression argued that he hadn't enjoyed it.

"He begs me—that's his word, not mine—not to use atom bombs on the territory of the Federal Republic," Truman answered. "He says the damage they would cause outweighs any military advantage they'd give. He says his people would have a hard time staying friends with a country that did that to them."

"If we don't do it, in another week or two there's liable to be no Federal Republic to worry about," Marshall said.

"I understand that," Truman said, with another harassed glance toward the map. "The trouble is, I'm sure Adenauer understands it, too. He may have the tightest asshole in Western Europe, but he's no dope."

Marshall sent him a quizzical look. Truman had seen a few of those from the distinguished soldier and diplomat since succeeding Franklin D. Roosevelt. He knew exactly what they meant: that FDR never would have said such a thing. *Well, too stinking bad,* the President thought. When he slogged through Tacitus in the Latin, he'd been horrified to discover that the Roman historian called a spade an implement for digging trenches. As far as Truman was concerned, a spade was a spade, or maybe a goddamn shovel.

"Of course, sir," Marshall said, "if we drop atom bombs all over the Federal Republic, Adenauer won't have much left even if they do drive the Russians back."

"That's what he said in the wire." The President sighed. "It's his country."

"Only about as much as Japan is Hirohito's." As usual,

Marshall had a point. The United States called the shots in western Germany. Or the United States had called the shots till the shooting started. The Secretary of Defense went on, "He doesn't say anything about atom bombs on the Russian zone?"

"No. I told you, he's no dope. He knows he can't make us pay attention to him on anything outside his borders." Truman drummed his fingers against the side of his leg. Then, suddenly, he grinned. "I bet he hopes like anything the wind's blowing from west to east when we bomb his ex-countrymen."

Marshall's face twitched in a sort of vestigial smile. "I bet you're right, Mr. President."

"If we do it again, it won't just be the Russian zone there," Truman said. "We'd better clobber the other satellites, too. That will slow the reinforcements going through them, and it may give them a hint they're backing the wrong horse in the race."

"I wouldn't count on that, sir." Marshall explained why he sounded dubious: "Those regimes are full of Stalin's hand-picked men. Rokossovsky, the Polish Minister of War, was a Russian marshal during the war."

"I understand," Truman said. "But you'd hope that, after a few atom bombs, even people with the MGB sitting on them might get frisky. No guarantees—I understand that, too. Still, you'd hope."

"Ah. I see what you're saying." Marshall nodded. "Yes, you would hope—you do hope. At the end there, the Italians rose up and shot Mussolini and his mistress and Achille Starace."

Truman snapped his fingers. "Starace! Thank you! I never remember that Fascist bastard's name."

"He was a big wheel in Italy once upon a time," Marshall observed.

"Sure he was. But he's not important enough for anybody to want to keep him in mind now—anybody who doesn't have your head for details, I should say." The President sent what was almost a bow in Marshall's direction. Then he continued, "Those Red bosses in Warsaw and Prague and Budapest and East Berlin, they're smart enough to see the writing on the wall. If it looks like people are gonna shoot them and hang them upside down from lampposts, how long will they stay in love with Stalin?"

"That's a good question, all right," George Marshall said.

"If we bomb Warsaw and Prague and Budapest and East Berlin, those people won't be around to worry about it. Stalin will have to find someone else to pass on his orders."

"I don't want to do that. It would be like dropping a bank vault to squash an ant. Most of the people in those cities despise Communism as much as we do." Truman hadn't worried about such things when he ordered the Manchurian cities hit. Europeans were people to him, people who could have ideas like his. Chinese were just . . . Chinese.

"So you want to take out smaller towns, then? More places with important rail lines?" Marshall said. "Shall I make a list for your approval?"

"Yes, do that. We'll break a lot of eggs, but I don't want to drop the whole bushel basket at once, not if I can help it," Truman said. "And it will get Adenauer off my back—for a while, anyway."

Konstantin Morozov stuck his head out of the cupola and warily peered ahead. His T-54 sat hull-down behind a low swell of ground nobody who hadn't been a tank commander for a while would even have noticed, much less exploited. You got to be a veteran commander by starting to notice such things—and by killing the new fish and the jerks who didn't.

The T-54, he was discovering, had a design flaw nobody in the Red Army'd talked about. Talking about it would have cost some engineer his cushy dacha or his Stalin Prize or maybe his neck. Not talking about it meant tank crews had to find out about it the hard way, in combat . . . or buy a plot before they could.

Trouble was, the 100mm gun wouldn't depress as far as the main armament on the American and British tanks the swarms of T-54s were facing. That meant the Soviet machines, when they were on a reverse slope like this, had to come farther forward and expose more of themselves when they fired. The enemy had an easier time getting a clean shot at them than they did at him.

He studied the terrain ahead with Zeiss binoculars he'd taken off a dead German major somewhere in western Poland at the end of 1944. He'd hung on to them ever since. They were so much better than the junk his own country made, it wasn't even funny.

A few enemy foot soldiers had dug foxholes half a kilometer farther west, not far from a burnt-out farmhouse. They were Americans, or maybe the Nazi retreads who fought alongside the imperialists. Had he been sure they were Fritzes, he would have sent a few shells at them, more to scare them out of a year's growth than in serious hope of killing them. Fighting Americans was a professional responsibility. Even in this new war, fighting Germans was a savage pleasure.

He let himself slide back down into the turret. "What's going on, Comrade Sergeant?" Pavel Gryzlov asked.

"Not much, not right this second," Morozov told the gunner. He asked the loader, "How are we doing for ammo, Mogamed?"

"Could be better, Comrade Sergeant," Mogamed Safarli answered. "We're down to maybe eight rounds of AP, half a dozen HE, and a couple of those canister shells."

"Fuck me! That's not enough!" Morozov said. You could go through eight rounds of armor-piercing in five frantic minutes. The T-54 had already done it more than once. "What are we supposed to do if we run dry? Hit the goddamn Pershings with our dicks?"

"You'd need a hell of a hard-on to get it in," Gryzlov said. All three men in the turret laughed goatishly.

But Konstantin didn't keep laughing for long. "That really isn't enough, Mogamed—nowhere near. Why didn't you say something sooner?"

"Comrade Sergeant, please excuse me, but I told you we were running low yesterday afternoon. We haven't bombed up since. In fact, we used some high-explosive shells knocking that tavern flat."

Morozov thought back. "Well, up my cunt," he remarked without rancor. "You did say that. Went clean out of this chamber pot that's supposed to be my head." He didn't mind getting on his crew when they screwed up. You kept them sharp that way. But they hated you if you came down on them when they hadn't done anything wrong.

He'd had a couple of superiors like that. Neither one of them lived through the Great Patriotic War. It could have been a coincidence. It could also have been that nobody went out of his way to lend a hand when the hardasses landed themselves in trouble.

He got on the radio with regimental HQ and said, "Things

are pretty quiet in front of me. Any chance I can pull back long enough to fill up my racks?"

"How are you fixed for shells?" asked the uniformed clerk in the colonel's tent. Konstantin repeated what Mogamed Safarli had told him. The clerk said, "You'd better hang on where you are. We've got some tanks drier than you, and we aren't feeding them any shells, either."

"*Bozhemoi!* Why not? What'll we fight with if the Yankees counterattack? Rocks?" Morozov didn't want to talk about his dick with someone he didn't know well. If the clerk was a prissy little shit, as so many clerks were, he could get his tit in a wringer for throwing *mat* around. People like that were allergic to the filthy Russian slang.

"I can't give you what I don't have." By the way the man said it, he'd used the same words with those other tank commanders before he talked to Morozov. "It isn't reaching the front in the quantities we've requisitioned."

"Why the hell not? If we don't have ammo, we'll lose the war!" Konstantin yipped.

"Haven't you been paying attention to Radio Moscow?" the clerk said coldly. "The imperialists dropped more atom bombs on our supply routes last night. We have to be careful expending ammunition and fuel till the situation stabilizes. Out." He broke the circuit.

"Bugger me with a pine cone!" Morozov said in disgust, yanking the earphones off his head. "They can't give us any more, not right now. They're low on diesel, too, or they say they are, the stingy turds." He called to the driver through the speaking tube: "Hey, Misha!"

"What do you need, Comrade Sergeant?" Mikhail Kasyanov asked.

"How are we fixed for fuel?"

"Half full—a hair under. How come?"

"Because only the Devil's auntie knows when we'll get any more," Konstantin replied. When a Russian started talking about Satan's near relations, things had gone wrong somewhere. Well, things *had* gone wrong somewhere, and the Devil was loose on earth. For all Morozov knew, his near relations were loose with him. The tank commander went on, "They've dropped more atom bombs—that's what's happened. They want to fuck over our logistics, is what they want, and they know how to do it."

"That's no good," Kasyanov said. "What happens if we get

the order to advance, and we run out of gas before we've gone ten kilometers?"

"What do you think happens?" Morozov answered irritably. "Either the Americans shoot us because we're out of shells, too, or the MGB shoots us because we didn't send the tank forward without fuel."

He regretted the words as soon as they were out of his mouth. As usual, that was just exactly too late. Everybody who wasn't a snitch hated the MGB. Even some polecats who were snitches hated the MGB while they informed on their friends and neighbors and spouses and parents. Hating the MGB was simply a fact of life in the Soviet Union.

But *saying* things that suggested you hated the MGB . . . When you did that, you gambled with your freedom. You gambled with your life. Konstantin had given the other three men in the tank a grip on him. It wouldn't matter that his T-54 was at the spearpoint of the Soviet advance. If one of them let a Chekist know what he'd said, they'd yank him out and send him to the gulag or shoot him, depending on how annoyed and how busy they happened to be.

They might also do the same to the crewmen who hadn't reported him. Disloyalty was one of the worst crimes a Soviet citizen could commit. What was not reporting disloyal speech but a disloyal act? Nothing else at all, not the way the security apparatchiks eyed things.

To keep from worrying about it, he poked his head out of the tank again. A couple of Soviet infantrymen had come up alongside it. One of them carried the new rifle, the AK-47. It was wonderful, like giving a soldier his own private machine gun.

"Careful, friends," Morozov called to the men in grimy khaki. "The Americans are on the far side of the rise, maybe half a kilometer from here. Don't show yourselves when you move up."

"Yes, Granny dear," the man with the Kalashnikov said. His pal snickered. They figured a tank commander didn't know the first thing about fighting on foot. For all Morozov knew, they were right. He shrugged. At least he'd tried.

Boris Gribkov smiled as he walked from the barracks to the airstrip. "Isn't that something?" he said, his breath smoking as he spoke. "Makes me wish I spoke English, damned if it doesn't."

His Tu-4, like all the heavy bombers at Provideniya, had turned into a B-29. *Maskirovka* was a many-splendored thing. The paint job had always been the biggest visual difference between the original and its reverse-engineered half brother. The other Soviet features—the engines, the cannons that replaced .50-caliber machine guns in the turrets—didn't stand out to the eye.

Now the red Soviet stars and numbers were gone. White U.S. stars inside blue replaced them. So did American numbers and group markings. If you saw Gribkov's plane or any of the others here, you would swear it came out of a Boeing factory, not one from half the world away.

Vladimir Zorin came out with a nasty chuckle. "We may not speak English, but the imperialists will understand what we tell them," the copilot said.

"You're right about that, even if they don't understand us," Gribkov said. His big hope for accomplishing his mission was that any American fighter pilot who happened to spot the Tu-4 would take it for a B-29 and pay no attention to it.

No guarantees, of course. No guarantees about anything that had to do with what they were about to try. All the aircrew knew that. Everybody understood it. No one had shied away or refused to fly, even though Colonel Doyarenko swore there would be no reprisals against anybody who wanted out.

Gribkov didn't believe him. He didn't believe any of the other flyers did, either. Maybe they wouldn't give you a bullet in the nape of the neck. Maybe. But you would get an enormous black mark on your record. You would never see another promotion or another assignment you actually wanted. And what would happen to your family? They had all kinds of ways to make you sorry if you stepped out of line, and to make the people you loved even sorrier.

Two ladders led up into the bomber. Gribkov, Zorin, and Alexander Lavrov, the bombardier, climbed up into the one that led to the cockpit. The radioman, the navigator, the flight engineers, the radar operator, the fire-control scanners, and the poor, lonely tail gunner boarded through the bomb bay.

As soon as Gribkov was installed in the left-hand seat, he started running through checks with Zorin and Gennady Gamarnik, the engineer. The engines powering the Tu-4 were only cousins to those the B-29 used, but they had the same problems. They ran hot, and they were barely powerful enough to get a fully laden bomber off the ground. You had to be careful with them, or you wound up dead—to say nothing of all over the landscape.

When the engines started, the roar and vibration filled the cockpit. One by one, the Tu-4s in B-29's clothing rumbled down the runways and climbed into the air. None of them climbed very high. They all turned southwest after takeoff: away from the questing radars near Nome and on St. Lawrence Island. Fighter-bombers were attacking those, but who could say if they'd knock them out?

After the Tu-4s had flown that way for twenty minutes or so, they swung to the southeast, toward the United States. They scattered across the North Pacific like wandering albatrosses, separating from each other one by one. Even if the Americans should spot them and come hunting, they wouldn't have an easy time knocking them all down. And every single bomber packed a massive punch.

The sun sank behind Boris Gribkov. His Tu-4 flew almost half as fast as the line of night traveled. Since he was moving against the cycle, sunset came on sooner than it would have otherwise. Now it would be up to Leonid Tsederbaum, the navigator, to get them where they needed to go. *He's a smart Jew,* Gribkov thought. *He'll take care of it.*

He kept his fuel mixture lean and the throttles as low as he could while staying airborne. His target wasn't at the far end of the Tu-4's range, the way so many were. He wasn't necessarily on a one-way trip. Not necessarily, no, but he knew damn well that remained the way to bet.

"Want to hear something funny?" Vladimir Zorin said.

"I'd *love* to hear something funny, Volodya," Gribkov answered. "What have you got?"

"I was just thinking—if this really were a B-29, we could fly it."

"Bet your cunt we could!" Gribkov exclaimed. The dials and labels would be in English, but he knew what they did without reading them. The measurements would also be in the English units that had driven Tupolev's aeronautical engineers to distraction. That could prove a bigger problem, but as long as the indicators stayed out of the red it wouldn't be anything he needed to worry about.

Tsederbaum's voice on the intercom sounded in his earphones: "Comrade Pilot, please bring the plane two degrees farther north. I say again, two degrees farther north."

"I'm doing it." As Gribkov spoke, his hands on his yoke and his feet on the pedals made the course correction with next to no conscious thought from him. He kept his eyes glued to the altimeter, the artificial horizon, and the angle indicator. You had to trust your instruments when you flew at night. Your senses would fool you and betray you. You'd think everything was fine till you went into the drink.

When he yawned, Zorin passed him a flat pressed-tin package of benzedrine tablets. He dry-swallowed one. "Shame I can't wash it down with some vodka," he said. His copilot gave back a crooked smile.

Gribkov's eyes opened wider. His heart pounded harder. His mouth got dry. He'd been sniffling a little, but his nose dried out, too. His gaze darted from one instrument to the next like a hunted animal's. The little white pill was on the job.

"You should take one, too," he told Zorin. The copilot did. Benzedrine made you pay later, but that would be later. For now, Gribkov felt like a new man. And, right now, what would happen when he came down from the pep pill was the least of his worries.

He flew on. He saw nothing through the windshield but darkness and his own reflection, faintly lit up by the lights from the instrument panel. It might have been better that way. The USSR hadn't tried making Plexiglas—much less curved sheets of Plexiglas—till it set out to duplicate the B-29. The result wasn't perfect. In the daytime, you got a distorted view of the world. Darkness looked the same any which way, distorted or not.

More than three thousand kilometers from Provideniya to the target. More than two thousand miles, if you were going to think like an American. More than seven hours of flying. You just kept going. You monitored the course as best you could. Every so often, Tsederbaum gave you another small correction. You applied it.

How many more Tu-4s were in the air, from Provdeniya and Vrangel Island and other Soviet Far East bases? Gribkov had no idea. But the number wouldn't be small. How many of those eleven-man crews would ever see the *rodina* again? He feared the number wouldn't be large.

"Comrade Pilot, time to gain altitude for the attack run," Tsederbaum said.

"Thank you, Comrade Navigator." Gribkov pulled back on the yoke. The Tu-4's nose rose. This was where things got tricky. He had literally stayed under the Americans' radar on the way across the Pacific. But he had to rise to deliver the bomb. They'd spot him. His IFF would have outdated codes. If they were on their toes, they could scramble fighters. If the *maskirovka* didn't fool them, they could shoot him down.

But there was the western coast of the USA, dead ahead. It was supposed to be blacked out, but it wasn't. With the radar in the plane, that wouldn't have mattered much, but a proper blackout would have made things harder. As they were, he could guide himself as if by a road map.

"Are we ready, Comrade Bombardier?" he asked as they flew 9,000 meters over sleeping Seattle.

"We are, Comrade Pilot," Lavrov said. "I bomb at your order."

"Bomb!" Gribkov said. The Tu-4 got five tonnes lighter as the egg of death fell free. He banked toward the ocean and mashed the throttles to the red line.

# 10

MARIAN STALEY GOT LINDA to bed a little past eight o'clock. Linda didn't much want to go to bed—when did she ever?—but she didn't pitch one of the famous fits that make four-year-olds lucky to live to five, either. After a while, the wiggling and soft singing from her bedroom settled down toward quiet. After a little while longer, surprisingly deep snores floated out. Marian smiled. Linda was down for the count.

To celebrate, Marian went into the kitchen, took a can of Olympia out of the icebox (actually, it was a refrigerator, but the old name stuck), and opened it with a church key. She started to pour the beer into a glass, then shook her head and drank from the can. She didn't have anybody to impress. Besides, this way she wouldn't have to wash the glass.

She always remembered savoring that beer. It had been a busy day, with a lot of running around: the grocery, the bank, the laundry, a secondhand bookstore. Linda'd been . . . not terrible, but enough to keep Marian on her toes. She felt she'd earned the Oly.

Everything else about the day seemed the same way. She worried about Bill, over there in Korea. She worried about the war in Europe, too. But all of those concerns lay thousands of miles away. They were noises from another room, like her daughter's snores.

She turned on the radio to catch some news. "It's nine P.M. on Thursday, March 1, 1951," the broadcaster said. "Mayor Bill Devin has announced that Seattle's civil defenses are being beefed up. Air-raid warnings are scheduled to begin next week. Mayor Devin said, 'We did this after Pearl Harbor, too. We turned out not to need it then. I don't expect we'll need it now, either. But, as the Boy Scouts say, it's always better to be prepared.'"

Everett actually lay about twenty miles north of Seattle. Unless the suburb did the same thing as the big city, the air-raid alerts wouldn't matter here. *Just as well,* Marian thought. If the sirens weren't enough to throw Linda into a tizzy, she didn't know what would be.

The broadcaster bragged about how many planes the Boeing plant was turning out. "Full speed ahead for the war effort!" he said. As Boeing went, so went business in Seattle and all the bedroom communities. Sometimes you wondered which was the tail and which the dog.

She listened to the radio till nine o'clock, then turned on the TV. KING-TV was the only station in Seattle—the only station in the Pacific Northwest, come to that. They'd beaten Portland to the punch. Unfortunately, the comedian prancing around on it lacked the essential quality of humor known as being funny. She gave him five minutes, made a face that would have got Linda a swat on the fanny, and turned him off again.

Maybe a murder mystery would be more interesting. It was, for ten or fifteen minutes. Then she found herself yawning and reading the same paragraph three times. Was the beer making her that sleepy? Or was it taking care of a little girl by herself while her husband fought a war on the other side of the Pacific?

Whatever it was, going to bed before ten o'clock seemed a depressing way to end the day. When she was a kid, staying up as late as she wanted seemed one of the big attractions of turning into a grownup. No bedtime! What could be better than that?

Marian yawned. Not being so goddamn tired could be better than this. She yawned again. Staying up as late as you wanted could also mean going to bed as early as you wanted. It could, and tonight it did. Linda would be up at the crack of dawn, one more habit that failed to endear little kids to their parents.

The bed was cold. She often thought that when she slid into it by herself after Bill got summoned to active duty. It seemed especially bad tonight, though. She shivered under the covers till her own body heat warmed things up a little.

Then, with a sigh, she gave up and went to sleep. That was five minutes after she lay down—six, tops.

She woke in the middle of the night from a confused dream of howling dogs. The howling went on after she stopped sleeping. *Sirens?* she thought, more confused than ever. But Mayor Devin had said they would start next week, and that was in Seattle, not here. A couple of guns went off. Big guns. Cannons.

All the windows were closed. The shades were down to the bottom. She'd made sure of that—there'd been a Peeping Tom in the neighborhood the year before. The curtains, dark ones, were drawn. The light that filled the room was brighter than the sun even so, brighter than a thousand suns. If a flashbulb the size of a car had gone off in front of her nose, it might have felt something like that. Her left cheek felt as if someone had pressed a hot iron to it.

She screamed and buried her face under the covers, which helped not nearly enough. Blast hit the house while she was doing that. Had the Jolly Green Giant put on hobnailed boots before kicking the place, that might have come close. It slid off the raised foundation as all the windows broke and everything that could fall down did. The bed suddenly developed a tilt. The roof beams creaked and groaned and then shrieked as they pulled apart. Chunks of plaster rained down. One, luckily not a big one, hit her in the head.

*"Mommy!"* High and shrill and terrified, the squeal overrode everything else. "Help, Mommy, *help*! It hurts!"

Marian jumped out of bed. "I'm coming, darling!" she yelled, and ran toward the bedroom door. Halfway there, she tripped over a fallen nightstand she couldn't see in the now-returned dark and took a header.

She landed on her face—luckily, not on the burned side. When she brought her hand up to her eyebrow, it felt wet. She tried to blot the cut with the sleeve of her nightgown. She smelled gas. She also smelled smoke. She didn't see fire anywhere, but that proved nothing. They had to get out of there right now.

"Linda?" she called.

At the same time, Linda was calling, "Mommy?" They ran into each other in the pitch-black hall. They both screamed. Then they both laughed. Marian snatched up Linda and ran for the back door. It was closer than the front door, and also downhill in the new, off-kilter world inside. As she ran, she noticed her feet hurt. Then she wondered how much broken glass she'd stepped on, and how much was still in her feet. Glass didn't show up on X-rays.

That was the least of her worries about X-rays. How big a dose of them had the bomb just given her . . . and Linda? She couldn't do anything about that. That she couldn't do anything about it made her hate herself.

The back door stood open. She'd locked it, but atom bombs, like love, laughed at locksmiths. She stumbled out into the chilly night.

"What's that, Mommy?" Linda pointed to the southern sky.

"It's the horrible bomb that did this to us," Marian answered. The mushroom cloud, still swelling, still rising, towered high into the night sky. Though fading, it glowed with a light of its own. The colors had a terrible beauty: goldenrod, peach, salmon. She also discovered that Linda had a flash burn on her neck like the one on her own cheek.

Here and there, fires were beginning to burn, some on her block. How far from the terrible cloud were they? Too far to be erased in an instant, like the people peacefully sleeping under the bomb when it went off. Too close to get off scotfree.

Neighbors were calling to one another. People were screaming, too, people who'd had pieces of furniture or big pieces of their house fall on them and people who were burning. A man ran shrieking down the street. His hair was on fire—bright yellow flames shot up at least six inches. Maybe he used too much greasy goop. Maybe he'd slept with an uncurtained window facing south. Maybe, maybe, maybe . . . Whatever exactly had happened, it was dreadful and funny at the same time—unless you happened to be him, in which case it was just dreadful. He shrieked and tried to beat out the flames with his fists as he dashed along the street in his pj's.

With a sudden thrill of horror, Marian recalled that *this* was what her husband did to other people. He did it for a living. He incinerated them and smashed their houses and set them on fire. You took that for granted when it happened to other people, dirty Japs or Commies, thousands of miles away. Of course you did. It didn't seem real then.

But when it happened to *you* . . . That was when you saw what atom bombs were all about. They were city-killers, nothing else but. And the Russians had killed her city. Sirens began to wail. But there wouldn't be enough fire engines or ambulances on the whole West Coast to deal with the disaster here.

A sudden, hot rain pelted down on her and Linda. "Eww! That's disgusting!" her daughter said. It was bound to be radioactive, too.

"Come on. We'll get in the car and roll up the windows," Marian said. That might help a little. Or they both might already be cooked in a fire invisible, but no less deadly—more so, in fact—because of that.

Leon Finch was still a little guy. He wouldn't turn two till the end of May. He didn't always sleep through the night. When he woke up, he usually needed to be changed. Sometimes he wanted a bottle. Sometimes he just needed cuddling till he could go back in his crib.

Except once in a while on weekends, Ruth took care of all that. Aaron went out and made a living; she stayed home with the baby. More often than not, Aaron didn't even wake up when Leon fussed. He was tired enough to have a good excuse for staying asleep till the alarm clock bounced him out of bed.

Ruth would take Leon out to the living room and rock him in the rocking chair till he settled down. Sometimes she would turn the radio on softly and listen to music or the news. It didn't bother Leon, and it gave her something to do without turning on the lights, which would have.

The first thing Aaron did when Ruth shook him awake was grab his glasses off the nightstand. It was still dark, but that had nothing to do with anything. He had to be able to see, and without them he damn well couldn't.

"What is it?" he asked as soon as he had them on his nose.

"They've bombed Seattle," she said, "and Portland, too."

"Oh, Lord!" he said. He had relatives near Portland. Or maybe he had had relatives near Portland.

"I almost dropped Leon when I heard," Ruth said. "The news from Seattle had already come in when I got him. Portland just happened, or they've just said it happened, anyhow."

"What time is it?" Aaron looked at the glowing hands on the alarm clock. It was a few minutes past four. He yawned. "Well, I'm awake. Thanks for telling me. You want to put some coffee on? I'll get by without an extra couple of hours today, that's all."

"Okay. I'm sorry, dear," Ruth said.

"So am I." Aaron turned on the lamp on his nightstand. After blinking against the sudden light, he grabbed his cigarettes and lit the first one of the morning. The first drag made him cough. After that, it felt wonderful. As he got out of bed, his wits started working. "Honey!"

"What is it, dear?" Ruth asked.

"They bombed Portland after Seattle, not at the same time?"

"That's right. Or I think so."

"If they had warning in Portland, why were they asleep at the switch?"

"Because nobody really believed anybody could attack the United States, I guess," Ruth said. "We got caught by surprise at Pearl Harbor, too, and then the next day the Japs were still able to bomb the airports in the Philippines."

"They should have court-martialed MacArthur for that." Aaron had never been an admirer of the general's. But Ruth's brother, who'd been in the Army in the South Pacific and come back to the States with malaria, swore by MacArthur, not at him.

"They must have decided they needed him." Except for marrying a man ten years older than she was, Ruth showed good sense. Aaron had quickly learned to respect her judgment.

He said, "If Portland got it about an hour after Seattle . . ." He paused to picture distances. "If all their planes took off together, San Francisco should get hit about two hours after Portland, and we'll catch it an hour or an hour and a half after San Francisco."

"Let me make you breakfast," Ruth said. "Maybe you'll be happier after you eat." She fixed bacon and eggs for both of them, frying the eggs in the bacon grease. She'd kept kosher till she married him. He'd never bothered—his father prided himself on being a freethinker. Ruth hadn't minded quitting. With toast with butter and jam, a breakfast like that gave you enough ballast to last till lunch.

They listened to the radio while they ate. From what the excited newscaster said, someone had shot down a B-29 that had no business being anywhere near Spokane when it didn't respond on the radio. Or maybe it was a Russian bomber pretending to be a B-29. The newsman didn't seem sure, which made it a good bet the authorities weren't, either.

After breakfast, Aaron showered and put on his work clothes: gabardine trousers and a white shirt with *Aaron* embroidered in red script on his right breast and BLUE FRONT in blue capitals on the pocket. His shoes looked ordinary but had steel toecaps under the leather to keep his feet from getting mashed. He'd also used them to advantage in a bar fight or two.

When he came out of the bedroom, Ruth said, "Are you sure you should go to work today? If the bomb does come—"

He cut her off. "I can't call in for something like that. If the bomb doesn't fall, Weissman'll can me so fast, it'd make your head swim. Maybe even if it does. He's like that."

She looked unhappy, but she nodded. They'd both gone through the Depression. If you had a job then, you clung to it the way an abalone clung to a rock. Somebody was always trying to pull you away from it.

Just before he was going to head out the door, the radio newsman said, "Flash! And I'm afraid I mean that literally. A flash of light was seen above San Francisco moments ago, and communication with the city appears to have been lost. Further details as they become available."

"Jesus!" Jewish or not, Aaron swore like any other American.

"Don't go," Ruth urged him again.

"Honey, I have to," he said. "They won't hit the Blue Front warehouse. They'll bomb downtown, and we've got the hills to shield us."

"They're not high enough," she said. He shrugged. They probably weren't. But they weren't high enough to protect the house, either.

When he got to the warehouse just before sunup, Herschel Weissman was standing out front. "Good to see you. I wasn't sure I would," the boss said. He spoke in Yiddish, in a *Nobody here but us chickens* way.

"I'm here—for as long as I'm here," Aaron answered in the same language.

They went inside. Not everybody had shown up, or would. Weissman grumbled, but not too hard. Aaron realized he wouldn't have got fired for staying home after all. Well, he'd feel like a jerk for leaving now.

And it was too late anyway. Sirens started going off. A

minute later, he heard jet engines screaming overhead. Jet engines meant warplanes, nothing else. If there was a bomber, maybe they'd shoot it down before it could unload. Or maybe it was a drill, or a false alarm, or even a bad dream.

But it wasn't. The sunflash made Aaron and Mr. Weissman and everyone else in the place shout and scream. Seconds later, blast rattled the building. It didn't fall on the people inside—the bomb must have gone off a little too far away. All the lights inside went out.

Aaron was already running for the open door. "See you later," he called over his shoulder. Washing machines weren't the biggest thing on his mind right now. He jumped into his Nash and started home. He hadn't even looked at the mushroom cloud rising above downtown Los Angeles. He had more urgent things on his mind.

He was only a couple of blocks from his house when a parachute-wearing airman landed in the street in front of him. He swore under his breath—all the goddamn traffic lights were out, and now this? What else would slow him down? Then he saw the red stars on the man's flight suit.

He jumped out of the car and ran toward the Russian, who was struggling to free himself from his harness. Aaron grabbed a pocket knife, the only weapon he had except for his shoes. "You're my prisoner!" he yelled. The man spread his gloved hands and gave forth with palatal gibberish. On a what-the-hell hunch, Aaron repeated himself in Yiddish.

"*Ach,* prisoner," the Russian replied in what had to be German—close enough to Yiddish to be comprehensible. "Yes, I am prisoner. I surrender." He raised his hands.

"Come on back to the car with me. I'll take you . . . somewhere." Aaron wondered where. He'd never captured a prisoner in the merchant marine. Then inspiration struck. He put the car in gear and headed for the Glendale police station. It wasn't far. They could stick the Russian in a cell so nobody lynched him till after he was questioned.

Afterwards? How many people had the bastard just killed? What would the Japs have done to the crew that bombed Hiroshima? That was what Aaron wanted to do to this guy. He kept driving. He was more civilized than he'd thought.

It was daylight over the North Pacific. Boris Gribkov felt as if he'd been flying forever. The little white pills kept his eyes wide open anyhow. He wouldn't start paying for them till after he got down. If he got down.

All he could see was water. All he'd been able to see for a long time was water. The USSR was the biggest country in the world. You could drop it into the Pacific and it would go splash and disappear. He hadn't imagined an ocean could be so vast. Till now, he'd done his flying over land. This was a different business—about as different as it got.

"How are we doing, Leonid Abramovich?" he called back to the navigator.

"Comrade Pilot, change course three degrees to the north. I say again, three degrees to the north," Tsederbaum answered. He and Gribkov were trying to bring the Tu-4 to a precise dot of latitude and longitude, a dot marked only by waves.

"I am changing course three degrees to the north," Gribkov said as he applied the correction. "We're what—fifteen minutes away?"

"More like twenty or twenty-five. We've been fighting some nasty headwinds on the way west," Tsederbaum said. Gribkov must have made an unhappy noise, because the navigator asked him, "How are we fixed for fuel, sir?"

"We're low." Boris didn't need to look at the gauge to answer that. Flying from Provideniya to Seattle took more than half the Tu-4's range. All the land between Seattle and Provideniya belonged to the USA or Canada. If only the Tsars hadn't sold Alaska to the Americans! A long lifetime too late to regret that now.

And so Red Fleet vessels were supposed to be waiting at that designated dot of latitude and longitude. If the Tu-4 got there, if it ditched as it was supposed to, if the sailors were on their toes . . . If all those things went right, the bomber crew might possibly survive. It gave them something to hope for, anyhow.

A lot of the Tu-4s taking off from the bases in the Soviet Far East would use all their fuel, or almost all, reaching their targets. Their crews couldn't even hope for waiting ships. They would have to drop their bombs and either make an emergency landing at whatever airfields they could find or bail out and hope the Yankees who caught them didn't string them up or burn them alive.

He'd done what he was ordered to do. The bomb lit up the night when it blew. Two separate shock waves buffeted the

Tu-4. He'd expected only one. Maybe the second came from a ground reflection. He didn't know. It hadn't knocked the plane from the sky. Nothing else mattered.

Time crawled by. After twenty-five minutes—and after the fuel for the first engine fell into the red zone—Gribkov said, "Well, Leonid Abramovich?"

"Another . . . two minutes on this heading, Comrade Pilot," the navigator replied. "Then start flying the search spiral. We'll find them—or we won't." Better than most, Tsederbaum understood their chance wasn't a good one. A dot—an invisible dot—on an unimaginably enormous ocean? A dot where his navigation had to match that of the pickup ships?

After two minutes, Gribkov did begin the spiral. He also began flying lower. Two engines were in the red zone for fuel now. He needed power for ditching. They could bob in their rafts for a while if they went in smoothly. Maybe the Red Fleet would find them. Maybe the Americans would, and take them captive. Maybe no one would, and they'd all wish they'd crashed and got it over with in a hurry.

He peered through the Plexiglas, hoping to see ships below. In the right-hand seat, Vladimir Zorin was doing the same thing. Alexander Lavrov, the bombardier, had the best view of anyone in the crew.

"Fuck your mother!" Lavrov shouted suddenly. "Fuck *my* mother! There they are—about two o'clock, not even far away!"

*"Bozhemoi!"* Boris whispered. Now that the bombardier had spotted them, he could see them, too. He put the intercom on the all-hands circuit. "We have spotted the rescue vessels. We are preparing to land on the sea. Get ready to use the water-landing procedures we have learned."

One of the interned B-29s had a manual that covered the drill for ditching the big plane. Translators had carefully turned it into Russian. No one in the Red Air Force had actually practiced the drill, not so far as Boris Gribkov knew. He knew damn well he'd never practiced it himself, though he'd read the translated manual. Well, there was a first time for everything.

They shrugged out of their parachute harnesses. Lavrov left the bombardier's station and took his place by the flight engineer. You wanted to come in as slowly as you could—ideally, under sixty meters per second—and land on top of a swell with the nose slightly up. Gribkov lowered the flaps to cut his speed as much as he could. At first, even the Americans hadn't been sure that was a good idea. They finally decided it was, though, and he wasn't about to argue with them.

"Brace yourselves!" he called one last time as the green-gray water rushed up to meet the plane. "We're going in!"

There were two slaps, as there'd been two blast waves. The first, when the tail touched the water, was light. The other, when the fuselage and wings went in, almost threw Gribkov against the yoke in spite of his safety harness. He hoped everyone was well strapped in.

"Come on, Volodya," he called to Zorin. "We'll get the rafts out." The Tu-4 rode higher than he'd expected. That was one advantage of dry fuel tanks, anyhow. He grabbed the raft near the pilot's seat. The copilot was doing the same thing on the other side. They inflated the rubber rafts with $CO_2$ cartridges.

Boris opened his escape hatch. He pushed the raft out ahead of him, and didn't inflate his own life jacket till he'd got outside—the hatch was tight. A light line connected the raft to the plane. It would break if the bomber quickly sank, so as not to pull the raft down, too.

Other men were coming out of the hatches farther back along the fuselage. Damned if Vitya Trubetskoi wasn't splashing forward from the left tailplane toward the left wing. Rear gunner was the loneliest spot on the plane. You were all by yourself for the whole flight—unless the enemy gave you company, of course. And Boris had put the plane down tail first. He'd feared he'd drowned poor Vitya. But there the corporal was. He was made of stern stuff. He waved as he paddled forward, held up by the life vest. Boris had no idea whether he could swim without it.

He scrambled into his own raft. The first man he pulled up was Leonid Tsederbaum. The navigator kissed him on the cheek. "Thank you, Comrade Pilot."

"Thank *you*, Comrade Navigator. You guided us to where we were supposed to be."

Everybody got out. His raft held six men; Zorin's, five. He wouldn't have bet on that when he ditched. The Tu-4 was no seaplane, made to land on water. All you could do was put it down and hope, the more so with an unpracticed crew. But they'd made it work. He cut the umbilical line.

Here came the boats from the rescue vessels. One ship in the flotilla was a destroyer, the *Stalin*. The others were smaller: patrol ships and a couple that looked like fishing boats. The sailors waved and cheered.

"You did it!" shouted the bosun in the lead boat. "You stuck a big one right up the Americans' cunts!"

"We serve the Soviet Union!" Gribkov answered. It wasn't as if he never used *mat,* but it didn't seem right for an officer who'd managed to survive a mission where survival wasn't really expected.

"Pull these heroes in!" the bosun told his sailors. They did. Behind the abandoned raft, the Tu-4 settled lower and lower in the water. Before they'd got back to the patrol ship that had sent out the boat, the bomber sank forever. Gribkov saluted it. Like him, it had done everything asked of it and more.

"I thought you were going into Kiev today," Ihor Shevchenko told his wife. "It's Sunday, after all."

Instead of answering, Anya sneezed. It was one of those horrible, wet sneezes that show somebody has a genuinely awful cold. She blew her nose—a mournful honk—into a handkerchief. Ihor got a glimpse of her snot. It was yellow, almost green, the kind you would expect to see dribbling from a three-year-old's snoot.

"Never mind," Ihor said. "I see why you're staying here."

Anya made a feeble, get-away-from-me pushing gesture. "Go to the common room. Go outside. Go somewhere," she said. "If you stay around me, you'll catch this. Believe me, you don't want it." As if for emphasis, she sneezed again.

"Bless you," he said, and then, "I'm going, I'm going." Sometimes arguing with your wife was a losing proposition. That had to be doubly true when she wasn't fit company any which way.

Ihor did go outside. If he didn't want Anya's company, he didn't want anybody's. Besides, if he went to the common room, he'd start drinking. The *kolkhozniks* were celebrating the news of the blows the Red Air Force had struck against the West Coast of the United States—and against Newfoundland and a city called Bangor, Maine. Yuri Levitan bragged about the devastation the Soviet bombers had left behind.

Ihor lit a *papiros*. Yuri Levitan hadn't said a word about what the USA was liable to do next. The Americans and the Russians were playing a game like the one snockered Ukrainian peasants sometimes enjoyed. Two men stood facing each other. One slapped the other's cheek. Then the second guy slapped him back. They took turns till one man either couldn't stand the pain or fell over.

Blowing out smoke, Ihor remembered he'd played that game a few times. You had to be drunk, the drunker the better. When you were, it was funny and full of ridiculousness. If you tried it sober, it would just hurt. Not much fun in that.

He smoked and walked, walked and smoked. The Soviet Union had just slapped the United States hard enough to stagger it. He wished the slap would have been harder. Why not some really big cities on the U.S. East Coast? Maybe the Soviet bombers couldn't reach them. Or maybe they got shot down trying. But was this slap hard enough so the Yankee imperialists couldn't whack you back? How could you know? All you could do was wait and find out.

Snow still lay on the ground. The trees near the stream remained as bare-branched as if they'd never heard of leaves. Spring was on the way, but winter always hung on as long and hard as it could. Summer was the season that seemed to vanish as soon as you looked away.

And this was the Ukraine. Up in Russia, things were worse. No wonder the Russians thought they were tougher than their cousins down here. It wasn't just that there were more of them. They had to put up with more to get anything out of where they lived.

He walked on. A weasel stared at him. Pretty soon, its white winter coat would turn brown. It hadn't yet, though. The weasel darted behind a tree trunk and disappeared. Disappeared from Ihor's view, anyhow. But the mice and voles would find out it was still around.

He looked back at the clump of buildings that made up the heart of *Kolkhoz* 127. They were all cheap and shabby, punished by winter cold and summer sun, their paint faded, roof tiles coming loose and blowing off. They didn't get fixed up as often or as well as they should have.

But the buildings were collectively owned, along with almost everything else on the collective farm. What everybody owned together, nobody cared about individually. And so things wore out, and mostly didn't get repaired. Ihor had never heard of a *kolkhoz* that worked any differently, whether in the Ukraine, in Russia, or, for that matter, in Bulgaria.

Three women rode by on bicycles, bound for Kiev. Ihor stared after them, scowling. Had Anya decided she was going, horrible cold or no horrible cold? She'd be lucky if she didn't come back with pneumonia. But he didn't think she was one of the riders. For her sake, he hoped not.

Fifteen or twenty minutes later, something started to squeal, far off at the edge of hearing. Not a pig kind of squeal—a machine-made kind of squeal. Rising and falling . . . Air-raid sirens? Ihor lit another *papiros*. Stalin had sown the wind. Was the whirlwind on the way?

Screams in the air—those were jet fighters taking off and getting as high as they could as fast as they could. Could they get high enough fast enough? Everybody anywhere near Kiev would find out soon.

Through those urgent, even desperate, screams, Ihor's ear caught another jet roar, this one high and distant, as if the airplane making it had already got as high as it needed to get and didn't have to worry about any interlopers late for the party.

Off in the distance, as far away as the sirens, guns began to pound. Ihor hadn't thought they had antiaircraft guns that could shoot as high as the plane moving from west to east was flying. For all he knew for sure, they didn't have flak like that. Whether they could reach high enough or not, they were shooting for all they were worth. Why not? What harm would it do?

None, probably. Whether it would do any good, though . . . That question got answered moments later. It did no good at all. For all the antiaircraft fire, for all the screaming MiGs, a new sun burst to life over Kiev. Even from kilometers away, the heat of that burning was fierce on Ihor's face.

He threw himself flat on the cold ground and tried to dig himself into it like a mole, the way he had when the Germans started throwing 105s around. But shells from a 105 were gravel on a tin roof next to that mountain of flame incinerating the ancient city.

"God, have mercy! Christ, have mercy!" He gabbled out the Old Church Slavonic prayers again and again, hardly knowing he was doing so. Had anyone heard him, he might have got in trouble for it. But if they weren't also praying back at the *kolkhoz,* he would have been mightily amazed. They were praying wherever they could . . . wherever they weren't dead. And he had to pray Christ had had mercy on those bicycle riders out for a shopping trip to the city—and that Anya really wasn't one of them.

Not half a dozen centimeters in front of Ihor's frightened eyes, a corpse-pale mushroom no taller than the last joint of his little finger pushed its way out of the Ukraine's black earth. There above Kiev, that monstrous mushroom thrust its way untold kilometers into the Ukraine's gray-blue sky. Lightnings crackled about it.

Blast picked him up and flipped him over. It didn't fling him into a tree and smash him; it wasn't quite strong enough for that. But it did lift snow and send it skirling along. It lifted pebbles, too. One hit his boot, hard enough to hurt his foot. A little nearer and it might have pierced him like a rifle round.

"Thank you, Lord! Thank you, Jesus!" Suddenly, Ihor was praying in earnest, praying as he hadn't prayed since he was a boy, not just spitting out words by reflex the way the least pious man would do when in danger of his life. He wasn't thinking about *his* life now. There was Anya, rushing out to see the terrible cloud for herself.

If not for that miserable head cold, she *would* have got on her bicycle and gone into Kiev with the other women. She wouldn't have been there yet, but she would have been much closer than Ihor was. How much closer? He couldn't know. Close enough for her clothes to catch fire from that blast? Close enough for her hair to catch fire? Close enough for her to catch fire?

"Thank you, Jesus! Thank you, Lord!" Ihor still had his wife, still would have her for as long as the two of them could go on putting up with each other. In the circle of villages and collective farms around Kiev, how many people would tell their children and grandchildren those stories down through the years? And how many wouldn't be there to tell them, because they'd gone into the city after all?

By the nature of things, you couldn't answer such questions, not unless you were God. But you could worry at them, the way a dog worried at a bone. Worrying at questions like that was what made human beings human. Sometimes the question was more important than the answer.

And sometimes not. *What did the bomb do to me?* Ihor wondered. He couldn't answer that one, either. But the answer was already written inside him, whatever it chanced to be. He would have to keep turning the pages of his life to discover it.

# 11

MAJOR HANK MCCUTCHEON HAD to be confident as he spoke for everybody in the B-29 as it took off from the airfield north of Pusan. "Payback," McCutcheon said solemnly, "is a bitch."

Sitting in the right-hand seat next to the pilot, Bill Staley knew damn well that McCutcheon spoke for him. "You betcha, sir," he said, sounding like he felt: the fiercest bookkeeper on the face of the globe.

After bringing the yoke back a little farther to pull the bomber's nose up, McCutcheon nodded. "You'd be the one to agree with me, all right. Hear anything from your wife yet?"

Bill shook his head. "Not a word. All I know is, that bomb went off between Seattle and Everett. They're calling it the Seattle bomb in the papers and on the news, but I got the straight skinny from a G-2 guy on Harrison's staff. I have no idea whether Marian's alive or dead." He didn't know whether Linda was, either. That hurt even worse, or maybe just as bad in a different way. A little girl had no idea what war was all about, or why people could be willing—even eager—to kill one another in the sacred name of politics.

"You've got to be going out of your tree," the pilot said as he swung the plane east, toward the Sea of Japan. McCutcheon went on, "Me, I'm glad I stayed in Omaha. The West Coast is pretty, yeah, but look at all the chunks the Russians bit out of it. They can't get to Nebraska."

"Yet," Bill said. "Three or four years ago, they couldn't get to the West Coast, either. And it's not just the coast. Salt Lake City got it, for Chrissake. Denver!"

"Yeah, and the guys who smoked Denver landed with dry

tanks at that Air Force Field outside of Colorado Springs, got out of their plane, and put their hands up—and nobody knew what to do with them till they started speaking Russian," McCutcheon said in disgust. "Fucking Tu-4 looks just like a Superfort even before you give it the same paint job. Afterwards? Brother!"

"I don't care if they came out of the same pussy when they were born," Bill said savagely, which made McCutcheon guffaw. Jaw set with fury, Bill continued, "The air-defense people ought to get their balls handed to them in a sack. They knew the Russians were liable to attack. How many of those bombers did they shoot down? Two or three, that's it. Spokane made it. Las Vegas is still safe for the gamblers. Happy goddamn day!"

"That one might've been going after Hoover Dam, not Vegas," McCutcheon said. "If it was, the guys who shot it down really earned their paychecks that day."

"Okay, fine. Those guys weren't asleep at the switch. But everybody along the Pacific sure was. We don't have a decent port north of San Diego any more." Bill grabbed his yoke and squeezed as if it were a civil-defense coordinator's neck.

"Well, Vladivostok's going to glow in the dark like a radium clock dial for nobody knows how long," McCutcheon said. The Air Force had hit the Soviet port near the border with North Korea with several A-bombs. But only one of those bombers came home again. The Russians had known they were coming and baked them a cake.

Staley's B-29 and its comrades droned along just above the surface of the sea, to make themselves as hard for radar to spot as they could. The Ivans had done that on the way to the West Coast. It had worked for them. Imitation might or might not be the sincerest form of flattery. Bill hoped like hell it was the most effective kind.

Some of the planes in this flight were bound for Yuzhno-Sakhalinsk, the main Russian town on the island north of Japan whose southern half Stalin reconquered in 1945. Some were heading for Magadan, on the Sea of Okhotsk. Though ice closed the port for close to half the year, roads connected it with the rest of Russia. Things delayed there might not get anywhere else in a hurry, but they eventually would.

And some B-29s, like this one, would call on Petropavlovsk on the Kamchatka Peninsula. Only the sea and air joined Petropavlovsk to the outside world. It was a major Soviet naval base all the same. It had been a naval base under the Tsars, too. During the Crimean War, the English and French attacked the place, but couldn't take it. What they would have done with it if they *had* taken it was beyond Bill. That that siege had happened at all was one of those worthless bits of history he happened to know.

"You're jiving me," McCutcheon said when he mentioned it.

"Honest injun." Bill held up a hand as if swearing an oath.

"Wow!" The pilot whistled softly. "That must've been the lost fighting the lost. Like that German pest in East Africa during the First World War who stayed in the field a month after it was all over everywhere else."

"You wonder what was going through those admirals' minds a hundred years ago. Honest to God, you do," Bill said. *"We've got these ships here, and there are the Russians, and if we don't watch out they could sail around the Horn and bombard England year after next.* Had to be something like that. Why didn't they just sit tight and watch 'em?"

"Beats me," McCutcheon replied. "Remember, the Russians did sail out of the Baltic, around Africa, and up to the Sea of Japan in the Russo-Japanese War."

"And the Japs walloped the snot out of them, too," Bill said. "Yamamoto was at that fight. He lost a couple of fingers there, if I remember straight."

"You know all kinds of stuff nobody in his right mind gives a crap about, don't you?" the pilot said, not without admiration.

"Useless information is my specialty, yes, sir," Staley answered, not without pride. "Sometimes even useful information. If you want your taxes done after you get out of the Air Force and start making some real money again, come see me if we're anywhere in the same part of the country."

"Do I get a discount?" McCutcheon asked.

"Sure, and you won't even have to jew it out of me. Everybody on the crew gets the special helped-keep-me-alive discount."

"I like that." McCutcheon straightened in his seat and pointed ahead and to the left. "I think those are the two islands that lead up to the Kamchatka Peninsula. We're down mighty low, but I'm gonna swing away from 'em anyhow. The Reds are bound to have radar stations on 'em. Hell, I would." He spoke over the intercom: "I'm changing course five degrees east."

"Noted," answered Roger Williamson, the navigator.

The islands were lumps of dark mud in the sea, which the waning crescent moon dappled nicely. North of the second, smaller, island, the peninsula was more darkness—mountainous darkness. There was a big volcano just a few miles inland from Petropavlovsk. It made a perfect target marker.

Hank McCutcheon spoke over the intercom again, this time to the radioman, who sat on Bill's side of the plane behind a bulkhead: "Radio traffic give any sign the Russians know we're in the neighborhood?"

"Well, you know how well I don't speak Russian," Hyman Ginsberg answered, "but what I'm picking up doesn't sound excited or anything."

"Works for me," the pilot said. When he spoke again, it was to the navigator: "Let me know when we're about seventy-five miles south of the target. I'll start climbing then."

"Seventy-five miles. Yes, sir," Williamson answered.

When McCutcheon pulled back the yoke and the B-29 left the comforting clutter and cloak of the Pacific Ocean, Bill gulped. This was the bad time. If the Russians could scramble fighters, the aircrew wouldn't last long enough to drop the bomb on the naval base. Their plane was painted midnight-blue all over, but radar didn't care. The controllers could vector in the MiGs. . . .

"Boss, they're starting to have conniptions," Ginsberg reported.

"Well, fuck 'em. I can see the damn volcano now, blotting out the stars. Another couple of minutes." McCutcheon eyed his watch and the target ahead. You had to think of it as a target, not as people. And gunners around the target were starting to shoot: fireworks that confirmed where to aim. "Bombs away!" McCutcheon shouted.

"It's gone," Steve Bauer said from the nose. As the bomb fell free, McCutcheon heeled the B-29 away to the east and gave all four engines full emergency power.

Hell burst on earth, the way it had over Harbin. The light was dazzling, stunning. Bill stopped worrying about Russian fighters. They'd have no one down there to guide them to their target now.

\* \* \*

Los Angeles writhed like a snake with a broken back. As befitted a city so sprawling and spread out, it had got hit by two bombs, one just a little south of downtown and the other to smash the ports at San Pedro and Long Beach. City Hall was gone. So was the downtown police station. Water and power in the city were both erratic.

It mattered less to Aaron Finch than he would have guessed. Like him, his wife and son were as all right as you could be if you'd wound up a little too close to an atom bomb going off. The house hadn't fallen down on them. Only a couple of windows had blown in. Glendale, a city in its own right, had its own utilities, and they kept working . . . most of the time.

He was even a local celebrity. Some of the Russians who'd parachuted from their bomber were still missing. One had got stomped to death by a mob, one hanged from a lamppost, and one shot by somebody with a deer rifle before his feet even touched the ground. But Aaron was the only person who'd actually captured a Soviet flyer.

The *Glendale News Press* interviewed him. So did the *Pasadena Star-News.* The Los Angeles papers had had a large circulation in the suburbs, too. But the *Times,* the *Mirror,* the *Examiner,* and the *Herald-Express* were among the casualties of the downtown bomb.

"You know what?" Aaron told Ruth. "I'm not sorry the *Times* went up in smoke. It's been a union-busting right-wing rag for as long as I've been alive, and I don't miss it a bit."

"That's a terrible thing to say!" Ruth exclaimed. "They blew them up! There's nothing left of the *Times* Building. Even City Hall downtown is only a melted stub." City Hall had been the one L.A. building exempt from the twelve-story height limit imposed to cut earthquake damage. It had always stood out on the skyline as a result. It still did . . . what was left of it.

"If anyone on earth misses the Chandlers, I'd be amazed," Aaron said stubbornly. He raised a finger to correct himself. "Maybe some of the Nazis hiding out in Argentina and Paraguay do. Nobody else."

"You're horrible," she said. He nodded, more pleased than otherwise.

Three days after the bombs fell, someone knocked on the door. When Aaron opened it, a Glendale flatfoot stood outside, his patrol car parked at the curb. "You Aaron Finch?" he asked.

"Yeah," Aaron said. "What's going on?"

"Somebody down at the station wants to talk to you," the cop answered. "You don't gotta come. I'm not arresting you or nothin'. But he wants to."

"Who is he?" Aaron asked—reasonably, he thought.

"Somebody down at the station," the policeman repeated. "That's what he told me I should tell you, so that's what I'm sayin'."

"Somebody who wants me to buy a pig in a poke," Aaron said. The cop didn't deny it. Aaron thought for a moment, then shrugged. Getting in bad with the local police wasn't something a sensible guy wanted to do. Glendale *was* a city, but not a great big city. If the clowns in the black-and-whites wanted to make someone's life miserable, they could. "Okay. I'll play along." He called back over his shoulder to let Ruth know where he was going, then walked out into the night.

He slid into the front seat alongside the cop. The fellow sent him a quizzical look, but kept quiet. The back was where you went when they arrested you. Had the cop insisted that he sit there, he would have got out and gone back inside.

More police cars than usual cruised the streets. Glendale hadn't got so badly damaged by the bomb that smashed downtown L.A. No doubt because it hadn't, refugees flooded north into it. Some slept in cars, others in parks or alleys or anywhere else they could find. A lot of them had no cash. They begged. They stole. Some of the women peddled themselves. You couldn't blame them for any of that. But you could try to slow it down, and the Glendale cops were.

Aaron also saw two rifle-toting National Guardsmen in full combat gear checking somebody's papers. Following the lead of Fred Payne of Maine when Bangor got hit, Governor Warren had mobilized them as soon as the bombs fell. His counterparts along the West Coast had done likewise. In Utah and Colorado, the state capitals had got hit, so the Feds took care of it for the governors who weren't there to do it for themselves.

The police station was a low-slung stucco building fronted by trees. The policeman took Aaron inside, led him past the fat sergeant at the desk (who was eating a jelly doughnut to make sure he didn't get any skinnier), and took him into a room next to the chief's office.

The man waiting inside wore a blue uniform, but he wasn't a cop. He was an Air Force lieutenant colonel. Aaron nodded to himself. He'd expected either military brass or an FBI man. To himself, he'd bet on J. Edgar Hoover's boys. Himself would have to find some money to pay off.

"Mr. Finch?" the officer asked. When Aaron nodded, the fellow went on, "I'm Del Shanahan. I'm with Air Force Intelligence." He held out his hand.

Aaron took it. "Pleased to meet you," he said, which might or might not prove true, depending on how things worked out here. Shanahan's grip said he didn't spend all his time behind a desk.

"I asked you to come in here," he said, "to talk with you about how you captured Lieutenant Yuri Svechin. He was the navigator on the Russian bomber."

"Was he? I didn't ask him anything about that. I just got him into my car and took him here," Aaron said. "I'll tell you what I know, Colonel, but I don't know a whole heck of a lot."

"You could talk with him, though. Isn't that correct?" Shanahan asked.

"A little bit," Aaron admitted.

"Do you speak Russian? I know he doesn't speak English."

"Nah." Aaron shook his head. With Senator McCarthy bellowing about Communists like an enraged elephant, you didn't want to admit you spoke Russian, even if you did—but he didn't. "I know some Yiddish, though, and I tried that on him. He turned out to speak German, so he could pretty much follow me and I could pretty much follow him."

"He was willing to give himself up to you?"

"When he saw I wouldn't hurt him, yeah. He was eager, in fact. Take a look at what happened to some of the other guys from that plane and I guess you can see why."

"That was . . . unfortunate. We've sent a note to the USSR through the International Red Cross apologizing and offering compensation to the slain flyers' families."

"You have?" Aaron said in surprise. "How come?"

"We'll have planes shot down over Russian territory. We don't want their civilians to have any excuse to lynch our downed crewmen."

"Oh." Aaron thought that over. He didn't need long. "Okay.

I gotcha. Makes sense, I guess. Of course, when the Russians watch one of their cities go up in smoke, they're liable not to need any other excuse. We sure didn't, did we?"

"No. As I say, unfortunate." Lieutenant Colonel Shanahan was in his early forties, with hair held in place by Vitalis and with a thin mustache like the ones that had been popular during the last war. Aaron had worn one then, too. He had a photo of himself with it, feeding the pigeons in St. Mark's Square in Venice. They weren't stylish any more. These days, Aaron's upper lip was bare. Shanahan didn't seem to have noticed the change. He'd probably have a thin white mustache if he lived to be ninety.

Aaron took out a pack of Chesterfields. "Do you mind?" he asked politely.

"Huh? No, not a bit." Shanahan flicked a lighter for him and lit up himself.

"It's funny," Aaron said. The Air Force officer made a questioning noise. Aaron went on, "They must have killed a million of us, at least, and maimed more than that. And we've got to be even with them, huh?"

"More than even," Shanahan said. "That's off the record, if you please, but it's no great big military secret. We can hit them harder than they can hit us."

"Pretty much what I figured," Aaron agreed. "But here we are, going through the motions over bomber crews. Isn't it like blowing a thousand bucks on the world's biggest spree and then getting all upset 'cause you can't find a penny in your pants pocket?"

Del Shanahan sighed and blew a cloud of smoke up at the ceiling. "You do what you can, Mr. Finch. You do what the laws of war train you to do. We send those men out. If we can save them, aren't we obligated to try our best to do so? Their families would want no less from us."

Once more, Aaron nodded after a moment. "If you look at it that way, you've got a point." He stubbed out his butt. "Need anything else from me?"

"No." Shanahan shook his head. "To tell you the truth, I just wanted to make sure you were only a chance passerby who rescued that Russian instead of, say, bashing in his head with a brick."

"What else would I be? A spy?" Aaron asked.

"You aren't, clearly. But we had to make sure," the officer said. That gave Aaron something to chew on as the Glendale policeman drove him back to his house. In Stalin's Russia, he supposed they would have kept him in jail on the principle that he *might* be a spy. This was better, but was it enough better?

"Mommy, I have to go potty!" Linda said.

Marian Staley sighed. Rain was drumming down on the roof of their Studebaker. They were living in it. That seemed better than the tents housing so many refugees from Everett. Her car was one of the few from so close to the bombing that was still in working order. Flash from the blast had set the paint on dark autos afire, but not their yellow one.

Another sigh. "Well, come on," Marian said. "I'll take you to the outhouse." That was a polite word for what they had: slit trenches with board seats inside tents to hold off the rain.

"They're stinky!" Linda said. And they were. Latrine workers sprinkled the trenches with lime chloride every day—or they were supposed to, anyway. They didn't always. The trenches got smelly even when they came through, and worse when they didn't. That also could have been worse, though. It could have been summertime, with flies swarming everywhere. Linda went on, "Can't I just tinkle out here? In the rain, who'd know?"

It would have been simpler. Not without a pang, Marian shook her head all the same. "No, that's disgusting. It lets germs get loose. Come on—we'll both go." Plenty of germs were bound to be loose regardless, with so many people crowded together and with hardly any way to get clean this side of standing naked under the rain.

"I wish I had my Mickey umbrella," Linda said when they got out of the Studebaker.

"I wish we had any kind of umbrella at all," Marian said. The ones back at their house had burned. Almost everything back there had burned. If she hadn't stashed a spare car key in a flower pot, they wouldn't have been able to drive away.

*Would we be that much worse off?* she wondered as they squelched through the mud toward the outhouse. They were both wearing tattered secondhand clothes—handouts, and what the National Guardsmen and State Police who ran this camp had had in their storerooms. None of it fit well. It was warmer than nothing, and that was about what you could say for it. The blankets they wrapped themselves in at night were wool, and somehow managed to be scratchy and thin at the same time.

They got in and out as fast as they could, and looked at the other women and girls in there as little as they could. There were no stalls. What you did, you did for others to see. That was harder on women than on men, though Marian refused to believe even men relished taking a crap in front of spectators.

There were other things men didn't have to worry about. She really dreaded getting her period in a place like this. Not having privacy when you needed it most . . .

Linda's little hand in hers, she hurried back to the car. They were both alive. They still had a chance for things to turn around and get better. From what the harried, desperately overworked docs said, they had a good chance of staying alive for a while, too. Some of Marian's hair kept coming out when she combed it. So did some of her daughter's. Their flash burns were healing cleanly. When she put on enough powder, she could hardly see hers.

They hadn't gone bald, the way people with bad radiation sickness did. They weren't puking up their guts all the time, or passing blood, or roasted like a medium-rare leg of lamb. They would have to worry more about cancer down the line. Next to vanishing in a flash of light, next to getting your whole hide seared and your eyeballs melted, next to being too weak and too sick to eat, they were lucky.

*Some luck,* Marian thought as she let Linda in ahead of her. They had one ratty towel in there. She dried off Linda first, then used the wet towel to get some of the water off herself, too. She sneezed. They could catch pneumonia. Then they'd end up in a hospital till penicillin cleared it up. If penicillin cleared it up.

Marian had to keep both front windows open a half inch or so, or the inside of the Studebaker got impossibly stuffy. But that let in half-inch slices of rain—one more thing to keep the towel busy. *Boy, this is fun,* ran through her mind. *Yeah, sure.*

Just when she was ready to believe things couldn't possibly get any worse, two National Guardsmen came by carrying a corpse. The weary men in olive drab didn't even bother with a stretcher. One had the head end, the other the feet. Cloth shrouded the body, but not well. At least the workers wore camouflaged ponchos, and helmets to keep the water out of their eyes.

"There goes another dead one, Mommy!" Linda adapted to things like this faster and more easily than Marian could.

Well, she saw enough of them. People here died all the time, of radiation sickness and burns and bodies broken by the bomb—and of heart attacks and strokes, and of knife wounds and gunshots when they brawled. More bodies went into the new graveyard by the camp every day. Whenever they filled a new layer in the mass graves, they shoveled dirt over the corpses. They used lime chloride on them, too. As with the latrines, it helped some but not enough.

At seven in the morning, at half past noon, and at six at night, bells rang throughout the camp. That was meal call. Getting food, maybe running into people you knew: the highlights of the day. Keeping the car windows open a smidgen did make sure they heard the bells.

Most of what they got was C-rations and K-rations— canned and packaged stuff—out of the National Guard armories. Like the rest of the camp, it kept you alive without leaving you overjoyed to stay that way. The K-rats sometimes included a starvation allowance of cigarettes: not even enough to keep you from getting the jitters if you'd smoked regularly before the bomb fell. There was a lively trade between people who needed tobacco more than anything else on earth and those who didn't care about cigarettes and were out for whatever else they could get.

When Marian got her ration pack and a real sandwich for Linda ("Dog meat" was her daughter's take on the bologna), someone waved to her from one of the crowded tables in the mess hall. She peered that way, smiled, and waved back. "Mr. Tabakman!" she said. "It's good to see you!" It would have been good to see anyone she knew, but she didn't say that.

"You can eat with my friends and me if you want," the cobbler said. "We'll make room for you and Linda."

More than anything else, his remembering her daughter's name decided her. "Come on, dear," she said, shepherding Linda forward.

Fayvl Tabakman's friends were a couple of other middle-aged Jews. He introduced them as Yitzkhak and Moishe. They both spoke English with accents thicker than his. Plainly, they would have been more at home in Yiddish, or perhaps Polish or Russian. But, like him, they stuck to America's language while talking to lifelong Americans. Any other speech was for when they were amongst themselves.

They were no dopes, even if they did have heavy accents. They talked about how the war in western Germany was going and about how Stalin thought as if they belonged on the Joint Chiefs of Staff. "I saw Stalin once, in Minsk," Moishe said. "I was lucky—Stalin didn't see me."

Accent or not, he made Linda laugh. "That's funny!" she said, and was amused enough (or hungry enough) to take two more bites from her sorry sandwich.

He looked at her over the tops of his bifocals. "Funny now, sure. I can sit here and tell the story. Not so funny then. Stalin is a very scary man. Even in a crowd of people, I was nervous." Marian got the idea that to him the atomic bomb was only the latest catastrophe he'd lived through, and that he didn't expect it to be the last—or the worst.

Marian got down her own canned-beef ration. Two of the Jews were eating Spam instead. Since they didn't say anything, she didn't, either. Moishe gave her the hard candies from his pack for Linda. She passed back the cigarettes from hers. She didn't smoke enough to miss them much, and his yellow-stained index and middle fingers said he did.

Fayvl walked her and Linda back to the Studebaker. "Thank you," she said. She'd never had trouble, but she knew she might.

He touched the brim of his old-fashioned cloth cap. "It's nothing," he said. "Once upon a time—" Breaking off, he turned and walked away fast. Marian wondered just what he was remembering. Whatever it was, she could tell how much it hurt.

In all his flying time, Boris Gribkov had never been airsick. Less than a day aboard the *Stalin* had him puking up the sausage and sauerkraut he'd eaten an hour before. The destroyer's skipper, a commander named Anatoly Edzhubov, was sympathetic. "I'm sorry, Boris Pavlovich," he said. "The North Pacific in the wintertime can be a nasty roller coaster. Here, drink this to get the taste out of your mouth." He held out a tumbler of clear liquid.

Gribkov drank, expecting it to be water. It was vodka: fine, smooth vodka, but strong as a plow horse. He got it down without choking. Had Edzhubov wanted to make him splutter, or did the skipper really think he was helping? "Thank you, Anatoly Ivanovich," Boris said when he could speak again. "That hits the spot—with a grenade."

"There you go! Good for what ails you, see?" Edzhubov beamed. He had a round, ruddy, peasanty face with several gold teeth he showed in a perpetual smile. He didn't seem the sort who would have tried to make Boris feel worse on purpose, but you never could tell.

The destroyer and the rest of the little rescue flotilla were steaming west now, into the teeth of the swells. Boris dosed his seasickness with more vodka. It helped him sleep, if nothing else. The bunk in the officers' quarters included a belt to keep him from suddenly waking up on the steel deck. He wasn't too drunk to use it.

They changed course two mornings after rescuing the Tu-4's crew. "I'm sorry, Comrade, but we'll be at sea a little longer than I expected," Edzhubov said.

"What's gone wrong?" Boris asked. The skipper still seemed cheerful, but his eyes had a faraway look.

"Well, we were bound for Petropavlovsk," Edzhubov answered. "There's . . . not much point to that any more, I'm afraid."

"Not much point?" Boris realized what that had to mean as soon as the question was out of his mouth. "Oh! The Americans?"

"Yes, the Americans," the naval officer agreed. "They gave the place a dose of the same medicine your crew served to Seattle. They got Petropavlovsk and Magadan and Vladivostok. They hit Provideniya, too."

Provideniya wasn't a port, except for a few months at the height of summer. In this season, the ice ran kilometers out from the land. But the Yankees wouldn't be hitting it because it was a naval base. Colonel Doyarenko had been a good man. He was still a good man if he remained alive, but Gribkov feared he didn't.

Trying not to think about Colonel Doyarenko and what might have happened to him, the bomber pilot asked, "Where will we go, then?"

"I have orders to put in at Korf—or rather, to get as close to Korf as we can," Edzhubov replied. "It isn't a big city, which is probably why the Americans didn't bother to bomb it."

"I'm sorry, Anatoly Ivanovich. Please forgive a dumb landlubber, but I have no idea where Korf is." Tu-4s didn't fly into or out of the place—Boris knew that much.

"It's on the east side of the neck of the Kamchatka Peninsula," the skipper answered. "You get there by sea, by sled in the wintertime, and these days by air, too. They catch salmon in the river, and there are mines for platinum and brown coal close by."

"All right." A town out here would have natives living in it, natives and *zeks* who'd served their sentences but were held near the gulags by the terms of their internal exile. Gribkov grinned a sly grin. "I bet they brew a lot of *samogon,* too."

"Well, what else is there to do in a place like that?" Edzhubov said. "Not as if a lot of real vodka gets there."

Boris nodded. Russian moonshine flourished wherever there were Russians but not enough official booze. Some of it was as good as anything the state distilleries turned out. Some was poison, literally. It was cheaper than the official product, because you didn't have to pay the tax that went into the government's pocket. That was the other thing that made it so widespread.

They sailed through a storm. If Gribkov had thought the North Pacific was bad before, now he admitted he hadn't known the first thing about it. Any dog as sick as he was, they would have shot. His fellow airmen suffered with him. Misery sympathized with company even if it didn't love it.

Most of the sailors took it all in stride. A couple of them also puked their guts out, but only a couple. You could get used to anything. You could, or you could die trying. Boris rather felt like it.

Little by little, more news trickled in to the *Stalin.* Radio Moscow went off the air suddenly and without warning. When it came back, several hours later, it had a weaker signal and unfamiliar broadcasters. That alone would have made Gribkov guess something horrible had happened to the station and to the city that housed it.

He supposed it made sense that the Americans would strike the heart of the *rodina* as well as the Soviet Far East. Except for Vladivostok, the Russian cities in this part of the world were small towns compared to the ones along the Pacific Coast of the United States. And supplies for the war in

Europe traveled from and traveled through the cities in the USSR's heartland.

But how much of the world would be left in one piece if they kept blowing up city after city? That was a question Boris couldn't begin to answer. It was also a question he couldn't ask anyone else. If he did, the MGB would soon be asking questions of him.

Stalin came on the radio not long before the destroyer that bore his name reached Korf. "The reactionary imperialists have murdered good Soviet citizens by the million," he said, his Georgian accent flavoring the way he spoke as it always did. "They have done their best to murder me, but their best is not good enough. The struggle for socialism, for Communism, will continue to its final, inevitable triumph against the Americans as it did against the Hitlerites. Forward, progressives of the world, to victory!"

It wasn't a great speech. Stalin seldom made great speeches. But it did show he was alive. Gribkov was amazed how good that made him feel. He'd been a baby when the Revolution came. He didn't remember anyone else at the Soviet Union's helm. He couldn't imagine how the immense country would go on without its leader.

Boats took the bomber crewmen from the *Stalin* to the edge of the pack ice. Dog sleds took them across the ice to Korf itself. The hamlet—it might have held a thousand people, or it might not—sat on a sand spit. People clumped over the snow on skis and snowshoes.

They gave the men from the Tu-4 as much of a heroes' welcome as they could. The toasts they drank, they drank with *samogon,* but it was good *samogon.* The roast they served was enormous, tasty, and, best of all, on dry land. However tasty it was, it didn't seem familiar. "What kind of meat is this?" Gribkov asked.

"Bear," answered a flat-faced local. "I shot it myself." The pilot had got hungry enough aboard the *Stalin* that the news hardly slowed him down.

Korf had a rudimentary airstrip. Rudimentary airplanes buzzed down to take away the Tu-4's men. Boris eyed the Po-2s in delight. "I learned to fly on one of those!" he exclaimed.

"Me, too," Vladimir Zorin said. "I can't imagine a Soviet pilot who didn't."

These particular wood-and-canvas biplanes sported skis

for landing gear. Snow didn't faze the *Kukuruznik,* either. As if he were still a student, Gribkov climbed into the front seat.

The pilot revved the little radial engine. The plane taxied along till it sedately rose into the sky. Icy wind in his face, Gribkov grinned like Christmas. This was what flying was supposed to be!

# 12

GUSTAV HOZZEL SPRAWLED IN the ruins of the suburbs west of Alsfeld, forty kilometers northwest of Fulda. He'd never visited Alsfeld in all the time he'd lived in Fulda. He didn't want to be here now, but the Russians had barged through the Fulda gap and were doing their best to overrun all of Western-occupied Germany, plus anything else they could get their grabby mitts on.

The Americans *were* fighting. Gustav had to give them that much. They'd battled the Ivans street by street, house by house, inside Alsfeld. That was why Gustav could still lie here on the outskirts of town. The Amis had smashed a lot of Russian tanks. They'd kept snipers in the cathedral bell tower till Russian artillery leveled it. Those guys had to know they would die if they went up there. They did it anyhow. They were soldiers, in other words.

Even if they were soldiers, Gustav still hated their helmet. It didn't cover enough of a man's head. A few German auxiliaries had put on the *Wehrmacht*'s *Stahlhelm* instead. But the Russians didn't take prisoners from men who did that. They killed them in cold blood, and left them on display with swastika placards by the bodies. Gustav got the message, and kept his Yankee pot.

He didn't care for the egg grenades on his belt, either. You could throw a German potato-masher farther. He had nothing against the Springfield the Amis had issued him. It was as good a rifle as a Mauser. But now he carried a PPSh he'd taken off a dead Russian. Close-range firepower was what he wanted, and the submachine gun gave it to him.

He *really* craved a Russian assault rifle. Some *Landsers* on the Eastern Front had carried weapons like that as the war drew toward its end, but never enough to hold back the Russian tide. Keeping the PPSh in ammo was easy: it fired ordinary pistol cartridges. The assault rifle used a special round, halfway between pistol and rifle. Feeding it might prove a chore if he got his hands on one.

In front of him and off to the left, a machine gun opened up. That was a Russian piece; he knew the sound as well as he knew Luisa's heartbeat when he laid his head on her left breast. He hoped his wife was all right. He could only hope right now.

More submachine guns went off. American M-1s answered, a rhythm halfway between a bolt-action rifle and an automatic. They could hit somebody with a PPSh or a PPD before he got close enough to hit them. But if the guy with the submachine gun did get that close, he had the edge.

Very cautiously, Gustav looked out from behind the burntout carcass of the Mercedes that gave him cover. The Mercedes sat a good many centimeters lower than it had before fire swept over it. The tires were gone, so it rested on the metal wheels. Whatever color the expensive car had been, it was charcoal-gray now.

Not seeing anything dangerous coming his way, he pulled back. "How's it look where you're at, Max?" he called.

His friend and comrade lay behind an overturned steel file cabinet. The Mercedes probably gave better cover, but that wasn't bad. "I'm smoking a cigarette," Bachman said. "I think I have time to finish it."

"Sounds about right," Gustav said, and then, after a moment, "You know, it's funny that all this doesn't seem funny. We're used to it. We know what to do, and we know how to do it, too."

*"Ja, ja."* Max sounded exaggeratedly patient. And he had his reasons: "Wait till they start throwing atom bombs around here. See if you know what to do then."

"Of course I know what to do then. I fucking die, *nicht wahr?*" Gustav said. They both let out black chuckles. The Americans weren't using atom bombs because this was the part of Germany they wanted to protect, not to wreck. The Russians hadn't used them yet because . . . well, who the hell knew why? Maybe because they were still advancing without them. Or maybe because, with Moscow and Leningrad and Kiev radioactive dust, no one who could give the orders was still alive.

"Do you think it's true Adenauer asked Truman not to use the bombs in the western zones?" Max asked.

"Why wouldn't Adenauer ask? What does he have to lose?" Gustav said. "Whether his asking has anything to do with why they haven't fallen—that, I can't tell you." Adenauer, at least, had the courage of his convictions. He'd been jailed for opposing the Nazis. That gave him some clout with the Amis. How much? Well, who could say for sure?

The firefight off to the left died away. The Russians' hearts didn't seem to be in it. Maybe all the bombs that had fallen between the front and where their supplies came from meant they didn't have enough. It would be nice to think so, anyhow.

Then fire rippled on the eastern horizon—the other side of Alsfeld. Gustav knew too well what that meant. "Get down!" he shouted to anyone who could hear him. "Flatten out! *Katyushas!*"

Just to make themselves scarier, the rockets screamed when they came in, as if they were Stukas with Jericho trumpets. The whole salvo burst in the space of a few seconds. It could chew up most of a square kilometer. It wasn't an atom bomb, but was in the running for next worst thing.

Blast kicked Gustav around and slammed him into the dead Mercedes, hard enough to hurt but not hard enough to do any real damage. A chunk of sheet iron from a rocket casing gouged a hole in the fender only thirty or forty centimeters from his head. Too often, whether you got up or they planted you depended on luck like that, stuff you couldn't do anything about.

*"Urra! Urra!"* That was Russian infantry, probably snockered from the vodka ration, getting ready to charge. If the hair on Gustav's nape hadn't risen for the *Katyushas,* the rhythmic roar would have turned the trick. The Russians would come forward till they got slaughtered or till they cleared out whatever stood in their way.

Gustav felt terrified and exhilarated at the same time. He'd spent most of his youth in the *Wehrmacht*—spent it the way a gunner spent shells. He'd never felt so alive as on the Eastern Front, not least because he always knew life could end at any instant. Going back to Fulda was quiet, peaceful . . . and just a bit dull. All right, nightmares woke him screaming every so often. Did he feel so intensely about anything in the town, even Luisa?

To his own sorrow, he knew the answer. He hoped she was alive. He hoped she was safe. He hoped she was hiding—as the Russians had proved in 1945, they were swine around defeated women.

Hope was all he could do—hope and fight like hell.

*"Urra! Urra!"* The chant got louder, and higher in pitch.

He knew what that meant. "They're coming!" he bawled, and peeped out from behind the Mercedes again.

Coming they were, and just as he remembered from the old days: rank after rank of men, arms linked, greatcoat skirts flapping around their legs, the troops in front firing as they ran. Gustav squeezed off a short burst, then scuttled to the far end of the dead car. Other Germans and Americans were also shooting back at the Red Army men.

When he looked out at the Russians again, soldiers were falling like ninepins. The ones who still lived closed up, linked arms, and trotted on. You had to admire courage like that. You also had to wonder what inspired it. Were the Russians more afraid of what would happen to them if they didn't advance than they were of what happened when they did? God help them if they were, because this was suicidal.

Staying low, he fired at them again. They were close enough now for him to see his burst tear into them again. Then he wished for the Yankee Springfield and a long bayonet, because here they were, right on top of him. He fired till his magazine ran dry, then struck at the Russians with the PPSh's hot barrel. He waited for someone to shoot him or stab him from behind.

But then the Ivans, the ones who could, were running back as fast as they'd run forward. Even Russian flesh and blood had limits. Sometimes. But you could never count on when or even whether.

Maybe one of the dead Ivans nearby had carried an assault rifle. Gustav wasn't crazy enough to find out now. Later, when things calmed down a little, though . . .


The tiny, gray-haired Chinese woman sent Vasili Yasevich the fishiest of fishy stares. "You sure you know what you're doing?" she snapped.

He bowed his head and looked down at the muddy ground.

"This person does his humble best to follow the training in compounding medicines given to him by his father, who now, sadly, is among the ancestors."

"Oh, cut the crap." Her accent and her manner both shouted that she came from Peking. Her husband was one of the commissars charged with getting Harbin back on its feet as fast as humanly possible—or a little faster than that. Still giving him the fishy eye, she went on, "You can fix something to perk up Wang, keep him going?"

"Yes, ma'am," he said. He didn't know as much as his father had. He hadn't listened so hard as he might have. But that one he could handle. "The wise and distinguished lady will have heard of the herb called *ma huang*?"

"I told you to can the crap," she said, but Vasili could tell it flattered her at the same time as it annoyed her. The Reds from Peking were often holier-than-thou when it came to aggressive egalitarianism. Almost as often, though, they expected to be treated as rulers. So he wasn't amazed when she giggled before going on, "Yes, I know about *ma huang*. I'm surprised a round-eye would."

"It's used in our medicines, too," Vasili said, which wasn't even a lie. From what his old man had told him, the chemical that gave *ma huang* its kick was related to benzedrine.

"Ah. That I didn't know." The woman's glare sharpened again. "You can get me some in this miserable, bombed-out, backward province?"

She wasn't supposed to say things like that. She wasn't even supposed to think them. He might be able to land her in trouble if he repeated them to the right people. He didn't want to land her in trouble, though. He just wanted to make some money off of her. He wanted her to pass his name on to her friends, too, so he could also sell them drugs.

And so he nodded. "Yes, great lady. I have been lucky enough to secure a supply of the highest quality. . . ."

He'd found some in a wrecked medicine shop. He'd tested it by chewing a little. It sped up his heartbeat and made him lose a night's sleep no matter how tired he was. That was *ma huang,* all right.

"Well, what do you want for it?" she demanded.

"You understand how hard it is to bring things in these days—"

She interrupted: "I understand you're going to gouge me."

He was, too, but politely. When he told her how much he

wanted, she called him some things that weren't from the Peking dialect of Mandarin at all. He knew most of the insults that one offered. He wondered where the commissar's wife had grown up, to come out with those catfight-sounding curses. When she ran down, he gave her his politest bow. That inflamed her more, as he'd known it would.

They haggled for a while. He let her beat him down a little further than he'd expected. He didn't want her leaving angry. If she did, she wouldn't tell her friends about him.

She paid him. He gave her the *ma huang,* and told her how much to use. He didn't want the commissar dying of a heart attack or stroke, either. That would be bad for business. "Don't think that if a little is good, more is better," he warned. "*Ma huang* is strong medicine. You should always respect it."

"You are not my mother or my father," she said tartly. A Russian would have told him *Don't teach your granny to suck eggs.* They both amounted to the same thing. He bowed again. He'd done his best.

Away she went. It was the first day of spring—Vasili thought it was, anyhow; he'd been too frazzled lately to keep close track—but her breath smoked. In her shapeless trousers, quilted jacket, and cap with earflaps and a red star on the front, she might have been an undersized People's Liberation Army private—except she carried herself like an empress. He wondered what she would do if he told her so. Probably have him shot. If her husband was who Vasili thought he was, she could arrange that with a word or two.

Instead, she did talk to the wives of other high-powered organizers who'd come into Manchuria. Vasili had to scout around for more *ma huang.* Luckily, it was easier to come by than he'd made it out to be.

One of the officials went back to Peking very suddenly. People said he suffered from nervous exhaustion. Maybe he did. Certainly, his wife had been one of Vasili's best customers. If she'd brewed her tea too strong for too long, she was the only one who knew it. Vasili could only suspect—and, since he knew what was good for him, keep his mouth shut.

Railroad workers started rebuilding the line that ran through Harbin. It was one of the most important in China, since it connected North Korea to the Trans-Siberian Railway. Repairing the stretch the atom bomb had destroyed was important. Vasili understood as much. All the same, he was glad he wasn't spending twelve- or fourteen-hour days breaking rock and laying track right where that bomb had gone off.

He wondered whether the workers knew radioactivity could be dangerous—or that there was such a thing as radioactivity. It made sense for their overlords not to tell them. After all, they wouldn't pay any price for years.

Some of the railroad workers bought *ma huang* from him, too, so they could work harder longer. Like the official's wife, they thought it was funny to be getting a Chinese herb from a Russian. Funny or not, as long as he had it, they wanted it.

Some of them tried to buy opium from him. They didn't want to work harder; they wanted not to care about the work they had to do. Not without regret, Vasili told them he had none to sell. That wasn't quite true, but he wouldn't sell to strangers or even to a good many acquaintances. For opium, he had to trust his customers with his life. Mao had gone to war against the drug. Unlike earlier Chinese leaders who opposed it, he was serious to the point of killing people who grew it, people who sold it, and people who used it.

Vasili had enough money in his pocket so as not to need to take chances like that. He'd got a shack off to the west of the part of central Harbin the bomb had leveled. He picked one on that side of town on purpose. The winds here rarely blew from east to west. Whatever poisons remained in the seared ground, they wouldn't come his way.

He wished he could move somewhere else, to a place where no atom bomb had fallen. But then he would have to start fresh, from nothing. And he would have to start someplace where no one had ever seen a white man before. In Harbin, at least, people were used to fair skin, blond hair, gray eyes, sharp noses, heavy beards. They mostly didn't stare and point when he walked by. Some of them even spoke bits of Russian.

Every once in a while, he wondered if he could head north, slip over the border, and take up life in the Soviet Union. He might be able to pass himself off as somebody just out of the gulag. But everything his father had told him about the land argued against it.

Yes, there he would look like other people. He wouldn't have papers like other people, though. Even released *zeks*—especially released *zeks*—had identity papers detailing who they were, where they could live, where they were allowed to travel.

Without those papers, you couldn't get bread. You couldn't get vodka. You couldn't get cabbage. Unless you were a hermit in the woods who killed all his own food, you had to have papers.

*Even if I looked like everyone else, I'd be a stranger there,* he thought. Here in China, although people who'd never seen him before did double takes when he walked by, he knew how to fit in. He knew how things worked. The way the Chinese put it was, he had his bowl of rice. For now, that would have to do.

Any time they wouldn't let you sleep at night, any time they put you to work or put you on the road instead, you were going to get the shitty end of the stick. Even a conscript like Tibor Nagy had no trouble figuring that out. He grumbled as he climbed up into the battered truck that would haul him and his countrymen out of Schweinfurt and into . . . into whatever disasters waited at the other side of the ride.

Istvan Szolovits put it a little differently. As he scrambled into the truck, he muttered, "Out of the frying pan, into the fire."

Sergeant Gergely heard that. Tibor didn't think he was supposed to, but he did. He had ears like a rabbit's. With a harsh laugh, he said, "You got it backwards, Jewboy. All the fires are behind us. The frying pan is where we're going. What's the worst they can do to us at the front?"

"Shoot us. Blow us up. Fry us with flamethrowers . . . Sergeant," Szolovits answered. All that was much too true, but he might not have come out with it unless Gergely delivered that endearment.

The sergeant could have given him hell. Instead, Gergely just nodded. "That's about the size of it, yeah," he said. "When you put it next to one of those fucking atom bombs that still kill you even when they miss by two kilometers, it's nothing."

"Nice of the Russians to give us the chance to die for their country," Tibor remarked.

"I don't think they would if they had a choice," Sergeant Gergely said. Once under canvas himself, the veteran lit a cigarette. The brief red glow of the match gave his sharp features a satanic cast. He went on, "But the way it looks to me is, they're having trouble getting their own guys up to the front on account of everything that's fallen between there and here. Lucky us, we're already forward, and so they'll use us."

"They'll use us up," Szolovits emended. Gergely didn't hear that—or if he did, he thought it was too obviously true to need comment.

With an out-of-tune roar, the truck got rolling. German roads were damn good. All the same, every jolt, every pothole, went straight from Tibor's tailbone to his head. The workers at the factory must have given the truck springs once upon a time. They'd long since died of old age, though.

And the road, while good, had been bombed and shelled more than it had been repaired—and the men doing the repair work were Russian military engineers, not fastidious German roadbuilders. The only thing that mattered to the Red Army was keeping traffic going. Comfort was for capitalists and fairies and other socially undesirable elements.

No one had bothered fixing the truck's muffler, either. The rear compartment stank of exhaust. The noise was also impressive—or depressing, depending on how you looked at it. Tibor was used to riding in such clunkers. They were what the Russians could spare for their satellite forces. The racket from this one, though, might keep the driver and him from hearing enemy fighter-bombers overhead till too late.

He couldn't do anything about that but worry. Worry he did, even as he knew it wouldn't do him any good. He didn't want to fight the Americans. He would rather have shot at the Russians who'd flung him into this war that wasn't his. He had no doubt that he wasn't the only conscript in the truck with such notions.

Sergeant Gergely wasn't a conscript. But he'd been riding herd on reluctant soldiers since the Hungarian Army did its halfhearted best to help the Nazis try to keep the Red Army away from Budapest, away from Lake Balaton, away from the oilfields west of the lake. . . . He knew how they thought. He knew what kind of odds they were weighing.

Not at all out of the blue, he said, "Listen, you sorry sacks of shit, don't be any dumber than you can help. If you bug out, people on our side will shoot you in the back. The Americans or limeys or Germans or whoever the hell we bump up against will shoot you in the front. And the Russians and our own security forces will make your families pay like you wouldn't believe."

He didn't gloat about that, the way a movie villain might have. No—he sounded as matter-of-fact as a butcher telling a customer the price of a leg of mutton. *If you do this, that will happen.* As far as Tibor was concerned, he seemed scarier as he was.

The farther north and west they went, the worse the roads grew. They were passing through land that had been recently fought over, land the Red Army had taken away from the Americans. Dawn began to leak into the compartment through the opening in the rear. Through that opening, Tibor got glimpses of wrecked and shattered vehicles—everything from motorcycles all the way up to Stalin heavy tanks—shoved off to the shoulder so the ones that still ran could get through.

Not long before sunup, the truck convoy halted. The brakes on the machine that carried Tibor squealed like a kicked dog. "Out!" Sergeant Gergely yelled. "Out and under cover! The Americans spot us in the open in broad daylight, we deserve to get killed. They'll sure think so, anyhow."

Out Tibor went. They were at the edge of a large village or small town. Trenches and shell holes already marred the landscape. Tibor slid into a hole in the ground and started improving it with his entrenching tool. He hadn't seen much fighting yet, but air attacks had already taught him that a well-made foxhole would save your life if anything would.

Sometimes nothing would. If one came down right where you happened to be, all your digging in just meant digging your own grave a little deeper. But you did what you could.

Artillery up ahead bellowed. The Russian guns didn't sound very far up ahead. Tibor wondered whether American shells could reach this far. They had at some point, or the village wouldn't be a jumble of wreckage with dead, swollen dogs—and, no doubt, dead, swollen people who hadn't been planted yet—perfuming the air. But maybe the Russians had pushed them out of range.

Then again, maybe it didn't matter. American fighters—prop jobs, left over from the last war—screamed by at just above treetop height, pounding the place with rockets and heavy machine guns. Tibor had never faced a couple of trucks' worth of *Katyushas*. He no longer felt he was missing anything.

Several of the trucks that had brought the Hungarians here were ablaze, sending their smoke screens up into the sky now that smoke screens didn't matter any more. They'd gone under camouflage netting as soon as the soldiers piled out of them. The enemy flyers might not have seen them, but they'd hit them just the same. Tibor did hope the drivers had got out.

Someone behind him shouted something: guttural consonants mired in palatalized nouns. Tibor recognized Russian without being able to speak it. He looked around and found himself on the receiving end of a Red Army major's glare. Saluting, he said, "Sorry, sir. I don't speak your language"—in Magyar. That didn't make the major any happier. Tibor called, "Sergeant, there's a Soviet officer here." He didn't say what he thought of the Soviet officer. The bastard might understand more than he let on. Trusting Russians didn't come naturally to their fraternal socialist allies.

Sergeant Gergely climbed out of his hole and walked over. Saluting the Russian, he said, "What do you need, sir?" He also used his own language. The major gave forth with something impassioned. Gergely only shrugged. Scowling, the Russian switched to German to order everyone into the front line at once. Tibor followed that only too well. Gergely also must have. But he just spread his hands and stuck to Magyar: "Sorry, sir. I can't understand a word you're saying."

The Red Army major scorched him up one side and down the other. But he couldn't *prove* the Hungarians were playing dumb. He stormed off, his face as red with rage as a baboon's backside. "Good job, Sergeant!" Tibor exclaimed. "They won't throw us into the sausage machine yet."

"Yet. Yeah." Gergely nodded. "Gimme a cigarette, will you? I stalled him this time, but they'll use us up pretty damn quick any which way."

During the Twenties and Thirties, Harry Truman had read a good deal of science fiction and fantasy. He'd enjoyed the stories; they'd kept his mind loose and elastic. When even ordinary reality could stretch and twist like taffy, a loose, elastic mind wasn't the least useful thing to have. He sometimes wished he had time for that kind of reading now.

*Wish for the moon while you're at it,* he thought sourly. Reports of the disaster the Russians had visited on the West Coast (and even on Maine) clogged his Oval Office desk. He hadn't dreamt Stalin could hit that hard. Yes, the USSR had been paid back in spades, doubled and redoubled. That didn't mean the United States was in anything like great shape.

But even as Truman was reading about the devastation in Los Angeles, science fiction and fantasy bubbled back into his thoughts. Somebody'd said *Do not call up that which you cannot put down.* He thought it was H.P. Lovecraft, but he wasn't sure. Lovecraft hadn't been one of his favorites.

That might have been because Lovecraft was a strange, gloomy New Englander, not at all in tune with Truman's Midwestern optimism. Lovecraft's style was overblown and ornate, too: out of step with the straightforward prose that flowed from Truman's pen. But strange and gloomy or not, overblown and ornate or not, old H.P. had hit that particular nail square on the head.

*Do not call up that which you cannot put down.* In the Second World War, it hadn't mattered. The USA could go ahead and incinerate Hiroshima and Nagasaki and lose no sleep afterwards. The Japanese were already on the ropes, even without the A-bombs. No matter how much they wanted to, they couldn't hit back. All they could do was endure the unendurable and surrender.

Well, Red China couldn't hit back, either, when the United States threw those Manchurian cities onto the pyre. The Red Chinese couldn't, and neither Truman nor Douglas MacArthur had believed that Joe Stalin would. Didn't he see he was in over his head against America?

Whether he did or not, he must have decided he didn't care. If he couldn't avenge his biggest and most important ally, who would want an alliance with him afterwards? He had an almost Oriental sense of face. So he'd dropped bombs in Europe, and so. . . .

And so now his country and Truman's, and Western Europe and his satellites and Red China as well, wouldn't be the same for years, decades, maybe centuries to come. No matter who wound up dominating Korea, no matter how the European land war turned out, nobody would come out better off than he'd been going in. Nobody.

*Do not call up that which you cannot put down.* The really terrifying thing was, it could have been worse. And, had the war waited another few years—maybe two, maybe four—it would have been worse. Incalculably worse.

No, not quite incalculably. The physicists who were hard at

work on the next generation of bombs worked those calculations as a matter of course. They had to. That was part of their job. Making the calculations mean anything to somebody who didn't take a slide rule to bed instead of a Teddy bear, though . . . That was a different story.

The biggest ordinary bombs the limeys dropped from one of their Lancasters in the last war weighed ten tons. The A-bombs that flattened Hiroshima and Nagasaki and ended the last war packed the punch of ten or twenty *thousand* tons of TNT. So did the ones both sides were throwing around now. That was a hell of a big step up, the equivalent of putting on thousandfold boots.

And another step, every bit as big, lay right around the corner. So the boys with the high foreheads and the funny haircuts kept telling Truman, anyhow. The kinks lay in the engineering, not the physics. And the engineering, they assured him, was the easy part.

They'd convinced him. He believed them, even when believing them scared the living bejesus out of him. Because they talked glibly about bombs with blasts worth not thousands but millions of tons of high explosives.

What could you do with a few bombs like that? Blow not just a city but a medium-sized state clean off the map. Or, if you happened to drop them in Europe instead, the map might be missing a country or two.

Truman muttered to himself. He knew Senators who kept a bottle of bourbon—or, if they came from the Northeast, a bottle of scotch—in their desk drawers to lubricate the thought processes and shield them from the slings and arrows of outrageous constituents. He'd never been a teetotaler, not even during Prohibition. But he'd always been clear that he had hold of the bottle. The bottle didn't have hold of him.

He'd always been clear about that, and he'd always been proud of it, too. Now he felt like getting blotto. He was presiding over a disaster, a catastrophe, a horror beyond the eldritch dreams of H.P. Lovecraft. The world wouldn't recover for years and years, if it ever did.

And yet . . . And yet . . . The USA and the USSR were only doing the best, or the worst, they could with the halfway tools they had right this minute. Give them a few of the scientists' new toys, and what would they come up with?

The end of the world. That was how it looked to the President. Life would go on after this war, however it turned out. After the next one, if they used the new goodies?

Einstein had said, or was supposed to have said, that he didn't know what the weapons of World War III would be like, but that he did know what they would use to fight World War IV. Rocks. What worried Truman was, Einstein might have been looking on the bright side of things.

Had the bushy-haired physicist really said anything so cynical? It didn't sound like him. Truman was tempted to pick up the phone, call the Institute for Advanced Study at Princeton, and find out. When you were President of the United States, you could satisfy whatever whim you happened to have.

You could. Truman suspected Franklin D. Roosevelt, a man of more than a few whims and whimsies, would have. As for himself, he refrained. His hard Midwestern frugality was as much a part of him as his bifocals—more, because he'd had it longer. So was the relentless drive to get on with the job.

He muttered again, this time with the kind of language he'd used while his battery was throwing shells at the Huns during the First World War. Scientists here told him the new bombs, the end-of-the-world bombs, were coming soon.

Joe Stalin, damn his black, stubborn heart, had scientists working for him, too. Good ones. He wouldn't have been so dangerous if they were a pack of thumb-fingered clods. Hitler hadn't expected the Russians to make such good tanks, or so many of them. Truman hadn't expected Stalin to pull the Bull bomber or the MiG-15 out of his hat.

And nobody had expected the Russians to make their own atom bombs so fast. General Groves, who'd ramrodded the Manhattan Project through to its triumphant completion, hadn't figured Stalin would learn to build an A-bomb for twenty-five years, if he ever did. Which proved . . . what? That Groves made a better engineer and manager of engineers than a prophet.

No doubt those Soviet big brains were working just as hard for their boss as their American counterparts were here. They might be working even harder. Stalin, like Hitler, made unfortunate things happen to people who didn't satisfy him.

Truman muttered one more time. Even assuming the United States won this war—even assuming a war like this was winnable—what was he supposed to do about Russia, or with it? It was too big to conquer and occupy in any ordinary sense of the words. Napoleon had discovered that; despite far greater resources at his disposal, so had the *Führer.*

You couldn't just leave it alone, either. When you did, the Russians got frisky. That was bad enough before, when all they exported was world revolution. Atomic bombs gave the question new urgency—but, dammit, no new answers.

# 13

IHOR SHEVCHENKO WAS NOT a religious man—
not an outwardly religious man, anyhow. He'd lived his
whole life through the Soviet Union's aggressive campaigns
against supernatural belief of every kind. Only a man with
the urge to become a martyr or one with an insatiable curiosity about what a gulag looked like from the inside could be
outwardly religious in this day and age. Assuming there was
any difference between those two types.

Things had loosened up a little during the war against the
Nazis. With the country's fate in the balance, Stalin had decided he'd be a Russian patriot first and a good Communist
only later. If believing helped people kill Germans, he was
all for it.

If you looked at things the right way, that was funny. Stalin
was no more Russian than Hitler was. The thick accent with
which he spoke Russian showed he was a Georgian, a blackass from the Caucasus. Again, though, if you were smart
enough to see the joke there, you needed to be smart enough
to know better than to tell it to anybody else.

After victory, the powers that be seemed willing to let ba-
bushkas and a few old men keep going to services without
getting into trouble. Even a younger woman might get away
with it, though it would be noted and wouldn't look good on
her record. A man of Ihor's age who stuck his nose inside a
church would still catch it. Since going with the current was
always easier and safer than swimming against it, that was
what he did.

All of which meant he had no real idea how to pray, only
bits he remembered from when he was a little boy. For the

first time in his life, he found himself regretting that. He wanted to prostrate himself before the icon of some mournful-eyed, white-bearded saint and give the holy man reverence for not letting Anya go to Kiev and get caught in the Americans' atomic fire. He wanted to light candles in front of the icon to show his gratitude.

When he told his wife as much, she said, "Don't be an idiot." It wasn't so much that she was a New Soviet Woman, someone for whom religion was a relic of the primitive past. She was, however, a practical woman. Proving as much, she continued, "Do you want to bring the Chekists down on your head?"

They both spoke in whispers, in the darkness of their cramped room in the middle of the night. Such talk was safe then if it ever was. Sometimes, of course, it never was. Ihor answered, "A lot of them went up in smoke along with the rest of Kiev."

"A lot of them, sure, but not all of them. You can bet on that—not all of them," Anya said. "Can you imagine us without people watching to keep other people in line?"

Ihor shook his head. He and his wife both usually called the Soviet secret police by the name the Tsars' secret police had used. That said everything that needed saying about the permanence of secret policemen in this part of the world. Even if the Soviet Union stopped being the Soviet Union and for some reason went back to being Russia, whoever was in charge would use them to keep an eye on things. Unless, of course, he happened to be a secret policeman himself.

Anya responded to the motion, saying, "Well, there you are."

"*Tak.* Here I am." Only after the word was out of his mouth did he realize he'd said *yes* in Ukrainian. The language he'd learned from his mother and father was for moments like this—and for when he wanted to seem like a clodhopper to someone in authority trying to give him a hard time. Otherwise, he used Russian. He went on, "Here you are, too. I'm glad of it." He squeezed her.

She squeaked in surprise. "So am I," she said when she got her breath back. "If I hadn't come down with the sniffles—"

"If God hadn't sent you the sniffles," Ihor broke in.

But his wife only laughed. "Have you got any idea how silly that sounds?" she said.

He listened to himself. "It does, doesn't it?" he said, self-conscious and embarrassed at the same time. You thought about God—if you thought about God—as throwing thunderbolts around, not giving somebody a head cold.

He kissed her. This time, her arms tightened around him. Things went on from there. When you weren't doing it for the first time, messing around wasn't embarrassing. You didn't run the risk of saying something foolish, the way he had a moment before. In fact, you didn't have to say anything at all. Ihor liked that fine.

The other thing making love let Ihor do was show Anya how glad he was that she hadn't gone to Kiev. He'd told her, of course, told her over and over, but this seemed so much better. Words weren't enough for some things. He'd heard once from somebody—maybe during the war; he couldn't remember now—that writers said the trick was showing readers things, not telling them about things. Ihor barely had his letters, but that made sense to him.

Losing Kiev meant more to the collective farm than fewer visits from the MGB. It also meant gasoline didn't come out to the *kolkhoz* for the spring plowing. At some collectives, progressive and advanced, that would have been a disaster. Here, it was an annoyance that cost people extra work, but no more. Horse-drawn plows sat slowly rusting in a barn. After the Red Army reconquered the area from the Hitlerites, plowing with horses again rather than people had seemed the height of modernity.

One night near the end of March, just before plunging headlong into exhausted slumber, Ihor did think to ask Anya, "What will we do with our grain once we harvest it? We sent it in to Kiev, but Kiev doesn't need so much any more."

"No, it doesn't," Anya agreed. Nobody knew how many people had died in the capital of the Ukrainian Soviet Socialist Republic, not to the nearest ten thousand—maybe not to the nearest hundred thousand. Or if anyone did know, he wasn't saying.

More people still had fled the city. The *kolkhozniks* had herded refugees away. Some of the injuries those poor bastards sported were ordinary, the kind Ihor had seen over and over in the last war. The burns, though . . . He hadn't seen anything like that before, except a couple of luckless men who wound up on the wrong end of a flamethrower. But these didn't seem to want to heal. Raw, oozing meat . . .

With an effort of will, he pulled his mind away from all that. "So what *do* we do?" he asked.

"I don't know," his wife said. "We won't have to worry about it till fall. By then, I'm sure somebody will have come around to give us orders."

"I suppose so," Ihor said around a yawn. All the same, he found time to wonder some more before sleep dragged him down. The people who gave orders like that would have come from Kiev before the Americans lashed it with fire. If they didn't come from Kiev, wouldn't they come from Moscow? When you got right down to it, in the end everything came from Moscow.

If it could. The Americans had desecrated Moscow along with Kiev. They hadn't killed Comrade Stalin; he still spoke on Radio Moscow. But Ihor had no way of knowing whether Radio Moscow still came from its namesake city, or from somewhere like Magnitogorsk or Irkutsk. He did know Yuri Levitan and the other regular broadcasters weren't reading the news on the radio any more. He couldn't prove that meant anything, but it probably did.

The people who were reading the news on the radio warned against going into the ruins of cities struck by atomic bombs. The warning was twofold. The authorities declared looting a crime punishable by summary execution—a bullet in the back of the neck. And they warned of poisonous radio-activity lingering in the air and water and on the ground.

Maybe the radio told the truth. Maybe it served up a fresh helping of government lies. Ihor didn't try to find out himself. It wasn't as if he hadn't looted in Soviet, Polish, and German cities retaken from the Nazis. When you were in the Red Army, you were supposed to be your own quartermaster sergeant. Anything over and above keeping yourself fed was a bonus.

But plundering Kiev felt different to him. He couldn't have said why, but it did. Not everybody on the *kolkhoz* thought the way he did. People pedaled off, saying they wanted to see what the ruins looked like. If they came back with more than they had when they set out, how could you prove it?

Then again, sometimes they didn't come back. A *kolkhoz-nik* named Orest Makhno rode away to see what he could see. That was the last anyone at the collective farm saw of him. He might have come across an enormous cache of gold-

pieces stamped with the shaggy visage of one Tsar or another, enough to set himself up as a prince of thieves. If you
wanted to look on the bright side of things, that was how they
would look to you.

More likely, though, he'd met a stocky, unsmiling man in a
bad suit, one who'd heard enough protestations of innocence
to laugh at them or ignore them altogether. And, more likely,
Orest had found nine millimeters' worth of answers: as much
as he would need for the rest of his life.


Cade Curtis cradled his M-1 carbine. They'd congratulated
him for making it from the Chosin Reservoir to the UN lines
far to the south. They'd asked him how he'd done it, and
taken careful notes as he spun his story. Fair enough. Knowing what had worked for him might let them give other soldiers in trouble tips that would really help.

Afterwards, they'd promoted him to first lieutenant. They'd
given him a Bronze Star with a V for valor. And they'd given
him not just a platoon but a company of his own. Officers
were scarce in Korea, officers with combat experience even
scarcer.

The war here ground on just the same, even if the wider
world, distracted by atoms and mushroom clouds, hardly
bothered looking this way any more. Despite the bombs that
had fallen on the Manchurian cities, the Red Chinese kept
throwing as many troops into the fight as they could. And the
North Koreans, though reduced to rifles and submachine
guns and homemade grenades, went on fighting, too. They
were bastards, but they were brave bastards.

Cade wished he had a Russian-made submachine gun
himself. Having lugged one most of the way south, he'd
come to like it better than the weapon with which the USA
armed its officers. The Russian guns were more reliable than
his carbine, more compact, and had a much higher rate of
fire. They didn't jam in cold weather. His piece looked like a
rifle. Unfortunately, it didn't perform like one—or like a submachine gun. It combined the worst of both worlds.

There was a loophole in front of the trench. You could,
if you were so inclined, examine the enemy positions up
ahead through it without exposing your whole head. Cade
Curtis wasn't so inclined. He figured some sniper with a
scope-sighted Russian rifle was watching it. If the son of a

bitch saw an eyeball looking back at him, the family of the eyeball's owner would get a Deeply Regrets wire from the Department of Defense.

So Curtis looked up over another stretch of the entrenchment. He showed more of himself, but only for a couple of seconds. Then he ducked out of sight again. Nothing looked to be stirring. All he saw was snow and dirt and rusting wire. That proved only so much, of course. The Red Chinese and North Koreans had learned plenty about the fine art of camouflage from their Russian instructors. But you did what you could. In this imperfect world, that was all you could do. This imperfect world's weather worked the same way. The calendar said it was spring, but nobody'd told the countryside.

"All quiet, sir?" Staff Sergeant Lou Klein asked. He was about forty, with graying whiskers and sagging jowls. The Germans hadn't killed him in North Africa or Italy, though the ribbon for the Purple Heart with two tiny oak-leaf clusters said they'd tried hard enough. He could have run the company better than Cade, but he'd never bothered going to OCS.

"Looks that way," Cade said. "I mean, you can't tell with the Chinks, but I didn't see anything stirring."

Klein lit a Camel. "Mind if I look for myself?"

"Be my guest." If the career noncom thought Cade would get huffy about the question, he had another think coming. Curtis did say, "You may not want to do it right where I did, though."

"Nope. That wouldn't be so real great." If the warning offended Klein, he didn't show it. He walked along the trench till just before it kinked, popped up to check things, and promptly disappeared from sight. Somebody fired at the place where he'd been, but he wasn't there any more.

"You reckon we'll ever see the tanks they keep promising us?" Cade asked him.

"Sir, I been in the Army about as long as you been around, so I gotta say stranger things have happened." Klein paused to think. "You ask me to name two of 'em, though, I'm gonna have some trouble."

"That's how it looks to me, too. I was hoping you would tell me I was wrong," Curtis said. The Reds hated and feared American armor. They hadn't had that many old Russian T-34/85s to begin with, and a lot of the ones they had had were wrecks now. Even a new T-34/85 wasn't a match for a

Pershing. And the enemy wasn't likely to get new ones, or T-54s, not when Stalin needed tanks a hell of a lot closer to home.

Of course, that shoe also fit the American foot in Korea. With the Red Army trying to crash its way to the Rhine, every American, British, and French tank around was busy doing its best to hold the Ivans back. After World War II ended, the French had taken on some ex-Nazi Panthers to tide them over till they built up their own tank factories again. If any of those brutes were still running, the froggies had probably thrown them into the fight, too.

All of which left Korea half forgotten, dangling from the ends of both sides' ridiculously long supply lines. And it turned the fighting here into something out of the war before last: trenches and artillery and grenades and machine guns. The fighters that sometimes strafed the trenches were more modern than Sopwith Camels. But, with the aviation world swinging at top speed from prop jobs to jets, they were hardly less obsolete than those cloth-and-wood-and-wire biplanes.

Just to show you never could tell, a regiment's worth of Pershings clanked up to the front under cover of darkness a couple of days later. Astonishment made the cigarette in Klein's mouth twitch. "Fuck me," the noncom said. "We went and won the Irish Sweepstakes." Cade couldn't have put it better himself.

The attack was to be in the direction of Chongju. The way the higher-ups put it showed they didn't think it would get that far. Cade noted that without much surprise. The Americans had more and better planes and tanks and big guns than the enemy. The Red Chinese and North Koreans had committed far more soldiers to the fight. Their tactics often reminded Cade of smothering a fire by piling bodies on it till it went out, which didn't mean they wouldn't work.

As it had on the Somme thirty-five years before, artillery thundered to soften up the foe. It had gone on for days then, throwing away the advantage of surprise. Generals had learned since—not quickly, but they had. After three hours, the 105s and 155s fell silent. The tanks went forward, foot soldiers in their wake.

Enemy machine guns started barking as soon as the barrage shut down. Unless you used an A-bomb, you wouldn't kill all the troops in front of you. Even if you did, you might not get them all. And this stretch of Korea wasn't worth splitting atoms.

Nor did it need them. England had invented tanks during World War I to deal with the Kaiser's machine-gun nests. They still did the job. The Pershings' 90mm main armament smashed sandbags and knocked reinforced concrete to pieces. A few Red Chinese soldiers carried rocket-propelled grenades—what the Russians used for bazookas. They knocked out a couple of American tanks, but only a couple. The rest ground ahead.

Cade and his men loped after them. You couldn't let tanks get too far out in front of infantry. Or you had better not. If you did, brave enemies would shove Molotov cocktails into the engine compartment or chuck grenades through open hatches and make the crews unhappy.

Here and there, live Chinks fought back with rifles and submachine guns. After the pounding the forward trenches had taken, there weren't too many of them. They didn't stay alive very long, either. Cade picked up a PPSh whose former owner wouldn't need it any more. He scavenged as many magazines of pistol ammo as he could to keep it fed.

Klein eyed him. "You weren't shitting me when you said you liked those Russian jobs, were you? Uh, sir?"

"Not even a little bit," Cade said. "They're like Model T's. They'll run forever, and they don't wear out."

"Sir, you weren't even born yet when they quit makin' Tin Lizzies," Klein said.

He was right. Even so, Cade answered, "There were still plenty of 'em around when I was a kid. People down the road from us had one."

"Me, I got my face slapped in my old man's Model T," Klein said. "If she'd come across instead, I might've married her and never joined the Army. Just goes to show, don't it?" He didn't say what it showed. Chances were he didn't know, either. They slogged on through the ruined Korean countryside.

It was what would have been a lazy Sunday morning in Glendale. Aaron Finch hadn't seen a lot of lazy Sunday mornings in his life. He'd known a few after he married Ruth. He might have known more with her, but then Leon came along. Babies didn't believe in lazy mornings, not even after they turned into toddlers.

And the bombs that had smashed Los Angeles made Aaron only too sure that nobody around here would know any lazy Sunday mornings for a long time to come. The people the bomb hadn't killed were too busy scrambling to kick off their shoes, pour some more coffee, and relax with the paper (assuming the paper they were used to relaxing with had survived, which the big ones hadn't). Aaron found himself no less busy at the game of survival than anyone else.

"You ready, Leon?" he asked his little son.

Leon was fidgeting, which made it hard for Ruth to finish tying his shoes. He fidgeted a lot. He had more energy than he knew what to do with. But he nodded, which made the baby curls bounce up and down on top of his head. And he said, "Ready, Daddy!"

Aaron and Ruth looked at each other. They knew Leon knew what *ready* meant. But he hadn't said it himself till just now. Kids came out with new stuff every day. From everything Aaron could see, coming out with new stuff all the time was a big part of what being a kid was about.

"Well, come on, then." Aaron stubbed out his cigarette. "Let's go see what the Kasparians want for eggs. And you can pay your respects to the ducks."

"Ducks! Quack!" Leon jumped up and down in excitement. He wasn't a whole lot taller than a duck or a chicken, but he did act oddly solemn around the mallards. If he wasn't paying his respects to them, Aaron didn't know what else to call it.

They walked down the street together, Leon's little hand in Aaron's big one. No cars went past them. It was still early, but even so. . . . Gas was scarce in and around Los Angeles, and cost upwards of half a buck a gallon when you could get it. That was one reason Aaron was down to part-time at Blue Front. Another was that nobody was hauling appliances into L.A. Even if people had brought them in, nobody was buying them. Herschel Weissman cursed the way his business was going in Yiddish and in accented English.

No cars drove the street, but a beat-up station wagon and a newish De Soto that didn't belong in the neighborhood were parked on the far side. The windows on both were steamed up, which meant somebody, or a family's worth of somebodies, slept inside. Aaron locked his doors all the time now, which he hadn't bothered doing before the bombs fell. He kept a heavy iron fireplace poker and a carving knife where he could grab them fast if he had to, too. He hadn't needed them, but he was ready if he did.

Leon suddenly yanked his hand out of his father's. "Flarn!" he said. "Flarn!" He plucked a yellow dandelion on the next-door neighbor's lawn. *Flarn* was what he said when he meant *flower.* He knew what he meant, and so did Aaron and Ruth, but not everything that came out of his mouth was what strangers would recognize as English. His parents didn't always recognize it right away, either. He'd gone *Drin-drin!* for a couple of weeks before Ruth figured out it was the noise he made for a ringing telephone.

The Kasparians had a hand-lettered sign on their front lawn: POULTRY & EGGS FOR SALE HERE. Clucks and quacks floated up from the back. Leon picked another flarn. One of these days, he'd probably tear up somebody's prize tulips and catch hell for it, but so far he'd stuck to dandelions.

Aaron knocked on the front door. When it opened, a woman of about his own age looked back at him. She had a nose more "Jewish" than his and eyebrows that met above it. He found that off-putting, but somebody'd told him it was a beauty mark for Armenians. *To each his own,* he thought with profound unoriginality.

Her smile was nice. "Hello, Aaron," she said, and then, "Hello, Leon."

"Flarns!" Leon showed off the dandelions.

"Morning, Elizabeth," Aaron said.

"You need eggs today?" Elizabeth Kasparian had a faint guttural accent. She'd come to the States after surviving the Turkish massacre of Armenians during World War I.

"And a chicken, if you've got one to sell," Aaron answered.

"We do, yes." She nodded. "Go around the back, and Krikor will let you pick one out for yourself. Do you want him to do the honors for you?" She meant killing and gutting the bird.

"Thanks, but I'll take care of it myself and save a quarter. We kept poultry in Oregon when I was a kid, and I used to do it then. Chopped wood, too." Aaron didn't tell her that he'd also chopped off the last joint of his younger brother Marvin's right little finger. He hadn't meant to, which didn't make Marvin—or their father—any happier.

"However you please," Mrs. Kasparian said. "Some people don't care to do the killing themselves. They would rather not think about that—only the eating."

"They've never raised livestock, then," Aaron said. Mrs. Kasparian nodded again. If you ran a farm or even kept a few chickens for eggs and meat, you couldn't get sentimental about your critters. Of course, most city folks knew animals only as pets. Aaron steered Leon toward the gate by the side of the Kasparians' house. "C'mon, kiddo-shmiddo."

Leon bounded ahead. Aaron wouldn't let him watch when the chicken met the hatchet. He was too little for that. But he sure did think live chickens, and especially ducks, were fascinating as all get-out.

Krikor Kasparian had a graying mane of wavy hair and a mustache bushier than Joe Stalin's. He was shorter than Aaron, but wider through the shoulders. He puffed on a stogie foul enough to fall under the Geneva Convention rules against poison gas.

"Hallo, Aaron," he said, his accent thicker than his wife's. "Eggs this morning?"

"A dozen, yes, and a chicken. That one, I think." Aaron pointed at a plump bird pecking corn and bugs from the dirt. Leon ran past the rooster toward the muddy little pond the ducks used. He stared at them, wide-eyed. He didn't bother them or anything—he just stared. He really did seem to be paying his respects. He got muddy doing it, which wouldn't thrill Ruth, but he was a little kid. Little kids drew mud the way magnets drew nails.

"Feed has got more expensive since the bomb fell," Krikor said gravely. "And we have more demand, because the supermarkets that get birds from far away cannot do it so easily. So it will cost you half a dollar more than last time."

*I've got you over a barrel,* was what he meant. He was one of the price gougers big shots in Sacramento and Washington went on about. But he was also a neighbor, and he could have tried to extract more than he had. Aaron paid him without haggling. Life was too short. As long as you had the money, life was too short. For the moment, he did.

"Hey, Leon!" he called. "Come on! We're going home!"

Pretty soon, from what Ruth said, Leon would start saying no whether he meant it or not. He hadn't done it yet, though. He started back toward Aaron, but stopped to go eye-to-eye with the rooster. Maybe he enjoyed doing that with something that was shorter than he was. The rooster's golden eyes bored into his brown ones. Leon reached out—Aaron was convinced he was experimenting, not being mean—to touch the bird's red comb.

"Careful, kid," Aaron said. He knew, as Leon didn't, that a rooster was boss of the henyard and had no use for intruders—especially not for intruders who weren't much bigger than it was.

He spoke up just too late. The rooster hauled off and kicked Leon in the shin. Since Leon was wearing short pants, it hurt even more than it would have otherwise. He let out a squeal that literally ruffled the rooster's feathers, then dashed back to his daddy. Aaron picked him up to inspect the damage.

"I am very sorry about that," Mr. Kasparian said.

"Doesn't seem to be much harm done," Aaron said. Leon had a red mark on his leg and might get a bruise, but the rooster hadn't broken the skin. "You have to watch out for things like that," Aaron told him.

Leon had no idea what he was talking about. He'd keep finding out the hard way how the world worked for quite a while yet. But, as long as Aaron had hold of him, things couldn't be *too* bad.

After a minute or two, Aaron set him down. He paid Krikor Kasparian, took the eggs and the chicken, got hold of Leon's hand, and went home. He'd have a new story to tell Ruth.

They said you never saw the one that got you. As far as Sergeant Konstantin Morozov was concerned, they said all kinds of silly crap. This once, though, they happened to be right.

Morozov was frantically traversing the T-54's turret so the tank's big gun would bear on an English Centurion—he thought it was a Centurion, anyhow, since it looked more angular than the American Pershings. Next thing he knew, something slammed into the T-54 hard enough to smash his face into the periscope eyepiece. Blood ran down his cheek.

"Fuck your mother!" Pavel Gryzlov bawled. "We're hit!"

"Fuck your own mother," Morozov said irritably. "I never would have known without you."

From the front of the tank, Mikhail Kasyanov reported the situation in two words: "Engine's dead."

"Oh, fuck your mother, too," Morozov told the driver. If that round, wherever the hell it came from, had hit the turret or bored through the hull into the fighting compartment, they wouldn't still be here banging their gums about it. With luck, they would have died before they knew they were dead. Without luck . . . Morozov didn't want to think about that, so he didn't.

"What do we do, Comrade Sergeant?" Mogamed Safarli asked.

Morozov marveled that even a blackass could be so goddamn dumb. "We get the hell out, that's what," he answered. In his mind's eye, he pictured an American or English tank commander ordering his gunner to put another round into the Red Army tank with the black smoke pouring out of the engine compartment—he couldn't see that smoke, but he knew it had to be there.

Out they went. The driver had a floor hatch behind his seat. The others escaped through the one in the floor of the fighting compartment. They crawled forward as fast as they could—burning diesel fuel was dripping down from the stricken engine.

"I feel naked," Gryzlov said.

"Tell me!" Morozov exclaimed. Under the tank wasn't so bad. But they had to get out, get away. That meant exposing themselves to bullets and shell fragments and all the other things the T-54's thick, beautifully sloped armor had held at bay . . . till it hadn't.

Sure as hell, as soon as Morozov came out from between the tracks, a bullet cracked past him. More rounds stirred the grass in front of the tank. Staying as low as he could, he slithered along to put the T-54's bulk between him and those unfriendly strangers out there. How the devil did any infantryman live longer than a minute and a half?

Misha Kasyanov yipped in pain. He clutched at the calf of his left leg. Red began to soak through the khaki of his coveralls. "Keep going if you can," Morozov called to him. "We'll get you bandaged up as soon as we find cover."

"I'll try," was all Kasyanov said. That was as much as anyone could do. Morozov knew how lucky he was not to have stopped something himself.

Another armor-piercing round did hit the T-54 then. It brewed up. Flame and smoke shot from all the turret hatches.

The turret itself didn't blow off, which was also a matter of luck. One perfect smoke ring did come into the sky from the cupola, as if the Devil had paused in the middle of smoking a cigar.

"Heh!" Pavel Gryzlov said. "They wasted ammo there. That pussy wasn't going anywhere anyhow."

"I don't know," Morozov responded. "If we recovered it, we might have been able to slap in a new engine."

"I don't believe it for a minute," the gunner said. Then, remembering to whom he was talking, he quickly added, "Uh, Comrade Sergeant."

"Right." Konstantin Morozov's voice was desert-dry. He pointed to the east. "I think those are our men in the holes there." He hoped like anything those were Red Army men there. Neither he nor anybody from his crew carried anything more lethal than a Tokarev automatic. That was fine if you were shooting somebody trying to clamber aboard your tank. If you had to hit anything out past twenty meters, you might do better throwing rocks.

The tankers made for the holes. They all yelled *"Tovarishchi!"*—Comrades!—at the top of their lungs. Bullets kept cracking past and clipping the young, so-green grass—with April here, everything was sprouting like mad—but none hit any of them. And whoever was in the holes didn't slaughter them, which would have taken next to no effort.

Morozov tumbled into a foxhole beside the burnt-out ruins of a shack. A Red Army corporal with one of the new Kalashnikovs grinned at him. "Look what the cat drug in," he said. "I didn't know they let you people out of your cages."

"When the cage starts burning, you go," Morozov assured him. "Listen, help me bring my driver in, will you? He's got a wounded leg."

"I'll do that," the infantry noncom said at once. Wounded men were serious business.

He was less leery about leaving his foxhole than Morozov had been of bailing out of the dead T-54. To him, going around in the open was all part of a day's work. Morozov couldn't very well hang back himself. They bundled Mikhail Kasyanov into their arms and got him into the hole.

"Let's see what we have here," the corporal said, as he used his bayonet to cut Kasyanov's coveralls so he could examine the injury. "Doesn't seem too bad." He began to bandage it with skill that told of experience.

*"Aii!"* Kasyanov said, and then, "Up yours, you whore! It isn't your motherfucking leg!"

"That's a fact," the corporal agreed placidly. He examined his handiwork. "Not bleeding *too* much now. You'll be on the shelf a while, for sure. If the war's still going when you get better, though, I bet they let you serve again."

"Happy fucking day," Kasyanov said. "You have a morphine shot? It hurts like they shot the head of my dick off."

"Ouch!" The corporal cupped his hands in front of his crotch. Morozov wanted to do the same thing. The foot soldier took a syringe from a pouch on his belt and stuck the tank crewman. He said, "This ought to do the trick. I took it off a dead American. Those whores carry all kinds of goodies. They must all be millionaires over there."

Someone who wanted to land him in trouble could do it if he kept talking like that. The Soviet Union declared over and over, at the top of its ideological lungs, that the American proletariat, like the proletariat in other capitalist countries, was oppressed by the bourgeoisie and especially by the magnates, the plutocrats. What would an American soldier be but a member of the proletariat, dragooned into service by his vicious overlords?

And yet . . . During the last war, Morozov had seen for himself that even Poland was richer than the workers' and peasants' paradise, and that people lived better there. He'd seen that Germany was *much* richer than the USSR, though he hadn't seen any parts of Germany that weren't knocked flat before he got to them.

During this war, he'd seen that the Western-occupied parts of Germany were richer and were rebuilding faster than the section the USSR controlled. The corporal must have seen some of those things, too. Unlike Morozov, he didn't know enough to keep his big mouth shut.

So the tank commander without a tank just asked, "Where's the closest aid station?"

"Back that way, not quite a kilometer," the corporal said, jerking his thumb to the east. "You want your other two guys to take him? Once they get away from the front, he can probably drape his arms over their shoulders and go on his good leg."

"How's that sound, Misha?" Morozov asked.

"Fine by me." Kasyanov spoke as if he hadn't a care in the world. Morphine was good stuff, as Morozov had also seen before. The wounded driver let his comrades take him to the sawbones. Morozov went back with them, wondering what the Red Army would do with him next.

# 14

BACK IN THE BLACK days of October 1941, the Soviet Union had chosen Kuibishev, on the Volga just west of the Urals, as the capital in case the Nazis took Moscow. There'd been a panic and a skedaddle out of Moscow that October, when it looked as if the Hitlerites would do exactly that. These days, people talked about the skedaddle in whispers when they talked about it at all.

Boris Gribkov understood why they whispered, and why they didn't like to speak at all. That was called a working sense of self-preservation. Underlying the reticence was the question of whether anyone would have paid attention to Stalin had he tried to give orders from a provincial town dusty in the summer and frozen in the winter. The Soviet Union was lucky: it hadn't had to find out.

But Kuibishev was now what it had been intended to be then: the alternative capital of the USSR. Jackbooted SS men didn't goose-step through Moscow's streets. Atomic fire, though, had burnt too many of those streets out of existence. Too many commissars and generals were burnt out of existence, too.

So the authorities hadn't brought Boris and his bomber crew to Moscow to congratulate them on dealing a similar blow to Seattle. No, they'd pinned Hero of the Soviet Union medals on them here in Kuibishev. They'd photographed them for *Pravda* and *Izvestia* and *Red Star.* And, after that, they hadn't seemed sure what to do with them next.

"You know what really bothers me?" Leonid Tsederbaum said quietly as he and Gribkov walked from their barracks to the mess hall at the Red Air Force base where they were being kept. *Confined,* Gribkov judged—and hoped—was too strong a word.

"No. What really bothers you, Leonid Abramovich?" the pilot asked. It wasn't as if he didn't also have a list of things that really bothered *him.* Tsederbaum was a clever *Zhid.* He might be bothered by some things that hadn't even occurred to Gribkov.

"What really bothers me," he said, pausing to light a *papiros* and blow a stream of smoke up toward the watery sky, "is that, as far as I can tell, we're the *only* Tu-4 crew that bombed America they're making propaganda about."

"Oh." Gribkov felt vaguely disappointed. "That crossed my mind, too." He nodded to himself, admiring the understatement. "Even so, though, considering what we all did, you have to say the *rodina* got a good return on its investment."

"How capitalist!" Tsederbaum exclaimed. Boris eyed him. In the USSR, a man could disappear without ditching in the Pacific or having the Americans shoot him down. A Hero of the Soviet Union could become a nobody in nothing flat. But the navigator didn't look like someone getting ready to report him to the MGB. He just looked like somebody cracking wise. Of course, what somebody looked like didn't mean a thing.

"Have you heard anything about our next assignment?" Gribkov asked. Being a clever *Zhid,* Tsederbaum was liable to have connections in all kinds of interesting places.

Just because he was liable to didn't mean he did. He shook his head. "Not a word. Since you're the pilot, I was hoping you could tell me."

"Sorry," Gribkov said. "I serve the Soviet Union, but they haven't told me how they want me to serve it next."

He wondered how much Soviet Union would be left to serve by the time the war ended. The Red Army was still advancing in Germany, at least if you believed Radio Moscow. Here, Gribkov did. He knew the signs a newsreader used when he was hedging—or, for that matter, when he was just lying. He hadn't noticed any of those in the reports.

Even if the advance stopped, even if the Americans and their Western European lackeys somehow turned the tide and fought their way through Russia's allies in Eastern Europe and invaded the USSR, they wouldn't be able to conquer and occupy it. Boris was sure of that. If Hitler hadn't been able to, nobody could.

Which might not have anything to do with anything. He knew what the bomb his Tu-4 had dropped did to Seattle. How many of those bombs had fallen on the Soviet Union? How many holes did you need to blow in the fabric of a country before it was more holes than fabric? Boris Gribkov didn't know, but he did know the experiment was going on right this minute, both here and in America.

He and Tsederbaum walked up three wooden steps to the mess hall. His nose twitched as soon as he opened the door. A cook with a ladle stood next to an enormous cauldron of borscht. Another stood next to an equally enormous cauldron of shchi. Beet soup or cabbage soup? That had been the Russian question for as long as there'd been Russians. The cauldron of kasha—buckwheat groats—was smaller but still formidable. There was also black bread and peppery sausage coiled like rope.

Gribkov loaded up his tray. So did Tsederbaum. They both took twenty or twenty-five centimeters' worth of sausage. The stuff was bound to have pork in it. Gribkov couldn't imagine a Soviet military kitchen worrying about kosher food. To Russian military cooks, the meals they turned out were like gasoline: fuel for the body, nothing more.

He didn't say anything about it to Leonid Tsederbaum. The Jew had to know what kind of meat went into the sausage—and the shchi, and the borscht—as well as he did. If Tsederbaum didn't care, that was the navigator's business.

Glasses of tea from a samovar completed the meal. Gribkov and Tsederbaum spooned in sugar, then sat down on one of the long benches and ate. It wasn't the kind of meal anyone would go looking for in a restaurant. All the same, Gribkov knew he was getting more food and better food than most civilians did.

"What now?" Tsederbaum asked after they put their dishes in a basin and their trays on a mountainous stack.

"I don't know. What now?" Gribkov answered. "We spent all that time getting ready to fly the mission. Then we went and flew it. And we didn't just fly it—we came back from it."

"And now they have no idea what to do with us," Tsederbaum continued for him.

"And now they have no idea what to do with us," Gribkov agreed. "So we wait around till they make up their minds."

"Let's go outside," Tsederbaum said. When they couldn't be easily overheard, he went on, "Do you want to bomb Paris or London or Rome?"

"I serve the Soviet Union!" Gribkov said, which was never the wrong answer. But it wasn't always enough of the right answer. After a moment, he went on, "Do I *want* to? Of course not. Who in his right mind could? Will I, if they give me the order? I will, because I do serve the Soviet Union. And I'll worry about what I want some other time."

Leonid Tsederbaum opened his mouth, then closed it again. Whatever went on behind his eyes, Gribkov couldn't read it. A couple of seconds later, he tried again: "That's a good answer, Comrade Pilot."

"How about you?" Gribkov wasn't happy about the way the navigator had put him on the spot. "What would you do if they gave us an order like that?"

"Oh, I'd get the plane where it was supposed to go," Tsederbaum replied. "After all, I've already done it once. And I'm a great coward."

"I don't think so!" Whatever Gribkov had expected, that wasn't it.

"Oh, but I am," Tsederbaum said. "If my choice is between a bullet in the back of the neck now and generations yet unborn spitting on my name later, they can spit all they please."

"It isn't like that," Gribkov insisted. "We'd be doing it for the proletarian cause, for the socialist cause."

"If you say so."

"We would!"

"Even if we would, do you think anyone would be glad to remember us for melting the Eiffel Tower down to a stump about this high?" Tsederbaum drew a line across his own belly, just above his navel.

Gribkov winced. He couldn't help it. Even so, he said, "That didn't stop the Americans from hammering the Kremlin. If they're hard, we have to be hard, too."

"I understand that, Comrade Pilot. Just because I understand it doesn't mean I like it," Tsederbaum said. "And do you think for a minute that those American pilots don't have bad dreams, too?"

The *too* was what pierced Gribkov to the root. He hadn't told anybody about his fiery dreams. He most assuredly hadn't told Leonid Abramovich Tsederbaum. Yet the Jew knew. He knew much too well.

\* \* \*

The Yanks were back at the Owl and Unicorn! So were the RAF men who flew out of Sculthorpe with them. Daisy Baxter cared more about the Americans. April would indeed have been the cruelest month without them. Her own countrymen were a thrifty lot, keeping tabs on every ha'penny and turning loose of it only when it was forcibly extracted, as if by a dentist's grippers.

Americans, though . . . Americans spent as if there was no tomorrow. The base remained on high alert. The people who gave orders, though, discovered that the men who carried them out were human beings, and needed an escape valve to relieve the pressure of what they did. Except perhaps for a brothel, a pub was the best escape valve around.

"You gotta make that getaway turn as quick as you can, you know?" an American said, his accent sharp and hard. He used his hands to show what he meant, continuing, "If you don't, if the blast wave catches you when you're halfway through it, it'll flip you around like a leaf in a breeze."

"That happens to you, you're lucky—*damn* lucky—if you ever pull out again, too," another Yank said.

Working the tap, trying to keep up with their orders for bitter, listening with no more than half an ear, Daisy needed longer than she might have to realize they were talking about the blast wave from an atomic explosion. No wonder they spent as if there was no tomorrow! For the people they visited, there wasn't.

A man at a slaughterhouse could knock cattle or sheep over the head day after day for years and years without ever thinking about what he was doing. Back in bygone times, executioners had hanged people the same way. But you needed imagination to be a good flyer. And if you had it, how could you help thinking about what you were doing?

An American first lieutenant she hadn't seen before asked her for a pint. She drew it for him. He gave her a crown. When she started to return his change, he waved it away. "All funny money anyhow," he said.

"Well, thanks very much." She wondered if he knew how much he was overpaying. A lot of Americans, used to decimal coinage, had trouble with Britain's more arcane system. If he did know, he didn't care.

"Mud in your eye." He raised the pint in salute, then started to take a long pull. But he stopped in surprise before it was well begun. He stared at the deep-amber liquid in the mug with sudden, astonished admiration and blurted, "This is *good* beer!"

"Glad you like it." Daisy hid a smile. She'd seen that reaction before from Americans downing their first pint of best bitter.

This Yank had more enthusiasm than most. "I mean to tell you, Miss, this is *good* beer," he said again. "The stuff you get in bottles in America, it tastes like they strain it through the kidneys of a horse—a sick horse, too. Draft beer's a little better, but only a little. This here, though, this is great." By the way he finished the pint, he meant every word of that.

"We aim to please." Now Daisy did smile. She couldn't help it, not with such an enthusiastic customer.

"Sweetheart, you hit the bull's-eye." She'd gone from *Miss* to *Sweetheart* in a couple of sentences. Well, beer and enthusiasm could do that. Having mentioned a bull's-eye, the American waved toward the dartboard down at the end of the snug. Pete Huntington, a local man, was matched with an American sergeant. The Yank had some idea of what he was about. That put him ahead of most of his countrymen, who thought of darts as nothing more than a silly lark. But Pete was taking him to the cleaners just the same. No one would have told the sergeant his foe won tournaments all over East Anglia. The U.S. Air Force man standing in front of Daisy said, "Let me have another glass of this . . . what do you call it?"

He didn't even know that. He was a new fish, all right. "Best bitter," Daisy said patiently.

"You got that right!" He grinned and nodded. "It is the best—you better believe it!" He slid another fat silver coin at Daisy. "Big old coin," he remarked, eyeing it. "Bigger than a cartwheel."

"Cartwheel?" Whatever that Americanism meant, Daisy hadn't run into it before, at least not where it had to do with money.

"Silver dollar," the Yank explained. "They haven't made 'em since the Depression—they just make halves, and use dollar bills instead."

"Notes, we say."

"Do you? How about that? Anyway, though, I'm from

California, and there's still lots of silver dollars around out West."

She took one more stab at not gypping him: "Let me give you your change, please."

He shook his head. "Nah, don't bother. Way things look, I'm not likely to live long enough to care what I've got in my pockets when I go down."

*What has he got in his pocketses?* Memories of some children's book flickered in Daisy's mind. Where did that line come from? As the Yank had, she also shook her head. The title wouldn't come back to her. Letting it go, she said, "Well, your next couple are on the house, then."

He touched the patent-leather brim of his officer's cap. "Much obliged, dear, but you don't have to do that."

"I'm not doing it because I have to. I'm doing it because I want to," Daisy said, in lieu of something like *You've already bought them anyhow, you silly twit.* He wouldn't have paid any attention to that unless it made him mad.

"Well, that's mighty nice of you." He touched his cap again, coming closer to a real salute this time. "What's your name?"

"I'm Daisy Baxter. I run the Owl and Unicorn."

"Mighty pleased to meet you, Daisy. My name's Bruce—Bruce McNulty." He eyed her. "You run this joint? For real?"

"That's right." She nodded. "Why?"

"I just figured they hired you to tend bar on account of you're so pretty—they figured you'd draw guys the way sugar draws ants."

She chuckled. She'd heard more lines than she could remember; that was better than most. As was her habit, she replied as if he hadn't been strewing compliments around: "No, the pub's mine. It's been mine since a little before the war—the last war, I should say—ended. My husband was fighting in Germany, and he didn't come home."

"Oh. I'm mighty sorry to hear it. I was there myself—I was flying a B-25 then. Just dumb luck I came back in one piece. The krauts, they sure did their best to see that I didn't."

She would have guessed him for a year or two younger than she was. Probably not, though, not if he'd fought in World War II. "What do you fly now?" she asked him.

"One of the Superforts down the road," he said, which surprised her not at all. "Guys who were in the B-25 and B-26 kind of have a head start on the big bird, since they all come with nose wheels. A little harder when you're used to tilting up because you were in a B-17 or some other plane with a tailwheel."

"I hadn't thought of that," she said, which was true enough.

Bruce McNulty wagged his hand, as if to say it didn't matter one way or the other. "Enough about me," he said, so earnestly that she could tell the best bitter was doing some of the talking. "What I want to know is how come a pretty gal like you never found another fella."

Daisy would have retired rich long since if she'd had a quid for every lecherous flyboy who asked her that. For *another fella,* they always meant *me.* Now she shrugged. "At first, I wasn't at all interested, which I'm sure you'll understand. Since the worst of the grief passed away, I haven't met anyone who suited me."

She waited for this McNulty to volunteer his services. That was what they did. Except he didn't. He just said, "Well, I hope you do one of these days." Such restraint so amazed her, she drew him another pint on the house. Why not? She was still far ahead of the game.


Gustav Hozzel didn't know exactly where he was. Somewhere between Frankenberg and Arnsberg—he knew that much. Along with the Amis—and with Max Bachman, who also remained lucky—he was still retreating to the north and west. And the Red Army was still coming on. Not much seemed to have changed from the last war, in other words.

He was filthy. He couldn't remember the last time he'd bathed. He couldn't remember the last time he'd shaved, either. His beard had streaks of gray on the chin that hadn't been there the last time he went to war. But he wasn't lousy, which he surely would have been then. A couple of weeks earlier, an American aid man had sprayed him with DDT. He had no idea what went into DDT. Whatever it was, it did to lice and fleas and ticks and other little pests what Zyklon-B had done to Jews.

Russian mortar bombs whispered in and blew up with sudden, startling bangs. After one of those bangs, someone started shrieking for his mother—in English, so he was an American. You felt bad when somebody screamed liked that. No human being who wasn't desperately hurt could make such horrible noises. Gustav would have felt a trifle worse had the wounded man been a fellow German.

Then he blinked and whipped his head around. That noise like a giant tearing heavy canvas was a blast from the past in the most literal sense of the words. That couldn't be anything but a German MG42—no other machine gun in the world had such a high rate of fire. Whoever was shooting it had found enough 7.92mm cartridges to satisfy its appetite for ammo.

Some of the Russians knew what it was. They cried out in alarm. They'd hated and feared the MG42 from the moment the Germans started using it. It spat death at rates unmatched. Because of that and because of the noise it made, they called it *Hitler's saw*. The Amis and the Tommies hadn't loved it, either.

Most Russian private soldiers, like their American counterparts in this fight, would be too young to have heard it before. The old sweats, the corporals and sergeants and officers from captain's rank on up, would have to warn the kids what they were facing.

*I bet the Amis are glad it's not shooting at them this time,* Gustav thought. He crawled toward the snarling gun. That noise brought back happy memories to him, memories of Russian soldiers falling over and Russian soldiers running away.

He wanted to find the crew that had brought such an excellent weapon out of retirement. If they needed him to help serve the gun, he would gladly do that. He could handle it. By the end of the war, each German squad had centered on an MG42 (or, occasionally, an older, more finicky, MG34). The riflemen were there more to protect the machine gun than for the sake of their puny firepower. Everybody learned to handle the piece in case the regular guys got hurt.

Gustav looked for a detachment of emergency militiamen, figuring only Germans could properly appreciate the wonders of the MG42. But the men serving the machine gun—and doing it with the same unflustered competence *Landsers* would have shown in the western Ukraine in 1944—were Yankees, jabbering away in English.

Gustav hadn't worried about English during the Second World War. He'd picked up tiny bits in the years since. Because Fulda lay so close to the border with the Russian zone, it had swarmed with American soldiers. The Amis had run the town till they finally let it elect its own *Burgomeister.* Gustav and Max had printed for them, in English as well as German. So he had those bits. Max, now, Max could really use it.

He waited for the crew to notice him, and to make sure he wasn't a Russian but wore pretty much the same uniform they did. Then he pointed at the MG42 and asked, "Where find?"

As soon as they figured out he was one of the gun's original users, they burst out laughing. One of them spoke better German than Gustav did English. "We found it in a warehouse," he said, his speech painfully correct, like a clever schoolboy's. "We found some friends who knew where cases of cartridges were kept. It uses a great many cartridges."

"You've sure as hell got that right," Gustav said. Then he said it again, more slowly. The Ami didn't understand what he heard very well. He must have studied German in school and forgotten it till he came over here.

"It's a wonderful gun, though," another American said, in English. He added *"Wunderbar!"* in case Gustav hadn't got it.

But Gustav nodded—he had. "Do you change the barrel often?" he asked the fellow who had a little *Deutsch.* Because the MG42 put so many rounds through the barrel so fast, it heated up in a hurry. The *Wehrmacht* had issued an asbestos mitt to handle the hot metal. With it, you could take off the old barrel and swap in a new, cool one in seconds.

The Americans didn't have an asbestos mitt. Stowing those along with the machine gun would have stretched even German efficiency. But they did have a folded-up wool blanket that now showed scorch marks. The Ami showed it to Gustav to let him know they weren't burning out the barrels. He nodded again. People said Americans were good at improvising.

Russians, on the other hand . . . Russians were good at muddling through, at keeping at it when anyone sane would have given up. *"Urra! Urra!"* the infantrymen shouted, a sound to make the hair of anyone who'd heard it before want to stand on end. They were nerving themselves for a charge.

*"Urra! Urra!"* Here they came, a great khaki flood of them.

For a bad fraction of a second, Gustav thought he was back in the other war, trying to hold a position in Poland or, later, in eastern Germany. Then the flashback, the nightmare, merged with reality, and reality was just as bad. Armed with the Russian PPSh, he had to sit tight as the Ivans rushed forward. Some of them still wore billowing greatcoats; it might be spring, but it wasn't warm. His submachine gun was just a peashooter—it couldn't reach them yet.

Some of them tripped in holes in the ground or over hastily laid barbed wire. A few stepped on land mines. One must have set off a big charge, because he and two of his neighbors vanished into scarlet mist. But the rest of the Red Army men closed ranks, linked arms, and came on. They were as impervious to doubt or damage as they had been on the *Ostfront* a few years before. Vodka and fear of their own secret police both had to play a part in that.

*Rrrriiiippp! Rrrriiiippp!* The MG42 cut loose. The Amis fired short bursts to keep from overheating the barrel as best they could. They traversed it so the stream of bullets knocked down Russians across a broad stretch of the line. Riflemen and Yankees with grease guns—which fired heavier cartridges than the PPSh—also took a toll. That khaki wave was liable to roll over these defenses anyhow.

An American took another belt of ammo out of a wooden crate and fed it into the MG42's insatiable maw. The old crate had an eagle with a swastika in its claws burned onto its side. That emblem was illegal in the new Germany the Allies had made and then broken. It was mighty welcome to Gustav just the same.

Bullets snapped past the machine gunners. Some of the Ivans were shooting as they ran. It wasn't aimed fire, or anything like it. With enough bullets flying, that didn't matter. Gustav started shooting back from behind a large chunk of broken brickwork. The Ivans were close enough for him to have a decent chance of hitting them with the PPSh—not a good sign.

Then another machine gun opened up. Its bass stutter put even the MG42's growl to shame. During the last war, Gustav hadn't had to face the Americans' .50-caliber machine gun. He counted himself goddamn lucky he wasn't facing it now. Those big, heavy slugs didn't just drop the Russians they hit in their tracks. They threw the poor, sorry bastards every which way, like crumpled wastepaper.

Flesh and blood, even vodka-numbed flesh and blood, had their limits. Between them, the MG42 and that heavy monster not only reached but exceeded those limits. Instead of rushing forward, the Russians still on their feet turned and ran away. They wouldn't break through on this stretch of the line.

One of the Americans on the MG42 tossed Gustav a pack of Camels. *"Danke,"* Gustav said. His hands trembled when he stuck a cigarette in his mouth. He needed three tries before he could light it. The Amis didn't laugh at him. They were having the same trouble themselves. They'd lived through a nasty firefight. The shakes came with the territory.

Tibor Nagy had a bandage on his right thigh, under his dirty trousers. He had another one on his ribs. Both wounds were just grazes. They'd bled. They'd hurt. They'd left him with horrendous bruises, too. Try as he would, he couldn't find a comfortable way to sleep.

People kept telling him he was lucky. If they meant he was lucky not to be dead, they were right. As far as he was concerned, though, real luck would have involved not getting hit at all or getting wounded badly enough to have to leave the front without getting crippled.

Instead, he crouched in a muddy hole in the ground. Artillery fire burst not nearly far enough away. Shell fragments screeched and whined by overhead. Pretty soon, the Russians would tell the Hungarian People's Army to attack the Americans again.

No matter what the Russians told him, Tibor didn't want to fight Americans. He didn't want to fight anybody, but he really didn't want to fight Americans. If you were on a schoolyard playground, did you poke the biggest kid in the eye, especially when he came from the richest family in town? Not unless you were out of your mind, you didn't.

Or unless the mean kid at school told you he'd wallop the snot out of you unless you took a poke at the big, rich kid. That was what had happened to everybody in the Hungarian People's Army. No matter what its soldiers thought, Stalin didn't give them much choice. As a matter of fact, he gave them none.

"Come on, you sorry dingleberries," Sergeant Gergely called. "Like it or not, we're going up to the front. Move forward through the communications trenches."

Reluctantly, Tibor came out of his foxhole. Like any other

young Hungarian man, he recognized communications trenches when he saw them. He was too young to have used them during the last war, though Gergely surely would have. But the nomenclature of trench warfare was second nature to him. Everybody in Hungary had a father or grandfather who'd done his time in the trenches when the Kingdom of Hungary (much larger than the current Hungarian People's Republic) went into World War I along with the rest of the defunct Empire of Austria-Hungary.

Tibor zigzagged along the trench. You didn't dig them in a straight line; that would have invited one bullet or shell fragment to knock down a whole file of men. Even this trench had fewer kinks than a persnickety military engineer would have liked. It was also punctuated here and there by shell craters. Two burnt-out tank carcasses, one Russian, one American, sat no more than fifty meters apart. Tibor wondered whether they'd fired at each other at the same time.

Whether they had or not didn't matter. The fighting around here had been rugged any which way. Those steel hulks said as much. So did the shell holes. And so did the faint but unmistakable death stink in the air. Not all the men who'd died in the past few weeks—or all the pieces of them, anyhow—had gone into the ground the way they would have in a well-ordered world.

Istvan Szolovits trotted along behind Tibor. Both of them hunched forward to make sure they didn't show themselves above the lip of the trench. "Well, here we go," the Jew said in a low voice.

"Some fun, huh?" Tibor answered.

"Fun? That's one word, I guess," Szolovits said. "We've got to be nuts, even trying this."

Since the same thought had gone through Tibor's mind not long before, he couldn't tell Szolovits he was full of crap. He did say, "If you have a better idea, I'd love to hear it."

"What we ought to do is give up the first chance we get," Szolovits replied, even more quietly than before—he wanted to make sure no one else heard.

"That's desertion," Tibor said automatically. "You know what they do to people who try to bug out on them."

"That's if we don't make it convincing," Szolovits said. "They're sending us up there to fight. Wouldn't you rather spend the rest of the war in a POW camp than in some scratched-out grave? Do you give a shit for Stalin and our fraternal socialist allies? C'mon!"

"If Gergely hears you, you're dead meat. He'll take care of that personally," Tibor said.

"If you rat on me, I am. Otherwise? Maybe not," the Jew returned. "You think Gergely doesn't want to live, too? You think he isn't figuring the angles? He's so crooked, he can look down the crack of his own ass."

Tibor snorted—not because Szolovits was wrong but because he was right. Anyone who could serve both the Arrow Cross and the Communist Party figured the angles better than a pool shark. If Tibor did rat on his fellow soldier, Szolovits would get it in the neck. And then? Then they'd commend Tibor and send him forward so he could get it in the neck, too. The Americans would give it to him, not his own people, but what difference did that make?

His heart sank when he saw soldiers in the forward trenches: Russians, dammit. A lieutenant came over to Sergeant Gergely and spoke to him in slow, accented German: "Half an hour from now, after artillery, we advance. You understand?"

Tibor hoped the sergeant would do as he'd done farther back, and pretend not to understand the only language a Magyar and a Russian were likely to have in common. But Gergely saluted, nodded, and said, *"Zu Befehl, mein Herr!"* He might have fallen straight out of Franz Joseph's time.

*"Gut, gut,"* the young Soviet officer said. "You tell your men, so they know what to do."

*"Jawohl!"* Gergely said, with another precise salute. He did everything but click his heels. Then he spoke in Magyar: "We go in in half an hour, after they shell the Americans. Good luck, boys! Stay as safe as you can."

The Russian lieutenant sent him a fishy stare. Few who weren't Hungarians learned Magyar. It had no close cousins in Europe. But that lieutenant might have understood more than he let on. Well, even if he did, Sergeant Gergely hadn't said anything to upset him. You weren't going to tell the soldiers you led to go out and get themselves killed as fast as they could.

Freight-train noises in the air, thunder on the ground: big shells flying in to tear at the Americans' lines. From things Sergeant Gergely had said, the Red Army had always been strong in artillery. This wasn't a crush-everything barrage. It was just designed to knock the Americans back on their heels. The infantry would do the hard work.

That Russian junior officer stuck a brass whistle in his mouth and blew a long, shrill blast. He yelled something in his own language and shouted "Forward!" in German for the Magyars' benefit. Then he scrambled out of the trench and ran toward the Americans' holes. His men followed. So did Tibor and his countrymen.

Bullets cracked past him. He clamped down on his bladder and his anus as hard as he could. Not five meters from him, Gyula Pusztai went down with a bubbling wail, clutching at his midsection. The big man thrashed like a cat hit by a car. He was no great brain, but how smart did you need to be to know you were dying in agony?

Tibor yanked the pin from a grenade and chucked it into the foxhole ahead of him. A Yank in there screamed just the way poor Gyula had. Tibor felt terrible. He'd been thinking about giving himself up to the Americans, not killing them.

That didn't mean they weren't still thinking about killing him. Their semiautomatic rifles fired faster than the bolt-action pieces he and his friends carried. A few of the Russians had submachine guns or assault rifles, which put still more rounds in the air, but only a few.

An American popped out from behind a bullet-pocked freezer. What the hell was *that* doing in the middle of a battlefield? Tibor swung his Mosin-Nagant toward the man in olive drab. The American fired first: three bullets, one right after another. Two caught Tibor in the chest. It hurt like hell, but only for a few seconds. Then merciful blackness swept down forever.

# 15

"LUNCHTIME, MOMMY!" LINDA SAID.

Marian Staley wondered how her daughter knew. Tummy Standard Time, she supposed. She didn't have a watch. The Studebaker's clock had quit a couple of months after she and Bill bought the car. She'd never seen an auto clock that wasn't a piece of junk.

Linda didn't know how to tell time anyway. That didn't mean Tummy Standard Time wasn't pretty good. Here and there, people were heading for the refugee camp's mess hall. Maybe that helped give Linda a hint, too.

"Well, we can go," Marian said. She rolled up the windows and made sure the Studebaker's doors were locked. She didn't have much in there, but she wanted to keep the little she did have. Someone could still break one of the windows and help himself, but that would—or at least might—make someone else notice and raise a ruckus. It hadn't happened yet, for which Marian was duly grateful.

It wasn't raining right this minute, but it was muddy. The stuff pulled at Marian's shoes. She hadn't known a day since they came here when it wasn't muddy. She wished she could go somewhere, anywhere, else. Right at the moment, there didn't seem to be anywhere else to go.

Three sets of stretcher-bearers carried bodies from the hospital tent toward the graveyard. One bunch came from the National Guard. The others were refugees working for their keep or because they were bored out of their skulls. The atom bomb's poison kept on working even six weeks after the damn thing went off. Marian touched her face. She'd healed well enough, and so had Linda.

More and more people bombed out of their homes converged on the big tent that housed the mess hall, like iron filings drawn by a magnet. Here and there, somebody would nod to her. If it was somebody she knew, like Fayvl Tabakman or one of his friends, she would nod back. If it was some man trying his luck with a woman he'd never seen before because he liked the way she looked, she pretended not to see him. She had enough troubles as things were. She needed more like she needed a hole in the head.

When she realized what she'd thought, she smiled. That sounded like something Fayvl would say—as a matter of fact, it was something he *did* say. The cobbler with the number on his arm had rubbed off on her in ways she hadn't even noticed.

Tummy Standard Time must have run a little fast. The line curled around the mess-hall tent, which hadn't opened yet. "Phooey!" Linda said. She enjoyed waiting no more than any other four-year-old.

"Phooey is right," Marian agreed. "Phooey and pfui!" The two terms of annoyance sounded just about the same. She meant something different by each one, though. Her *phooey* carried the same message as Linda's. She didn't like waiting in line, either. That was one of the reasons she hated the camp so much.

Her *pfui,* now . . . Another reason she couldn't stand the place was that the people stuck here didn't bathe as often as they should. She and Linda didn't bathe all that often themselves. It wasn't as if the camp had enough hot water. It also wasn't as if you could bathe without hot water in this weather unless you wanted pneumonia or frostbite.

But Marian and her daughter were nowhere near the worst offenders, as she got forcibly reminded every time they had to queue up. Some people either didn't notice they smelled like walking garbage piles or didn't care. Some people, in fact, seemed to glory in their BO. Animals used piss and shit to mark their territories. Some of the stinkers seemed to use their bad smell the same way.

Not so long ago, a camp like this, with thousands of people crowded together and with only the most primitive plumbing arrangements, would have had all kinds of horrible diseases tearing through it. There wasn't much of that. Drinking water carried so much chlorine, it tasted horrible, but it didn't make anyone sick. National Guardsmen with

DDT sprayers and Red Cross armbands went through the place once a week. Hardly anyone had lice or fleas. Health workers spread a thin film of oil over every nearby puddle they could find. It was probably still too cold for mosquitoes, but nobody was taking chances. So the inmates might be unhappy, but they weren't unhealthy.

Fayvl Tabakman and his friend Yitzkhak came by. They talked with each other in Yiddish till they saw Marian waving to them. Then they immediately switched to English. "Here—you can wait with us if you want to," Marian said.

"Thank you, but we should go to the end of the line," Tabakman said. Yitzkhak nodded. The cobbler went on, "No one likes somebody who jumps his place."

"Cuts," Yitzkhak corrected him. "They say 'cuts in line' in English."

"You're right. They do." Fayvl thumped his forehead with the heel of his hand, as if to show what an idiot he was.

"In places where there is not enough food to begin with, it may matter more than it does here, where there is usually enough," Yitzkhak added. "But you make yourself no friends doing it anywhere." He and Fayvl Tabakman touched forefingers to the brims of their cloth caps, then walked on.

They'd invited Marian and Linda to join them when they were ahead in line. She'd done it without thinking twice. Now she wondered if she should have thought twice. Did people talk about her because she took cuts? She was a mother with a little girl, but even so. . . .

After she and Linda got their ration packs—Linda's was cut down to child-size; the powers that be wouldn't let anybody get away with overeating because of a kid—they saved places at one of the long tables for Fayvl and Yitzkhak. No one grumbled about that; people did it all the time.

Halfway through yet another military ration, Yitzkhak remarked, "I don't like lining up for food, you know? It makes me remember the last time I had to do it." He also had a number on his arm.

"Food now is better. More of it, too," Fayvl Tabakman said. "What the little girl has there, that would have fed one of us for a week."

"Ah, you're stretching things," Yitzkhak said. "Six days at most." He smiled to show he was kidding. The smile never reached his eyes. Marian decided he wasn't kidding very much.

"They aren't trying to work us to death here, neither," Tabakman said. "If they didn't manage that, they just got rid of us, the way we'll get rid of the trash from lunch."

"How could people do that to other people?" Marian asked.

"I'm the wrong one to answer that," the cobbler said. "The ones who should answer it are the Nazis. Only now, what's left of the *mamzrim* are on the same side of us." He screwed up his face as if at a bad smell. Marian decided against asking what *mamzrim* were.

"*Nu*, you're not wrong, but the Russians, they're no bargain, either," Yitzkhak said. "Lucky me, I was in camps from both sides over there. Such luck! You wound up in one of Stalin's, they wouldn't kill you because you were a Jew. They wouldn't even put you in because you were a Jew. You'd go in because they said you were a reactionary."

"What's that?" Linda asked.

"Anything they said it was," Yitzkhak told her. Tabakman nodded. Yitzkhak went on, "And they didn't kill you with poison gas or anything fancy. They just worked you till you dropped or else shot you. Maybe not so bad as the Nazis, but like I say no bargain. And they got Germans on their side, too. *Feh!*" As Fayvl had before him, he mimed smelling something foul.

Marian didn't even know which questions to ask them. Had she known, she wouldn't have had the nerve. She was just an American: someone who'd been comfortable her whole life till the bomb hit Seattle, and who only thought she and her daughter were uncomfortable now. Next to what these two men had known, this camp was a rest cure.

Fayvl Tabakman walked her and Linda back to the Studebaker near the edge of the encampment. When they got close, Marian let out a yelp: "Hey!" Some young punk with pimples and a greasy pompadour was messing with the door on the driver's side. She yelled "Hey!" again, louder and more angrily.

The would-be thief looked up again from what he was doing. He had some kind of pry bar in his hand. Seeing only a woman, a little girl, and a small, skinny man, he let out a yell of his own—a thirteen-letter unendearment—and rushed them, waving the bar.

Marian shoved Linda behind her. Tabakman bent, picked up a rock about the size of a baseball, and let fly. He hadn't played baseball wherever he came from, but he knew how to throw. It caught the kid right in the nose. He started to grab at himself, but fell on his face, out cold, before the motion was well begun.

"Go get a camp cop or a Guardsman," the cobbler said calmly. "This jerk needs real trouble, or he'll come around bothering you again."

"Okay." Marian stared at him. "Where did you learn to do that?"

"With grenades," he answered, calm still. "Go on, now." Marian went, herding Linda with her. Tabakman stayed right there, in case the thief came to. Marian didn't think he would.

Konstantin Morozov's new T-54 wasn't new as in coming right off the factory floor. It had already seen hard action. He knew as much as soon as he slid down into the fighting compartment from the hatch atop the cupola. The inside of the tank stank of kerosene.

He'd discovered in the last war why repair crews used that stunt. If a crew got chewed to sausage meat by an armorpiercing round that did its job, you could weld a patch into place on the steel outside. And you could clean up whatever was left of the poor sorry pricks who'd got killed. But blood and bits of flesh would linger no matter how well you cleaned things out. Pretty soon, the fighting compartment would start smelling as if you'd forgotten a kilo of pork in there for a couple of weeks.

So after the repairmen did the best they could with the tank crew's mortal remains, they would swab down the inside of the fighting compartment with a mop soaked in kerosene or gasoline. Konstantin didn't know whether that actually killed the dead-meat stench or just overwhelmed it. Kerosene wasn't what he would have called a pleasant odor. Next to what he could have been smelling in there, it seemed ambrosial.

When he stuck his head out again, the look on his face must have shown what was going through his mind. The corporal at the tank park who'd led him out to the T-54 donned a faintly embarrassed expression. "You've been through the mill a time or two, haven't you, Comrade Sergeant?" he said. "Sorry about that, but we do want to get 'em back into action if we can."

"Yes, yes," Morozov said. "Show me where this pussy got it the last time, why don't you?"

That *why don't you?* made the order polite, but an order it remained. The corporal took him to the front of the tank and pointed out to him the rough patch under some new greenish-brown paint. That AP round wouldn't just have penetrated the frontal armor. It would have slammed through the driver and the back of his seat on its way to tearing up the rest of the interior.

Thoughtfully, Morozov said, "I think I'll hang some spare track links or something in front of that. I don't *know* it's a weak spot in the armor, but why take chances?"

"Sounds like a good idea to me." The corporal gave him a sidelong look. "And I like the way you said that—so it wouldn't piss me off if I happened to be a welder. I'm not, but just the same. . . ."

"Life is too short when you start quarreling with the guys who're supposed to be on your side," Konstantin answered. "Doesn't the enemy give us enough grief?" He set his palm on the weld.

"Did your crew get out with you?" the corporal asked.

"We all got out—we took a hit in the engine compartment. My driver was wounded before we made it to cover, though, so I have a new man there." Morozov resolved not to say anything about the welded spot to Yevgeny Ushakov for a while. The replacement driver was barely eighteen. He'd have enough trouble telling left from right and getting into the proper gear. He didn't need to dwell on what had happened to the man who'd sat in that seat before him.

Horrible things would have happened to all the men in the earlier crew. Morozov didn't need to dwell on them, either. If you started wondering whether your tank was unlucky . . . If you did, you were liable to bring down the curse you were trying to avoid.

"Why don't you get them, then?" the corporal said. "The beast has a full tank, and we bombed it up. You can go straight to regimental headquarters and see what they need you to do."

"I serve the Soviet Union! Don't go away. I'll be back with them in a few minutes." He trotted to the far edge of the tank park. Mechanics and welders worked on damaged T-54s and Stalins—and on a few damaged T-35/85s, leftovers from the last war pressed into service again. A cursing crew used a crane to drop a new engine into a T-54. The number on the side of the turret was different, or Konstantin would have wondered if that was his old machine.

"Well?" Pavel Gryzlov asked when Konstantin came up to the crew.

"Well, it's a T-54," the tank commander reported.

"That's good," the gunner said. "When I saw some of the old models here, I was afraid they'd try to palm one of those clapped-out cunts off on us. Fat chance we'd have in a T-34 against a Pershing or a Centurion!"

"We didn't do so well in our T-54," Mogamed Safarli put in between puffs on a pipe.

"We hurt them before they hit us," Konstantin reminded the loader. "Anyway, this isn't a brand new machine, but I think it's sound." *Well, except for that patch on the frontal armor, anyway.* "It's got a full load of ammo and a full tank of fuel. We just have to put it back into action."

"Let's do that, then! We serve the Soviet Union!" Yevgeny Ushakov's voice cracked with excitement. For the veterans, *I serve the Soviet Union!* was a catchphrase with no more meaning than *Yes, sir!* or *I'll take care of it.* Ushakov, still wet behind the ears, said it as if he meant it.

Well, he'd find out. Or maybe he was playing a role, and what seemed like excitement and enthusiasm and patriotism was in fact acting ability. You never could tell to whom people really reported.

"Come on over, then," Morozov said. "Climb in and fire it up. We'll find out what the regiment wants us to do, and hop back on the merry-go-around again. Doesn't that sound like fun?"

"*Da,* Comrade Sergeant!" By the way Ushakov said it, he *did* think it sounded like fun. Gryzlov and Morozov eyed each other for a moment. Yes, the kid would find out. He'd never had to flee a burning tank. He'd never watched a crew-mate suffer and bleed. He'd never watched enemy soldiers machine-gunned from the turret, or seen an enemy tank afire and known it could as easily have been his own.

Safarli's nostrils twitched when he got into the tank. "Smells like the lamps at my grandfather's house," he said.

Pavel Gryzlov glanced at Morozov again. The loader must not have known why the fighting compartment smelled that way. As plainly, Gryzlov did. "Well, there are worse odors," he said. He didn't name any of them. In this business, you didn't keep your innocence long. If Safarli and Ushakov had some left, more power to them.

"Start it up," Morozov called to the driver.

"I serve the Soviet Union!" Ushakov replied, as Konstantin had guessed he would. The engine belched to life. It ran more raggedly than the one in Morozov's old machine, but it did run. The new driver shifted well enough. Morozov guided him toward regimental HQ. As they rumbled along, Konstantin watched Gryzlov fiddle with the sights on the main armament and the coaxial machine gun. He couldn't do as much as he doubtless wanted to without some leisure, but he was doing whatever he could.

As it happened, Captain Gurevich was back at regimental headquarters, seeing to something or other, when the T-54 chugged in. Morozov waved to him from the cupola. He didn't ride buttoned up unless he had to. "You've got a runner again, do you, Sergeant?" Gurevich called.

"Sure do, Comrade Captain," Konstantin answered. "Where do I go with it?"

"We're still trying to break into Arnsberg, four or five kilometers up the road there," the company commander said. "They'll be glad to see another 100mm gun. Why don't you give them a hand?"

Morozov sketched a salute. "I'll do it, Comrade Captain," he said, and ducked inside to deliver the word to the men who couldn't have heard it. The tank headed for Arnsberg. Morozov's belly knotted. Another chance to serve the *rodina*. And another chance to get horribly killed.


Bill Staley cherished the postcard as he'd never cherished any piece of writing before. *The house is a wreck, but Linda and I are OK*, it said. *At the refugee camp, sleeping in the car. Will get out when we have somewhere to go. Much love, Marian.* Not a long message, but more precious than rubies to him.

The night after he got the card, he slept well for the first time in he couldn't remember how long. He found himself too much reminded of *O God! I could be bounded in a nutshell and count myself a king of infinite space, were it not that I have bad dreams.*

Bad dreams he had. They woke him, again and again, in one kind of a cold sweat or another. Sometimes his wife and little girl went up in radioactive fire. Sometimes he did himself—till he woke with thundering heart. Sometimes all the Chinese and Russians he'd helped incinerate rose from the graves they mostly didn't have, hungry for revenge.

How many people had died from the bombs his B-29 dropped? He couldn't begin to guess. When he was awake, he didn't try. Indeed, he did his best not to think of what he did on his missions. When he couldn't help calling it to mind, he told himself he did it strictly in the line of duty—and shoved it out of his thoughts as fast as he could.

All of which worked fairly well . . . while he was awake. But the more he shoved things aside by day, the more they came out at night. He'd woken up screaming only once. The cold sweats bothered no one but himself. That didn't make them—and the nightmares that spawned them—any less horrible to him.

Once, over frosty-cold Falstaffs at the officers' club, he asked Hank McCutcheon, "Sir, do you ever, um, dream about any of the things we've done?"

"Dream?" The pilot paused with his glass halfway to his mouth. "Oh, maybe once or twice. Nothing too much. Nothing too bad. How about you?"

"A little more than that," Bill said, which was true in the same sense that water was moist or a jet of molten metal was warm.

"Ah." For all they showed, Major McCutcheon's eyes might have been made from green and white glass. "Still able to handle your job okay when you aren't sleeping?"

"Oh, hell, yes," Bill answered quickly. That was true, too. True or not, though, it wasn't what he wanted to talk about.

Regardless of whether he wanted to talk about other things, Hank McCutcheon plainly didn't. "That's good, Billy-boy," McCutcheon said. "That's what you need. Can't let the hobgoblins and fantods get you down, right?"

"Sure," Bill said tonelessly, and emptied his own beer. He'd been drinking more than usual lately, in the hope that it would dull or blot out the nightmares. It hadn't, but he hadn't cut back again, either.

"There you go. You're a good man, Bill. Nothing to worry about, not in the long run, hey?" Without waiting for an answer, McCutcheon stood up, patted Staley on the shoulder, and walked out of the club: back straight, stride long, the image of a professional military man on the move.

*Fuck.* Bill silently mouthed the word. He wasn't a professional military man himself, and didn't want to be. Maybe that made the difference.

Or maybe there was no difference. Maybe Hank jerked awake in the middle of the night with icy rivers running down his back, too. Or maybe his bad dreams got to him some other way. Maybe he just didn't feel like admitting that to Bill. Maybe it felt too much like showing weakness. Maybe Hank didn't feel like admitting it even to himself.

Maybe. How could you know? You couldn't, not when Hank didn't want to talk about it. For all Bill could prove, the pilot really did sleep the sleep of the just every goddamn night. *If you do, you're a better man than I am, Gunga Din,* Bill thought.

He raised his right index finger. A waiter—a colored Army private—came over and put the empty beer glasses on a tray. "You like another one, suh?" he asked.

"You bet I do," Bill said. "Thanks." Beer might not be the answer, but he kept hoping it would deflect the question.

"Comin' right up," the kid said.

Bill drank the next one a little more slowly. As he did, he looked around the inside of the officers' club. Just by looking, he couldn't have proved that he was in Korea rather than, say, Milwaukee or Portland.

He grimaced and shook his head. He could tell he wasn't in Portland, all right. Portland was one of those West Coast cities that wasn't there any more, along with Seattle and so many others. He was anything but happy about the job the Air Force had done defending the American mainland. It had screwed that up even worse than the Navy botched Pearl Harbor back in 1941.

At least Marian and Linda came through in one piece. He'd hoped they had. He'd prayed they had. He was pretty rusty at things that had to do with prayer, but he'd given it his best shot. Still, not knowing had eaten at him till Marian's card finally got here. Probably the mail service in Seattle was as snafued as everything else in the shattered city. The card had taken more than a month to cross the Pacific in spite of its Air Mail stamp.

One piece! He had a family to go home to if he managed to live through the war. After this stretch, he promised he would never put on another uniform for the rest of his life. He'd get a bookkeeping job and be happy—ecstatic—about columns of figures in ledgers. A dark blue flannel suit, a fedora, a topcoat in the wintertime . . . That would be as much uniform as he needed.

If he landed a place at a big company, it might have its own softball team. He'd never been good enough to try out for the pros or anything like that, but he made a pretty fair middle infielder. He'd played baseball during the last war, softball when he went back to civilian life, and baseball again here in Korea. Even the gooks were starting to pick up the game.

If they let him play in blue jeans and a sweatshirt, he'd join the company team. If the firm that hired him was big enough to pay for uniforms, though, he figured he'd look for some rinky-dink neighborhood team instead. The ball wouldn't be as good, but he'd feel free.

Whatever neighborhood he'd live in. By the couple of lines from Marian, he wouldn't be in the house he'd left when Uncle Sam called him back to active duty. If that house was smashed, his wife and daughter were extra lucky to have lived. Not only would the place have done its best to fall down on them, but they would have been close enough to ground zero to pick up a nasty dose of radiation.

He grimaced once more, not caring for that thought at all. If they'd got radiation sickness, Marian hadn't mentioned it. Even if they had, they should be better now. But who could guess what that kind of thing might do to you years down the line?

Grimacing yet again, this time in a new way, he drained the glass of beer. He'd wondered before how many Russians and Chinamen died when the Superfort dropped its bombs on them. But that wasn't the real question, was it?

No. It wasn't. It was tiptoeing around the real question. It was ducking the responsibility the real question held. The real question was *How many people have we killed?* Or, more directly, *How many people have I killed?* Or, more directly yet, *How much blood is on my hands?*

That was the real question, all right. And, with that being the real question, was it any wonder he had nightmares? How could you not have nightmares with a question like that weighing on you? The only way he could see was to have no conscience at all, like the Nazis who ran the gas chambers and crematoria at their extermination camps.

Fortunately or unfortunately—however you chose to look at it—he came equipped with that invisible but inescapable piece of his moral fiber. And, because he did, he wondered whether he might not do best by taking his service pistol and sticking it in his mouth.

The colored enlisted man appeared out of nowhere. "Want I should fetch you a fresh one, suh?"

"Why the hell not?" Bill answered. He wasn't going to fly today. If he felt like getting snockered, he could. If he did, maybe he wouldn't think so much about that real question.

He was doubly glad he'd got the postcard from Marian. Knowing he did have people to go home to, people who loved him, also helped armor him against the temptation to start fiddling with his .45.

Boris Gribkov and his Tu-4 crew took the train from Kuibishev to just east of Moscow. From there, they climbed aboard an Li-2 for the trip to an airfield not far from Leningrad. In normal times, they would have gone the whole way by train. But almost all of the European Soviet Union's rail lines ran through Moscow. Kilometers of those lines were twisted, melted metal now. Till workers replaced them, rail transportation was going to be, in technical terms, a mess.

That was one of the reasons saving the capital from the Nazis had been so important. Yes, Moscow was the USSR's biggest city. But it was also the country's transport hub. With it in enemy hands, too often you really couldn't get there from here.

Hitler hadn't been able to seize it or damage it badly. The *Luftwaffe* wasn't up to the job. The United States Air Force, by contrast, damn well was. Gribkov used his rank to ensure that he had a window seat when the military transport flew low above Moscow on its way west and north. The weather was good. Here a month after the equinox, spring was coming for real as opposed to on the calendar.

Three roughly circular holes, each a kilometer or two across, were gouged from the fabric of the city. One, close by the Moscow River, was centered on the Kremlin. Nothing was left of the famous cluster of onion domes. Whatever air defenses the authorities had emplaced around the beating heart of the Soviet world, they hadn't been good enough— and that heart beat no more.

Instead of buildings, the blast sites held rubble. Toward the heart of each one, everything was melted flat. The farther out from right under the explosions you went, the more the wreckage started to resemble what Boris recognized as bomb damage.

Vladimir Zorin held the window seat right behind his. *"Bozhemoi!"* the copilot said as the plane passed over the last devastated circle.

Good Communists weren't supposed to mention the Deity. All the same, Boris answered, "I couldn't have put it better myself." What else but *My God!* could you say when you saw something like that?

Zorin found something. "As a matter of fact," he said in clinical tones, "it looks more as though Satan's got loose on earth."

"It does, doesn't it?" Boris agreed. Someone who heard that agreement and didn't care for him might report him to the MGB. Someone might, yes, but that worried him less than it would have most of the time. The Hero of the Soviet Union medal on his chest could shield him from informers. And the Lubyanka, the Soviet secret-police headquarters since the days of the Russian Revolution, was one more smashed, radioactive ruin.

Leonid Tsederbaum sat next to Zorin. In a low, troubled voice, he said, "Now we know what we did to Seattle."

"Well, Leonid Abramovich, if the Americans do it to us, we don't have much choice but to do it to them, do we?" Gribkov said.

"Of course not, Comrade Pilot, not when you put it that way," Tsederbaum replied. "But if they keep hitting us and we keep hitting back, will anyone or anything be left by the time we get through?"

That was a better question than Boris wished it were. After a moment, he said, "We don't have to worry about such things. Our superiors tell us what to do, and we do it."

"Of course, Comrade Pilot," the Jew said. Four innocuous words, and he sounded as if he was calling Gribkov a liar.

On droned the Li-2. The United States designed excellent airplanes. The Soviet Union made excellent copies of them. The United States had designed the first atom bombs. The ones the USSR made worked just as well, as Gribkov had seen. Whether their design also copied American originals, he didn't know, but he wouldn't have been surprised.

The plane passed over Leningrad on the way to the new base. Patchy clouds there didn't let Gribkov see as much of the USSR's second city (Kiev would have thought of it as the third; it thought of itself as the first) as he would have liked, but he did see that its cityscape also had chunks bitten out.

So did his comrades. "The Americans called here, too," Vladimir Zorin said glumly.

"Did you think that they hadn't?" Tsederbaum asked.

"No. But I wished they wouldn't," Zorin said. "This was a hero city above all hero cities in the last war. The Nazis laid siege to it for three years, but couldn't take it. Now the Americans killed who knows how many people in the blink of an eye."

However many the atom bombs had killed, it was probably fewer than had died during the siege. Those people mostly hadn't died in the blink of an eye, though. Most of them had starved to death, especially in the first winter. The bread ration in Leningrad got down to something like a hundred grams a day, and even that tiny bit was stretched with sawdust or sometimes dirt. People whispered of cannibals—well-fed, rosy-cheeked cannibals—roaming the streets in search of corpses or living men and women they could make into corpses . . . and meat.

But that wasn't what bothered Boris Gribkov. "We knew their bombers were coming!" he said. "We *knew,* dammit. We should have done a better job of stopping them. The way it looks, we couldn't even slow them down."

"They couldn't stop us, either, Comrade Pilot," Tsederbaum reminded him. "If they'd been able to, we wouldn't be sitting here now talking about how bad our own air defenses were."

He was right. Gribkov hadn't looked at it that way. Now that he had to, he said, "Yes . . . and no. We were hitting their coast, so they wouldn't have had much warning—"

"Maybe not for Seattle," the navigator broke in. "But they should have been waiting for us at every city south of that. They should have been—only they weren't."

"They were dickheads," Boris said. "Just because they were dickheads, should we have been dickheads, too? We had radar! We had jet fighters! To hit places like Moscow and Kiev, the Americans had to fly over our territory for hundreds of kilometers. They got through."

"They lost planes." Tsederbaum sounded uncomfortable.

"So did we. Not enough, either way, to keep the cities safe," Boris said. No one said anything in response to that.

His crewmates had to be remembering, as he was, the holes burnt into the hearts of the great Russian cities, and all the people who'd lived in those places and lived no more.

The Li-2 flew under the clouds toward the camouflaged airstrip. Gribkov had spoken of jet fighters. Now two of them streaked past the transport's windows. He knew a moment of alarm. Leningrad had always been Russia's window on the West. It might not be impossibly far for American fighters with drop tanks to reach.

But no. Those were MiG-15s, familiar as the back of his own hand. Their tails and fuselages and swept wings were blazoned with the *rodina*'s red star. Their jet engines weren't copies of an American design. They were copies of a British design, and far better than the copies of Nazi jet engines the Soviet Union had used before.

*Bump!* The Li-2 touched down on the dirt runway and taxied to a stop. One of the gunners opened the door on the right side of the passenger compartment. Cool, moist air came in. So did the noise of the props, which were still spinning. The blast of air from them almost knocked Gribkov off his feet when he jumped out. As soon as the whole bomber crew had left the Li-2, the pilot taxied toward the men who waited with *maskirovka* off to the side of the airstrip.

What looked like a big farmhouse was the only building in sight. Boris and his crewmates walked over to it. When he opened the door, a Red Air Force major greeted them all. Inside, the place looked like an air base. A radioman with earphones and a mike tended to his set. A sergeant flicked beads on an abacus as he did paperwork. A battered samovar sat over a low flame on a table in a corner. Tobacco smoke fogged the air.

"Well, we're home," Leonid Tsederbaum said. Gribkov felt the same way.

# 16

MORE AND MORE GERMANS flooded into the emergency militia. Konrad Adenauer still wasn't calling it an army, but it sure looked like one to Gustav Hozzel. He, of course, was on the inside looking out. However much it looked like an army, it didn't look like the old *Wehrmacht.* The men wore American olive drab, not *Feldgrau.* They wore U.S. rank badges on their sleeves, not German ones on shoulder straps. They still wore those U.S. helmets, too. Gustav did miss his old *Stahlhelm,* but not enough to risk getting caught by the Russians with one on his head. And they used American weapons, with a few British Sten guns and mortars mixed in.

No matter what they looked like, most of them behaved as if the last war had ended week before last—or maybe as if it hadn't ended at all. Some of the volunteers were kids who'd been too young to take on the Ivans before . . . although boys of twelve and thirteen had fought in Berlin. A far larger number were old *Frontschweine,* ready for another go at the Bolsheviks.

The Germans didn't enjoy the good, hard physical shape they'd had six or eight years before. A stretch of peacetime would do that to you. But they made up for it by knowing every trick in the book. Anybody the Russians hadn't been able to kill was good at his trade almost by definition.

Some of them fought with a reckless disregard for life and limb that startled even Gustav. "Rolf, what unit were you in the last time around?" he asked a fellow in his company after the man charged a Russian machine-gun nest. He made the

Ivans keep their heads down with his Sten, then finished them off with grenades.

Rolf's cheeks hollowed as he took a drag on a cigarette. After blowing out a stream of smoke, he answered, "LAH. How come?"

"Oh," Gustav said. The *Leibstandarte Adolf Hitler* was part of the *Waffen*-SS, not the *Wehrmacht*. It had started out as the *Führer*'s personal bodyguard unit, and ended up as one of the best German panzer divisions. But the *Waffen*-SS combat style was more aggressive than the one the *Wehrmacht* favored. (So was the SS taste for atrocities, though the *Wehrmacht* wasn't a dewy pink innocent there, either.) After a moment, Gustav did ask, "Have you got a blood-group tattoo?"

"Not any more. Had it cut out years ago. Hurt like a bitch when I did, but the scar hardly shows now," Rolf said.

"All right." Gustav left it there. The Russians slaughtered the men with those tattoos they caught, the same way they bumped off soldiers with German helmets. To them, both were marks of Nazism.

Well, if Rolf came out of the LAH, he damn well had been a Nazi, and doubtless still was. He might well have been an officer then, too. The tattoos were required for them, voluntary for other ranks. That he'd made a point of obliterating his argued he'd needed to. Here, he was just another private . . . who happened to fight like a homicidal maniac.

Gustav let it go. That kind of stuff was ancient history as far as he was concerned, even if the Russians saw things differently.

Rolf held out the pack of cigarettes. "Want one?" he asked. He could be plenty friendly—as long as you were on his side.

"Thanks." Gustav took one and leaned close to get a light from his comrade's glowing coal. He drew in smooth, mild smoke—they were American Luckies.

"We are going to lick the Reds," Rolf said in tones that brooked no contradiction.

"Well, sure." Gustav wouldn't have put his one and only, irreplaceable body on the line if he hadn't thought so.

"We're going to lick them," Rolf repeated, as if Gustav hadn't spoken. "We should have lined up with the Amis to do it at the end of the last war, but better late than never. We'll lick them, and we'll clean out all the puppet regimes they set up in Eastern Europe, and we'll drive them out of all the land they stole. And Germany will take its natural place in the sun again."

*"Aber natürlich,"* Gustav said, though he feared Rolf wouldn't recognize irony when he heard it. And the ex-LAH man had to mean *at the top of the heap* when he said *natural place in the sun.* Gustav added, "The Americans and the Russians have the bomb. We don't. That's a problem, you know."

Rolf looked at him the way a *Waffen*-SS soldier would have eyed someone accused of defeatism. "We will. Our scientists are plenty smart enough—the best in the world, in fact. All we have to do is clear the foreign soldiers from our soil."

Some of the foreign soldiers on German soil opened up with a machine gun. Gustav started to reach for his own weapon, then relaxed. The Ivans weren't close enough to be dangerous—yet. To take Rolf's mind off dreams of world domination, Gustav said, "I've got another question for you."

"Go ahead—shoot," Rolf said, amiably enough.

"You were with the *Leibstandarte* at the end, right? Through the last attack in Hungary after Budapest fell?"

"Operation Spring Awakening? Yeah, I was there for that. We drove them back for a solid week, but in the end they just had too goddamn many tanks and too many men."

In the end, the Russians had had too many tanks and too many men—to say nothing of too many allies—everywhere. That wasn't what Gustav wanted to talk about, though. "When the retreat started again, the *Führer* ordered LAH to take off their cuff titles with his signature, didn't he?"

"Yes." Rolf scowled. "He didn't understand the situation down there."

By the end of the war, from everything Gustav could gather, Hitler hadn't understood the situation anywhere. But that wasn't what he wanted to talk about, either. He said, "I heard that, when you guys heard about that order, what you took off were your medals—and you sent 'em to him in a chamber pot."

"Oh. *That* story. I've heard it, too." Rolf nodded. "It isn't true. It's cute, but it isn't true. Sepp Dietrich was commanding the Sixth SS Panzer Army then. The order came through him, and it never got past his headquarters. He figured the *Führer* was having a bad day, so he didn't forward it."

"So you wore the cuff titles to the end?"

"When things fell apart, we all started shedding the SS stuff. You didn't want to be wearing it if the Bolsheviks caught you." Rolf drew a finger across his throat. Now Gustav nodded; he knew about that. The SS man continued, "But we didn't cut off the titles right after Spring Awakening."

"I get you," Gustav said. He wondered whether Rolf was telling the truth about the medals in the chamber pot. The LAH man had been on the spot; Gustav hadn't. But he'd heard the tale from people he had no reason to doubt. Rolf might be sanitizing things for the sake of his unit's reputation.

Or he might not. Gustav knew he couldn't be sure himself. He also knew *Leibstandarte Adolf Hitler* had a reputation worth protecting only among the most pro-Nazi Germans. To the Russians and the Americans, it had just been an uncommonly nasty enemy outfit.

A jeep rolled up. This second-string, hastily equipped unit was more motorized than the fanciest SS panzer division had been. That casual show of American wealth was another reason the Third *Reich* had lost the war.

Sitting next to the driver was Max Bachman. The back seat was full of ration boxes—more American goodies. Max started tossing them to the resting men. "Eat up! Eat up!" he cried merrily. "Hearty meals for the condemned men!"

"Put a sock in it, Max," Gustav said, but not before he'd snagged some food for himself.

"You know that loudmouthed clown?" Rolf asked, tearing open his own C-ration package.

"Know him? Back in Fulda, I work for him." After a moment's thought, Gustav amended that: "Worked for him, I mean. God only knows what it's like with the commissars giving the orders there."

"Not good." Rolf took the bayonet off his belt and opened a can of stew with it. That was a common use for bayonets these days. Another was candlestick: the socket was just the right size to hold a typical German candle. A bayonet could still be a fighting knife or a spearpoint on the end of a rifle. It could, but hardly ever was.

"Nowhere near good. My wife's back there. I hope Luisa's still back there," Gustav said, and opened his own can of soggy ham and eggs.

Rolf set a surprisingly gentle hand on his shoulder. "Sorry, pal. That's hard." They set their cans on a grill over the fire to heat.


The cook gave Istvan Szolovits a chunk of black bread and a chunk of ham. He cut the bread in half with his bayonet and surrounded the ham with it. The sandwich was the neatest way he could think of to eat what he had.

One of the other soldiers said, "I'm gonna tell your rabbi on you!"

"He won't be able to hear you, Andras," Szolovits answered, and took a bite. It was pretty good ham.

"What? Why the hell not?" Andras Orban demanded, as Istvan had hoped he would.

"Because your head's so far up your ass, no noise can get out." The Jew gathered himself. If Andras wanted a fight, he'd give him one. He'd had more fights like that than he cared to remember. Knuckling under seemed worse.

Andras' jaw dropped. If he was looking for a deferential Jew or a cowardly Jew, he was looking in the wrong place. He started to get to his feet, but the snickers from the rest of the Magyar soldiers eating and smoking and resting there made him hesitate.

Then Sergeant Gergely snapped, "Cut the crap, Orban. You ragged him, he ragged you back. I think his crack was funnier than yours, but what the hell? It evens out. Your face is funnier than his."

That made more soldiers laugh at Andras. He turned a dull red. He wasn't particularly handsome, though Szolovits wouldn't have called him funny-looking. *Well, you aren't all that handsome yourself,* Istvan thought. He also wasn't all that Jewish-looking. He had light brown hair, hazel eyes, and an ordinary nose. Only his mouth and the shape of his chin hinted at what he was.

But Gergely hadn't finished. "I'm going to keep my eye on you, Orban," he went on. "You think we don't have enough trouble fighting the Americans and the Germans? You have to stir something up with your own countryman?"

"Him? My countryman, Comrade Sergeant?" Andras Orban looked astonished. "Isn't he just a waddayacallem? A rootless cosmopolite, that's it."

*Rootless cosmopolite* was what a good Marxist-Leninist

said when he meant *kike*. It had a fine ideological ring to it, but what lay behind it was old as the hills.

However it sounded, it just made Gergely roll his eyes. "He's here, you stupid sack of shit. He's got our uniform on. He carries a rifle just like yours. He points it at the enemies of the Hungarian People's Republic. From everything I've seen, he's done fine since we came over the border. You haven't exactly been the world's biggest hero, so keep your fucking trap shut till you are, right?" Andras didn't say anything. Sergeant Gergely fixed him with a stare like twin flamethrowers. *"Right?"*

"Uh, right, Comrade Sergeant." The soldier looked as if he wished he'd never opened his mouth. He also looked as if he wished the ground would open up and swallow him. There Szolovits sympathized. It wasn't as if he hadn't felt the same way himself plenty of times.

The next interesting question was whether Andras Orban would decide that bothering him was more trouble than it was worth, or whether the other soldier would want to get even. Szolovits had never wished harm on anybody from his own unit, but in Andras' case he might make an exception.

As evening fell, he took his turn in a foxhole a couple of hundred meters west of the main Hungarian position. In case the Americans or the Germans tried a sneak attack, he could give the alarm and start shooting . . . unless they were too sneaky, and murdered him before he got the chance.

Just to ensure that he'd be able to spot them from a long way away, rain started coming down no more than ten minutes after he went out there. He buttoned up his greatcoat collar tight, to keep out as many drips as he could. The fabric was supposed to be waterproof, but it wasn't.

He remembered German motorcyclists scooting through Budapest before the city fell to the Russians. They'd worn rubberized greatcoats that really did shed water. Next to those, his was—and performed like—a cheap imitation.

He thought about lighting a cigarette, but didn't bother. In the wet, he doubted he could keep it going long enough to get any enjoyment from it. The bottom of the hole turned muddy. Puddles started forming. His boots were supposed to be waterproof, too. From what he'd seen so far, they came closer than the greatcoat did, anyhow.

As long as the Americans stayed farther than ten meters or so from his post, they could hit the Hungarian troops behind him with a whole armored division, and he'd never know it till the shooting started. The way the rain was coming down, even that might not do it. He pushed the helmet farther forward on his head so the drips from the brim wouldn't hit his nose. But that made the drips from the rear of the helmet dribble down the back of his neck, so he fiddled with it again.

Was that a noise? Would the Americans be daft enough to try something on such a miserable night? Clutching his rifle, he called, "Halt! Who goes? Give the password!" He hoped he didn't sound too much like a scared kid. If those were Americans or Germans, they wouldn't understand Magyar, and they would open up on him.

But, like a sign from the heavens, the password did come, followed by a wry chuckle he knew too well. "Just wanted to see if you were on your toes," Sergeant Gergely said.

"Of course I am," Szolovits answered, giddy with relief. "If I weren't, I'd be drowning in here."

"Cute," Gergely said, but he chuckled again. After a moment, he went on, "You know, I was gonna bump Nagy up to lance-corporal till he caught one."

"I'm not surprised," Istvan said, though he was surprised the sergeant told him. "Tibor was a good guy." He hadn't even thought about how much he missed the fallen soldier. It wasn't that he hadn't let himself, only that he'd been too busy trying to stay alive in his own right.

"What I'm thinking now is, maybe you're the one I ought to tap for that slot," Gergely said slowly.

What Istvan Szolovits was thinking now was that, when the sergeant was fighting for Ferenc Szalasi's Arrow Cross regime, Gergely would have shoved him into a train bound for Auschwitz and then toasted the departure with a glass of Tokay. Life could get very peculiar. So could the way people talked to each other. Szolovits came out with as much as he thought he could: "In spite of everything?"

"Yeah, in spite of everything." The noncom didn't pretend to misunderstand him. "You've got your head on straight, and that counts for more than whether your cock's clipped."

"Gosh, Sergeant, you say the sweetest things," Istvan said.

This time, Gergely laughed out loud, which didn't happen every day. *"Menj a halál faszára,"* he said. Szolovits hadn't dreamt anyone could tell him to go sit on death's dick and sound affectionate doing it, but Sergeant Gergely managed.

"What happens if you promote me and I order somebody

to do something and he tells me that?" Szolovits asked. "Somebody like, oh, Andras?"

"Well, there's two things you can do. You can tell me, and I'll take care of it. Or you can whale the shit out of the pussy yourself and go on about your business. The less a sergeant hears about the little stuff, the happier he is."

Istvan wasn't sure he could whale the shit out of Andras Orban. He was ready to try, though; a Jew who wasn't ready to fight in post-Fascist Hungary would be a doormat all his life. You did what you had to do, not what you wanted to do.

Gergely's other comment was also interesting. Szolovits asked, "Is the captain happy when he doesn't hear much from you?"

"Sure he is," Gergely answered. "He doesn't hear about picky crap because I take care of it. The colonel doesn't want to hear about garbage the captain ought to handle, either. Hell, you think Stalin wants to listen to arguments about which army goes into which front? That's why he's got generals, for Christ's sake."

"I . . . hadn't thought much about what Stalin wants," Szolovits said. If he had thought about it, it was to assume that whatever Stalin wanted, he got.

"In that case, you're even. Stalin hasn't thought about what you want, either." Gergely chuckled once more. So did Istvan, dutifully. A superior's jokes were always funny.

When you looked at a *kolkhoz,* you saw the residence halls and the barns and the other buildings at the center. Spreading out from them, you saw fields of grain and meadows where the collective farm's cattle and sheep grazed. As Ihor Shevchenko knew, you also saw that the buildings were shabby and faded and that no one worked like a Stakhanovite to bring in extra cubic meters of barley or to get the cows to give extra liters of milk.

What was the point? If you did work like a Stakhanovite, the state would take the crop and whatever it needed from the livestock. You wouldn't get anything extra for doing more. You wouldn't get in trouble for doing less, not unless you did so very little that the commissars couldn't even pretend you weren't sitting there playing with your dick. So people did as little as they could to get by, or maybe a touch less than that.

Almost everywhere on the *kolkhoz,* that was so. It was so

almost everywhere on every *kolkhoz* anywhere in the Soviet Union, and on the collective farms that had sprouted in Stalin's Eastern European satellites after the Soviet victory in the Great Patriotic War. Ihor didn't know whether the People's Republic of China and the Democratic People's Republic of Korea boasted *kolkhozes* of their own. If they did, it was bound to be true almost everywhere on those collective farms as well.

Almost. Near the buildings at any *kolkhoz,* women tended tiny private plots. No careless turning of the soil there. No slipshod weeding. What they grew on those little plots, they could keep. They could eat it themselves or take it to unofficial markets and sell it or trade it for things they needed but wouldn't get through regular channels for years, if ever.

As women raised carrots or cucumbers or tomatoes or radishes or onions or lettuces on their plots, the men on collective farms tended to a pig or two or some chickens or ducks. Those animals, those birds, had care lavished on them that the beasts the *kolkhoz* as a whole was responsible for never saw. When you slaughtered your own pig, you made damn sure it had a nice layer of tasty fat under its hide. A scrawny, razor-backed collective-farm pig? Who wanted a beast like that?

When you took care of your own pig, it got as friendly as a dog. You got to like it. Or, at least, Ihor got to like the shoats he raised. But, while he got to like them as animals, he knew he would like them even better as meat. So he patted this one's head and scratched its ears, but he had a knife in his other hand even so.

"Sorry, Nestor," he said. Nestor snuffled. He was good-natured even for a pampered private pig. That wouldn't do him any good, but he didn't know it. Plenty of good-natured people had tried to stay friendly when the Chekists grabbed them in the great purges before the Hitlerite war. They turned into sausages, too. Ihor turned to Anya. "Bucket ready?"

"Right here." She tapped the galvanized pail with the side of her foot.

*"Dobre,"* Ihor said. "Put it in place." Steering it like a footballer, she slid it under Nestor's neck. Ihor patted the pig one more time. Then he cut its throat.

He hung on while Nestor thrashed and made horrified drowning noises. Red and hot and iron-smelling, blood poured into the bucket. After half a minute or so, the pig went limp. Ihor thought about blood pudding and blood sausages and ham and ribs and chops and potatoes fried in lard.

He waited till he was sure Nestor was gone before gutting the pig. He didn't want it to suffer any more than it had to. He'd seen too many suffering men during the war to care to inflict needless pain. Some people didn't care. They were the ones who hit their dogs and kicked their cats after they fought with their wives. *It's only a dumb animal,* they would say. Ihor thought they were the dumb animals.

Guts meant sausage casings and chitterlings. Liver, kidneys . . . The less you wasted, the more you had.

Another *kolkhoznik* ambled by as Ihor went on with the butchering. "You're my good, true friend, aren't you, Ihor?" he called.

"Mykola, you look like a hound sitting in front of a butcher's window with its tongue hanging out," Ihor said.

"The hound hopes he gets some scraps. So do I." Mykola threw back his head and howled.

"We'll see what we can work out," Ihor said. Mykola wasn't anywhere close to the best pigkeeper or chicken farmer on the collective farm. But his clever hands could fix anything that broke. When you had something somebody wanted and he could do things for you, you'd cook up some kind of deal.

Meat to eat fresh, meat to salt, meat to smoke, meat to pickle, fat to render . . . Nestor would keep Ihor's belly full, and Anya's, for quite a while. Even so, they wouldn't be able to eat all of him by themselves. Some would get traded to Mykola and other people like him.

And Ihor took a slab of ribs to Petro Hapochka. In the days of the Tsars, Petro would have been a village headman. Most of the Ukrainians who had been village headmen then died in Stalin's famine. Hapochka's title was *kolkhoz* chairman. He had to deal with more senior Soviet functionaries at the oblast level. But on the collective farm he did what a village headman would have done in his village in the old days. He made sure the work that had to be done got done. He kept quarrels among the *kolkhozniks* from getting out of hand. He tried to stop drunks from gumming up the works.

He also got the rewards a village headman would have in the old days. If you didn't want your life to be one nuisance after another, you kept him sweet. No law said you had to. Laws, in fact, said you had to do no such thing. The USSR's constitution made it look like the freest country in the world. You couldn't count on what laws said.

"*Bozhemoi,* Ihor, what have you got there?" he said when Ihor came up to him. Petro was in his late forties. He walked with a limp worse than Ihor's, and well he might have: he'd lost his left foot in a German minefield in the fighting near Voronezh in 1943.

"I finally went and slaughtered Nestor," Ihor answered. "I figured you might find somebody on the *kolkhoz* who could use these."

"I might. *Tak,* I just might." That Hapochka used Ukrainian showed he was pleased; Russian was the tongue of official formality. Had Ihor come out and said he was giving the chairman the ribs, that would have been bad form. Had Petro given any hint he would keep them for himself, that also would have been bad manners. They understood each other, and the game, perfectly well.

"Comrade Chairman . . . ?" Ihor switched gears.

"What is it?" Hapochka's tone was expansive, not suspicious. Those ribs paid for a question or two.

"Do the people who're supposed to know such things know when they'll put Kiev back together again?"

"Nobody has any idea, Ihor. Not a hint. Some of the people who would plan things like that were in Kiev when the bomb hit. They aren't there any more." A village headman would have crossed himself. Petro didn't, but looked as if he wanted to. He went on, "And the people who would have told the people in Kiev what to do were in Moscow, and Moscow took a worse pasting than Kiev."

"That's what I've heard, too." Ihor had mixed feelings about Moscow, as which Ukrainian did not? Moscow forced them to be part of a country where they weren't quite first-class citizens. Then again, Moscow had saved them from being part of a country where they'd get worked like draft animals and knocked over the head if they faltered. Next to Hitler, Stalin seemed a bargain. Before the Great Patriotic War, who could have imagined *that*?

"We just have to go on about our business till things straighten out," Petro said. "Sooner or later, they will. They're bound to."

"Sure, Comrade Chairman." Ihor nodded. He wondered whether either of them believed it.

\* \* \*

Herschel Weissman puffed on his Havana and said, "We have an order for a refrigerator down in Torrance."

"We do?" Aaron Finch said, in place of telling his boss *You're kidding me, right?* If you drew a line between the Blue Front warehouse and the South Bay suburb of Torrance, downtown Los Angeles would be somewhere close to the middle. Or rather, it would have been till the Russian A-bomb forcibly removed it from the map.

"We do," Weissman said. "I want you and Jim to take the truck down there. You do the driving. It's liable to be too complicated for him."

"How did we get the order, anyway?" Aaron asked. Telephone connections between that part of the L.A. area and this one weren't just spotty. For the most part, they didn't exist.

"The lady wrote me a letter," Weissman answered. "A very nice letter. It got from there to here. Since it did, I expect you can get from here to there."

"A letter doesn't have to worry about radiation sickness."

"Maybe not, but the people who carry it do. It's okay if you go around downtown, Aaron."

"Thanks a bunch!" Aaron said. Weissman was feeling generous, wasn't he? It wasn't just okay for him to skirt downtown. It was mandatory. Inside a circle more than a mile wide, there not only weren't any roads, there wasn't much of anything. Inside a considerably wider circle, the road hadn't been cleared of all the buildings and poles and walls and fences the explosion had littered them with. People had been evacuated from a wider circle yet, a circle without electricity or running water. They filled three or four town-sized refugee camps.

You could say that area centered on downtown was a circle the twentieth century didn't touch. But the twentieth century had touched it pretty goddamn hard if you looked at things another way.

Jim Summers grumbled, "I oughta wear my lead-lined skivvies for a trip like this."

"If you've got 'em, wear 'em," Aaron said. As far as he knew—it wasn't as if he'd gone looking—no one had been selling lead-lined clothes before the war started. You could sure buy them now. How much good they did was a hotly, so to speak, argued question.

"I don't," Jim said. "So the closer we go to downtown, the better the chance we got of fryin' our nuts. Or am I missin' somethin'?"

"Sounds about right," Aaron said.

"What we oughta do, then, is go way the hell over to Pacific Coast Highway and head down it so we keep the hell away from them atoms," Summers said.

"That's wasting an awful lot of time and gasoline," Aaron said dubiously.

"Gas is cheap."

"Not since the bombs hit. It's still over fifty cents a gallon. I've never seen anything like it."

Jim Summers rolled his eyes. "Anybody'd reckon you was the Hebe, not old man Weissman." He pulled his wallet from his hip pocket and took two singles out of it. "This oughta cover the difference."

He was right; two bucks would more than take care of the gas for the extra distance. All the same, Aaron set his chin and said, "Can you pull two or three hours out of your back pocket the same way? We can get over the hill through Sepulveda, maybe even through Laurel Canyon."

"I know what's eatin' you." Summers wasn't smart, or anywhere close to it. He could be shrewd, though. "You want to see what the bomb wreckage looks like, from as close as you can git. I got news for you, pal—curiosity killed the cat."

"Satisfaction brought it back," Aaron retorted. He didn't like being so easy to see through.

"Not if it was glowin' in the dark to begin with."

"Mr. Weissman said I should do the driving for this run." Aaron didn't tell Jim that was because the boss didn't trust Summers not to make a hash of it.

"Says you! We'll see about that." Jim stumped off to have it out with the boss. Aaron could have told him that wasn't such a hot idea, but he didn't think Jim would have listened to him. As Aaron expected, Jim came back in short order, more crestfallen than he'd set out. Aaron had pulled punches; Herschel Weissman wasn't the kind of man who'd see any reason to bother. After muttering to himself for a few seconds, Jim said, "Awright, smart guy. We'll do it your way. But if your next kid has green hair and eyes on stalks, don't say I didn't warn you."

Aaron didn't worry about that. From what the doctors said, Ruth was lucky to have had Leon. She'd lost a girl before she managed to do it. They said she'd have to be *meshiggeh* to try again. Aaron didn't love rubbers, but he didn't want to endanger his wife. Rubbers it was, unless they did something that didn't risk getting her pregnant.

As for the green hair and the eyes on stalks, Aaron couldn't imagine Jim reading a science-fiction pulp with a story about mutants. That had to come straight from the comic books.

Aaron did decide to go as far west as Sepulveda before turning south. Laurel Canyon and Coldwater Canyon might still let out into bomb-damaged parts of town. Before the bomb fell, it would have been an easy trip. The Pasadena Freeway—people also called it the Arroyo Seco, the Dry Wash—had been there for a while; they were calling its southern extension the Harbor Freeway even if it hadn't come close to the harbor yet. After it ended, Vermont or Western would have finished the route. Now they were finished. The newer Hollywood Freeway met the Pasadena downtown. That would have worked, too. No more.

The Blue Front truck chugged up to the top of Sepulveda Pass, then down the other side. As the Santa Monica Mountains shrank to foothills and then flatland, Aaron craned his neck so he could look east. So did Jim, for all his complaining.

"Oh, Lord," he said softly. Aaron nodded. They couldn't see well, because closer buildings that still stood kept getting in the way, but the background to those buildings that should have been there . . . wasn't. It had been swept away, as if by the fist of an angry child—an angry child who happened to be several miles tall.

At Sunset, Aaron resisted temptation. He got his reward, if that was what it was, by driving past an enormous refugee encampment. National Guardsmen patrolled a barbed-wire perimeter. People dejectedly mooched about from one tent to another. The wind came out of the west, from the direction of the camp. Despite a cigarette in his mouth, Aaron made a face.

"Pew!" Jim Summers said. "Buncha stinking skunks. Don't they ever take a bath?"

"I wonder how often they get the chance," Aaron said.

"If they ever get it, they don't use it," Jim said.

At Wilshire, Aaron yielded, turning left. Jim called him

some amazing things when he did. "I love you, too," he answered, deadpan. That produced more creativity from Summers. Aaron kept heading east, toward the blast zone, anyhow.

Wilshire stayed open for some distance. Even when buildings had fallen down, the ruins were bulldozed off the street. Finally, at Crenshaw, sawhorses kept him from going any farther. A sign declared that it was A FEDERAL RECLAMATION PROJECT. Under the stenciled words, hand-painted letters added WE SHOOT LOOTERS! NO QUESTIONS ASKED FIRST! To drive home that point, more National Guardsmen and some cops prowled the area. All of them, men in blue included, carried rifles with fixed bayonets. Aaron turned right and headed south.

Bulldozer crews kept shoving rubble out of the way. Like most of the soldiers and policemen, the drivers and a lot of other workers wore masks like the ones doctors used in operating rooms. Seeing that, Aaron thoughtfully rolled up his window. It might not help, but it couldn't hurt.

He rolled it down again when they got farther south. He could look east and see what was left of the Coliseum. It had hosted the 1932 Olympics; the Trojans and Bruins and Rams played there. Or they had. The great stone-and-concrete bowl looked more battered than pictures he'd seen of the ancient Colosseum in Rome.

"What a mess!" Jim said. "What a fuckin' mess!"

Aaron nodded. That he could see what remained of the Coliseum said that everything in the two or three miles between him and it had been knocked flat. Farther north, City Hall, which had been by far the tallest building in an earthquake-wary town, was only a melted stump. *If the earthquakes don't get you, then the atoms will,* he thought. Los Angeles would be a long time getting back on its feet, if it ever did.

The farther south he went, the easier that was to forget . . . for a while. Then the truck passed a lamppost with a body hanging from it. Around the dead man's neck was a placard: THIEF. Jim Summers whistled softly. "They ain't fuckin' around."

"No," Aaron said in a voice quieter than he'd looked to use. "They aren't."

Damage from the downtown bomb faded as they kept on; they hadn't come far enough to see any from the one that took out the port. Mrs. O'Brynne of Torrance was lucky. Her little suburb, full of fig and orange orchards, seemed untouched.

Aaron and Jim lugged the refrigerator inside, being careful to keep it upright while they did. They plugged it in. She signed the paperwork. A baby started to cry while she did. "My little girl," she said.

"They do that," Aaron agreed. "Not very old, is she? A couple-three months? I've got a little boy who'll be two in May." She handed him the clipboard. He checked. She'd put her Jane Hancock everywhere it needed to be. "Much obliged, ma'am."

"Purty gal," Jim said when they got back in the truck. "Reminded me a little o' that Katharine Hepburn."

"If you say so." Aaron didn't want to argue. Mrs. O'Brynne wasn't bad, but he didn't think she was in that league.

"A little, I said." Summers changed the subject. "When you head back north, can you kindly stay farther away from the bomb, huh? You seen what you wanted to see."

"Oh, all right." You had to give to get. Aaron put the truck in gear.

# 17

A TRAIN WHISTLE BLEW, off to the north. Along with the other laborers who'd worked so hard rebuilding the rail line through Harbin, Vasili Yasevich stood by the track and waited for the train to roll by. Like his comrades in socialist labor, he wore a padded cap and a quilted jacket. But he was pink and fair and round-eyed, so he stood out in spite of his ordinary clothes.

"Here it comes!" Somebody pointed. All the workers craned their necks up the line.

Here it came indeed, black smoke puffing from the locomotive. The engineer leaned out the window and waved to the crowd. He looked no more Russian than Vasili.

A claque set up a cheer: "Long live Sino-Soviet solidarity!" The engineer couldn't possibly have heard them over the din of the mechanical monster he controlled. Even if he had heard them, he wouldn't have understood what they were saying. The cheer was for the benefit of the Chinese onlookers.

He tried to keep his breaths as shallow as he could. Maybe that wouldn't do any good, but it couldn't hurt. He hadn't wanted to come into the blast zone to greet the Soviet train. When your gang boss told you to come, though, what you wanted stopped mattering.

The train was a long one. Some of those tarpaulined shapes lashed to freight cars had to belong to tanks. They would help Mao and Kim Il-sung twist the Americans' tails down in Korea.

Those covered tank shapes looked to be the same T-34/85s that had driven the Japanese from Manchukuo with their tails between their legs in August 1945. Vasili had heard that the Russians had a new model, bigger and lower to the ground and generally meaner than their old warhorses. People who knew about such things—or made noises as if they did—complained that Stalin was giving his allies the junk he didn't use himself any more.

Vasili had no love for the Soviet Union. With his upbringing, it was unlikely that he should. But he didn't have anything in particular against their Chinese allies. Mao's men made better overlords than the Japanese had.

They did unless they decided to give him to the MGB, anyhow. It hadn't happened yet, and they'd seized control of Manchuria well before they took the rest of the Chinese mainland. Vasili dared hope they would keep leaving him alone. If they didn't actually like him, indifference would do.

He also didn't have anything in particular against the United States. Even if the Americans had wrecked Harbin, they were the biggest reason Manchukuo was no longer a going concern. The Chinese Nationalists and Communists could have fought Japan for the next hundred years without beating it.

More flatcars rumbled past. If *those* tarp-shrouded mysteries weren't airplane fuselages, he couldn't imagine what they would be. And if they were fuselages, the flat things strapped down by them would be wings. Could you bolt them on and start flying? He didn't see why not. Maybe not flying saved wear and tear on the engines. Maybe it just gave the U.S. Air Force less of a chance to shoot down the Russian planes.

Then again, the U.S. Air Force might shoot up the train, or bomb it, or fire rockets at it. Vasili was glad none of the cheering Chinese around him could tell what he was thinking. He'd go to the MGB in a hurry if they could.

Another Soviet railroad man waved to the crowd from the caboose. That seemed to be what he was there for: waving to the people he passed. It was a nice, easy job—unless you happened to run into American planes.

A Chinese man next to Vasili nudged him and said, "You're the round-eyed barbarian who sells *ma huang,* right?"

"That's me," Vasili answered with a mental sigh. If you were Chinese, anyone unlucky enough not to be was a barbarian by definition. And the man was right about which kind of barbarian he was.

"I want to buy some," the fellow declared, as if sure Vasili had brought some to the ceremony to cater to his needs.

But Vasili had come to the ceremony because he got a day off from work and because he was ordered to show up, not to do business. By Chinese standards, that made him a lazy man. The Chinese were ready—eager—to do business anywhere, any time. "I'll sell you some tomorrow after work. Where do you want to meet?"

"I need it. I'll come home with you now," the man said.

"No." One of the things Vasili had learned was that there were times when Chinese were the most formal, flowery people in the world. There were others when nothing but out-and-out rude got through to them. This looked to be one of *those.* "Tomorrow after work. Where?"

"I'll come home with you now," the man repeated.

"I said no, you stupid turtle. Do you think I want you in my house?"

The Chinese man's eyes opened so wide, they almost went round themselves. He hadn't looked for a round-eyed barbarian to behave—and to sound—like one of his countrymen. Then he bristled, as if getting ready to fight.

Vasili reached inside a jacket pocket. He carried a straight razor in there, just because you never could tell. He didn't threaten with it. He didn't even show it. He had no intention of starting anything. But if the Chinese man did, Vasili aimed to finish it.

The man didn't know what he had in his pocket. A knife? A pistol? Nothing at all—only a bluff? The Chinese decided he didn't want to find out. He stomped off, cursing as he went.

"Good job," another man told Vasili. "I know Wu there a little bit, I'm sorry to say. I wouldn't trust him inside my house, either. You may be a round-eye, but you're nobody's fool."

"Thanks." Vasili wasn't ready to take this stranger on trust, either.

"Being a round-eye, do you know how other round-eyes think?" the man asked him.

He shrugged. "I don't know. Being a Chinese, do you know how other Chinese think? That's the kind of question you're asking."

"Is it? I suppose it is." The man chuckled. "A lot of the

time, I do know how other Chinese would think—they'd think the way I do. Isn't it the same with round-eyes?"

"A lot of the time, it is," Vasili admitted. "Not always, though. Different kinds of round-eyes often don't think alike, any more than Chinese and Koreans and Japanese do."

"Koreans?" The stranger sounded dismissive. "Japanese?" He sounded disgusted. But then he nodded to Vasili. "All right. I see what you mean. What I wondered was, when the Americans find out the railroad line through Harbin is fixed, will they drop another one of those terrible bombs on the city?"

"Oh." Vasili shrugged again. "I can't begin to guess. I hope not. They're busy over on the other side of the world. Maybe that will keep them from noticing Harbin—for a while, anyhow."

"Ah. Yes, that makes sense." The Chinese man nodded. Around them, the crowd that had come out to celebrate the railroad's reopening was breaking up. Men who had the day off were probably looking for ways to enjoy it as best they could. The stranger changed the subject: "Was nasty Wu there right? You have *ma huang* to sell?"

"A little," Vasili answered. "My father trained me as a druggist. He knew what an excellent medicine it was. When I have the chance, I follow in his footsteps." Chinese honored and respected their parents more than Russians were in the habit of doing. Putting it like that was calculated to please.

And it did. "Will you sell *me* some?" the man asked. "I'll meet wherever you want."

Vasili smiled. Even if Wu hadn't listened, this fellow had.

The *Independence* touched down at Los Angeles International Airport, a landing as smooth as a baby's cheek. "Well, we're here," Harry Truman said. A cross-country flight, even on an airliner as luxurious as this one, was always wearing.

"Quite a view, wasn't it?" asked Joseph Short, who'd taken over from Stephen Early as Truman's press secretary. His deep-South drawl made Truman's Missouri twang sound almost New England-y by comparison.

"It was, yes. The kind I hope I never have again," Truman said. Sitting on the right side of the DC-6 as it descended across Los Angeles from east to west, he'd got a good look at what the Russian bomb had done to the heart of the city. After a moment, he went on, "Who was that guy who captured their flyer and turned him over to the cops?"

"His name is Finch, Mr. President. Aaron Finch." As a good press secretary should have, Short had the facts at his fingertips. "He drives a truck and installs appliances for a local company called Blue Front."

"Oh. Blue Front. That's Herschel Weissman's outfit, isn't it?" As a good politician should have, Truman recognized a prominent contributor to his party.

Short nodded. "I believe it is, sir."

"Okay. Maybe we can play it up. Is this Finch a veteran? That'd help."

"No, sir. He served in the merchant marine. The military wouldn't take him—he can't see past his nose without Coke-bottle specs."

"He served his country, anyhow. That'll work," Truman said.

As the plane taxied over to the terminal and stopped, the props spun down to stillness. Airport workers wheeled a portable stairway to the door. Truman expected it to be warm when that door opened. This was Southern California, after all! But it was still only April, and the airport lay close by the Pacific. The air that came in was chilly and moist. He set his fedora on his head before he stepped outside.

Reporters and photographers stood on the runway. So did National Guardsmen. The military was practically running the West Coast these days. It was in decent working order and could get directions straight from Washington. That put it several steps ahead of the battered state and local governments. Putting the Humpty-Dumpty of civilian administration back together when peace came back—if peace came back—might not be so easy. Well, the country had managed it after the Civil War. It could again.

Truman shoved such worries out of his mind—one more time. Flashbulbs popped. The President waved to the members of the Fourth Estate. "Hello, boys!" he called. They were vultures, hoping he'd trip halfway down the stairs or do something else stupid so they could write a story about it.

A couple of Secret Service agents pushed past Truman, hurried down the stairs, and took stations near the base of the wheeled platform to keep the newshounds from coming too close. They no doubt felt virtuous about that. But if one of the gentlemen of the press pulled out a pistol and started shooting, he could fill the President full of holes before the Secret Service men knocked him down with their guns.

No one fired. Truman had been seventeen, almost a man but not quite, when that crazed anarchist shot William McKinley. No one had assassinated a President since then. A nut had taken a shot at FDR, but he'd only managed to kill the mayor of Chicago. And those Puerto Rican independence fanatics had hunted Truman himself, but they hadn't made it into the White House.

Truman's mouth twisted. Other, even worse, madness was running wild now. He wouldn't be visiting this ravaged city if that weren't so. How many had died here, in the two blasts? Hundreds of thousands. Put a President's life in the scales against so many and it didn't seem like much.

"How did those Russian bombers get through, Mr. President?" a reporter called. "Up and down the West Coast, sir, how did they get through?"

"I wish I had a good answer for you," Truman said, a reply that came from the heart. "I wish I did, but I don't. The best I can tell you is, they must have used the same kind of tricks we've used to strike at their territory. And I promise you, we've hit them harder than they've hit us."

"That doesn't do people here a whole lot of good," another man said.

"I understand that. I've come to see the damage with my own eyes. I'll go up to San Francisco and Portland and Seattle afterwards, too," the President said. "I want to make sure this can never happen again."

"The Russians are still advancing in Germany, too," said a fellow with a loud necktie. "How can they be doing that if we're hitting them with fire and brimstone like you claim?"

"Because there are swarms of them. It's the same trouble we had in Korea facing the Communists from the North and the Red Chinese," Truman snapped. "We cut our military to the bone after we whipped the Germans and the Japs. Joe Stalin didn't. We probably put too much faith in the power of our atom bombs, and didn't look for the Russians to build theirs as soon as they did. We can see all that now. We couldn't then, no matter how much I wish we'd been able to. Hindsight is always 20/20."

Behind him, Joe Short had to be pained. To a press secretary, admitting you'd made a mistake was an unpardonable sin. Truman couldn't see it. The *Führer* was always right. He'd said so, repeatedly. Teachers had taught German schoolkids to believe it. Stalin was the same way—Mao, too.

Hitler hadn't turned out so well. Stalin and Mao killed anybody who dared disagree with them. Truman had wanted to punch a reporter in the nose a time or three, but that was as far as it went. He knew damn well he wasn't always right. The people deserved to know he knew it.

"Will we drive them back?" Mr. Yellow-and-Orange Necktie persisted. "Why can't we smash their army with more A-bombs?"

"Because that army is on the soil of a land we're allied to, a land we're committed to defend," Truman said. "We use atomic weapons as a last resort, not as a first one. We don't want to wreck our own friends."

Another reporter found a different kind of question for him: "Do you think anybody in the whole country will want to vote for you in 1952 after . . . this?" His wave took in all of shattered Los Angeles and, by extension, all of the shattered country.

"I don't know. I don't care. I'm not worrying about it right now," Truman answered. They'd proposed the Twenty-second Amendment, limiting a President's tenure to two terms of his own and half of a predecessor's minus one day, in 1947. They'd got enough states to ratify it just weeks earlier. But it didn't apply to the President in whose administration it was ratified. If he could get people to keep reelecting him till 1976, it would be legal.

For now, though, he tended to agree with the snoopy reporter. He'd have a hard time getting elected dogcatcher next year, let alone President. That didn't necessarily prove anything. A lot could change in a year and a half. The USA might have won the war by then.

Or the Russians might have dropped one on the White House, the way the United States had dropped one on the Kremlin. The American effort hadn't got rid of Stalin, which was too bad. *Maybe the Russians won't get me, either,* Truman thought. If they did, the USA would have an easier time going on than Russia would without Uncle Joe. If the United States could get along without Roosevelt, it could definitely get along without Truman.

He held up both hands. "Boys, I didn't come to chew the fat on the runway," he said. "I came to see what Los Angeles looks like now, and how we can get it back on its feet as soon as possible." He'd also come to eat rubber chicken at a banquet that would swell Democratic coffers, but he didn't mention that.

He'd hoped for a convertible so he could see better, but they put him into a sedan. The fan was uncommonly noisy. That turned out to be because it wasn't just a fan. "This car has an air-conditioning and filtering system, sir," explained the Air Force colonel who played tour guide for him. "Some of the dust in the air is still radioactive in the damaged regions. We don't know how much long-term harm it can do, and we don't want to experiment on the President."

"No, eh?" Truman said. "Well, thanks for that much."

In the air-conditioned car, he got close to ground zero. Nothing much stirred there. The area had been comprehensively flattened. But a crow hopped around on the glassy ground before flying off in search of a place that offered better eating. The bird didn't worry about radioactivity.

The bird also didn't have to decide whether and when to launch new strikes against the Soviet Union. All it worried about were cats and hawks. It didn't know how lucky it was.

Cade Curtis watched the distant plumes of black exhaust heading his way. Sure as hell, more T-34/85s had made it into Korea. Tanks with diesel engines had all kinds of advantages over ones powered by gas. They went farther on the same amount of fuel. They were easier to maintain. If hit by an AP round, they were far less likely to explode into flame.

But they didn't run clean. You could see them coming if they moved by day. You could, and Cade did. He went down the trench to the radioman. "Let division know we've got half a dozen tanks coming toward us," he said. "An air strike would be nice, or some artillery if they can't do that."

"Yes, sir," the kid with the heavy backpack said. Some kid—he was likely a year or two older than Curtis. He hesitated, then asked, "What if they can't do it?"

"Well, in that case we just have to figure out something else, don't we?" Cade hoped he sounded more cheerful than he felt. They did have a couple of bazookas, but no foot soldier relished the prospect of taking on tanks without help.

"Right." The radioman sure didn't relish the prospect. He got on the horn with divisional headquarters. He did look happier when he took the earphones off his head. "They say they can give us some air, but they'll need half an hour—maybe a whole hour."

"Better than nothing, I guess." Cade stuck his head up for another look at those oncoming smudges of diesel smoke. They weren't going to wait an hour, or even thirty minutes. He tried for a nonchalant chuckle. Whether he succeeded, he wasn't sure. "Well, we'll just have to keep the Indians busy till the cavalry rides over the hill, that's all."

"Right," the radioman said again. By his tone, whatever Cade had managed, nonchalant wasn't it.

He had no time for another rehearsal. He hurried through the trenches, saying, "They'll have infantry with them. If we can knock those guys over or make them take cover and not come forward with the tanks, we've got a better chance." That mostly meant there wouldn't be so many enemy foot soldiers to shoot at the American bazooka teams.

A bazooka round could kill a T-34/85 from a hundred yards, maybe from a hundred fifty. Past that, you'd probably miss. The tank could shell a bazooka team out of existence from better than half a mile if its crew knew where the men were.

Along with the bazooka tubes, Cade had a couple of machine guns, one with a bipod that could go anywhere and the other on a heavy tripod in a sandbagged nest. "Fire one burst, then take it off the tripod, get the hell out, and use it as a light gun," he said.

"We have a lot more accuracy with the tripod, sir," said the sergeant in charge of the gun. He was old enough to be Cade's father, and spoke as if he expected Cade to take his advice.

Not this time. "Do what I tell you, O'Higgins," Cade said sharply. "How long do you think this position will stand up to shelling?"

Bernie O'Higgins scowled. In spite of his name, he looked more like a dago than a mick. Thick black stubble rasped under his fingers when he rubbed his chin. "Awright, Lieutenant, you got a point," he allowed. "We'll play it your way."

Lou Klein nodded when Cade said what he'd done about the machine-gun nest. "Good job, sir," the staff sergeant said. Then he spoiled it by adding, "I woulda talked Bernie around if he kept giving you grief."

No doubt he would have, too . . . which had nothing to do

with anything. "It's my company," Curtis said. "I'm supposed to be in charge of it."

"People are supposed to do all kindsa things they can't always handle. Sometimes they need a little help—uh, sir." Klein paused, eyeing the young officer. "You've seen more and done more'n most guys your age, ain't you?" He paused again, this time for a smoke. "Tell you what. If we're both alive a coupla hours from now, we can talk about it some more. How's that sound?"

"Works for me," Cade said.

Mortar bombs started whistling down. The Red Army had always been in love with them. It passed on its doctrine—and a bunch of tubes—to the North Koreans and Red Chinese. The company had an 81mm mortar, too. Cade also liked it. How could you not like portable artillery? It fired back. If he got very, very lucky, a bomb would come down on a T-34/85's turret top, where the armor was thinnest, and brew it up. That kind of luck, he didn't have. But the mortar rounds would maim some of the enemy troops and make others take cover. They could do that from longer range than machine guns.

As soon as O'Higgins' gun started hammering away, the approaching tanks stopped. Their turrets swung toward the sandbagged nest. Taking out protected enemy machine guns was one reason tanks had been invented, half a lifetime ago now. After four or five hits, not much was left of the nest. Not much would have been left of the machine-gun crew, either, had they stuck around. But the gun, now on a bipod and much more portable, had already escaped.

Another reason tanks had been invented back during the First World War was to clear paths through the bramble patches of barbed wire both sides strewed about with such abandon in front of their lines. Less wire than Cade would have liked stood between him and the enemy. He wanted the T-34/85s to come flatten it, though. That would get them closer to his position, and give the bazooka men better shots at them.

Unfortunately, the tank commanders weren't so dumb. They stayed back and lambasted the American trenches with shells and with bursts from their machine guns. Cade wondered if they were Russians. The Koreans who'd crewed tanks in the earlier days of the fighting wanted to get as close as they could to whatever they were attacking. They seemed to think squashing a foe flat was the best way to dispose of him.

A shell slammed into the dirt ten yards in front of Cade. Fragments whined overhead. He got mud in the face, harder than somebody would have thrown it at him. He spat and blinked and rubbed his eyes, trying to clean the crud out of them.

Wounded soldiers yelled for corpsmen. Standing up on the fighting step and looking out to see what the enemy foot soldiers were up to was asking to get shot in the face. He knew the bastards were moving forward, but what could he do? Men popped up for a few seconds, fired half blindly, and ducked down again, with luck before they got hit themselves. The machine guns delivered quick bursts.

One of the bazooka men launched a rocket at a T-34/85. It fell well short. All the same, it warned them not to get too cute. And it made them send some heavy fire toward that part of the trench. By the time they did, the guy with the sheet-metal launcher had prudently vacated.

Cade stuck his head up to spray some bullets around with his PPSh. He was alarmed to see some Chinese soldiers—or maybe they were Koreans—close enough for him to hit. He fired a couple of short bursts. The PPSh pulled up and to the right like a son of a bitch if you just squeezed the trigger and let 'er rip. The enemy soldiers shrieked and went down. Maybe he'd hit them. Maybe he'd just scared the shit out of them. That would do.

A distant buzz in the sky swelled to a deep-throated roar. Four Navy Corsairs zoomed low over the little battle, ripple-firing rockets and blazing away with the .50-caliber machine guns in their wings. Cade whooped and waved. Those inverted gull wings were the most gorgeous things he'd ever seen. In Europe, they'd be obsolete. They held their own here. This was a long way from MiG Alley, and a Corsair stood a good chance against anybody's prop job.

They made four passes in all. By the time they waggled their wings and rode off into the sunset, three tanks were on fire and the other three on the run. The foot soldiers who'd advanced with them decided they didn't want this stretch of American line all *that* much, either. They fell back with the surviving T-34/85s.

Some of the dead in front of the trenches would have ammo Cade could feed to his Russian-speaking submachine gun. He'd go out and scrounge . . . eventually. Now he turned to Lou Klein and said, "Made it through another one."

"Yeah, we did," the veteran agreed. "Another million to go and we win the fuckin' war."

"Think anybody back home'll give a good goddamn?" Cade asked. Klein shook his head.

Air-raid sirens woke Daisy Baxter out of a sound sleep. They hadn't sounded when the Russians bombed Norwich. If this wasn't a drill or a mistake, the enemy was hitting somewhere closer to Fakenham now.

"Sculthorpe!" Daisy gasped, and jumped out of bed. She hurried down to the cellar, trying not to break her neck on the dark stairs. Whether going down there would do any good if an A-bomb hit the air base, she didn't know. She didn't see how she could be any worse off, though.

Antiaircraft guns began to hammer. Sculthorpe lay just a couple of miles from Fakenham. If an A-bomb did hit there, this little town would catch it hard.

Explosions thundered. The Owl and Unicorn shuddered above Daisy's head. She whimpered like a terrified animal. If the pub fell down above her and blocked the stairs, would she have to stay here till she starved or suffocated?

Explosions, she realized. Plural. With an atom bomb, there'd be only one. But watch out for that first step—it's a dilly!

So the Russians were dropping ordinary high explosives on Sculthorpe. They didn't think the airfield was important enough for fancy, expensive atomic weaponry. Fakenham wasn't in danger unless they missed badly—which, from everything she'd heard about bombing last time here and in Germany, they might well do.

But, unless the Owl and Unicorn took a direct hit, it wouldn't collapse like that. She breathed easier. She also hoped that whatever the Reds were dropping, it would miss the runways and Nissen huts—the Yanks called them Quonset huts—to the west.

The sirens wailed for about fifteen minutes. No new bombs had fallen for some little while when the all-clear finally warbled. Daisy went up to the ground floor, opened the door, and looked around. Not much to see, not when Fakenham was blacked out. A couple of other people were also peering about.

"That was fun, wasn't it?" George Watkins called from across the street.

"Now that you mention it," Daisy said, "no." They both laughed shaky laughs and ducked back inside.

More sirens sounded in the distance. Daisy tensed, fearing a second wave of Russian planes. Then she realized they weren't air-raid warnings. They were the sirens fire engines used. One thing she could be sure of: with fuel and planes and bombs and buildings, plenty at Sculthorpe would burn.

She didn't know what time it was. The night was clear. She found the moon. By where it stood in the sky, she guessed it was about two in the morning, give or take an hour. She could go back to sleep . . . if she could go back to sleep.

She decided to try. She had nothing to lose, and it was cold down here. It wouldn't be warm in her bedroom, either. She had a coal brazier and a hot-water bottle, very Victorian but not very effective. Steam radiators and gas heat were little more than rumors in Fakenham.

A glance at the glowing hands of the clock on her nightstand told her it was twenty-five past two. She nodded, pleased her celestial timekeeping had come so close. Then she burrowed under the blankets. They were all wool except for the quilted comforter on top. Nothing wrong with them at all. What the feeble outside heat sources couldn't do, they could.

Whether they could calm her leftover fear and jitters was liable to be another story. Somewhere in the bathroom—or was it downstairs?—she had a packet of fizzing bromide powders. The stuff was supposed to calm your nerves and help you sleep. Getting out to look for it seemed more trouble than it was worth, though. She snuggled under the familiar weight of bedclothes. Either she'd sleep or she wouldn't. If she didn't, she'd pour down tea all day—and probably wouldn't sleep much tomorrow night, either.

The alarm clock's insistent bells woke her at a quarter after six. As she silenced the clock, she realized she hadn't killed it when the air-raid sirens wailed. As fuddled as she'd been then, that was a stroke of luck.

She went downstairs, heated water for her morning cuppa, and fried a banger on the stove. Then she warmed up some leftover mash she had in the icebox: a fine British breakfast.

She turned on the wireless to listen while she washed the dishes. If you didn't stay ahead of the game as best you could, you'd be hip-deep in rubbish before you knew it.

"Russian aircraft attacked several landing strips in England, Scotland, and Northern Ireland last night," said a suave BBC newsreader with an accent so perfect, you wanted to sock him in the face. "Relatively little damage was done, and only conventional bombs were dropped. Alert RAF and U.S. Air Force night fighters have claimed three enemy bombers shot down, with two more so badly damaged that they appeared unlikely to make a safe return to their distant bases."

He made it sound as if the Russians had carried out nothing worse than nuisance raids. It hadn't seemed that way to Daisy. But then, when you measured attacks on air bases against leveling Norwich and Aberdeen, their importance on the grand scale of things shrank.

She readied the pub for another day's business. A fresh barrel of bitter went under the tap. All the ashtrays were clean and empty; all the pints and halves behind the bar gleamed. She ran the carpet sweeper to get rid of ashes and potato-crisp crumbs in the rugs. She kept telling herself she ought to buy a Hoover, but she hadn't done it yet.

As she worked, she wondered whether anyone but the locals would come in. If the airmen at Sculthorpe were confined to base, as they might well be, she'd lose most of a day's trade. She shrugged. She had to get ready. If she was and they didn't come, that would be annoying. If she wasn't but they did, that would be disastrous.

Come they did, as soon as the Owl and Unicorn opened for business. For them, the raid the night before seemed to have been more exciting than terrifying. "We must have irked Ivan, or he'd not have come after us like that," an RAF flying officer opined between pulls at a pint.

"How bad was it?" Daisy asked.

"Well, it wasn't good," the officer said. "They hit a barracks and wrecked a couple of planes and smashed up the runways. We'll have bulldozers and steamrollers the way a picnic has ants."

"A barracks? No, that doesn't sound good at all," she said.

"It wasn't," the RAF man said. "Actually, the bomb didn't hit square. It blew in one wall, and then the roof fell down. One bloke—a Yank; this was an American barracks—has to be the luckiest sod ever hatched. He was near the far wall. The blast blew him out of his cot and through the window next to it . . . and all he has to show is a cut on one cheek. You wouldn't care to play cards against a chap who can do that."

"I don't know. He may have used it all up there," Daisy said. "If he were a cat, that would be eight lives out of nine, wouldn't it? Eight and a half, maybe."

"Hadn't looked at it like that. You may be right." The flying officer flashed what he no doubt thought of as his best lady-killing smile. "You're as smart as you are pretty, dear."

"Oh, foosh!" Daisy said. That and the look on her face made the flyer deflate like a punctured inner tube. Later, she thought she might have let him down more easily. But sometimes such a stale line made her not care what she came out with.

Bruce McNulty strode in that afternoon. He had a bandage taped to his left cheek. For a moment, Daisy thought nothing of it. Several RAF men and Americans had shown up with one minor injury or another—or with one and another. But then she made a guess: "Are you the bloke who went through the window during the raid?"

"Oh, you heard about that, did you?" He made as if to chuckle, but his face clouded over instead. "Yeah, I made it. Some buddies of mine didn't. I almost feel like I shouldn't be here myself—know what I mean?"

"I suppose I do." She drew him a pint. "Here. This is on me. *I'm* glad you're here." He tried to argue. She wouldn't let him.

**18**

BILL STALEY WATCHED THE ordnance men bombing up his B-29. The bombs had yellow rings painted on their noses. They were ordinary high explosives. The Superfortress didn't always visit radioactive hell upon its targets. Sometimes ordinary hell was thought to be enough.

Hank McCutcheon stood beside him. The pilot reached for his breast pocket, as if to take out the pack of cigarettes in there. An ordnance sergeant wagged a finger at him. Major McCutcheon dropped his hand. "Yeah, I'm too close to all this good stuff to smoke," he said sheepishly. "But I still want to."

"Can't imagine why," Bill said. "Pyongyang's a milk run, right? A piece of cake. Nothing to it."

"Nothing to it," McCutcheon echoed, his voice doleful.

The North Korean capital wasn't far. They could get there and back in a couple of hours. Whether they could get back at all, though, was very much an open question. Stalin had lavished on Kim Il-sung air defenses stouter than any city had enjoyed during the Second World War. Radar to spot approaching bombers, radar to direct the fire from the anti-aircraft guns, radar-carrying night fighters to hunt through the black skies and attack with heavy cannon of their own . . . Yes, the B-29s carried window to make the enemy radar operators' lives more difficult. Yes, the radar-carrying F-82 Twin Mustangs escorted them and tried to keep off the North Korean La-11s.

*Tried* was the word, though. It wasn't the way it had been going against the Japs, some of whose fighters couldn't even climb up to the B-29s. Japan was on the ropes before the bombs on Hiroshima and Nagasaki knocked it through them. With their big Red brothers helping out, the North Koreans remained much tougher customers.

"I should've driven a milk truck instead of one of these babies. That'd be a milk run for sure." McCutcheon sounded like a man kidding on the square.

"Hey, I'm a bookkeeper," Bill said, "or I would be if Uncle Sam let me." He imagined a gloomy office full of dusty ledgers, none of which added up the way it should. Next to what the plane would be facing tonight, he wouldn't have minded spending several weeks—or years—in a place like that.

They took off around 2300. This wasn't anything like a lone-wolf mission, the way some of the atomic strikes had been. A swarm of Superfortresses would visit Pyongyang. With luck, something from one of them would blow Kim Il-sung to kingdom come. Just because it hadn't happened yet didn't mean it couldn't. Without Kim telling them what to do, the North Koreans might just throw in their cards and give up the war. Quite a few Americans—some with stars on their shoulders—thought it could happen.

Bill wished he could believe it, but he didn't. With Kim Il-sung gone, he figured the North Koreans would find some other hard-nosed bastard to order them around. And, even if they didn't, the Red Chinese seemed here to stay. Short of turning all of North Korea into radioactive glass—an approach which, if you'd been fighting here for a while, definitely had its points—this war wouldn't dry up and blow away any time soon.

Meanwhile, he kept his eyes on the glowing instrument panel in front of him. B-29 engines had run hot in the last war, making every takeoff an adventure. Sitting in mothballs for half a dozen years hadn't improved their performance one bit. When everything worked, they hauled the big plane off the ground. When it didn't . . . that happened some of the time, but, in the brutal economics of war, not often enough to make the authorities quit using them.

Bill had heard that the Soviet copies of the B-29 didn't duplicate the American engines, but used a Russian power-plant of about the same performance. He wondered if it had the same trouble, too. He guessed it did. A B-29 copy wouldn't have been a real copy without overheating engines.

As they crossed the front, a little antiaircraft fire came up at them. They were up past 33,000 feet; most of it burst well below them. Front-line flak was there mostly to make enemy fighters show a little respect when they strafed trenches.

But the sons of bitches down below would have radios or telephones or telegraph clickers. In case the radar operators farther north had decided to turn in early, somebody up there would know to wake them up and put them back to work.

The country down there was pretty well blacked out. Electricity hadn't been widespread in Korea before the war started. Many of the generators that supplied it had been knocked out as fighting ground up and down the peninsula. Soldiers on both sides would shoot without warning at houses showing lights they shouldn't. No wonder the blackout was good.

Hyman Ginsberg's voice resounded in Bill's earphones: "The Twin Mustangs have picked up what have to be Lavochkins heading our way," the radioman reported.

Hank McCutcheon heard that, too, of course. He glanced over at Bill. Bill nodded back. They were nearing Pyongyang. They had to expect a welcoming committee. Here it was, evidently. The Lavochkin La-11 was a neat little fighter, its lines not too different from a German FW-190's. It was about as good a prop job as anybody could make, in other words. Not its fault that the rise of the jet had left it obsolete.

Of course, the rise of the jet had left the B-29 even more obsolete. Like the La-11, it soldiered on regardless. Small jet engines helped the even larger B-36 get off the ground. The B-47 was all-jet. Neither of those planes had been manufactured by the thousands, though. Lots and lots of leftover B-29s around. Why not use them? Why not use them up?

Flak rose toward the Superforts again. This stuff came from the heavy guns, the guns designed to throw it so high. It didn't burst below the bombers. It burst among them. The big plane shook from near misses, as if on a potholed road.

Out through the Plexiglas windshield panels, Bill also spotted tracers zipping back and forth across the sky. The B-29s and Twin Mustangs spat .50-caliber cartridges. The La-11s carried four 23mm cannons apiece. Their tracers, though scarcer, were more impressive.

Fire burning from engine to engine along the left wing, a Superfort spun toward the ground. "How much longer till we can drop, dammit?" McCutcheon demanded of the bombardier. The gunners were firing at something out there.

"Another minute, sir," Charlie Becker answered. A fragment sliced through the plane's aluminum skin; Bill heard the snarling clang.

"Fuck it," McCutcheon said. To Becker, he added, "Get rid of 'em, Charlie!"

"They're gone!" the bombardier said from the nose. The plane grew lighter as the bombs fell free and more aerodynamic as soon as compressed air shoved the bomb-bay doors closed. Hank McCutcheon pulled it into a tight turn to port, a turn designed to get away from Pyongyang and all the unfriendly people there as fast as he could.

Another B-29 took a direct hit and blew up. The flash of light left Bill night-blind for several seconds. Blast buffeted his Superfort—not the way it had right after an A-bomb burst, but noticeably all the same. The big engines roared as they got out of there. The roaring wouldn't help with an La-11 on their tail, though. The Russian fighter had something like an extra hundred miles an hour on them.

No fat shells blew out their pressurization or smashed up an engine or tore a crewman to bloody shards. Bill began to breathe normally again. *Another mission down,* he thought. *Sooner or later, they have to let me quit.*

They were talking with the flight controllers at the strip north of Pusan when the men there suddenly started cussing a blue streak. Bill could see explosions ahead. Somebody's planes—North Korean? Red Chinese? Russian?—were pounding the field.

"Divert! Divert! Divert!" the controllers chorused. Diverting, here, meant diverting all the way to Japan. Bill glanced at the fuel gauge. They had enough in the tanks. They could go. They could, and they would—McCutcheon swung the B-29 to the east. But getting hit, here as anywhere else, was a lot less fun than hitting.

Konstantin Morozov saw the Centurion crawl out from behind the battered barn about the same time as the tank commander in the English machine spotted his T-54. But his gun pointed right at the Centurion, while the other tank had to traverse its turret ninety degrees to bear on him.

"Armor-piercing!" Morozov screamed. "Range—five hundred! Give it to him!"

*Clang!* The round slammed into the breech. *Blam!* "On the way!" Pavel Gryzlov shouted.

"Another!" Morozov commanded. Even as Mogamed Safarli muscled the shell into the breech, the tank commander knew it wouldn't matter. If the first one hit, the Centurion wouldn't get a shot off. If it missed, the limeys would smash them before they could fire again.

But Gryzlov knew his business. That first round caught the English tank before its main armament reached the T-54. It slammed through the thinner side armor and hit some of the ammo stowed in the fighting compartment. The Centurion brewed up. Smoke and fire burst from every hatch. Morozov couldn't imagine how the turret stayed on after a hit like that, but it did. The British built tough machines, even if this one hadn't been tough enough.

The men inside would hardly have had time to realize they were dead. That was good. Better to go out fast than to cook and know you were cooking. This side of being shot by an outraged husband when he was 104, Konstantin hoped he'd die the same way.

"Good job!" He thumped Gryzlov on the shoulder. "Fucking good job! We'll paint a fresh ring on the cannon barrel when we get the chance."

"My dick was on the block, too, Comrade Sergeant," the gunner said, which was true. The Englishmen wouldn't have missed. Morozov was sure of that. More Americans fought in western Germany, but the limeys seemed more dangerous. They were professionals, the Yanks brave amateurs still learning their trade.

In aid of which . . . "Back us up into cover, Yevgeny. Those sons of bitches may have friends up there."

"I'm doing it," Yevgeny Ushakov said, and the T-54 moved back toward the little apple orchard from which it had emerged.

"Mogamed, swap out that AP round and load us with HE instead," Morozov said. "It'll still hurt a tank, and confuse it—and it'll tear up infantry."

"Whatever you say, Comrade Sergeant." If Mogamed Safarli sounded like a man trying not to show he was irked, that had to be what he was. Those shells were heavy. Taking one out of the breech and slamming in another with your closed fist (to make sure you didn't snag your thumb in the mechanism) was hard physical labor. Safarli might have loaded the HE round with a little extra oomph to drive the point home.

Morozov sympathized . . . up to a point. The tank commander had started as a loader himself during the Great Patriotic War. Almost every crewman did. Loader was the slot that needed nothing but a broad back and strong arms. If you happened to have a brain, too, you'd get promoted out of it pretty quick. With the way the Hitlerites chewed up Soviet armor during the last war, there were always plenty of places to fill.

The T-54 stood a better chance against the latest American and British tanks than the T-34/85 had against the Panther and Tiger. But Morozov had fought on a broad front before, where Soviet armor could usually find a weak spot in the Germans' overextended lines and force a penetration.

Western Germany wasn't like that. Everything here was compact. If you outflanked some of the imperialists, you just ran into more when you tried to break through. They'd have tanks of their own nearby. Their foot soldiers would have bazookas. A bazooka wouldn't always kill a T-54, but it had a chance. And the USAF and RAF had rocket-firing fighter-bombers—not quite the same as Shturmoviks, but plenty to pucker your asshole and send your balls crawling up into your belly.

When peering through the periscopes set into the sides of the commander's cupola didn't show Konstantin what he needed to see, he put the Zeiss binoculars around his neck and stuck his head out of the cupola for a proper look around. It was the turtle's problem. As long as he stayed inside his shell, not much could get him, but he didn't know what was sneaking up to try. He was more vulnerable while he stuck his neck out, but he could see trouble a long way off.

Those fine German field glasses brought the Tommies moving by the dead tank almost close enough to yell at. So it seemed, anyhow. Some of the Englishmen carried rifles, others Sten guns. Neither they nor the Americans had anything like the AK-47. As more of those came into service, the enemy would regret that.

One of the Englishmen—a sergeant, by the stripes clearly visible on his sleeve—pointed in the direction of the T-54. Maybe he could still see it despite Morozov's pullback. Tanks weren't exactly inconspicuous. Or maybe he was just showing the direction from which the fatal round had come.

None of the soldiers Morozov could see carried a bazooka tube or wore a sack of rockets on his back. That made them unlikely to come tank-hunting. It wasn't a cinch—the limeys sometimes did brave, foolhardy things, like any fighting men since the beginning of time. But it did seem to be the way to bet.

He slid back down into the turret. When he reported what he'd seen, Gryzlov asked, "Want me to give them that HE round? I can see 'em pretty well through the magnifying sight."

After a moment's thought, Konstantin shook his head. "Not unless they start coming forward. We've already made them notice us, and we don't have a lot of support around here."

"That's what we get for being at the tip of the spear," the gunner said.

"That *is* what we get, Pasha," Morozov agreed. "We get it because we're good. They put us where we can fuck the imperialists the hardest." *And where they can fuck us.* That thought followed automatically on the other. But it wasn't something you said when you were trying to encourage your crew. He went on, "We finally smashed through that shitass Arnsberg place."

"Not much left of it now, that's for sure," Gryzlov said. "But more and more towns and cities ahead, right? This part of Germany's even more built up and built over than the Soviet zone."

Now Konstantin nodded. "I was thinking the same thing." In the USSR, there'd be a city. It would have suburbs around it. Villages and farms and forests and meadows would surround the suburbs for scores if not hundreds of kilometers around. Then you'd come to another city, one that might be hardly acquainted with the place from which you'd set out.

Things here were different. Cities in Germany ran together. You could hardly tell when you got out of one and into the next. This little stretch of farm country was unusual in these parts. Land wasn't just land. With none to spare, the Fritzes made all of it *do* something, not sit there waiting for someone to get around to it.

Shturmoviks roared in from out of the east, passing over the orchard so low that their landing gear might have brushed the tops of the taller trees had it been lowered. They shot up and rocketed the English infantry near the knocked-out Centurion. Morozov stuck his head out of the turret again to watch the fun.

Only it turned out not to be all fun. The Tommies had a

quick-firing flak gun that knocked down a Shturmovik. The way the planes were armored, that wasn't easy, but the anti-aircraft gun did it. The Shturmovik slammed into the ground behind the English line. A pillar of greasy black smoke marked the pyre of the pilot and rear gunner.

The other planes in the formation flew on. A few minutes later, RAF Typhoons did unto the Red Army as the Shturmoviks had done to the English soldiers. Konstantin dove back inside his tank in a hurry. A couple of bullets clattered off the armor, but that only chipped paint. A hit from a rocket might have been a different story, but none struck. One blew up close enough to shake the T-54, but close didn't matter. It didn't if you were a tankman, at any rate. For the poor, damned foot soldiers, that was a different story, too.

When the telephone rang in the Oval Office no more than five minutes after Harry Truman got there from eating breakfast, he didn't expect it to be good news. He rose early. His breakfast was simple: scrambled eggs, sausages, toast, coffee. Good news was patient. It usually waited till someone was ready to appreciate it. Bad news came when it came, and you couldn't do a damn thing about it.

"Truman here," the President said. "What's gone wrong now, Rose?"

"It's the Secretary of Defense, sir," Rose Conway answered. She'd been his personal secretary since he came to the White House. She was a frump, but an efficient frump.

"Well, put him through," Truman said.

"Yes, sir."

A couple of clicks on the line, and then George Marshall began, "Sorry to disturb you so early—"

"Never mind that," Truman broke in. "Just let me have it, whatever it is. That's what you were going to do, isn't it?"

"Yes, Mr. President, I'm afraid it is." Even after that, Marshall didn't seem to want to go on. Whatever the bad news was, it would be worse than anything Truman could imagine off the top of his head.

"Come on, George. Out with it," he said. "Whatever you've got, it's already happened.

'The Moving Finger writes; and, having writ,
Moves on: nor all thy Piety nor Wit

Shall lure it back to cancel half a Line,
Nor all thy tears wash out a Word of it.
I have to know what *it* is so I can figure out what to do
about it.'"

"Omar Khayyam. Yes, sir. My English instructor at West
Point said Fitzgerald made too good an English poem of *The
Rubaiyat* for it to be such a good translation." Marshall went
on beating around the bush. That was so very unlike him,
Truman upped the scale of the disaster again. At last, after
one more sigh, the Secretary of Defense said, "Sir, the Russians have wrecked the Panama Canal."

"Oof!" Truman said, for all the world as if he'd taken a
boot in the belly. He wished he had; that would have been
easier to bear. Gathering himself, he went on, "Well, you'd
better tell me how, hadn't you?"

"It was a Greek freighter—Greek registry, anyhow. The
*Panathenaikos*. A Liberty ship like five hundred other Liberty ships," Marshall said. "Cargo was listed as olive oil, bay
leaves, jute transshipped from East Pakistan, and something
else. . . . Oh, I remember. The other item on the manifest was
building stone—marble."

"No one went over it with Geiger counters before it passed
through the Canal?" Truman asked. "When you say the Russians wrecked things, I presume you mean they had an
A-bomb on the ship?"

"Yes, that's right, Mr. President," Marshall said unhappily.
"The best guess is, they used lead sheeting to shield the
bomb from the counters. If it was covered in raw jute or in
among blocks of marble, the inspectors would have had to be
lucky to discover it. And they weren't lucky."

"Where along the Canal did it go off?" Truman asked.
There was bad, and then there was worse.

"At the Gatún Locks, sir, by the Caribbean end," Marshall
said. Truman almost went *Oof!* again; that was as bad as it
got, the greatest change in water level anywhere along the
Canal. The Secretary of Defense continued, "The lock mechanism, of course, is literally up in smoke. There's a radioactive hole hundreds of yards wide and no one knows how
deep, with seawater and river water steaming in it. If they can
repair it at all, it's a matter of years, not months."

"Good Lord!" Truman had been close to thirty when the
Panama Canal opened. Before it did, goods bound from one

coast to the other by sea had to go around South America or get unloaded, shipped overland across Central America, and reloaded on a different vessel. Now the nineteenth century was back—with a vengeance. The President tried to look on the bright side: "Our railroad and highway systems are much stronger and more solid than they were back in the day."

"Sir, that's true . . . up to a point," Marshall said. "But if anyone knows how to put an aircraft carrier on a Southern Pacific flatcar and haul it from one ocean to the other, word hasn't got to the Defense Department yet."

Truman grunted. "Well, you're right—dammit," he said. "Around the Horn, around the Cape of Good Hope, through the Suez Canal—" He broke off, suddenly anxious. "The Suez Canal is still all right, isn't it?"

"I haven't got any reports that it isn't." George Marshall seemed unwilling to go any further than that, for which Truman didn't blame him.

"Call the Minister of War or the First Sea Lord or whoever in the British government is responsible for protecting Suez," the President said. "Never mind the telegraph—*call* him. Warn him about what just happened in Panama. I'm sure he'll know: no way in hell you can keep an A-bomb going off secret. Call him and warn him anyway. If we lose the Suez Canal along with Panama, we don't just fall back fifty years. We fall back a hundred."

"I'll do it, sir," Marshall said. "You're right. That wouldn't just ruin trade. It would do terrible things to our military logistics. Even worse to the British, of course. So if you'll excuse me . . ." Marshall hung up without waiting to find out whether Truman would.

Unoffended, Truman slowly set the handset on the desk telephone back in its cradle. Then he cradled his head in his hands much the same way. The USA still had an Atlantic Fleet and a Pacific Fleet, but the Panama Canal had made swapping ships between them quick and easy.

Had made. That was the right phrase, unfortunately. Now the naval situation was back the way it had been when Teddy Roosevelt sat in this chair. What was in the Pacific would stay in the Pacific or take its own sweet time getting to the Atlantic, and vice versa.

None of which was likely to make any enormous difference in how this war came out. Stalin had done it anyhow. "That miserable fucking bastard!" Truman snarled. When the Germans retreated through Russia as they began to lose the last war, they destroyed everything they could to keep the Red Army from getting any use from it. Scorched earth, they called the policy.

Destruction for the sake of destruction, the Allies named it. War-crimes tribunals convicted several German field marshals and generals because they'd ordered such devastation. He wasn't sure, but he thought some of them still sat behind bars.

That was the kind of thing Stalin was doing. What else was wrecking the Panama Canal but damaging America economically in a way that didn't have much directly to do with the war? Truman would have loved to see the mustachioed four-flusher in the dock at Nuremberg to answer for his crimes. Unlike the German generals, he couldn't claim he was only following orders. He didn't follow orders. He gave them.

Truman swore under his breath. Then he came out with the question that had been in his thoughts more and more lately: "Even if we win, what the hell do we do about Russia?" Hitler had planned to occupy it on a line that stretched from Arkhangelsk down past Moscow and all the way to the Caspian Sea. Chances were he wouldn't have had enough men to make that occupation stick even if he'd won all his battles. And, with the majority of the vast USSR still unoccupied and still in arms against him, all he would have bought himself was endless grief.

Suppose the United States eventually made Russia say uncle. Suppose it stripped away the Soviet satellites and turned them into free countries again. Suppose it kept a close eye on the Reds for years to come. Then what?

The unhappy example of the Treaty of Versailles leaped to mind. Only it was worse than that. Russia would still be enormous. It would still have swarms of people and tremendous industrial power. Some of those people would still know how to make atom bombs. It would still be a deadly danger to the rest of the world, in other words.

Stalin and his henchmen had to be looking at the United States the same way. The USA and Canada put together posed the same problem for the USSR as Russia did for America. Truman only wished that were more consolation.

Then the telephone rang once more. He picked it up. "Truman."

"It's the Secretary of Defense again, sir," Rose Conway told him.

"Thank you."

"Mr. President . . ." George Marshall sounded even gloomier than he had before. Truman hadn't dreamt such a thing possible. He could come up with only one reason why it might be. Before he could ask, Marshall went on, "I'm sorry, sir, but my call came too late. The British were on the point of ringing us—that's how the First Sea Lord put it—to tell us to watch out for the Panama Canal, because they'd just lost Suez."

"Oh," Truman said: a sound of pain disguised as a word. "Well, this is a hell of a morning, isn't it?"


Rain drummed down. The ground got muddy in a hurry. So did the soldiers on both sides fighting in Germany. Istvan Szolovits wore his shelter half as a rain cape, the way you were supposed to. He got muddy anyhow, and wet, and uncomfortable. Maybe he was a little drier than he would have been without the shelter half, but he wasn't dry enough to be happy about it.

He was happy that the rain had slowed down the fighting. Those dirty-gray clouds hung only a couple of hundred meters above the ground. Fighters couldn't tear along shooting up anything they saw when a pilot was liable to fly into a tall tree or a church steeple before he had the chance to dodge. It was wet enough for wheeled vehicles to make heavy going of it when they left the road. Tanks could still manage, and so could foot soldiers, but the rain also cut down how far anybody could see to shoot.

Pickets and snipers on both sides of the front still banged away, just to remind everybody the war hadn't gone on holiday. But if you were back a little way and you used some care and common sense, you could almost relax.

Istvan sat with a smashed tree trunk between him and the fighting ahead. He leaned forward to get some extra protection from the brim of his helmet and kept his hands cupped as he lit a cigarette. Even so, he needed a couple of tries. Considering how wet it was, he didn't think he'd done badly.

Other Magyars sprawled here and there amidst the wreckage of war. Some also smoked. Some ate. Some slept. Szolovits thought he might try that after the cigarette. He'd quickly learned you were more likely to be sleepy—tired to death, not to put too fine a point on it—at war than you were to be hungry.

More men with shelter halves worn as ponchos moved up to the Hungarians' left. Istvan saw they weren't countrymen of his. Their uniforms were of deeper khaki, and their helmets had a slightly different shape. He guessed they were Russians and forgot about them.

He forgot about them, that is, till Sergeant Gergely burst out laughing. Half the Magyars in earshot sat up straight when that happened. A bear playing the piano might have been more astonishing. On the other hand, it might not.

"What's up, Sergeant?" Somebody had to grab the bear by the ears. Szolovits took care of it for his comrades. Some of them would step up for him one day.

Gergely was laughing so hard, he needed a few seconds to check himself so he could talk instead. "Oh, the company we keep!" he said once words worked. "This stretch of Germany is turning into the slum of the war." Then he started laughing again.

"What do you mean, Sergeant?" another Magyar asked, military respect and annoyance warring in his voice.

"I mean you're a fucking idiot, Lengyel," the noncom answered. "Can't you see? No, I guess you can't—no eyeballs. They're pushing up a bunch of Poles alongside us."

*Urk,* Istvan thought. That could prove nasty all kinds of ways. The Hungarian and Polish People's Republics were fraternal socialist allies against the capitals and imperialist forces opposing them. The governments of both countries would jail or kill anyone mad enough to have any different opinion. But . . .

Poland was the first country Hitler overran in 1939. Hungary fought on Hitler's side during the war, though Magyar troops hadn't invaded Poland. To say things might be touchy summed them up pretty well.

Istvan could see other complications, too. Compared to Red Army soldiers, the Poles were as likely to be as underequipped as his own countrymen. That wouldn't be so good when the fighting heated up again. And . . . "How the devil will we talk with them?" Magyar and Polish had nothing in common.

Well, neither did Magyar and Russian. Gergely found the same solution he would have used when he didn't feel like ignoring Red Army officers. In his fluent German, he yelled, "Hey, you fucking Polack *Arschlochen*! C'mon over here and swap sausages with us!"

"Who're you calling assholes, you stupid, stinking piece of shit?" The Pole who answered didn't sound angry. He just sounded as if that was how he spoke German. Szolovits could understand him, but it wasn't easy. And every word with more than one syllable, he stressed on the next to last.

Some of the Poles did come over to swap food and smokes and booze. Neither they nor the Magyars got the Soviet hundred-gram firewater ration, but neither nation's soldiers had to do without. One of the Poles said, "Kind of fun to pay the Fritzes back for all the shit they dumped on our heads."

Most of the Magyars looked at one another when they heard that. They didn't have anything in particular against Germans or Germany. Istvan thought he understood how the Pole felt better than his countrymen did. He was a Hungarian, yes. But he was also, forever and inescapably, a Jew. Even if there were times when he might want to forget that, the Magyars wouldn't let him.

"So does it make you happy to screw the Germans for Stalin's sake?" one of the Hungarians asked, perhaps incautiously.

Their new friends—well, comrades—muttered to themselves in their own language. Not surprisingly, the accent went on the next to last syllable of every word in Polish, too. After a moment, the fellow who'd spoken before said, "Screwing the Germans makes me happy any which way." His buddies nodded. He went on, "Did you guys enjoy screwing the Russians for Hitler's sake?"

Not even the incautious Magyar felt like answering that. Admitting you enjoyed screwing the Russians could only land you in deep shit, no matter how true it was. Poles didn't love Russians, either; Istvan knew that. Down through the centuries, the Russians had screwed them as hard as the Germans had. The Germans had done it most recently, though, and this latest screwing was a rough one. That was what the Poles got for living between nations bigger and stronger than they were.

"I still think it's a kick in the head German's the only language we can use to talk to each other," Sergeant Gergely said.

One of the Poles pointed up toward the clouds, or toward

the heavens beyond them. "Somewhere up there, old Franz Joseph is smiling in his muttonchops," he said.

Until the end of World War I, southern Poland had belonged to Austria-Hungary. Franz Joseph, the Emperor of Austria, had also been King of Hungary. After the war, the victorious Entente stripped Hungary of all the lands it had ruled that didn't actually have Magyars living on them, plus some that did. Wanting to regain that lost territory had helped push Admiral Horthy into Hitler's arms.

"We may have one more language in common," a Pole said in German. Then he switched to his other choice: "Do any of you know English?"

A couple of Magyars nodded, but only a couple. Szolovits didn't speak the language. He would have liked to; his ignorance felt like a lack. But he'd never had the chance to learn.

Gergely recognized what tongue it was, even if he didn't know it, either. He jerked a thumb toward the west. "You can take it up with the Yanks and the Tommies, if you want."

"I have cousins in America. They mine coal there," the Pole said. "We haven't heard from them since the war, but they're still around." He scowled. "Not like their country got invaded."

Sweden. Switzerland. Portugal. Spain. Those were the countries on the European mainland that hadn't been invaded during the last war . . . and Spain had just finished its own civil war when the bigger fight exploded. Even so, Istvan trotted out his own indifferent German to say, "Now they have A-bombs falling on them instead."

"So do the Russians. So do we. So do you," the Pole said. "It's a fucked-up world, is what it is."

If it weren't a fucked-up world, Magyars and Poles wouldn't have squatted in the German rain, filling space the Red Army couldn't in its fight against the Americans, English, and French. Istvan got another cigarette going, but the rain put it out in short order. That was fucked up, too.

# 19

GUSTAV HOZZEL USED A hand-held mirror to peer through a broken window in a house on the outskirts of Schwerte. Schwerte itself lay on the eastern outskirts of Dortmund, while Dortmund was at the eastern edge of the Ruhr. The Russians were getting too damn close to the Rhine, in other words.

This bottom floor of the house was fortified, with bricks and rubbish piled up to waist height by the east-facing wall to hold off incoming bullets. Emergency militiamen had knocked out the wall between this house and the next one farther west. They could retreat to that one when they had to.

More emergency militiamen had dug a corridor from the cellar under this house to the one next door. Gustav had been one of them. His back still grumbled. He wasn't so young as he had been the last time he played these house-to-house games. He grimaced. The fee hadn't changed, though.

The Russians, as a matter of fact, were masters at this kind of combat and field fortification. The *Wehrmacht* had learned a lot from them, and paid a monstrous price in blood for the instruction.

That mirror didn't show him any Russians or other pests. Some of the Soviet satellites' forces were in action on this stretch of the front along with their Red Army big brothers. Hitler had used allies like that, too: Hungarians and Romanians and Slovaks. From what Gustav had seen, they were like bread crumbs in a sausage mix. You used them to stretch out the real meat.

They'd fought bravely—sometimes. But bravery wasn't always enough. No matter how brave you were, if you had only rifles and machine guns and the enemy came at you with tanks and truck-mounted rocket launchers and heavy artillery, you might slow him down a little but you wouldn't stop him. And sometimes the puppet troops wanted nothing more than to bail out of the fight without getting killed.

Max Bachman chuckled when he said that out loud. "I don't much want to get killed myself," the printer replied.

"Well, neither do I," Gustav said. "But I'm still here, same as you are. We haven't bugged out."

"And does that make us heroes or jerks?" Max asked. Gustav only shrugged; he had no answer. His boss went on, "I was looking at things from a different angle."

"Why am I not surprised?" Gustav said. Max made a face at him. Hozzel added, "Tell me what your angle is, then. You know how much you want to."

"Ah, kiss my ass," Bachman said without heat. "I was just wondering whether we'd run into any Hungarians we knew."

"Ha! That's funny! It could happen, couldn't it? They hung in there longer than almost anybody else." Gustav didn't bother mentioning that the Hungarians had hung in for so long because Hitler occupied their country and installed his own pet Magyar Fascists to run things there for him.

That Stalin was their other choice had no doubt kept them compliant, too. They'd had time to see how he treated other countries that yielded to him. Seeing it kept them in the *Führer*'s camp. So, instead of surrendering to Stalin, they'd got overrun by him. And now they were Russian cannon fodder, not the German kind.

"The guy who'll probably know some of the Hungarians is Rolf," Gustav said after a little thought. "He fought there till the end—till the Ivans drove us back toward Vienna."

Max made a production of opening a ration can. "I still think chow ought to come in tinfoil tubes, not these stupid things," he muttered. After a couple of bites, he continued, "Rolf's a pretty good soldier—for a *Waffen*-SS puke."

"There is that," Gustav said. Rolf lived up to, or down to, the *Wehrmacht*'s stereotypes about Himmler's rival service. He was recklessly brave. But he was also inclined to kill anybody on the other side who got in his way. For him, the laws of war were something out of a fag beautician's imagination. The *Wehrmacht* hadn't kept its hands clean on the Eastern Front. Nobody had, on either side. But the *Waffen*-SS hadn't just fought dirty. It had reveled in fighting dirty. That made a difference.

Not quite out of the blue, Max said, "I wonder what Rolf thinks of Israel."

"Matter of fact, I can answer that one," Gustav said. "He told me the bomb that blew up the Suez Canal should have gone off a little farther northeast."

*"Ach!"* Max pulled a face. "I never jumped up and down over Jews, but only an idiot would take the Nazi *Quatsch* about them seriously. An idiot or an SS man, I mean, if you can tell the one from the other."

"Sure." Gustav nodded. "You couldn't tell those people they were full of crap, not unless you wanted them to bust your balls. But I didn't go out of my way to give Jews grief."

"Me, neither." Max's head bobbed up and down, too.

As long as things outside seemed quiet, Gustav also opened a ration can. He shoveled pork and beans into his chowlock. It was nothing he would have eaten had he had a choice; as far as he was concerned, the Americans kept their taste buds in a concentration camp. Even a lousy ration, though, beat the hell out of going hungry.

As he ate, he remembered SS *Einsatzkommandos* leading scared-looking Jews out of a Russian village back in the early days, the days when victory looked sure and soldiering still seemed as if it could be a lark. He didn't know what happened to those Jews, or to others later on. He didn't want to know. It was none of his business.

Had Max seen things like that? He probably had. If he hadn't, he would have been looking away as hard as he could. Not impossible, but it didn't seem to be his style.

They'd hardly got done talking about Rolf before he poked his head up out of the cellar. "Anything going on?" he asked.

Gustav had found falling back into the military life easier than he'd expected. Rolf might never have left it. Gustav had heard that some old sweats went straight from the *Wehrmacht* and the *Waffen*-SS into the French Foreign Legion: one of the few outfits that didn't worry about where its soldiers came from. They really hadn't quit soldiering. Now they fought in meaningless little wars in places like Senegal and Indochina, places that could never matter to anybody in a million years.

"Not much," Gustav said. Afterwards, he had a hard time making himself believe he hadn't jinxed things. It *was* quiet. Then, without warning, it wasn't any more. A series of descending shrieks in the air made him yell "Down!" even as he threw himself flat.

The heavy shells slammed into the houses in Schwerte. Pieces of the houses started falling down. Gustav scuttled like a crab—arms and legs every which way, belly on the ground—toward a heavy table. He huddled under it. So did Max. They hugged each other, as much to keep from being knocked out of that problematic safety as for friendship and reassurance.

Something slammed into the top floor like a giant's kick. Big chunks of roof crashed down onto the table. Gustav sniffed anxiously for smoke. If the place started burning, he'd have to leave in spite of the barrage. He hoped he didn't shit himself before then. Lying under artillery fire was the worst thing in the world, as far as he was concerned.

After fifteen minutes that seemed like fifteen years, the shelling stopped as suddenly as it had started. He and Max both knew what that meant. "Come on!" they yelled in each other's stunned ears. Untangling themselves, they hurried to the window.

Sure as the devil, men in khaki uniforms and Russian-style helmets not too different from their own were nosing forward. Gustav chopped down one of them with a short burst from his PPSh. Max wounded another. A moment later, the machine gun down the block spat death at the Red Army soldiers. The Russians—or were they satellite troops?—pulled back and hunkered down. They wanted the German soldiers served to them on a silver platter. If the first round of shelling hadn't minced the Germans thoroughly enough, maybe a second would.

Aaron Finch nodded to his niece. "Give Leon dinner in half an hour or so. He'll probably go to bed between eight and eight-thirty. Make sure he's dry before he does. He shouldn't kick up too big a fuss—isn't that right, Leon?"

"No," Leon said. He'd been doing that a lot lately. He was younger than the books claimed all the no-saying was supposed to start. That made him advanced for his age. This once, Aaron would have liked him better normal.

"I'll handle him," Olivia Finch declared. She was Aaron's younger brother's daughter, and had just turned thirteen. Marvin lived up in the hills, in a nicer part of town than

Aaron did . . . and one farther from the downtown L.A. bomb. Olivia poked Leon in his belly button. "You'll be a good boy for your cousin Olivia, won't you?"

"No." Leon had strong opinions and a limited vocabulary.

"It'll work out, Uncle Aaron," Olivia said.

"Yup." He nodded. If he hadn't thought so, he wouldn't have let her babysit. He was forking over half a buck an hour for dinner and a movie with Ruth and—more important—without Leon. He raised his voice: "You ready, dear?"

His wife came into the living room. "I sure am." Aaron would have been amazed if she weren't. She was one of those people for whom right on time counted as late. She smiled at Olivia. "You look nice."

"Thanks, Aunt Ruth." Olivia smiled back. To Aaron, Olivia looked like . . . his niece, wearing whatever silly clothes thirteen-year-old girls wore this year. If Olivia thought of herself as a budding femme fatale—or, if you wanted to get down to brass tacks, as thirteen going on twenty-eight—that was Marvin's worry, not his.

Ruth, now, Ruth looked nice to him. She wore a sky-blue sweater over a white blouse, with houndstooth wool pants that did nice things to the shape of her waist and hips. Ruth *was* a woman; Olivia just wanted to be one.

"We're going out, Leon," Ruth said. "Wave bye-bye."

"No," Leon answered, but he did. His mouth said whatever it said. Sometimes it hardly seemed connected to the rest of him.

Out they went. Aaron held the Nash's passenger door open so Ruth could get in. Then he went around and hopped in himself. As he started the car, he said, "One of these days, hon, I *am* gonna teach you to drive."

"Okay," Ruth replied. He'd been saying the same thing ever since they got to know each other. It hadn't happened yet. As he backed out of the driveway, she added, "I feel funny going out and having a good time when there's that horrible—hole—gouged out of the city just a few miles away."

"I know what you mean." Aaron had seen for himself what the bomb had done at much closer range than she had. "But the horrible hole will still be there if you stay home every day for the next two years and let Leon drive you *meshiggeh.* You're entitled to a little fun."

"Twist my arm." She held it out so he could. He took his

right hand off the wheel to give it a token yank. She let out a theatrical squeal for mercy. "Okay, Buster—you talked me into it."

Aaron pulled into the parking lot at Bill's Big Burgers. The BBB lot was crowded; quite a few people were out for a good time on a Saturday night. They didn't let the war get them down, either, any more than they could help.

The Bill in question was a plump cartoon-y sculpture. He had amazing fiberglass hair, wore a shirt and shorts checked green and white, and clutched an enormous hamburger in his right fist and an equally enormous malt in his left. Aaron and Ruth rolled their windows all the way down and waited.

They didn't wait long. A carhop also wearing a green-and-white-checked shirt and shorts came up with a large professional smile on her face. Her figure was much nicer than Bill's. "Welcome to BBB," she said, handing Aaron and Ruth menus. "I'll be back in a minute to take your orders."

"What are you gonna do?" Ruth asked.

"I was looking at the cheeseburger with onions—"

"Good thing we're married."

"Well, I think so, too. Like I said, a cheeseburger with onions, the fries, and a strawberry malt. How about you?"

"Strawberry malt and fries sound good. I think I'll have the meat roosters to go with them."

"Meat roosters!" Aaron snorted. Bill's Big Burgers also peddled fried chicken. There was a picture of a strutting rooster in golf togs (why golf togs? God only knew) on the menu. Somehow or other, Leon had got that picture mixed up with fish sticks, which he loved. He'd started calling them meat roosters, he hadn't stopped, and now his mother and father did it along with him.

When Aaron told the carhop what they wanted, he had to make himself not say *meat roosters* to her. She hustled back into the building to give the kitchen the order. He watched her hustle, not too obviously. She was young enough to be his daughter. And he was with his wife. So he watched without making any kind of fuss about watching.

She came back with a food-filled tray in each hand. She fixed one to Aaron's door, the other to Ruth's. "Enjoy your dinners," she said, and hurried off to take care of another car.

BBB's wasn't fancy. When your mascot was a plump guy with silly hair, you weren't likely to be. The place served plain chow cooked well. Aaron's dinner was exactly that.

After he'd reduced it to a few crumbs, he asked Ruth, "How's yours?"

"Fine. If we weren't going to the Deluxe from here, I'd save Leon the last meat rooster. Since we are—" She ate it.

The carhop came back to unhook the trays and settle the tab. Aaron tipped her a dime more than he would have if she weren't cute. He'd heard somewhere that nice-looking people were more likely to be wealthy and happy than their plainer cousins. He was no beauty himself, but he was pretty damn happy with the gal he'd snagged. Wealthy? He shrugged, there in the old Nash. You couldn't have everything.

Parking meters in downtown Glendale didn't gobble coins from six at night to six in the morning. The City Council was talking about changing that, but hadn't done it yet, no doubt fearing outraged—and cheap—citizens would throw the rascals out if they got greedy. Aaron figured he'd vote that way, but so far everything was just talk.

A whiskery panhandler stood in front of the Deluxe with an upside-down Hollywood Stars cap in his hand. Aaron gave him two bits and waved aside his whimpered thanks. Ruth rolled her eyes. She had to figure he'd spend it on bourbon. Maybe she was right, but Aaron had got a closer look at smashed Los Angeles than she had. The guy might be an ordinary Joe just down on his luck.

Not a first-run house, the theater was showing *The African Queen*. They'd already seen it once (Aaron had read it, too—he liked C. S. Forester), but it was worth watching again. He also wanted to see the newsreel. You got more concentrated pictures of what was going on in the world there than you did on TV.

What was going on in the world was the world going to hell in a handbasket—an atomic handbasket. A big crater in the middle of a tropical jungle was the wreckage of the Panama Canal. An equally big crater in the middle of a sandy desert was the wreckage of the Suez Canal. A smashed Russian tank in northern Italy said the Red Army still hadn't muscled its way into Milan. A stream of refugees on a southbound road and the shot-up ruins of a train said the Italians still feared they might. A general pinned a medal on an Air Force pilot who'd downed his fifth MiG and become an ace.

After a stupid science-fiction serial, the movie came on. With A-bombs and jet planes and TV, the world was living a science-fiction life these days. Even so, that serial was dumb.

Not *The African Queen*. You could say a lot of different things about it. Dumb, it wasn't.

Aaron found himself eyeing Katharine Hepburn in a new way. After a moment, he worked out why. Jim Summers hadn't been so squirrely as he'd thought. That gal down in Torrance, the one to whom they'd taken the refrigerator, did look a little like her. Not a lot, but enough to notice.

When they got back to the house, Ruth asked Olivia, "How'd it go?"

"It was okay," she said. "He didn't want to eat his string beans, but I sprinkled magic dust on 'em, and after that he did."

"Magic dust?" Aaron said.

His niece waggled her fingers above an imaginary bowl. "Sure. Magic dust," she said. "Makes everything yummy."

"I bet it does." Aaron decided to give her an extra quarter for finding a way to get Leon to do what she wanted. Little as the kid was, that could be tricky. He did what *he* wanted, and to hell with the rest of the world. "Come on, then. I'll drive you back to your dad's house."


Boris Gribkov watched as the technician bolted the new IFF unit into its place in the radioman's equipment behind the bulkhead on the right side of the Tu-4's cockpit. The man began connecting wires to hook it up to the rest of the radio gear.

"This will really work?" Gribkov asked.

"Comrade Pilot, it ought to," the tech answered over his shoulder as he worked. "We took this IFF set from a B-29 we shot down in Poland only a couple of days ago. We've fixed it up as best we know how. It should convince the enemy that your machine is a B-29 itself."

"But our original IFF unit wasn't copied from the B-29's," Gribkov said. "They told me that when I started training on the Tu-4. They took the unit from a different American bomber, a newer one."

"Don't worry. The Americans have updated the ones in their B-29s now, too," the technician said. "And we've made this kind of swap before. I've done it myself, when I got my hands on a good unit."

"I serve the Soviet Union!" Gribkov said—a phrase with a multitude of meanings. Here, it translated as something like

*You prick, you'd better be right, because I'm stuck with it either way.*

"We all do," the technician agreed. "Do you know where they'll send you once you've got your new toy here?"

*"Nyet."* The pilot shook his head. Even if he had known, he wouldn't have told the tech. The man might be honestly curious. Or he might report to the MGB. Boris didn't want the Chekists landing on him for violating security. The Hero of the Soviet Union medal on his chest wouldn't save him. Nothing saved you from that. They'd call him a stupid hero while they knocked his teeth down his throat.

That afternoon, once the tech was happy with the way the new IFF box worked, the base commandant summoned Gribkov and his copilot, bombardier, navigator, and radio-man to his office. That was a tiny cubby, maybe the size of a submarine skipper's, in the farmhouse; the strip outside Leningrad was as cramped as if it housed fighter planes only thirty kilometers behind the lines.

Lieutenant Colonel Osip Milyukov would have seemed at home at an airstrip like that. He was on the happy side of forty, though his medals said he'd had a busy time in the Great Patriotic War. "Well," he said brightly, "so you're all set up to give the imperialists a surprise, are you?"

"Yes, sir, unless they change their IFF codes before we take off," Boris answered. "In that case, the joke's on us."

"They usually do that on the first of the month, so it shouldn't cause you any problems." Milyukov clucked in a peculiar form of military disapproval. "They ought to pick a day out of a hat, not do it on the same one every time. We'd have to work harder if they did. But if they want to make things simple for us, I don't mind."

"Simple is good," Leonid Tsederbaum said.

Milyukov nodded. Boris could almost see the slot-machine wheels spin behind his eyes. They went *Navigator . . . Jew . . . wise guy . . . but smart wise guy, so put up with him.* Boris had made those same calculations about Tsederbaum himself.

"Simple is excellent," Milyukov said. "So that's why you're going to bomb Bordeaux. The Americans are shipping things in there like you wouldn't believe. You'll put a stop to that, all right."

"Long flight," Gribkov said, and then laughed at himself. He'd flown from Provideniya to Seattle, and from Seattle a long way back across the Pacific. By comparison, any purely European mission was only a schoolboy jaunt.

Osip Milyukov got his pipe going. It was the same model as Stalin used. Boris wondered whether the other officer had chosen that style because Stalin used it. One more question he wouldn't ask. After sending up some smoke signals, Milyukov unfolded a map and used a capped pen for a pointer. "This is the route you'll fly," he said when he'd traced it twice.

"Sir, that isn't simple," Tsederbaum said. Boris Gribkov was thinking the same thing. By the looks on their faces, so were his crewmates. Being a smart wise guy—and the navigator—Tsederbaum could, and had, come out with it.

"I will have all the bearings and distances for you before you take off," Milyukov said. "And, while it may not be simple, you can see how it combines with the captured IFF box to improve the element of surprise."

"I serve the Soviet Union!" Tsederbaum said.

A tractor brought a fat bomb to the Tu-4. The special armorers in charge of atomic weapons winched the bomb off its trailer and up into the big plane's bomb bay. Like the one that had attacked Seattle, this bomber was painted in U.S. Air Force colors. If you were going to duplicate all the mechanisms on your enemy's expensive machine, why not confuse him some more by duplicating its markings?

Takeoff in a Tu-4 duplicated the anxiety B-29 pilots knew. Would you coax the huge, ungainly monster into the air? Boris breathed easier once the bomber climbed past two thousand meters. If you got going, you'd usually keep going— as long as you didn't run into enemy fighters.

He droned south and a little west. He flew right over Minsk, hoping MiG-15s wouldn't take him for a real B-29 and shoot him down. One A-bomb had already hit the Byelorussian capital. The crater reminded him of a canker sore on the world's gum.

The sun set just before the bomber left the USSR and entered Romanian airspace. Romania had joined the Soviet Union in the fight against capitalist imperialism, but, aside from contributing a few second-line divisions, hadn't done much.

Over a town called Craiova in the southwestern part of the country, Tsederbaum said, "Change course to 270, Comrade Pilot. I say again, change course to 270."

"I am changing course to 270," Gribkov replied, and swung the Tu-4 due west. He was up above 11,000 meters now, as high as it would fly. In a little while, they passed out of Romania and into Yugoslavia. Tito's Yugoslavia was socialist, but deviationist. He'd broken with Stalin, and he'd stayed neutral in the war. If his defenses detected the Tu-4, and if he had fighters that could get high enough, he might try to attack it.

No challenges came from the ground. No antiaircraft fire climbed into the darkness. No Yugoslav fighter planes made runs at the Tu-4. Gribkov guessed Tito's men had no idea it was there. He kept flying.

Yugoslavia gave way to the Adriatic between Zadar and Split. "Switch the IFF set to its American configuration," Gribkov told Andrei Aksakov.

"Comrade Pilot, I am switching the set to its American configuration," the radioman replied.

Now, as far as any electronic snoopers could tell, they were an American B-29 going about its business. Gribkov flew across the Adriatic, across Italy, and came to the Ligurian Sea near Pisa. He stayed over the water, passing south of Marseille, and entered France near Perpignan. Had he gone too far south and come into Spain instead, Franco's Fascists might have tried to meet him with leftover Messerschmitt-109s, though they probably couldn't have reached his height.

"There's the Garonne!" Tsederbaum sounded surprised and exultant at the same time. "Now all we have to do is follow it northwest to Bordeaux."

Alexander Lavrov let the bomb fall free at Boris' command. No one had wondered about them from Leningrad all the way here. Gribkov swung the Tu-4 into its escape turn. The parachute delayed the fall of the bomb. When hellfire burst out behind them, blast buffeted the Tu-4 but did it no harm.

"Now we see if we get back to the *rodina*," Zorin said with a wry chuckle. "They may not have known we were here before, but I bet they do now."

"They may," Boris told the copilot, "but will their IFF?" He was betting his life—all their lives—it wouldn't.


Cade Curtis had always admired George Orwell. *Animal Farm* told people what Stalin was like years before they wanted to hear it. Orwell's new one, *1984,* had come out just ahead of the day Cade traded in civvies for Army olive-drab. He read it in a night, and came away with his mind reeling at the totalitarian world and at the scrunched-down language that totalitarian world required. As far as he was concerned, *1984* was a doubleplusgood book.

And then there was *Homage to Catalonia.* Orwell hadn't just talked about fighting Fascism. He'd gone and done it, and got himself shot in the doing. While he was in Republican Spain, he'd also noted and written about Marxist doctrinal splits and how they hampered the war against Franco. (These days, having outlasted his Fascist pals, Franco was an American ally. Politics could be a mighty peculiar business.)

One of the other things Orwell had seen while in the trenches was that the Spanish Civil War was the first loudspeaker war. Phalangists and Republicans threw loud, amplified lies across no-man's-land at each other. Anyone on either side who believed the other's propaganda would no doubt regret it in short order. Both made the effort, though.

At the start of the Second World War, the Phony War between the Western Allies and Germany (the *Sitzkrieg,* the Germans had called it) was mostly a loudspeaker war, too. Again, both sides also used them later.

And loudspeakers were very much in play here in Korea. The Red Chinese used them whenever the fighting bogged down, which was often. Sometimes what came out of them was pretty thick stuff: people going on about how wonderful Marx and Lenin and Stalin and Mao were, all in an accent straight out of a Chinese laundry back home. That kind of crap was easy to ignore.

As time went by, though, they got smoother. More people who really spoke English started giving spiels for them. If somebody who sounded like you said you were fighting for the wrong cause and that things on Mao's side of the line were wonderful, you could be tempted to listen to him. You'd be a prime jerk if you did, but what army didn't have some prime jerks in it?

Uneasily, Cade wondered how many American prisoners the Reds had taken south of the Chosin Reservoir. Not everybody they overran there would have died. When you were surrounded and cut off, you might throw down your M-1 and raise your hands and hope for the best.

And then, once you were a POW, what if they said they'd

feed you better if you did some talking for them? What if they said they wouldn't feed you at all if you didn't? What if they worked on you the way O'Brien worked on Winston Smith in *1984*? Would some prisoners start to love Big Brother? The garbage that sometimes came from the loudspeakers argued they would.

The Americans used loudspeakers themselves. What they shouted across the barbed wire sounded to Cade like cats in a sack when you kicked it. He didn't find Chinese a beautiful language.

Every so often, though, one of the Reds would sneak across no-man's-land and give himself up. It didn't happen every day, but it happened often enough for Cade to notice. When his battalion CO came to the forward trenches to see how things were going, Cade asked, "Sir, what are we yelling at the Chinks? It seems to do something, anyway."

Major Jeff Walpole grinned a sly grin. "Ah, you haven't heard that story, huh?"

"No, sir," Cade answered. "What is it?"

"What we yell on the loudspeakers is something a psy-ops colonel named Linebarger cooked up. He speaks perfect Chinese—he's an American China big shot's kid. I mean somebody with clout. Sun Yat-sen was Linebarger's godfather, for cryin' out loud."

"Wow! Really?" Cade said.

"I wasn't there to see it myself. I haven't met Linebarger. From what I gather, he's not an easy guy to meet. But that's what I hear. And anyway, what we're telling them is, they can come in to our lines yelling Chinese words like *love* and *virtue* and *humanity*. And when they yell 'em in the right order, it sounds like *I surrender* in English. Lets 'em give up without losing face, you know?"

"Wow," Cade said again. "That's one sneaky guy. I thought I heard something like *I surrender* in all the Chinese jibber-jabber, but who can tell? I mean, it's Chinese, sir."

"Yeah, it's Greek to me, too." Walpole grinned. Cade winced. The older man continued, "We drop leaflets on 'em with the same message. It works. From what they tell me, it works better than most of the rest of our propaganda."

"If it works, we ought to stick with it," Cade said.

"Feels the same way to me." Like Curtis, Walpole wouldn't look out at the Red Chinese positions from any of the loopholes set up so American soldiers could do exactly that. Nine times out of ten, maybe ninety-nine out of a hundred, you'd get away with it. The odd time, a sniper would be waiting and put one through the eye you used to do the looking. The battalion commander found his own observation points. "Quiet for the time being," he remarked.

"Yes, sir, I think so," Curtis replied. "They tried that armored assault on us, and the Corsairs came in and smashed it up. They were like kids with new toys—they'd got some tanks through! Then we went and broke the new toys, so they've been sulking ever since."

"People who outrank me weren't very happy when those tanks showed up," Walpole said. "I mean to tell you, son— they were *not* happy. We dropped an atom bomb on Harbin, remember, and on the rail line through Harbin. And now the line's a going concern again. Nobody figured the Chinks could drive it through there anywhere near so fast."

Nobody had figured the Red Chinese would swarm over the Yalu the way they had, either. Nobody had figured they would be able to do such horrible things to the Americans and other UN troops south of the Chosin Reservoir. If they hadn't cut them off from Hungnam and started grinding them to bits, maybe Truman wouldn't have decided to use atom bombs in Manchuria. Underestimating Red China came with expensive consequences.

The major, though, wouldn't care about the political and strategic views of a shavetail first looey too young to vote or buy himself a drink. So all Cade said was, "Lord help the poor suckers who rebuilt that railroad. I bet every one of 'em glows in the dark."

"I bet you're right," Walpole said. "Considering how the Reds throw soldiers at us the way rich guys throw money at chorus girls—and considering how they lose 'em as fast as the rich guys burn through their cash—is it any wonder if they spend railroad workers the same way?"

"No wonder at all, sir," Cade said.

Once more, he didn't feel like arguing with his superior. It wasn't even that he thought Jeff Walpole was wrong. But the Red Chinese didn't have planes and abundant artillery and bunches of tanks. They had bunches of men with rifles and submachine guns. The Americans could spend ordnance to kill them. They had to spend men to kill Americans, and did what they had to do. That their commanders did it as cold-bloodedly as if they were snakes lent itself to Walpole's point, but to fight the war at all they would have had to do it whether they cared to or not.

Off in the distance, a rifle banged—once, twice. That was a Mosin-Nagant, probably in a Chinaman's hands, maybe fired by one of Kim Il-sung's finest. A Browning machine gun stammered death back at it. One more bang from the rifle. Another quick, professional burst from the Browning.

Cade hefted his own Soviet submachine gun. If things heated up, he was ready. But they didn't. One of the clowns on the other side had got excited about nothing, and that was as far as it went.

Walpole pointed to the PPSh. "Like that piece better than the carbine they gave you, huh?"

"You bet, sir," Cade said, in lieu of *You bet your ass, sir.*

But all Walpole said was, "You're nobody's fool, kid. The carbine's a piece of junk, but you can do yourself some good with one of those babies." They beamed at each other. For an old guy, Cade thought, the major was all right.

# 20

VASILI YASEVICH SHOOK HIS head in what he hoped was a convincing show of regret. "No, sir. I am very sorry, sir, but I have no opium to sell," he said. "Use of opium is not allowed any more, not under the just laws of the People's Republic."

"But you are a druggist. You can get medicines like this." The man was about fifty. His clothes were as plain as Vasili's. No one flaunted wealth in China these days. His voice, though, had the self-assured growl that said he was used to getting whatever he wanted.

He wasn't going to get opium from Vasili. "I am very sorry, sir," the Russian expatriate repeated. "Having the poppy is a capital crime. It is not the kind of chance a poor man, an honest man, wants to take."

"Comrade Wang's wife told me you could get her whatever she needed," the man said.

"Comrade Wang's wife never asked me for opium," Vasili said, which was true. "I got her *ma huang.* That's legal."

"She didn't talk about what you got her. She talked about what you *could* get her." The man bore down hard on the word that made the difference.

*Bitch! Cunt! Whore! Fucking whore!* When Vasili swore inside his own head, he swore in Russian, not Chinese. Maybe that was because he'd learned the one language slightly ahead of the other. Maybe it was just because Russian sounded and felt earthier, more obscene, to him.

The bow he gave the important man, though, was Chinese. It was so Chinese, getting it from a round-eyed barbarian, even one who spoke the language of the Middle Kingdom, visibly surprised the fellow. "Comrade Wang's wife is a wise woman," Vasili said. "I am sad to have to tell you, though, that even the wisest is sometimes mistaken."

"Curse you, I need the poppy!" the man said. He wasn't telling Vasili anything Vasili hadn't guessed. If the fellow had had the habit for a while, even laws that threatened death to people who used the drug wouldn't get its claws out of his head. He went on, "You want money? I'll give you money! I've got plenty of money."

He reached into a trouser pocket. When he opened his hand, gold coins from Russia and England and Austria-Hungary gleamed like the sun.

He had plenty of money, yes. What he lacked was sense. The shabby streetcorner where they stood talking hadn't seen that much gold in all the centuries Harbin was there. "Put it away!" Vasili hissed. "Do you want somebody to knock you over the head?"

"Who would dare?" The man had the arrogance of a high official, of someone who was likely to know Comrade Wang and his wife. Again, though, arrogance was no substitute for caution.

"Who? There are people in this part of town who would kill you for that many coppers." At various times in Vasili's life, he might have been one of them. Not mentioning that seemed smart.

"I can have everyone in this part of town machine-gunned tomorrow morning," the man snapped. "Don't play games with me."

"Do you think they care what you can do, Comrade Commissar?" Vasili didn't know the man's title, but that seemed a good bet. "They've had an atom bomb fall on them. After that, what are some machine guns?"

For a wonder, what he said seemed to get through to the Chinese. To Vasili's relief, the man closed his hand and got the intoxicating gold out of sight. He also seemed to slump a little. How bad were the demons in his head? How soon before his brain felt emptied from the inside out, before every muscle in his body knotted, before snot flooded out of his nose, before he started shitting himself?

"You have to get me the poppy," he said, but now with the first touch of doubt and pleading in his voice.

"Sir, please forgive this unworthy one, but he cannot do what he cannot do," Vasili said. "Before the glorious People's

Republic triumphed, the eastern dwarfs"—a snide Chinese gibe at the Japanese—"wanted people to use opium, because it made them tame. Not many of those people still walk under the sun. Mao's justice is fast and sure."

The commissar slapped him in the face. Vasili had the straight razor in his pocket and a knife in his boot top. Had he thought he could pay back the commissar without being seen, he would have done it. On a street corner in a Chinese city, though? No. He made himself stand still.

"You stinking turd!" The man's voice rose to something close to a scream. He wheeled and stormed away. Vasili didn't follow him. With any luck, before long the man's own body would do worse to him than he'd done to the Russian.

A skinny fellow with a tray of millet cakes held to his front by a rope around his neck said, "That guy didn't like you."

*"Da,"* Vasili agreed absently. The skinny fellow nodded; everybody in Harbin followed that. Vasili went on, "But he's a big man, so what can you do?" The phrase meant *an important person.*

"What did he want from you?" the cake-seller asked.

"Something I don't have. Something I can't get," Vasili said.

"Not so good when a big man wants something like that from you," the skinny fellow said shrewdly. "Especially when you're a round-eye. You stand out in a crowd."

Other Russians did still live here, but not so many of them. Vasili shrugged. "Nothing I can do about how I look."

"No, but if he wants to make you sorry, his friends won't have much trouble finding you."

Vasili bowed to him, too. "Thanks a lot, pal. You just made my day." It wasn't that the man who sold millet cakes was wrong. From now on, Vasili would have to worry every time somebody knocked on the door of the tumbledown shack where he was staying.

He did have some poppy juice there. He told himself he'd have to stash it somewhere else for a while. The commissar might come after it himself. Or he might send the secret police to search. If they found any, Vasili was out of business for good.

He decided to take care of that right away. He kept ducking into doorways on his way home, checking to see whether anyone was tailing him. As best he could tell, nobody was. He stopped at a little teahouse and drank a cup, watching

Harbin go by in front of the shop. Harbin didn't seem to care at all about Vasili Yasevich. That suited him fine.

"Do you want another cup?" the serving girl asked. She was pretty, even if she only came up to the bottom of Vasili's chin. He'd hardly noticed her when he asked for the first cup. He'd just wanted to keep an eye on things for a few minutes.

He noticed her now. With regret, he shook his head. "Sorry, dear. I have to get somewhere. Maybe I'll come back."

*"Khorosho,"* she said, so she knew a bit of Russian. She smiled after him as he left.

He stayed careful all the way to his place. He made sure he barred the door after he went inside. The opium was in a glass jar with a ground-glass stopper. His father had had dozens like it. He'd got this one in a junk shop. He stuck it in his pocket and left.

His hiding place wasn't wonderful, but it would do: a hollow under half a brick in a blacksmith's place that had been falling in on itself since before Harbin belonged to puppet Manchukuo. He didn't think anyone saw him go in. He left through a hole in the side wall. It was three blocks to his shanty. That was far enough, he hoped, to keep secret policemen from coming here when they didn't find anything in the place.

Of course, if they wanted him enough, they could plant their own opium and kill him on account of it. He couldn't do anything about that. With luck, he was too unimportant for them to bother. He headed back to the teahouse. "Hello, sweetheart," he said. "What do I call you?"

Bill Staley mooched away from yet another mail call with no card or letter from Marian. He wished she'd write. They had paper and pens in refugee camps . . . didn't they?

Or maybe she had written, but the Air Force hadn't figured out that he was in Japan, not at the field north of Pusan. One of the things he'd learned was that stuff could go south a million different ways. The poor sap for whom they went south wouldn't know which. He'd just know the world was fubar'd.

The field outside of Fukuoka was more like a base behind the lines and less like a forward airstrip than the one his B-29 hadn't been able to land at. The runways were paved. People slept in Quonset huts and prefab wooden barracks, not under canvas. A radar dish did spin to warn of trouble, but far fewer flak guns poked snouts toward the sky.

Hank McCutcheon noticed the same thing. "We're back in the peacetime Air Force," he said.

"Cripes, we've earned it," Bill answered. "We came way too close to buying a plot on that last run to Pyongyang."

"Place got bombed," McCutcheon said. "That's all Harrison and the other guys who give the orders care about. Lose some bomber crews? Hell, that's just the cost of doing business, like new spark plugs on a delivery truck."

"Cripes," Bill said again, on a different note this time. "Man, I don't like the idea of putting casualties on one side of the ledger."

"That's what those guys do. That's what they're supposed to do," the pilot said. "They go, 'if we can do this much damage and only lose that many men, then hey, it's worth a shot.'"

"How many cities have we lost? How about the Russians?" Bill said. "Whoever was working the cost-benefit analysis, he should have taken off his shoes so he could get the decimal point straight."

"Not like you're wrong," McCutcheon said. "But you were the one who reminded me a while ago that we haven't exactly been washing our hands with Ivory. Some of those mushroom clouds, we raised the mushrooms."

"Uh-huh. You try not to think about it. Sometimes I feel like Lady Macbeth just the same."

"Planning that shit is the generals' job. Doing it's ours," McCutcheon said. "The other choice is getting shot down. Bombing's better."

"Oh, yeah." Bill nodded. "I don't think I was ever so scared as I was on the last run over Pyongyang. How many Superforts did we lose that night?"

"Half a dozen," McCutcheon said, as if Bill didn't know that as well as he did. "And those two Twin Mustangs. And the airport down in the south. We didn't pay cheap for anything. But we plastered the target, and I promise we hurt Kim Il-sung worse'n he hurt us."

"Sure we did. We can blow up tons and tons of gooks. But they can only blow up one Bill Staley, and they came too goddamn close to doing it. I felt the goose walking over my grave."

McCutcheon studied him the way he might have looked

over a nose wheel with a slow leak, wondering whether he could take off on it. "Bill, old son, you think maybe you ought to sit out a few missions? You don't sound like you're in A-number-one shape right this minute."

"I'm not eager any more—I'll tell you that. I'll go, though," Bill said. "Yeah, I will. For whither thou goest, I will go; and where thou fliest, I will fly: thy crew shall be my crew, and thy Superfortress my Superfortress."

He hadn't thought he would—or could—go on butchering the Book of Ruth so long, but he got all the way through to the end of the passage. Hank McCutcheon eyed him with a mix of admiration and horror. "You're crazy as a fucking bedbug, Staley, you know that?"

"Marian always tells me so, yeah," Bill answered, not without pride. "'Course, she must be nuts herself, or she wouldn't've married me."

"I was gonna point that out in case you didn't," the pilot said. "Seriously, though, man, are you good to fly? I don't want you in that seat if you aren't up to doing the things you need to do."

Bill examined himself as he would have examined the instrument panel in front of the copilot's seat. Some of his internal dials didn't register as they would have if everything were running smoothly, but none was in the red. "Like I said, I'm not gung-ho these days. I've been shot at in two wars, and it never was any fun. I've got a wife and a little girl Stateside, and I want to see them again. I'm an old copilot, but I'm not an old, bold copilot. So I can do it. You want me to jump up and down about doing it, that ain't gonna happen."

"I wanna watch animals jumping up and down, I don't need you," Hank McCutcheon said. "I can look at the fucking Jap monkeys instead. Ain't they a kick in the nuts?"

"They're something, all right," Bill agreed. Most of the animals and birds and plants here didn't look too different from the stuff back home. They weren't identical, but you had to look twice to notice; the overall effect was similar. And then, in the middle of all that similarity—monkeys! He continued, "You could put 'em in uniform and they'd take over for our top brass without missing a beat. Nobody'd even notice."

"Like hell, nobody would," the pilot said. "The orders would start making more sense if the monkeys gave 'em."

"Yeah, you're right. And only a few of our generals have tails now, so people might spot that, too."

Chain-link fencing kept unwanted humans away from the runways. It didn't bother the Japanese macaques one bit. As Bill watched, a monkey swarmed up one side and down the other, grabbing the wire with hands and thumbish feet. Watching something the size of a dog climb nimbly as a squirrel told him he wasn't in Kansas any more. The monkey steered clear of him and McCutcheon. They were wary around men, though not too afraid of them.

"Wonder what it's after," Bill said.

"Anything that isn't nailed down," McCutcheon replied. "And if it wants something that is, it's liable to pry out the nails. Whatever else they are, the damn things are pests. If we had 'em back in the States, there'd be a bounty on 'em."

"No kidding!" Bill said. Macaques raided garbage cans. They sneaked into kitchens and storerooms and stole food from them. They were like giant rats with hands that worked. Not long before the B-29s that bombed Pyongyang had to land here, one of them had swiped an MP's .45. With its clever, curious fingers, the monkey managed to release the safety. That was its next to last mistake. It was pointing the pistol at itself when it found out what the trigger did. . . .

"You don't want to mess with 'em. Rile 'em up and they'll bite your face off," McCutcheon said.

That was also the truth, the whole truth, and nothing but the truth. A macaque could look amazingly manlike with its mouth closed. But when it yawned or screeched or did anything else with its mouth open, you saw that a man might be a monkey's nephew, but he sure wasn't a monkey's son. The chompers in there would have made a coyote think twice.

"I suppose it's because we don't have those teeth that we started hitting things with sticks, and then throwing rocks at things, and then making spears and bows and arrows and . . . and like that," Bill said vaguely. He glanced over toward the camouflaged revetment that held the B-29 McCutcheon and he flew. "If we'd kept our teeth, we wouldn't be dropping bombs on each other right this minute."

"No—we'd be a bunch of lousy, flea-bitten monkeys on the prowl for whatever we could scrounge," McCutcheon said.

Bill grinned a crooked grin. "And this would make us different from the way we are how exactly?"

"Hey, we aren't lousy and flea-bitten," McCutcheon said. "DDT takes care of that. We make the stuff that goes boom, but we make the stuff that lets life be worth living, too."

"Mm . . . maybe. Can I scrounge a butt off you, Major Monkey, sir?"

"Ook," McCutcheon said, and handed him a pack.

Marian had never seen Daniel Philip Jaspers after he tried to rob her car. She knew that was his name because a camp policeman pulled the would-be burglar's wallet out of his pocket while he was still groggy. Marian and Fayvl Tabakman and a couple of other people all told the cop what he'd been up to.

Glorying in his own self-importance, the policeman took Daniel Philip Jaspers away, poking him in the ribs with a billy club whenever he staggered. He staggered quite a bit. Marian was sure she would have, too. The rock Fayvl got him with hadn't been small, and he'd thrown it hard.

She didn't know exactly what happened to camp criminals. If you put them in a jail, would they notice? The whole camp was too much like a jail. Maybe they went into labor gangs, clearing wreckage on the fringes of the blast area. Wreckage like what had been the house where she and Linda lived, for instance. Those labor gangs had plenty of work. They were about the only kind of workers in these parts that did.

When Marian remembered, she did keep an eye out for Daniel Philip Jaspers. He might want to get even for not being able to steal from her. She peered every which way the first few days. After that, he began to move into the background of her worries.

Two big questions stayed in the foreground. Would Bill come back from the fighting in one piece? And, what the devil would she and Linda do till he did? She couldn't do anything about the first one but pray, and she wasn't much good at praying. The other . . .

She could drive out of the camp. The trouble was, she didn't know what she'd do then. The bombs that hit Seattle and Portland shot the whole Pacific Northwest's economy right behind the ear. She could type; she'd been a clerk-typist at Boeing during the war. That was about the only kind of job this side of waiting tables or sweeping floors she could do.

She'd been glad to walk away from it when Bill got his rup-tured duck. Linda came along shortly afterwards.

If she drove away, she might find a job, not that there were many around to find. If she did, who would take care of Linda while she worked, though? Where would she stay while she looked for work? Her bank account had gone up in smoke with her bank.

All of those questions felt like more than she could handle. And so she drifted from day to day in what seemed both a no-place and a no-time. She was just kind of going along.

She wasn't the only one at the camp who felt that way. Some people accepted it and joked about it. Nobody ever found out who first tagged the place Camp Nowhere, but the name spread like wildfire as soon as someone came up with it. Seattle-Everett Refugee Encampment Number Three, the camp's official handle, couldn't compete. Jokes helped, a little.

They helped some people, anyhow. More and more vic-tims of radiation sickness went into the graveyard alongside the camp. It got bigger and bigger.

More and more inmates who killed themselves found final resting places there, too. Guns, nooses, and poison ran a close, if ghoulish, race for most popular method. There were no tall buildings to jump off, or that would have been another favored choice.

When you were stuck in limbo like this, were you really living? The ones who took the long road out evidently thought not. Marian wondered herself. But wonder was all she did, or aimed to do. Whatever happened to her, she also had Linda to worry about. She wasn't selfish enough to leave a little girl all alone in the world.

The suicides bewildered Fayvl and his friends. "I seen plenty worse places than this," Yitzkhak said. "Hardly any-body kill himself in those. They die, yeah—they die like flies. They get killed. They don't kill themselves. Is crazy."

"You saw," Moishe told him. "You didn't seen. You saw."

"*Afen yam,*" Yitzkhak said without heat. When Marian asked him what that meant, he pretended not to hear.

"People give up," Fayvl said, puzzlement in his voice. "I don't understand it. In the other camps, the Nazi camps, peo-ple didn't give up. They tried to keep going as long as they could."

"Not the Mussulmen," Moishe said. To Marian, he explained, "This is what we called the goners, the ones who would die soon and knew it and didn't care."

"But they were goners," Tabakman said. "They were starving, they were sick, they were beat up like you wouldn't believe, like you hope you never see. If somebody with radiation sickness, he wants out of his pain, that I understand. But we got plenty food. We don't got guards with Schmeissers and whips. Don't gotta work sixteen hours a day. Don't *gotta* work at all. So what's to do yourself in for?"

"Americans is soft," Yitzkhak said.

"Americans are soft," Moishe said. Having corrected the phrase, he tasted it in his mouth and nodded. "Americans *are* soft. They never have to go through the things we went through. They don't know what it's like."

"Hitler's soldiers didn't think they were soft," Marian said.

Fayvl Tabakman lit a cigarette. "I watched Americans shoot SS guards," he said after a puff or two. "I watched them herd Germans from the town next door through my camp so they couldn't say they never knew what Hitler did. You're right, Mrs. Staley. That was not soft." Another puff. "I weighed forty-one kilos then."

Whatever Marian had learned of the metric system in school, she'd long since forgotten. "How much is that in pounds?" she asked.

The three middle-aged Jews went back and forth, fingers flashing as they worked it out. Finally Tabakman said, "Ninety—about ninety, anyways. And I was one of the healthy ones."

He wasn't a big man. He probably didn't weigh more than a hundred fifty pounds now. At ninety, though . . . She'd seen photos from the liberated concentration camps. Who hadn't? Men with fingers like pencils, arms and legs like broomsticks, necks too thin and weak to hold up the heads with skin stretched drumhead tight over skulls. Women so starved you couldn't tell them from men. You didn't want to believe photos like that. You didn't want to think people could do that to other people. You didn't want to—but there were the pictures.

Marian glanced over at Linda, who was happily chomping on a cracker from her ration pack while the grownups talked grownup talk she didn't care about. Marian asked the question she'd wondered about as long as she'd known the cobbler: "Did you have a family . . . before the war?"

"My wife and me, we had a boy and a girl," he said, looking down at the table. "We were partisans in the woods for a while after the fighting started. When we got caught, the Germans sent us to Auschwitz. We got there, the SS doctor, he told them to go one way and me the other. And that was the last I saw of them."

It was the last anybody saw of them, he meant. They would have gone to the gas chambers. Some German engineer would have designed false showerheads that didn't do anything but lull the people herded into those rooms. Some German chemical firm would have sold the SS the poison gas. Some German funeral-supply company would have sold the crematoria, to deal with what the gas chambers turned out. How could you contemplate any of that without going mad?

Marian didn't want to contemplate it. It made all her unhappiness here seem like a small child's temper tantrum. Maybe Americans *were* soft. "I'm sorry," she whispered. "I'm so sorry."

"Thank you," he said, which was gracious of him. What was *I'm sorry* against the memory of watching your wife and children, everything that mattered most to you, go off to be murdered while you stood there unable to do a thing about it? How could you go on after that?

Fayvl had. Marian glanced at Moishe and Yitzkhak. Their faces were both closed, inward. What were they remembering? Nothing very different, she feared.

No wonder seeing her and Linda sometimes seemed to sadden Tabakman. They had to remind him of what the Nazis had stolen. She wondered what the Jew's wife and children had looked like before . . .

Her mouth tightened. She shook her head a little, as if she were warning Linda to behave herself (not that Linda needed warning right now—she was fine). Whatever she asked Fayvl Tabakman, she would never ask him that.


"Attention, Moscow is speaking." No, it wasn't Yuri Levitan, even if it was his signature opening. And it wasn't Moscow, either, even if it was Radio Moscow. Ihor Shevchenko had no idea where the signal originated. The Soviet Union was a vast place. There were plenty of possibilities.

He didn't think much of the new chief newsreader. Roman Amfiteatrov had an annoying southern accent. He pronounced the letter *O* as if it really sounded like an *o*, rather than with the *ah* sound most Russian-speakers used. Ihor had fought alongside a few men like that. The other Russians said they sounded like mooing cows. Russian wasn't quite Ihor's language, but that accent seemed funny to him, too.

Amfiteatrov went on, "Today is Tuesday, May the first, 1951—the glorious holiday of oppressed peasants and workers all over the world. Red Army victories continue unabated, the troops fighting with great courage and passion for Marshal Stalin. Milan has now fallen to the Fifth Guards Tank Army, which is proceeding westward in the direction of Turin. Fierce fighting in Germany has also yielded further advances against the Fascists and imperialists."

He named places in Italy. That meant there was some chance he was telling the truth about how things were going there. *Further advances,* by contrast, could mean anything. Or it could mean nothing. It could, and odds were it did. Anyone who got his news from Radio Moscow learned to read between the lines.

"In the North Atlantic, heroic Red Fleet submarines have struck heavy blows against the convoys sailing from America to its jackal lackey, England," Amfiteatrov mooed triumphantly. "Ships have been sent to the bottom and convoys scattered. The naval link between the continents is being broken."

Again, he was longer on claims than details. Ihor wondered how much the men in the submarines could actually see. He also wondered whether there actually were any men in submarines in, or under, the North Atlantic. No one here in the USSR would know if there weren't.

He glanced around the common room. The other *kolkhozniks* were all listening attentively. They all looked happy about the victories Roman Amfiteatrov reported. Well, so did Ihor. Whatever doubts you might have inside the fortress of your mind, your face couldn't show them. If it did, somebody would report you.

Fewer people had gone into the gulags after the end of the Great Patriotic War. Well, fewer Soviet citizens had. German and Japanese prisoners of war took up a good part of the slack. Had Ihor felt more sympathy for them, he might have wondered how many would ever see their motherlands again. Since he didn't, his attitude was more along the lines of *Better those sons of bitches than me.*

"The bestial American aggressors, still slavering to spill the blood of innocent and peace-loving Soviet citizens, have sent their terror bombers over Kharkov and Rostov-on-the-Don," Amfiteatrov intoned. "In the latter city, bombs fell on a child-rearing collective. More than a dozen young lives were snuffed out."

Ihor's first thought was that Kharkov (as a Ukrainian, he thought of it as Kharkiv) and Rostov-on-the-Don had already suffered enough, or more than enough. Both went back and forth between Hitlerite and Soviet forces twice in the last war. He knew not much of Kharkiv was left standing. He'd never been to Rostov-on-the-Don, but he didn't think it would be in tip-top shape, either.

As for the child-rearing collective . . . Radio Moscow had made those claims before, too. Maybe they were true, maybe not. Ihor wasn't in Kharkiv now. Since he wasn't, how could he know for sure?

He couldn't, and knew he couldn't. He did remember that, in the last war, each side claimed the other made a point of massacring women and children. In the last war, the Nazis had really done it. So had the men of the Red Army, when they'd advanced far enough to get their hands on German women and children. Revenge spiced killing the way caraway seeds spiced pickled cabbage.

In the last war, the Americans hadn't had that kind of reputation. If anything, they were supposed to be softies then, too slow to start the Second Front and too easy on the Fritzes. But they'd been allies then. Now they were the enemy, with Harry Truman playing the role of Hitler.

Roman Amfiteatrov blathered on. Truman had dropped atom bombs—a large number; Ihor didn't know just how many—on the Soviet Union's biggest cities. Even so, the *kolkhoznik* wasn't sure whether they or the Germans had killed more of its people. Hitler hadn't had the weapons Truman used, but no one could deny the force of his will. He kept the Germans fighting for a year and a half after more sensible people would have seen they had no chance.

Ihor consoled himself by remembering all the extra fighting had cost the Hitlerites millions of casualties they wouldn't have taken had they surrendered. The trouble was, it had cost the USSR even more.

He'd heard the Nazis had killed 20,000,000 Soviet citizens. He'd also heard they'd killed 30,000,000. He had no idea which number to believe. He suspected no one else did, either.

He also had no idea how a country that had lost so many people—whichever enormous number came closer to truth— was supposed to pick itself up, dust itself off, and go on about its business. With Hitler's savage regime shattered and prostrate at its feet, the USSR had actually done a decent job.

Now it was at war again. Now somewhere close to the same number of Soviet citizens, men and women who'd lived through the Great Patriotic War, were suddenly gone. So were the cities where they'd dwelt. More still died in the fighting in Germany and Italy.

Could any country that had lost somewhere between one in five and one in three of the people who'd been alive on 21 June 1941 stand on its own two feet here ten years later and still be a country? The USSR was doing it. How the USSR was doing it, Ihor had no idea.

He glanced over at Anya. She was chatting with the *kolkhoz* chairman's wife. She must have said something funny, because Irina Hapochkova laughed till her plump cheeks turned even redder than usual. Anya'd almost gone to Kiev. She'd almost become part of the monstrous, murderous statistics. But she hadn't, and because she hadn't Ihor's life still meant something to him.

Now Amfiteatrov was talking about how foresters and factory hands had smashed production norms all over the Soviet Union. The factory hands labored in places like Irkutsk, which was hard for American bombers to reach, and in towns like Vyazma, which wasn't big enough for the bombers to waste A-bombs on it.

"And finally," the newsreader said, "on this great day Comrade Stalin, the beloved leader of the people's vanguard of revolutionary socialism, assures Soviet workers and peasants that, despite all the troubles we have had to overcome on the road to true Communism, the world—the entire world— will see it, and sooner than most people expect. The struggle continues. The struggle will be victorious. So the dialectic assures us. Thank you, and good evening."

"Moo!" Three different people in the common room said the same thing at the same time. Everyone giggled, even though Radio Moscow followed the news with Shostakovich's Seventh Symphony, the one he wrote in response to the Hitlerites' siege of Leningrad. Normally, you wouldn't want to laugh while that music poured out of the speaker.

Normally . . . but not this minute. Everyone in the *kolkhoz* lived in the shadow of things more terrible, or at any rate more instantaneously terrible, than Shostakovich had known while penning his great symphony. And when you lived in that shadow, you laughed when you could, to help hold it at bay. Any excuse would do. A newsreader mouthing silly slogans with a silly accent was as much as anyone needed.

Once upon a time, people had believed in the silly slogans. People had died for their sake, they'd believed with such passion. They'd gone to the gulag for them.

In the world of true Communism, there would be no gulags. Ihor chuckled again. That was pretty funny, too.

# 21

*WHY AM I HERE?* Istvan Szolovits wondered. The question was worth asking, on any number of levels. What kind of answer you got depended on how you asked it, which was true of most questions. A believing religious person (a dangerous thing to be in the Hungarian People's Republic, but not quite illegal as long as you didn't make a public fuss about it) would say he was here because God had placed him here as part of the divine plan. An existentialist would haughtily declare that such questions had no meaning.

Istvan knew less than he would have liked about existentialism. The Horthy regime had frowned on such decadent fripperies. So did the Red regime that took its place a couple of years after the war ended. But for those couple of years, Hungary had been Russian-occupied but not yet officially Communist. The new notions from Paris got in and . . . They were exciting, till suddenly you couldn't mention them any more if you knew what was good for you.

But for Istvan right now, *Why am I here?* meant *Why am I in a muddy trench in the middle of Germany with the Americans raining artillery down on my head?* In a way, he knew the answer. His own country's secret police would have tortured him or killed him if he hadn't let himself be conscripted. Their Russian overlords would have tortured or killed them had they shirked.

A big one—probably a 155—slammed into the ground ten or twenty meters in front of the trenches. Everything shook. Blast made breathing hard for a moment. A little closer and it could have killed, sometimes without leaving a mark.

Fragments screeched overhead. Mud flew into the air and thumped down in the trench.

He cowered in the dugout he'd scraped in the forward wall. He'd shored it up with wood the best way he knew how. If the best way he knew how wasn't good enough, it would collapse on him, and that would be that. A little closer and it might have collapsed anyhow.

In the dugout next to his, a Pole told his rosary beads and gabbled out Hail Marys and Our Fathers. Istvan recognized the Latin. He'd studied some. The Pole's pronunciation seemed strange to him, but he wasn't about to say so. He doubted the Polish soldier would have appreciated Latin lessons from a Christ-killing clipcock.

Any Jew who lived in Hungary heard such endearments. Any Jew who lived in Hungary while the Arrow Cross maniacs did Hitler's bidding heard them screamed in his face. Very often, they were some of the last things he ever heard.

The Communists didn't call Jews names like that. Several big shots of the Hungarian People's Republic, including Matyas Rakosi, who ruled the country, *were* Jews—exiles returned from Russia or survivors like Istvan. They were not, of course, observant Jews or even indifferent Jews like Istvan. They were ready to go after their own kind, knowing Stalin would come after them if they didn't. They didn't talk about Christ-killers. They talked about rootless cosmopolites instead. It sounded much more scientific. In practice? Six of one, half a dozen of the other.

Along with the heavy stuff, the Americans were throwing mortars around. Istvan had quickly learned to hate mortars. You hardly knew the bombs were coming in till they burst, and they could fall straight down into a foxhole or trench.

They could, and this one did. It burst right behind the Pole in the dugout next to Istvan's. The boom shook him. A fragment of hot metal buried itself in the mud a few centimeters in front of his nose. Another one, smaller, drew a bleeding line across the back of his hand. And one more, smaller still, clinked off his helmet. Like most people who'd seen both, he liked the German model better than its Soviet counterpart. But the Red Army lid did what it was made to do. Nobody's helmet would stop a bullet. Fragments? Yes.

He was so stunned—and so deafened by the near miss—he needed a couple of seconds to hear someone screaming, and a couple of seconds more to realize it was the Pole who'd sheltered in the dugout next to his. Though other bombs were still falling all around, Szolovits scrambled out of his shelter to do what he could for the foreigner who was here in a war no more his than the Hungarian soldier's.

"Oh," Istvan said, and then, "Oh, God." He'd already seen some things he'd be trying to forget for the rest of his life. This was worse than all of them put together.

He didn't want to look. He wanted retroactively not to have looked. It was that bad. It was . . . he didn't know what it was. He'd never dreamt even iron and explosives fired with bad intent could do—that—to a man.

Worst of all, despite mutilating the Pole as ingeniously as any torturer might have, the mortar bomb hadn't killed him. He wailed and moaned and shrieked and clutched at himself, trying to put himself back together. He wouldn't be in one piece again till the Christian Judgment Day at the earliest.

When the Pole wasn't screaming, he was shouting and crying out in a language Istvan didn't speak. Some of that was prayer in Latin mixed with Polish. Some was—Istvan didn't know what it was. But if he'd been torn apart like that, he would have been howling for his mother.

If he'd been torn apart like that, he would have wanted something else, too. He would have given it to a tormented dog smashed by a tram. You could do it *to* a dog, though. With a man, you ought to make sure it was all right first.

Istvan pulled the bayonet off his belt and held it in front of the Pole's wild blue eyes. *"Willst du?"* he asked. *Do you want me to?* German was the only language the two of them might share.

He didn't know the poor bastard spoke German. Even if the Pole did, he might be too far gone to follow now.

When his gashed mouth opened, more blood dribbled from the corner. But he choked out three clear words: *"Ja. Bitte. Danke."* He tried to make the sign of the cross, but his right hand wasn't attached any more.

*"Ego te absolvo, filii,"* Istvan said. He wasn't a priest, or even a Christian. He hoped the words would do the Pole a little good anyhow. In all the time since the beginning of the world, few men had been in unction this extreme. Not watching what he did, Istvan cut the fellow's throat.

The screaming stopped. Szolovits drew a deep breath. He plunged the bayonet into the dirt again and again to get the blood off it. It was a tool with all kinds of uses, though rarely as a spearpoint on the end of a rifle, its nominal purpose. He'd never thought he'd use it for *that,* though.

An unexpected hand on his shoulder made him jerk and start to use it as a fighting knife. No Americans in the trenches, though. It was Sergeant Gergely. "He shut up," Gergely said. "You shut him up?"

"Uh-huh." Istvan nodded miserably.

"Way to go," the noncom said. "Take care of it for me, too, if I get all ripped up like that."

"Once was bad enough, and he was a stranger," Szolovits said.

"You'd do it for a stranger but not for somebody you know? *Lofasz a seggedbe!*" The Magyar curse meant *A horse's cock up your ass!* Hungarians had come into Europe off the steppe, and their language still showed it a thousand years later.

"Are you volunteering, Sergeant?" Istvan asked. As soon as he spoke, he realized the joke might be too strong. But he was still feeling the horror of what he'd just done, and wanted to exorcise it any way he could. He'd also begun to suspect— though he wasn't sure yet—a human being might lurk somewhere under Gergely's thick, highly polished steel armor.

And the veteran noncom didn't get angry. He let out a harsh chuckle. "Not right now, thanks," he said. "If that day comes, you'll know. I'll be screaming the way that poor damned Pole was. Am I right? Did you try to shrive him before you put him out of his misery?"

"I didn't think it would do any harm." Istvan sounded more sheepish, more embarrassed, than he'd thought he would.

"My guess is, you did him as much good as a priest would've," the sergeant said. A good Marxist-Leninist was almost bound to say that. But you didn't have to follow the Communist line to feel that way. Anyone who'd been through a couple of wars and listened to too many people die in ugly ways might come to think it was true. More and more, Istvan was coming to think it was himself.


Boris Gribkov eyed the Tu-4 under camouflage netting at the field outside of Leningrad. "You know, we're lucky no real Americans have looked us over in either one of our planes," he remarked.

"Why?" Vladimir Zorin asked. "They look as much like B-29s as real B-29s do."

"But a lot of the real B-29s have naked girls on the nose, to remind the crews what they're fighting for. Not all of them, but a lot," Gribkov said. "I bet our *maskirovka* guys would have enjoyed their work more if they'd given us one of those."

"I would've enjoyed it more, too," the copilot said with a grin. "But I can't see the guys who give the orders telling them to slap one on."

"Mm, no," Boris said. The commissars who gave such orders were stiff-necked, strait-laced. . . . They were prudes, was what they were. They didn't have much fun, and they didn't believe anyone else should, either.

Leonid Tsederbaum said, "Our fighter pilots would sometimes paint a swastika on the nose for every Nazi plane they shot down."

"That's true," Boris said. "And some bomber crews would paint a bomb there for each mission they flew."

"Uh-huh." Tsederbaum nodded. "So I was thinking—maybe we could paint two cities on the nose of our beast here."

He owned a formidable deadpan. He sounded so calm, so reasonable, that the pilot started to nod before he really heard what Tsederbaum said. Then he made a horrible face and exclaimed, "Fuck your mother!"

"I love you, too, sir." Tsederbaum blew him a kiss.

Two cities. The Jew had asked him if he wanted to bomb London or Paris or Rome. He hadn't had to rip the heart out of a metropolis from which a great empire had been ruled for centuries. That was luck, if you liked. He had smaller places on his conscience. Seattle and Bordeaux didn't matter nearly so much to the people who didn't live in them. If you *did* happen to live in a city where an A-bomb went off, you wouldn't be happy afterwards. The best, the only, defense was to be somewhere else when that happened.

And if you were on the other end of the bomb, the only defense was not thinking about what you did in service to your country and to the world proletariat in arms. Gribkov remembered that the *Stalin* hadn't been able to land the crew at Petropavlovsk. He remembered the craters scarring the cityscapes of Moscow and Leningrad. He *was* defending his country.

The Americans who'd bombed Soviet cities were defending their country, too. A few of the Hitlerites who'd got hanged or shot for running death camps had killed more people than those Americans and their Soviet counterparts. A few, but not many.

That wasn't such a good thought to have. Gribkov wished he hadn't had it. Well, that was why they made vodka. One of the things vodka did was blot out thoughts you didn't feel like having. They'd eventually come back, but with Russians and the way they drank *eventually* could take a while.

There were also other ways to blot out those ugly thoughts. Hearing the base air-raid siren could do the trick, for instance. Pilot, copilot, and navigator looked at one another. Then they all started to run.

Maybe from force of habit, the construction crew that ran up this field had dug trenches by the quarters and others alongside the runways. Gribkov, Zorin, and Tsederbaum dashed for a runwayside trench. Tsederbaum was taller and skinnier than his Russian crewmates. He might have broken the Olympic record for the hundred meters. In any race, though, they would have won silver and bronze.

Tsederbaum leaped down into the trench. Gribkov and Zorin followed. They all crouched in the mud, careless of their uniforms. The trenches were there to protect base personnel from bomb fragments and from strafing fighters' machine guns. They'd done that well enough during the Great Patriotic War. They could again—if they were dealing with bomb fragments and bullets.

If, on the other hand, a B-29 was buzzing ten or eleven kilometers up in the air and dropped an A-bomb here, all this was nothing but a joke. Gribkov didn't think the Americans would send a B-29 into Soviet airspace in broad daylight. He wouldn't have wanted to fly a daylight mission against, say, England. But you did what they told you to do, not what you wanted to do.

And the fear remained. The fear, if anything, got worse. He'd dropped A-bombs. He'd seen the horrible gouges they tore in Soviet cities. So he knew what they did. If one did that here, he could only hope everything ended before he even knew the end had begun.

Jet engines screamed as fighters scrambled at some nearby airstrip. Looking up, Gribkov watched the MiG-15s climb almost vertically. That kind of flight was so different from the Tu-4's, it was almost as if he were watching a flying saucer perform. In the Tu-4, you counted yourself lucky to get off the ground at all, however slowly you did it.

The MiGs could reach a B-29's ceiling. They might even reach it fast enough to keep the Americans from doing whatever they wanted to do. *They might,* Boris thought. It wasn't a prayer. It wasn't that far from one, either.

Those jet banshee wails dopplered out as the MiG-15s rose against high-altitude invaders. No sooner had they begun to fade, though, than Gribkov also heard piston-engine growls.

He frowned. Before he could say anything, Leonid Tsederbaum exclaimed, "Those aren't ours!"

And they weren't. They were half a dozen American Mustangs. The plane had been developed as a long-range escort fighter. It had protected U.S. bombers all the way from England to Berlin. Mount a small bomb under each wing and it turned into a long-range fighter-bomber.

The Mustangs roared by low overhead. They dropped their bombs. They shot up the field. They zoomed away. They were gone.

*"Bozehmoi!"* Vladimir Zorin sounded shaken to the core. "I thought I was back in Lithuania in 1944, with Focke-Wulfs strafing my strip."

"If the MiGs can spot the Americans, they'll dive on them," Tsederbaum said. "Mustangs are fast, but not that fast."

"I wonder how many missions those Mustang pilots flew during the last war," Boris said. By the way they carried out this one, they had plenty of experience. Soviet fighter pilots with that kind of expertise were up at the front, not defending an airfield far behind it.

Boris stood up. The Americans had left holes in some of the runways. The Tu-4s wouldn't be taking off from here till people fixed them. Around the farmhouse that housed base personnel, everybody was running every which way. Well, everybody who could run. The Mustangs hadn't left the farmhouse unscathed.

"You know something?" Zorin said. "We were lucky to be where we were when the Americans came. If we'd been over there, we might not've made it to the trenches."

"It's all luck," Tsederbaum said. "Good luck, bad luck—what else is there?"

"The dialectic," Boris Gribkov said. "There's always the dialectic."

"Well, yes, Comrade Pilot." Tsederbaum smiled so charmingly, for a moment Boris thought he was watching a movie actor. "You're right. Absolutely. There's always the dialectic."

*Is he agreeing with me? Or is he mocking me, calling me an uncultured fool of a peasant?* Gribkov wondered. He wasn't sure. Leonid Tsederbaum left no room for anything so bourgeois as certainty. Then the pilot thought, *Don't you have more important things to worry about?* Deciding he did, he figured the navigator could wait.

The Canal Zone was American territory. Harry Truman couldn't imagine giving it back to Panama. The greasers down here could no more run or protect the Panama Canal than they could fly.

As the President stepped out of the *Independence* and into Panama's steamy tropical heat, he scowled. It wasn't as if the United States had done such a heads-up job of protecting the Canal. One bang, in fact, and there was no Panama Canal to protect any more.

"Welcome, Mr. President," Arnulfo Arias said. The President of Panama was a stout man of about fifty. He spoke English almost as well as Truman did; he'd studied medicine at Harvard.

"Thank you very much, Mr. President." Truman held out his hand. Arias took it. Holding the clasp, they turned toward the photographers and plastered political smiles on their faces. Flashbulbs popped. When the shutterbugs were happy, the two leaders let go of each other. As they did, Truman spoke in a low voice: "I'm sorry as hell about this."

"Yes. So are we." Arias shrugged. "Well, we can talk more about that after you've seen the disaster for yourself."

It was as much a disaster for Panama as it was for the USA. If anything, it was a worse disaster for Panama than for the United States. Panama had no reason to exist except for the Panama Canal. Without the Canal, there would have been no Panama. Up till the turn of the century, it had been a province of Colombia—not always a perfectly contented province, but also not one with secession on its mind.

Then the Colombian government refused the excavation

terms the American government offered. With amazing speed, the free nation of Panama sprang from Teddy Roosevelt's forehead the way Minerva sprang from Jupiter's. The United States recognized it almost before it declared its own independence. Colombia's choice was accepting the inevitable or going to war with the USA.

Thus the Panama Canal was born. And now, not quite half a century later, the Panama Canal had died. If any young Colombian lieutenants then were old Colombian generals now, they had to be snickering behind their hands.

A Cadillac convertible drove out onto the runway. "I will take you to the Presidential Palace," Arias said. "After the luncheon there, we will go the the Canal Zone so you can examine the damage for yourself."

Truman didn't want to go to the Presidential Palace. He didn't want to have lunch with a bunch of Panamanian big shots. That was all a waste of time. He wanted to get up there and see what the damned Russians had done. But, like it or not, he had to be diplomatic. "Sounds fine, Mr. President," he lied. "I'm at your service."

Secret Service men who'd flown down with Truman and Panamanian soldiers climbed into other cars. They made a small motorcade that wound through the streets of Panama City. A few people stood on the sidewalks waving American and Panamanian flags. If Arias' henchmen hadn't got them out there, Truman would have been amazed. That was one of the oldest ward-heeler's tricks in the world.

And one of the oldest assassin's tricks in the world was to attack from a high place. The guards wouldn't stop a rifleman or someone with a grenade if he popped out of a third-story window in one of the old Spanish-style buildings. Truman knew it but didn't let it worry him.

The Presidential Palace lay northeast of Independence Square, and took up a whole block. They'd declared independence in the cathedral in the square. The USA was in the background when they did it, but not very far in the background.

Big white egrets swaggered across the marble-floored palace lobby. Smiling, President Arias said, "The nickname for the building is *Palacio de las Garzas*—the Palace of the Herons."

Smiling back, President Truman replied, "None of those at

the White House. We have lobbyists instead, lobbyists and other vultures."

Like Arias himself, the dignitaries he'd invited to eat with Truman were educated men fluent in English. Some of them showed a better understanding of both sides' strategy in the war than most of the Congressmen Truman had conferred with. The lunch was excellent: lobster chunks simmered in spiced coconut milk and served with rice and beans. Rum flowed freely.

Not too much later than he'd planned, Truman got back into the Cadillac with Arias for the trip to the blasted lock. The Canal's geography was confusing; till you studied a map, you weren't likely to realize that the Caribbean opening lay west of the one on the Pacific.

A good highway ran from Panama City to Colón. It had gone on to Gatún, but Gatún was no more. Neither was Lake Gatún, some of which had boiled to steam and more of which poured out into the Caribbean after the bomb hidden in the *Panathenaikos* went off. Every drop that poured through the crater became radioactive as it went. Eventually, the Caribbean would dilute the poison till it didn't matter any more, but how eventually eventually was, Truman didn't know. Every alleged expert he talked to gave him a different answer.

Making sure the Japs didn't wreck the Panama Canal had been one of America's worries during World War II. Making sure the Russians didn't was a high priority this time around. High priority or not, the Russians had done it.

"My fault," he told Arnulfo Arias. "We were supposed to defend against this kind of savagery. We were supposed to, but we dropped the ball. I'm sorry, sir. I don't know what else to tell you."

"I have heard that you are a man who says what is in his heart," the President of Panama replied. "Now I find for myself that it is so."

"And you find that it doesn't do you one whole hell of a lot of good, hey?" Truman said. "I promise you this, Mr. President: after we've won the war, we *will* put the Panama Canal back together again. It's too important to leave it like—this."

"To the whole world, and to Panama," Arias said.

"Yes, and to Panama," Truman agreed. Without the Canal, Panama might as well go back to being part of Colombia.

The only drawback to that was, Colombia probably wouldn't want it.

President Arias had other things on his mind. "How long will the war go on before the United States wins it, Mr. President? How much of the world will be left in one piece by the time it ends?"

Those were both good questions. They were much better questions than Truman wished they were, in fact. "I'm not the only one who has something to say about that, you know, your Excellency," he said. "Stalin does, too. If the Russians pull out of western Germany and Italy and if the Red Chinese pull out of South Korea, we have nothing left to fight about."

"Yes, sir." Arias studied him with wide, sad eyes. "And what do you think the chances of that are?"

"Pretty poor," Truman said. "If he wanted to do that, he would've done it by now, and made Mao do it, too. But there is a way to get a man who doesn't want to do something to do it anyhow. If you keep hitting him, after a while he'll do what you tell him to do to get you to stop. That's how we finally made the Nazis and the Japs give up. Sooner or later, we'll make Stalin quit, too."

"Sooner or later, yes." Arias waved at the crater that marked the ruination of one of the greatest engineering feats mankind had ever brought off. "But in the meantime, Mr. President, Stalin keeps hitting back. He is still trying to make you quit."

"Well, it won't work," Truman snapped. "Korea won't go all Red, and if Joe Stalin doesn't like that, he can stick it in his pipe and smoke it. Western Europe won't be all Red, either."

"He's hurt you—not just here, but in your own country," Arias said.

"We've hurt him worse. We'll go on doing it as long as we have to," Truman answered. He fanned himself with his Panama hat. It was muggier than even a Missouri man who'd done time in Washington was used to. As an old haberdasher, he knew perfectly well that Panama hats came from Ecuador. He wore one anyhow; names counted, too. He went on, "In the last war, Admiral Halsey said the Japanese language would be spoken only in hell. Japan surrendered before we had to arrange that. If the Soviet Union doesn't, Satan will get himself a lot of new Russian customers."

Arnulfo Arias smiled. The expression slipped as he realized Truman meant it.

Wilf Davies walked into the Owl and Unicorn and said, "I'll take a pint of your best bitter, Daisy, if you'd be so kind."

"Well, I might have enough left to spare you one," she said, and winked at the mechanic with the hook where his left hand should have been.

"Here now, you watch that!" Wilf exclaimed as she worked the tap. "Anybody sees you and tells my missus, she'll think you're tryin' to lure me away from her."

The pub had just opened. They were the only ones in the snug. Wilf often stopped in for an early pint. Nobody but the two of them could have seen the wink. Daisy said, "Who knows? I could do worse."

"Don't go puttin' ideas in my head, dear," he said as he set money on the bar. They weren't likely to be practical ideas, not when he was happily married and old enough to be her father. Maybe he got them anyhow.

The worst of it was, she'd only been half kidding. Some of the RAF and USAF men who came into the Owl and Unicorn reckoned themselves God's gift to womankind. They acted as if she ought to fall into their arms right there in the snug—never mind wasting time going upstairs to bed.

You couldn't even tell those blighters anything that would dent their splendid opinion of themselves. The nicer ones would call you stuck-up if you did. The others would call you things that started with frigid bitch and went downhill from there.

Davies took a pull at the pint and smacked his lips. "That's good," he said. "That's mighty good." He drank again. "I've got a question for you, dear."

"What kind of question?" Daisy felt a certain small alarm. Was he going to get difficult, after so long being not just a customer but a friend?

But what he asked was, "Do you know how long a metal part stays radioactive and how dangerous that is?"

She stared at him. "Why in God's name d'you think I'd know something like that?"

"Well . . ." He looked sheepish, and stared down at his half-empty mug. "You've got those Yank officers comin' in here all the time. I wondered if maybe one of 'em talked about it, or somethin'." Embarrassment thickened his accent.

"Not a word," she said. "Not a single, solitary word. Why would you care about a crazy thing like that, anyhow?" She suddenly pointed a forefinger at him. It wasn't quite Balzac's *J'accuse!,* but it came close. "You're getting auto parts out of Norwich!"

"Hush!" He held his own forefinger up to his lips. "I've done no such illegal thing—not so they can prove it, anyhow. But I have me some friends who have some friends who can lay their hands on this, that, or the other thing—the kind of stuff what's hard to come by these days. I ask 'em no questions, and they tell me no lies."

Daisy wondered how outraged she should be, and whether she should be outraged at all. Of course scavengers would sneak into Norwich, never mind the Army and Scotland Yard. Autos at the edge of the blast area were more likely to have survived, or at least to be salvageable, than their owners were. You couldn't put a dead man's kidney or spleen on the market. A dead Bentley's pistons or mudguards were a different story.

"You might get yourself one of those Geiger counters," Daisy said. "If a part makes it click too much, don't buy it or don't use it."

"There's a good notion!" He looked at her admiringly. "I don't much fancy putting some gears in the gear train and poisoning my customers with 'em. There's the sort of thing that gives your business a bad name."

"Poisoning yourself whilst you're working on the repairs, too," Daisy said.

Wilf blinked. "Hadn't thought of that. Should have, shouldn't I?"

"I daresay!" she answered. *Am I killing myself on the job here?* would have been the first thing she worried about. She hoped it would, at any rate. She lit a cigarette.

The mechanic pushed more silver at her. "Have a half on me," he said. "You might just have saved my bacon there."

Daisy didn't care for beer so early in the day. But Wilf meant it kindly; she knew that. She filled one of the smaller mugs at the tap. Savoring the bitter, she said, "This *is* a nice barrel, isn't it?"

"You're the publican, sweetheart, so what else are you going to say?" Wilf returned. She made a face at him. He drank again. "I'm not pouring it down the sink myself, you see."

"You'd better not," Daisy said, and then, "Would you like another?"

He shook his head. "I'd like one fine, but I've got work back at the garage. I have a pint, it means naught. I have two pints, I'm liable to be clumsy and stupid and make a hash of what should be simple."

"Do what you need to do," Daisy said. That was her own motto; she could hardly resent it when someone else felt the same way.

Bruce McNulty came into the pub that evening. It was a noisier, busier, livelier place than it had been earlier in the day. Even so, Daisy asked him about how long metal parts stayed radioactive.

"That's a funny question," the American flyer said.

"A friend wondered," she told him.

"A friend?" he echoed, a certain edge to his voice.

"From in town," Daisy said, nodding. Then she realized the edge had to be jealousy. She felt like clomping the Yank over the head with a pint mug. Taking a deep breath instead, she went on, "For one thing, Mr. McNulty, Wilf was born before the turn of the century and came back from the First World War with a hook doing duty for one hand. And for another thing, *Mr.* McNulty, even if he were our age and handsome as a film star, that would be none of your bloody business." One more deep breath. "Am I plain enough, or shall I draw you pictures?"

He turned sunset red. She'd hit him too hard. Naturally, she saw that only after she'd gone and done it. "You're pretty plain, all right," he mumbled.

"Good," she said. Maybe briskness would help. "Do you know the answer to my friend's question, then? He wants to be able to use auto parts from, ah, around Norwich, but he doesn't want to hurt himself or any of the people whose cars they go into."

"Black-market parts. Stuff the buzzards bring home in their claws," McNulty said. To Daisy, a buzzard was a hawk; to the Yank, it seemed to mean vulture. She nodded again anyhow. That was what Wilf was dealing in, sure enough. Bruce McNulty shrugged and spread his hands. "Afraid I can't tell you—or even your *friend*." His mouth quirked. "I just deliver the junk. I don't know what all it does after it goes kablooie. How radioactive stuff gets, how long it stays that way"—he shrugged once more—"it's not my department."

"Fair enough. Thanks." After a beat, Daisy added, "I'm sorry I barked at you."

"Uh-*huh*. Listen, let me have one for the road, will you?" McNulty set a couple of shillings on the bar. He waved away change and drained the pint at one long pull. Then he said, "See you around, kiddo. It was . . . interesting, anyway." He tipped his cap and walked out into the night.

Only after he was gone did she understand that he wasn't coming back. Wherever he did his drinking from now on, it wouldn't be at the Owl and Unicorn. *Well, damn,* she thought as she drew another American a pint. She hadn't meant to offend him. She'd just tried to get an answer for Wilf. Things spiraled out of control from there. He'd had no cause to get jealous. None. But why was she so sorry he was gone?

**22**

SOMEWHERE OUT THERE, RUSSIAN tanks were prowling. Gustav Hozzel listened to the filling-shaking rumble of their big diesels. He could hear them, but he couldn't see them.

He was as ready for them as he could be when he did see them. Half a dozen Molotov cocktails stood on the floor of the second-story Dortmund flat, under the shattered window. Gasoline and motor oil and some soap flakes, all stirred together, filled the bottles. Each one had a wick. And Gustav had a Zippo. He'd got it from an Ami for some extra grenades. He admired tools that worked all the time. The American lighter qualified.

He sneaked a look out the window. Still no T-54s in sight. The brick façade of the block of flats across the street had fallen down onto the sidewalk and into the street. He could see into all the apartments over there. That would have been more interesting if fire hadn't gutted the building.

One or two 100mm rounds of HE would bring down the façade on this place, too. They might also bring down the rest of the building, and all the defenders in it. Just the same, he didn't think the Ivans were enjoying themselves in Dortmund, or anywhere else in the Ruhr. Street fighting inside cities melted armies like fat in a hot frying pan. Hitler'd discovered that the hard way in Stalingrad. Now it was Stalin's turn.

A heavy machine gun barked. It was a Russian gun, not an American M-2. Some T-54s mounted them on the turret as antiaircraft weapons. And just because they were billed like that didn't mean they weren't useful all kinds of other ways.

The Soviet machine gun powered its mechanism by gas; the American, by the force of recoil. A soldier hit by a 12.7mm slug from either was unlikely to care about the difference—or anything else, ever again.

Gustav glanced out once more, just in time to watch a Red Army soldier duck into a doorway. Another Russian stuck his head up from behind a jeep that some explosion had flipped onto its back. He ducked down as Gustav was ducking back. Gustav didn't think he'd been spotted.

"They're coming!" he called. His fellow emergency militiamen swore. Whenever you thought you could relax for a little while, the damned Ivans started trying to kill you again.

Another quick look showed more Russians sliding forward. Gustav was sure men he couldn't see were moving up with them. Russians disappeared into the woodwork like cockroaches if you gave them half a chance—even a quarter of a chance.

That diesel growl got louder and came closer, too. He nodded to himself. In the open, tanks trampled and smashed through enemy fieldworks so the foot soldiers could follow. But this wasn't the open. Dortmund stood at the eastern edge of one of the most heavily built-up areas in the world. The rules changed when you fought in terrain like this.

Tanks clattering down the streets of Dortmund without infantry guards wouldn't last five minutes. Somebody would shoot a bazooka round into the thin side armor or throw a grenade through an open hatch. Those Red Army foot sloggers were here to clear away the nasty somebodies so the armor could advance.

This particular tank took out the corner of a building when it turned on to the street where Gustav waited. The rest of the building fell down, not that the crew cared. The tank wasn't a T-54 medium. It was a heavy, an IS-3 (the IS stood for Iosef Stalin). It was, in a word, a monster.

It had much thicker armor than a T-54, sloped even more radically. The damned thing carried a 122mm gun, a piece of artillery that wouldn't have been out of place on a destroyer. No wonder even Tiger crews had treated Stalin tanks with respect in the last war. Stalins weren't fast enough to keep up with T-54s in open country, but all that armor gave them extra protection in city fighting like this.

The commander stood up, head and shoulders out of the open cupola hatch. He wanted to be able to see what was going on. He was a good tank commander, a brave man. Gustav could have potted him with his submachine gun, but held his fire. He was after bigger game.

A Russian foot soldier craned his neck up at the block of flats across the street, the one with the missing front wall. He turned to look at the building Gustav was holed up in. If he and his buddies decided to search this one, the Germans on the ground floor would open up on them. Gustav's chance would vanish.

If any of the men in here opened up on the Russians now . . . But these guys weren't rookies. They'd all learned their business the last time around. They had fire discipline. They knew how to wait.

Here came the Stalin, right past the block of flats at a slow walk. Gustav picked up one of his wicked bottles. He flicked the Zippo. First time, every time. He lit the wick and chucked the Molotov cocktail out through the glassless window.

The hatch on top of the cupola wasn't very wide. He needed to throw well enough to make a basketball player proud. The shot wasn't easy, but, because he was so close, it was a long way from impossible. If he missed, he'd spill fire down the outside of the turret, and the Stalin would probably keep working. It would also probably hose down the second floor here with machine-gun bullets. Better not to miss, then.

And Gustav didn't. The tank commander must have seen the bottle in the air. He ducked. Half a second later, he would have slammed the lid shut. In that half second, the Molotov cocktail followed him down the hatch and broke.

Smoke started pouring out of the turret. Tanks carried fire extinguishers inside, but would a startled crew have the presence of mind to grab one and use it? Even if it got used, would it kill the fire? Not just the gasoline-oil-and-soap mixture in the wine bottle would be burning in there. All kinds of things inside the fighting compartment could catch: paint, insulation, lubricating grease. Pretty soon, the ammunition in there would start cooking off.

But the Russian tank crew didn't wait around for that. As soon as they saw the extinguisher wouldn't stop the blaze, they bailed out. Two of them had their coveralls on fire. Gustav squeezed off a couple of short bursts at them as they rolled in the street trying to smother the flames.

He hit one man—he thought it was the tank commander. The other Ivan scrambled into shelter behind the Stalin.

More and more smoke belched from the stricken tank. Machine-gun ammo went off with cheerful popping noises. Pretty soon, the massive shells the main armament flung would go off, too. All that steel, though, would keep the explosions on the inside from hurting the tankmen on the outside.

Foot soldiers started shooting into the room from which Gustav had done his dirty work. The only trouble with that was, he wasn't in there any more. He knew they'd pock the back wall with as many bullet holes as they could. In their boots, he would have done the same thing. What else would you do, with a rifle or a PPD in your hand?

Some of the other Germans in the block of flats started shooting at the Russian infantry. The Russians gave back the fire. That didn't worry Gustav, except in the limited sense that he always worried some about getting wounded or killed. The important thing was, the Red Army wouldn't be bringing any more tanks up this street.

*Wham!* The block of flats jerked as if some giant had kicked an upper story. *Wham!* It shuddered again, convulsively. Those were two HE rounds from a 122mm gun. The Stalin had had a friend trailing it, and the friend was cranky. One more might bring the place down.

*Wham!* That one almost brought Gustav down. The other heavy tank had lowered its cannon. Another way to flatten a building was to knock out the props so the top fell in.

Coughing, deafened, ghost-white with plaster dust, Gustav didn't wait around for another love tap. He got the hell out of there. He could fight the war from the next building over. If the Russians wanted this one so much, they were welcome to it, as far as he was concerned.

In the last war, he might have won the Knight's Cross for killing a heavy tank with a Molotov cocktail. Here, he got to stay alive. That was a better decoration, in case anybody wanted to know what he thought.

"What's the trouble up there, Comrade Sergeant?" Pavel Gryzlov asked. "How come we aren't going forward any more?"

"I'll have a look, Pasha," Konstantin Morozov said. He flipped the cupola hatch open and stuck his head up to see what was going on. He knew he needed to keep doing that.

He also knew Dortmund was full of snipers. In the last war, Nazi snipers had loved blowing tank commanders' heads off. So had Soviet snipers. Things wouldn't have changed since.

He ducked back down. "Something's burning, dammit," he said. "I don't know for sure it's a killed tank, but it's that kind of smoke. And a killed tank in a place like this means a traffic jam."

"I don't like standing still in the middle of a place like this," the gunner said. "Too many bad things can happen."

"I know," Konstantin said. "But unless I crawl up the back of the next tank ahead and start humping it, what am I supposed to do?"

A bullet clanked against the tank's side armor. The people who'd fired it could do that from now till doomsday without hurting anything. But, where there were riflemen, there were liable to be pricks with bazookas. And a bazooka wouldn't clang off the armor. The shaped charge in the rocket's nose would burn through.

With a sigh, Morozov took his PPD off the brackets where it hung and opened the cupola hatch again. He glanced to the left, the direction from which the shot had come. All he saw were ruins. Like the other German cities he'd come through, Dortmund seemed far richer than a Soviet town of the same size. The shops looked fancier. They'd been looted, but even what was left was of higher quality than anything you could get back home. All the cars Morozov saw were abandoned hulks, but there were many more to see than there would have been on a Soviet street.

Dortmund had been heavily bombed during the last war. The Red Army and the imperialists were still banging heads for it now. Not all the old damage was repaired. It had new damage to go with it. The buildings still put to shame the cheap concrete blocks of flats that sprouted like toadstools near the statue of Lenin in any Soviet town's main square.

A foot soldier in Red Army khaki came out of one of those battered buildings. He carried a Kalashnikov in one hand and a bottle in the other. By the way he wobbled as he walked, he'd put a serious dent in the contents of the bottle. A silly smile on his face, he nodded to Morozov. "How the fuck are you, Comrade Tank Commander?"

"Well, I'm here," Morozov answered. "Looks like I'm stuck here, too, till they clear away whatever's on fire up ahead."

"That's a shame!" The infantryman was drunk enough so it seemed tragic to him. He looked down at the half-empty bottle in surprise, as if just remembering he had it. He probably was. "You want what's left of this? Can't hurt, not as long as you're stuck anyway."

"Sure. *Bolshoye spasibo!*" Morozov said.

The foot soldier stood by the tank. Boris leaned toward him. The guy had to toss the bottle. Gribkov caught it. Now that the foot soldier had a free hand, he waved and staggered away. Morozov guessed he was more interested in a place to sleep it off than in meeting the enemy.

*More power to him if he is,* Konstantin thought. He ducked down into the tank again. "Look what I found," he said. The liquid in the bottle was amber, not clear. He'd drunk schnapps before. He liked vodka better, but schnapps would cure whatever ailed you.

"Good job, Comrade Sergeant!" Pavel Gryzlov gauged the bottle with an experienced eye. "Plenty in there for a good knock for all of us."

"Just what I was thinking." Konstantin yanked the stopper, tilted his head back, and drank. The schnapps was harsh but strong. Warmth exploded out of his belly. He passed the gunner the bottle. Gryzlov also drank. He gave Mogamed Safarli the schnapps. Safarli was an Azeri, and so certainly a Muslim. He drank as eagerly as any Christian, though. Then he crawled forward to let Yevgeny Ushakov put paid to the bottle.

Ushakov's voice came back through the intercom as the loader returned to his place: "I killed it. Thanks!"

"Pass the body back here," Morozov said. "I'm going to look around again, so I'll chuck it out."

He threw the bottle onto the sidewalk. Watching it smash, he nodded to himself. No enemy would send it back full of burning gasoline. Just then, the T-54 in front of his belched more stinking black smoke from its exhaust and lumbered forward.

"Hey, Zhenya!" Konstantin called over the intercom. "They're moving!"

"I see it, Comrade Sergeant." The driver put the tank in gear. Whatever rubble lay in the streets, the tracks rolled over it with effortless ease. They ground most of it to dust.

A recovery vehicle had pulled a burning tank off into a side street to let the rest of the Soviet armor advance up the wider way the tank had blocked. It was a Stalin: the hardest tank to kill that the USSR knew how to make. Hard didn't mean impossible, though.

The Soviet Union might have been able to make tanks that were tougher yet. But it couldn't have made them in numbers worth putting in the field. In the last war, German tanks had had far more advanced engineering, most ways, than the good old T-34. But when there were five or six T-34s for every highly engineered Tiger or Panzer IV or Panther, what difference did that make? Quantity took on a quality of its own.

To Soviet planners, tanks were as expendable as bullets or rations. That was hard on the crews, but it made sense from a military point of view. Why waste too much quality on something that was sure to get smashed up pretty soon anyway? Turning out two or three of the pretty good instead of taking the time for the best worked out just fine.

In the same way, a swarm of half-trained soldiers spraying lots of lead in front of them would eventually wear down the smaller number of hardened professionals who faced them. The men who lived through their first few battles would learn their trade and leaven the new swarm that got seined into the Red Army after them.

That kind of approach had worked for Stalin the last time around. It was expensive, but the USSR had more men and more machines than it knew what to do with (by the way some generals performed, that was literally true).

A head popped up in the ruins. The helmet on the head was an American pot. Konstantin saw that just before he saw the bazooka tube on the broken masonry. He squeezed his PPD's trigger at the same time as the tube spat fire.

He never found out whether he got the American or German or whoever the son of a bitch was. The bazooka slammed into his T-54's frontal armor. He thought it hit near or on the patch the repair crew had welded on. The blast that consumed his crewmates flung him out of the turret and through the air instead.

He just had time to realize that his boots and the legs of his coveralls were on fire before he hit the sidewalk, hard. The thick leather tankman's helmet probably kept him from fracturing his skull. He rolled and beat at himself, trying to put out the flames before they burned him too badly.

A corporal jumped on him and rolled up and down his

legs, smothering the fire. The infantryman also had the mother wit to yell for a medic. He got one faster than Konstantin had thought he would. Between them, the medic and the corporal lugged him away from the front. "Do you want morphine?" the medic asked him.

The burns and the bruises all started to hurt at once. "Fuck your mother, yes!" Morozov exclaimed. The medic stuck him. The pain went away, or maybe Konstantin did.

Now that it was May, the snow had melted in Korea. The countryside turned muddy, then green. "Ain't that sweet?" Sergeant Lou Klein said. "Spring is in the air. La-de-da!"

"Nice to know you're enthused about it," Cade Curtis said.

"Fuckin'-A . . . sir," Klein replied. "The birdies'll be singing their heads off. And us and the Chinks, we'll be blowing each other's heads off."

"How long do you think this war can go on?" Curtis asked.

"I'm just a dumb sergeant. I don't know nothin'. I don't want to know nothin'," Klein said.

"You're a sandbagging dumb sergeant, is what you are," Cade told him. "C'mon—give."

"Well, I guess it kind of depends," the veteran noncom said. "Sooner or later, they're bound to run out of cities to plaster. When they do, I guess things'll just peter out. Not much point to blowing up forests or prairies or anything. That's how it looks to me, anyway. How do you see it?"

"I don't think we can last even that long," Cade said. "As soon as the logistics get so bad we can't support the armies, we've got to quit."

That applied with special force here in Korea, something he made a point of not mentioning to Lou Klein. The only functioning port on the West Coast was San Diego. All the ones north of there had taken A-bombs. With the Panama and Suez Canals gone, the harbors on the East Coast couldn't quickly take up the slack. Everything that didn't leave through San Diego would go around Cape Horn or the Cape of Good Hope. It would be only two or three days less than forever on the way.

Red China, in the meantime, sat right across the Yalu, right where it had always been. The logistics of a war in Korea had always been bad for America. With the ports and the canals destroyed, they'd gone from bad to worse.

Sergeant Klein looked amused. "Anybody can tell you're an officer," he said. "Officers go on and on about logistics."

"You've got to," Cade said. "They're important."

"As long as I've got ammo for my M-1, as long as the guys in the battery behind us have enough shells for their 105s, I won't worry about it."

Cade started to explain that that was what logistics were all about, that things would go horribly wrong if you didn't worry about making sure dogfaces had plenty of cartridges and howitzers had plenty of shells. He started to, but a glint in Klein's eye shut him up before the words came out. The sergeant was sandbagging again.

When Cade didn't walk barefoot through the obvious, Klein looked disappointed for a moment. Then he grinned a grin that showed off his nicotine-stained choppers. "You're learning, sir, damned if you ain't."

"Baby steps," Cade said. "Baby steps."

A moment later, they both dove for the dugout. Those screams in the air were incoming Red Chinese 105s. Klein dove no sooner than Cade—the young lieutenant really was learning. The dugout was cramped for two; it might have been cramped for one. As they huddled together, Klein said, "You come any closer, Lieutenant, you're gonna kiss me."

"No, thanks," Cade said. "I've been overseas a while, but not *that* long." The way they were twisted up with each other, he could just about whisper in Lou Klein's ear. They both laughed. It wasn't that funny, but Cade was glad for anything to take his mind off the artillery fire.

U.S. guns opened up, too, but they didn't shoot back as hard as he would have liked. *Save ammo* was the new watchword. With the troubles back home, it had to be. Stalin might give the Chinks only what he didn't feel like using himself, but he had plenty of old howitzers and rounds to shoot out of them. Artillery had always been an American advantage. It had been, but the balance was tilting.

When the shelling let up, Cade and Sergeant Klein untangled from each other and jumped up onto the firing step to see if the Red Chinese would follow it up with a ground attack. Not this time: no dun-colored wave of men slogging forward to get cut down. They'd shelled for the sake of shelling, because they had the tubes and ammunition. They'd made the Americans keep their heads down, and hurt or killed a few at no great cost to themselves.

By baby steps, they were learning, too.

A hundred yards down the trench, some unlucky GI was wailing for his mother. Curtis and Klein looked at each other. Their faces both wore the same expression. "Christ, but I hate that," Klein said. "Just dumb luck I ain't the one making those noises."

"Uh-huh," Cade said. "I've come too close to that too many times."

"Ain't we all?" Klein said. Cade remembered he had been wounded, and more than once. What kind of noises had he made when he got hit? Nothing so horrible as the ones rising now, or Cade hoped not. Those were the cries you let out when you were in agony, and death or lots of morphine were all you had to look forward to.

After what seemed like forever but was actually five or ten minutes, the wounded man fell silent. Either he was dead or they'd doped him not just to but past the eyebrows. Whichever, he wasn't making that horrible racket any more. Cade didn't care about anything else.

Klein lit a cigarette. He held the pack out to Curtis. "Want one, sir?"

Cade hadn't smoked at all till he put on the uniform, or, in fact, till he came under fire. He hadn't smoked much then; he hadn't really got the habit before he was cut off from the Army's logistical horn of plenty. So it wasn't as if he needed a butt. He took one anyway, saying, "Thanks. Now watch me cough my head off."

"I sure as hell did when I started smoking." Klein pulled a Ronson that had seen plenty of hard use out of his pocket. Cade leaned over to get a light. "There you go," the sergeant said when he took his first inexpert drag.

He did cough. It tasted terrible, as if he'd inhaled the smoke from burning leaves—which was just what he had done. He got dizzy and light-headed—no, he hadn't tried this for quite a while. He gulped as his stomach did an Immelmann.

"You okay, sir?" Klein asked with what sounded like genuine concern. "You look kinda green."

"I believe it." Spit flooded into Cade's mouth. His body was convinced he'd just gone and poisoned himself. Gulping again, he wasn't so sure it was wrong. "Hope I don't lose my lunch. Been too long since I did any of this."

"Yeah, you gotta stay used to it," Lou Klein agreed. "Even

when you are, it ain't like you get drunk or nothin'. Just kinda, I dunno, takes some of the edge offa things. Gives you somethin' to do when you got five minutes with nothin' goin' on, too."

"I guess so." Cade nodded and cautiously inhaled again. It was almost as rugged as his first try. He turned his head and got rid of some of that outpouring of spit. Klein chuckled, but softly. Cade said, "The Indians must have been crazy when they started doing this."

"I ain't gonna argue with you," the noncom said. "But the whole goddamn world sucks on coffin nails these days." He smoked in quick, harsh drags, and ground out his cigarette on the callused palm of his left hand.

Cade took more time between puffs. He didn't want to start puking his head off. His hands were hard, as any soldier's had to be, but not hard enough to do duty for an ashtray. He killed his cigarette with the sole of his boot.

"Here ya go, sir." Klein tossed him the opened pack. "I got plenty more."

"Thanks—I think," Cade said. The sergeant laughed, for all the world as if he were joking.

Behind the lines, more American guns started going off. Those were 155s, with plenty of range to strike the smaller Chinese pieces. As the 105s had before them, they stopped firing sooner than Cade would have liked. Yes, ammunition here was in short supply. Everything here was in short supply—everything except Red Chinese soldiers. With that on his mind, Cade warily lit another cigarette.

Marvin Finch had a swimming pool in his back yard. Even in Southern California, that was an uncommon luxury. When Aaron Finch took Ruth and Leon over to visit his brother's family, he looked at that pool with a proprietary air. And well he might have. When he moved in with Marvin right after the war, digging that pool was part of his rent.

He still had the shovel he'd used. About a third of the blade was worn away. He intended to keep it as long as he lived, as a reminder of the hard work he'd done.

Marvin was a couple of inches shorter than he was, and stockier, too. He had a double chin and a comfortable little pot belly. He wore horn-rimmed glasses and smoked a pipe. He had a million schemes, none of which had paid off the way he'd wished they would. He could talk anybody into anything . . . for a little while. After that, his charm wore thin. Aaron reflexively liked him—they were brothers, after all—but he'd learned to keep a hand on his wallet when Marvin started charming.

"No hatchet today, hey?" he said when he opened the door to let in Aaron and Ruth and Leon.

"I dunno. Got any wood you need chopped?" Aaron didn't let on that Marvin irked him. The accident was forty years old now, and Marvin hadn't forgotten it. He never forgot anything anybody did to him.

He squatted down in the front hall and tickled Leon. Leon giggled. He thought Marvin was great. Of course, he wasn't quite two, so his judgment left something to be desired.

"Hello, Aaron. Hello, Ruth," Sarah Finch said. Olivia's mother was a washed-out woman in her early forties. She'd been a Phi Beta Kappa at the University of Arkansas. Then she met Marvin, fell in love with him . . . and vanished into his shadow. If you gave him half a chance, he'd do that to you.

"Hi, Sarah," Aaron said. He liked Marvin's wife. By all the signs, he liked her better than Marvin did. Of course, he didn't sleep in the same bed with her.

He squeezed Ruth's hand. If he hadn't been living with Marvin, he never would have met her. That made him more forgiving than he would have been otherwise.

"Is Roxane here yet?" Ruth asked Marvin. Roxane Bauman was her first cousin, the gal who'd introduced her and Aaron. She was married to a working but not enormously successful actor named Howard Bauman. Their politics were very pink, almost if not altogether red.

Aaron hadn't seen them since the war started. Just before it did, Bauman had had to testify in front of the Un-American Activities Committee. Aaron wondered what they thought of Stalin now. That ought to be interesting . . . one way or another.

While Aaron wondered, his brother nodded. "They're out back by the pool," Marvin said. "I made a pitcher of martinis."

Odds were he'd fixed martinis more because they were in than because he particularly liked them. As far as Aaron knew, he didn't, but that was his style. Aaron drank beer because he liked beer. Ruth didn't drink a whole lot of anything, but when she did it was beer or scotch.

There was beer in the icebox. Marvin didn't go out of his way to be a bad host; sometimes it just happened. Aaron opened one for himself. He looked a question at his wife. She nodded, so he got her one, too. That she felt the urge probably said something or other.

They went out to the back yard. Olivia had outgrown the swing set there. Leon was just getting old enough to enjoy it when somebody big pushed him.

Caesar ran up, barking. Leon shrank back against Ruth. Ducks and chickens were okay, but Caesar scared him. Well, the dog outweighed him at least two to one. Caesar was a German shepherd who seemed in training to turn wolf. He had a mouthful of large, pointed teeth, and liked showing them off. He wasn't mean—he'd never bitten or anything—but he wasn't exactly friendly, either.

Aaron petted him. He deigned to wag his tail and trotted off, satisfied that he'd protected the household. Aaron and Ruth and (cautiously) Leon walked back toward the pool.

Howard Bauman was swimming. Aaron thought he was nuts, or else part polar bear. May or not, that water was cold. Roxane stretched out on a chaise longue. She had the same narrow chin and black hair as Ruth, but the rest of her face didn't look much like her cousin's. She had a higher opinion of her own cleverness than Aaron thought she'd earned.

She greeted him with, "How does it feel to be a hero to the plutocrats?"

"Give me a break," he said. "I caught the Russian when he parachuted down in front of me. What do you think I should've done? Run him over?"

"Maybe you could have helped him," she said.

"I did help him. I gave him to the cops. He didn't get lynched the way some of their flyers did." Aaron knew that wouldn't do him any good. When Roxane said *helped,* she meant *bought him a ticket to Moscow.*

"Terrible violation of the Geneva Convention," she said. "I don't want to think about what our police have done to him."

"Chance you take when you drop an A-bomb on somebody," Aaron said dryly. "You and Howard are lucky you're still here to give the Ivans a big hand." The Baumans lived in Hollywood—luckily for them, on the western edge of Hollywood. Their apartment building hadn't fallen down, and they hadn't got a lethal dose of radiation.

"We started dropping the atom bombs," Roxane said.

"They invaded South Korea," Aaron said. "None of the rest of this would have happened if that didn't."

"Our puppet government there is full of people who collaborated with the Japs," Roxane retorted. "They should have gone to jail. Instead, they were running a country—well, we called it one, anyway."

"Can we talk about something else?" Ruth asked. She couldn't stand arguments, which made Aaron wonder why she'd ever come to visit Marvin.

Aaron didn't say anything back at Roxane. For a wonder, she let it go, too. Howard Bauman came out of the pool and, dripping, made a beeline for the martini pitcher. It stood in a big bowl of ice, so the martinis would stay cold without getting diluted. Howard poured himself about half a liver's worth of booze. He was good-looking in a not especially Jewish way; he had a head of brown hair so thick, it was almost a pelt.

"How's it going, Aaron?" he asked. He had his politics, too, but, unlike Roxane, he didn't always try to ram them down your throat.

"Not as much work as I'd like," Aaron answered.

"Boy, I hear that," Howard said.

"I guess you do." Aaron didn't feel like quarreling. He had trouble getting as much work as he wanted because Blue Front was hurting as much as any other outfit that tried to sell things to people these days. Howard had trouble because he just wasn't that great an actor. Pointing out the difference might have influenced some people, but it wouldn't have won Aaron any friends. He kept his mouth shut.

Marvin came out and poured himself a martini almost as generous as Howard Bauman's. "Is everybody having a good time?" he asked.

"No," Leon said. He was still doing that. This time, it made all the grown-ups laugh.

Howard Bauman stood there drinking and dripping on the concrete deck (which Aaron had poured and leveled). No, the breeze off the hills wasn't what anyone would have called warm. Some of the refugees from the bomb were living in tents up there, getting by by hunting and begging and stealing.

"How come you're not turning into an ice cube yourself?" Aaron asked Howard.

"Antifreeze." Bauman raised the martini glass and made sure his radiator wouldn't boil over. He wasn't shivering. His teeth didn't chatter. Maybe he even meant it.

**23**

VASILI YASEVICH SMILED WHEN he walked into the teahouse. "What do you know, Mei Ling?" he said when the pretty serving girl came over to him.

"I know you're a nuisance," she answered, but she was smiling, too. "What can I get you this afternoon?"

"Tea and some buckwheat noodles," he said. The Japanese had introduced those noodles to northeastern China when they ran things here. People kept eating them even though the Japanese were long gone. They were tasty and cheap at the same time: the perfect combo.

She brought them back splashed with soy sauce and garnished with chopped scallions and leeks. Vasili handled chopsticks as if he'd used them all his life—which he had. He held the bowl up to his face and slurped away. He wasn't always neat, but neither were the Chinese. Neat eating was for aristocrats, the last thing you wanted to look like in Mao's People's Republic.

Mei Ling giggled behind her hand. "What's so funny, toots?" Vasili asked, though he already had a good idea of the answer.

Sure enough, she said, "It's just strange, watching a round-eye eat like a regular person. I always laugh when I see that."

"I am a regular person." Vasili used the same northeastern dialect of Mandarin she did. Why not? Hadn't he grown up in Harbin himself? After another slurp and a gulp, he went on, "I'm a regular person who has round eyes, that's all. How many other round-eyes have you watched eating like this?" His right hand shoveled more noodles into his mouth.

"A few," she said. "There aren't as many round-eyes here

as there used to be. And the ones who come over from Russia, they want knives and forks. Where am I going to get knives and forks?"

"Beats me," Vasili said. One or two surviving Russian eateries still had some for people who wanted them. A few Russian old-timers might use them at home. Vasili knew how; his mother and father had preferred them. But he couldn't remember the last time he'd picked up a fork. He really was a regular person: a fair-skinned, big-nosed regular person with a thick beard and round blue eyes.

People in some countries didn't all have the same general coloring and cast of features. Some looked like Vasili, some like Chinese; he supposed some were even Negroes (except for a few pictures, he'd never set eyes on one). China, though, wasn't like that. Everybody here looked Chinese . . . except for Vasili and a few other relics of bygone days.

Mei Ling said, "Even though you're a round-eyed barbarian, you talk and you act like a civilized person."

That was what she meant. What she said was *like a man from the Middle Kingdom,* which was China's name for itself. To Chinese, only Chinese could be civilized. Everybody else was a barbarian, somebody unlikely to speak the language (*very* unlikely to read it) and all too likely to make messes on the floor.

For hundreds of years, China had been the big wheel in the Far East. Japan, Korea, Indochina, Thailand, Burma . . . They all pretty much followed China's lead in style and culture. None of them got ahead of China. And the occasional Europeans were oddities when they weren't nuisances.

Then they turned into dangerous nuisances, nuisances who could do things the Chinese couldn't. For one of the rare times in history, foreigners ordered Chinese around, and had the strength to make their orders stick. Russians, Englishmen, French . . . even the Japanese started doing it. That had to be doubly humiliating, as if a wayward son beat up a proud but weak father.

So of course the Chinese distrusted foreigners. Vasili understood it no matter how much trouble it caused him. "I hope I am like a civilized person," he said. "I hope I am enough like a civilized person to keep you company every now and then."

Mei Ling giggled some more. "Well, maybe," she said, and then, tartly, "Took you long enough to get around to asking."

"Sorry," Vasili muttered. One of the few things he knew about Negroes was that white people often made rules against getting too friendly with them. Chinese sometimes felt the same way about whites. Knowing that had made him shy—but not too shy.

He left money on the counter and walked out whistling. He was as happy as he had been since the atom bomb fell, maybe as happy as he had been since his parents killed themselves instead of letting the Chekists take them back to the workers' and peasants' paradise of the USSR. They'd thought death was better than that. From the stories they'd told, Vasili could see why.

He stayed happy for about ten minutes: the time he took to walk from the teahouse to his own shanty. He rounded the last corner on his little alleyway—and stopped, and drew back. A jeep was parked there, probably one seized from Chiang Kai-shek's forces during the civil war. He wouldn't have thought the alley wide enough to let it squeeze through, but there you were—and there it was.

The men who'd come in it would be in the shack now, tearing it to pieces. He didn't need to see them to know that. They'd be looking for . . . for opium, of course. *"Yob tvoyu mat',"* Vasili whispered, aiming the obscenity at the official Wang's wife had sent his way. He should have known the son of a bitch would want to get even. Dammit, he had known.

*Now what am I going to do?* he wondered. Here he was, a fair round-eye in a land full of golden-skinned, black-haired people. He was as conspicuous as a snowball in a coal cellar. Running away seemed unlikely to do much good.

But he couldn't walk up to those policemen or whatever they were and go *Here I am!* He knew what would happen if he did: the kinds of things that would have happened to his father and mother had they got dragged back to the Soviet Union. Mao'd learned a lot from Stalin. He had native talent, too.

So, while running wasn't a good choice, plainly it was the best one he had. They might not catch up with him for a while. If he headed north, he'd stay in country that had some idea what Russians were. Maybe he *could* slip across the border. Being without proper papers in Russia was deadly dangerous. His parents had made that clear. He had Chinese papers. But if all they showed was *This man is wanted!,* that was even worse.

He headed for the abandoned blacksmith's shop. If they were after him for selling opium, he might as well start doing it for real. They couldn't kill him much deader for an actual crime than for an invented one. And selling the drug would get him more cash. He'd need that. They'd surely already stolen what he had in the shack.

He would have done better to have got some gold from the commissar with the craving. But Mao was so ferocious with anyone who had anything to do with opium, he hadn't had the nerve. So here he was, on the run.

As a matter of fact, he strolled along as if he had not a care in the world. Looking scared was the dumbest thing you could do. As long as he acted the way he usually did, people here took him for granted. If he started skulking or sprinting, they'd wonder why. They would till they added two and two and got four, anyhow.

He did glance around—as casually as he could—before slipping into the old blacksmith's shop through the hole in the side wall. Even after all these years, the place smelled faintly of horse. The odor was in the straw on the floor, and in the dirt. For all he knew, it had soaked into the planks of the walls.

He breathed a sigh of relief when he picked up the broken brick and found the apothecary's jar still under it. On the chance that other people had also used the place to hide things, he did some more searching after he retrieved it. And he found two tarnished trade dollars—some people called them Mex dollars—that had probably been there longer than he'd been alive. He took them, too. Silver was silver.

*Should I rest here for a while?* he wondered. The idea of sleeping on horse-smelling dirt didn't excite him. But neither did the idea of rushing out there and getting nabbed. He lay down. His jacket made a good enough pillow.

It was dark when he woke—the dark of a blacked-out city. He yawned, but didn't try to sleep any more. Time to get moving. He might be able to swap town for countryside by the time the sun came up.

Out in the *kolkhoz*'s fields, horses pulled plows. The tractors sat idle for lack of fuel. Sowers with bags of seed planted wheat and barley seeds in the furrows. Ihor Shevchenko was one of them.

The work was long and tedious, but he didn't mind. The black earth that made the Ukraine famous smelled as rich as some of the chops he'd cut from Nestor's loin. When you got a whiff of that newly plowed ground, you thought you could eat it instead of the crops that sprang from it.

Plenty of Ukrainian peasants must have tried that when Stalin starved them into collectivizing. They'd died, so it didn't work, even if it smelled as if it should. You had to do the rest of the work.

Ihor cast seeds here and there. He wasn't especially careful about it. Why bother? The fields were communal. He wouldn't get anything extra if they yielded a lot of wheat. If they yielded only a little, the *kolkhoz* chairman would lie to the people in charge of this area. They would lie to their superiors, and life would go on.

One of the other sowers waved an empty seed sack. A kid tore across the field with a full one. You weren't supposed to have used up all the grain in a sack so soon. It wasn't as if Bohdan cared, though. All he cared about was getting through the day so he could start drinking.

Petro Hapochka stood watching the workers from the edge of the field. He would have joined the sowing himself, or perhaps guided the horses up and down, if not for his missing foot. Ihor wondered if he'd give Bohdan hell for screwing around. He ought to, but Ihor doubted he would.

Ihor paused to light a Belomor cigarette. The White Sea name celebrated the canal dug from Lake Vygozero to the arm of the Arctic Ocean. One of the guys who used to live at the *kolkhoz* had helped dig it: he was one *zek* among countless others. From what he said, the idea was more to use up political prisoners than to make a useful canal. He hadn't had any idea how many died from overwork or hunger or cold. He'd pegged out himself, just after Ihor came home from the Great Patriotic War. The guy'd lived through his stretch in the gulag, but not with his health.

*Did as many die as an atom bomb kills?* Ihor wondered. The bomb gave an easy, quick way to measure the atrocities of Stalin and the MGB. The only trouble was, you'd see the gulag yourself if you told that to anyone you didn't trust with your life.

"We'll have a bumper crop this year," Bohdan said loudly.

"Sure we will," Ihor agreed, also loudly. You wanted people to hear you saying things like that. It showed you were loyal. If you talked that way, no one would care how much you screwed up the actual work.

The horse plodded up and down the field, plowing furrows and also manuring them. The tractor did much more in a day. Following the horse was more pleasant, as long as you didn't step in anything.

Every so often, Ihor would glance up to the sky. That seemed more important than watching out for horseshit on the ground. Contrails scared him, especially when they came out of the west or south. Those might be American bombers paying Kiev another call. Jet-engine noises also alarmed him. Either they were bombers or fighters trying to climb high enough fast enough to go after bombers.

"Stalin will be pleased with our harvest this fall," Bohdan declared.

"Of course he will," Ihor said. "Great Stalin is always pleased when the peasants and workers do well under the leadership of the glorious Communist Party."

He raised his voice, so as many of the sowers as possible could hear. Inside, he wanted to wash out his mouth with soap—or, preferably, vodka. You did what you had to do to get by. You couldn't just keep quiet about the man and the party ruling the Soviet Union. No, if you did that, your friends and acquaintances might think you kept quiet because you had nothing good to say about Stalin and the Communists. Someone who thought something like that was bound to report you to the MGB.

And so, every so often, people spoke up in hearty tones about how wonderful things always had been, were, and always would be in the USSR. Famine in the Ukraine, famine spurred on by fanatical Communist officials? War against Germany so badly botched, the country almost went under? American atom bombs landing everywhere from Leningrad to Petropavlovsk? All those were only bumps on the road to true socialism.

You had to say they were, anyhow, as long as anyone could hear you. You didn't dare say anything else, not unless you were in bed with your wife, in the middle of the night, all alone, with both your heads under the covers—and maybe not then, either, not if you knew what was good for you. You might have opinions about those other bits of business, but having them and voicing them were two different things.

"Great Stalin looks out for all the people of the Soviet

Union," Bohdan said. "Without his care, the country would fall to pieces."

"He does," said Ihor and some of the other sowers.

At the same time, others intoned, "It would." By the way their voices rose and fell in unison, they might as well have been giving responses to the priest in church. That was another point you made only in the dark and under the covers, if you were so crazy as to make it at all.

Ihor had got far enough west with the Red Army before stopping one to see that life in Poland was richer than life in the USSR, while life in Germany was far richer than life in Poland, much less here. For the life of him, he'd never been able to figure out why the Nazis, who already had a country with so much for everybody, tried to conquer one so much poorer. It made no sense.

But then, a lot of what the Nazis did made no sense. If only they'd treated Russians and Ukrainians halfway decently, they would have got more willing workers and volunteers to fight alongside them than they knew what to do with. Instead, they turned everyone they overran into slaves—except for commissars and people like Jews and gypsies, whom they killed outright. Next to that, even Stalin started looking, well, great.

Somewhere off in the distance, in the woods or on the plain, Banderists lingered. They flew the Ukraine's old blue-and-yellow flag, or their own red-and-black one. They still skirmished with the Red Army and the MGB. Sometimes the nationalists had fought Soviet soldiers alongside the Germans, sometimes on their own hook. When they went into the gulag these days, they won twenty-five-year terms, not the tenners that had been more common before.

Ihor wondered what *they* thought of great Stalin after the A-bomb fell on Kiev. He also wondered whether the bomb made people who hadn't been Banderists decide the great Stalin wasn't so great after all and join the rebels. He hadn't seen any Banderist propaganda around here for a while. Would it start showing up again?

Down the field. Up the field again. Wave for a bag of seed. Wait till one of the boys brought it to you. Pause at lunchtime to eat blintzes full of cheese and gulp kvass. Kvass was slightly fermented: on the way to being beer. You'd do nothing but piss for a month if you drank enough of the stuff to get a buzz, though.

Petro Hapochka stood at the edge of the field all day long, shouting encouragement to the men working out there—and occasional obscenities at them when they faltered. He took being *kolkhoz* chairman seriously. You had to, if you were going to do the job at all.

If . . . Ihor wouldn't have taken Petro's post for a suitcase full of hundred-ruble bills, a motorcar, and a house all his own the size of the communal barracks. Some things came at too high a price. Trying to keep both the *kolkhozniks* and the Communist higher-ups happy seemed to him to be one of them.

He aimed no higher than getting through another day, another month, another year. As long as nobody arrested him or shot him, he was ahead of the game. Oh—and as long as nobody dropped an atom bomb on him, either.

The briefing officer whacked the pull-down map with a pointer. If this had been Korea rather than Japan, Bill Staley would have guessed the light colonel was taking lessons from General Harrison. "Khabarovsk," the briefing officer said. "Khabarovsk and Blagoveshchensk."

Sitting in the folding chair next to Bill's, Hank McCutcheon whispered, "Gesundheit!"

Those were pretty good sneeze-names, all right, even by Russian standards. But Bill had to fight not to laugh out loud. You didn't want to get in trouble at a briefing. Sometimes it happened anyway, but not right then: somehow, he managed to hold a straight face.

*Whack!* "Khabarovsk and Blagoveshchensk," the lieutenant colonel repeated. "As you see, gentlemen, both cities lie along the Amur River, on the Russian side of the border with Red China." The U.S. government still didn't recognize that Mao had won the Chinese civil war. As far as it was concerned, he remained a usurper and Nationalist Chiang the legitimate President of China, even if all he held was the island of Formosa.

Then again, as far as the American government was concerned, Lithuania, Latvia, and Estonia were independent countries, not parts of Stalin's USSR. To Bill, the one seemed as surreal as the other. He wasn't a striped-pants diplomat. He didn't want to be any such silly thing, either.

He also didn't want to copilot Major McCutcheon's B-29.

When the Department of Defense recalled him to active duty, though, what other choice did he have but to put the uniform on again? Refuse and go to jail? He'd thought that was worse. He still did—except when the Commies were shooting at him.

"Khabarovsk and Blagoveshchensk." One more time! *Whack!* "Both cities are also important centers through which the Trans-Siberian Railway passes. By striking them, we will help interdict Soviet supplies flowing through Red China and down into the Korean peninsula. We will help the men on the ground by reducing the pressure the enemy can bring to bear against them."

When the briefing officer said *striking them,* he meant *sending them up in atomic fire.* That was what this mission was all about. Neither Siberian city had yet had A-bombs visited upon it. There were reasons why they hadn't, too. Khabarovsk lay about three hundred miles north of where Vladivostok had been. Blagoveshchensk was another three hundred miles farther west. Bill didn't know what kind of air defenses the cities boasted. To the best of his knowledge, neither did any other Americans. The crews on this mission would find out . . . the hard way.

"We are expending three atomic devices on each city." The briefing officer used the peculiarly bloodless language so beloved of militaries around the world. "We want to ensure that the interdiction process is successful. Other B-29s will carry high-explosive bombs to take out anything the large explosions happen to miss. They will also serve to divide the attention of the Russians' defensive personnel."

They would be decoys, was what they would be. No one—except the crews in those Superforts and their families back home—would care if the pilots in the MiGs knocked them down. The more effort the Russians put into shooting down the planes that couldn't hurt them badly, the better the chance of getting through the B-29s with the atom bombs had.

Bill was sure he wouldn't be on a plane loaded with ordinary bombs. Hank McCutcheon had already brought his B-29 back from repeated missions with A-bombs. To the brass, that would argue he was good at it, better than some rookie would be. And maybe the brass were right, and maybe they were full of crap. You could toss heads six times in a row, and it wouldn't mean a thing—just a statistical hiccup.

*I'm a fugitive from the law of averages,* Bill thought. That wasn't the way you ought to go into a mission. You needed confidence. Just because you needed it, though, didn't mean you'd have it.

"Any questions?" the briefing officer asked. Nobody said a thing. The men knew what they were getting into. This was what they'd bought when they let Uncle Sam teach them to fly. The officer with the silver oak leaves on his shoulders looked out at them. "Anyone who doesn't care to fly the mission?"

Some people in South Korea had walked out. Bill wondered if he should have. It was the fastest way he could think of to escape the Air Force. But it was also letting down his crew and his country. He'd sat tight then. He sat tight now. So did everybody else.

"Very good," the briefing officer said briskly. "Pilots— come forward to receive your orders for the mission."

Since Bill was but a copilot, he went on sitting right where he was. McCutcheon walked up to get the envelope with the bad news in it. Whatever the news in that envelope held, it was bound to be bad. The only question was, which kind of bad would it be?

"So who wins the Oscar?" Bill asked when McCutcheon came back. He hadn't broken the seal yet. Maybe he wasn't jumping up and down to find out, either.

"Funny, Billy-boy. Funny like a busted leg," he said, as if a broken leg was the worst they had to worry about. He slid his right index finger under the edge of the flap to make it come free. The noise of the glue breaking away from the paper reminded Bill of a small animal scratching to be let out. McCutcheon pulled out the folded sheet inside and unfolded it.

*Blagoveshchensk,* Bill read. He bit the inside of his lower lip. They'd spend an extra couple of dangerous hours over Russia, compared to the guys who'd hit Khabarovsk. The next line told him the B-29 *would* be carrying an A-bomb. By now, he wondered how much it mattered. His dreams couldn't get any worse than they already were. He'd killed his tens of thousands. What were a few more tens of thousands after that?

The rest of the sheet detailed courses and altitude. They'd stay as low as they could as long as they could, to give Soviet radar sets as much trouble as possible. *In the event that you should be intercepted, you will of course utilize your best judgment to extricate yourselves from the emergency,* the orders finished primly.

Bill pointed to that last sentence. "Nice of them, isn't it?"

"As a matter of fact, it is," Hank McCutcheon answered. "If we were Russians, that bit'd go *Keep following your assigned course no matter what.*"

"I guess it would," Bill said, but he wondered how much difference it would make. If a MiG-15 or even an La-11 came after them, they were dead meat. They could push the throttles over the red line. They could jink and dodge as much as they pleased—and as much as an elephant could tap-dance. None of it was likely to do them any good. Why not hold course? It wouldn't cost more than a few minutes of life.

All the B-29s took off in swift succession and roared northwest through the night toward the Siberian coast. It was as routine as anything else the crews had done before. Bill's nerves still twanged. That extra time over land gnawed at him.

He wondered if they would have done better to fly over Manchuria and hit Blagoveshchensk from the south. When he said so, Major McCutcheon replied, "Think the Chinks don't have radar there and down in Korea? Think they don't have jets ready to scramble? How much you wanna bet?"

"I'm already betting my neck," Bill said. "What else can I throw into the pot?"

They droned along not that far above what seemed endless taiga: pine forests that ran from west to east just below the frozen tundra. Khabarovsk lay somewhere south of their flight path. Just when Bill was wondering whether they'd come that far into Russia yet, flashes of blinding light in the distance told him some other Superfortresses had found their targets.

"One down, one to go," McCutcheon said.

"If they didn't know we were around before, they probably have a hint now," Bill said.

"Think so, do you?" the pilot answered.

Twenty minutes later, Bill wondered if he'd jinxed them. The radar operator started yelling about bogies. The B-29's defensive guns hammered. And shells from a night fighter's cannon ripped into the bomber. One of them tore off the left side of McCutcheon's face. The plane was suddenly Bill's, only it wouldn't answer the controls. There was fire—fire everywhere.

"Bail out!" he yelled. He couldn't himself, and it wouldn't have mattered. Not only were there flames between him and his escape hatch, but his parachute was already burning. So was he. The B-29 tumbled down toward the black, snow-dappled pines.

Marian had just dropped Linda off at the camp kindergarten. She didn't know why school had taken so long to get started in this miserable place. No, actually she could make a pretty good guess: too many other things for the authorities to worry about. But they'd finally noticed the swarms of kids too often running around in screaming packs.

So they said *Let there be school,* and there was school. And the parents looked on it, and they saw that it was good, and there was much rejoicing—among them, anyhow. And if their little darlings had a different opinion, too goddamn bad. Linda was out of Marian's hair for several hours a day. Somebody else could ride herd on her for a while.

Having left her own flesh and blood at the kindergarten tent, Marian walked away, wondering what she would do with time to herself and to herself alone. She hadn't had any since the bomb wrecked the house and left her and Linda with a Studebaker as a place to sleep. She kept looking behind her for the daughter who wasn't there.

The camp loudspeakers crackled to life. They did that every so often. Like everybody else, Marian paid them no more attention than she had to. She walked along for half a dozen steps before she realized they were blaring, "Marian Staley! Please report to the administrative center immediately! Marian Staley! Please report to the administrative center immediately!"

Again, like everybody else, she had as little to do with the camp administrative center as she could. You went there if you were in trouble or if you wanted to get someone else in trouble. She'd testified against Daniel Philip Jaspers after he tried to break into her car. She hadn't gone back since.

It was easy enough to find. In front of it flew a big American flag on a tall flagpole. Nobody seemed to know how the flagpole had appeared when so many more important things still hadn't. Most camp inmates thought it was stupid, not patriotic. Marian found herself among them.

Typewriters were clacking away when she walked inside. That was the only place in the refugee camp where she would have heard them. People came here with what they had on their backs, no more. Not even the craziest would-be author had a typewriter on his back.

Once she did go inside, the functionaries needed a couple of minutes to notice she was there. At last, a clerk looked up from whatever he was doing and said, "Yes? What do you need?" By the way he said it, it couldn't be as important as his job.

"I'm Marian Staley."

"Yes? And so?" He didn't listen to the loudspeakers, either.

"Marian Staley," she said again, more sharply this time. "The stupid speakers told me to come here. I want to know why."

"I'm sorry, I have no idea," the clerk said.

But another, older, man said, "Please come with me, Mrs. Staley. It is *Mrs.* Staley, isn't it?"

"That's right. Will you kindly tell me what's going on?"

"Please come with me," the older clerk repeated. Fuming, Marian followed him around a makeshift wall of olive-drab sheet-metal file cabinets taller than a man. The administrative center was a *big* tent. Sitting on a folding chair behind the cabinets was an Air Force major. He jumped to his feet as soon as he saw the clerk and Marian.

"Ma'am, your husband is First Lieutenant William Gerald Staley?" he asked her, his voice altogether empty of expression.

"That's right," Marian said automatically.

"Ma'am, I am sorrier than I know to have to inform you that the B-29 in which your husband was flying was seen to go down in flames over the territory of the Soviet Union. It is not believed that anyone could have survived the crash." Now the major did sound sad and sympathetic. He'd had to confirm who she was before he could start acting like a human being.

Her first dazed thought was *A B-29 carries eleven.* Were ten other officers telling ten other brand new widows or shocked mothers they'd just lost someone they loved? Or was she honored with a visit from an officer because Bill was an officer himself? Did enlisted men's kinfolk get only a wire?

Then she realized none of that mattered. The meaning of what the major said began to sink in. "Bill's . . . dead?" she whispered.

"Yes, ma'am. I'm sorry, ma'am." The officer nodded somberly. "I'm very sorry. He was on an important mission, and a dangerous one. Other planes succeeded in reaching and striking the target. Unfortunately, his was intercepted before it could."

*Important mission* had to mean *mission with an atom bomb,* while *striking the target* meant *doing to some Russian city what they did to Seattle.* The language of war was bloodless. War itself . . . wasn't. Bill's job was to visit radioactive hell on America's enemies. This time, they'd done unto him before he could do unto them.

Then all rational thought melted. She let out something between a shriek and a wail that made the older clerk hop in the air and startled even the sober Air Force major. She saw that in the instant before her own world dissolved in tears.

She wailed again, this time with words: "What are we going to do without Bill?"

"I'm sorry, ma'am," the major said once more. "I believe he has received a proper burial. The Russians have been respectful to our men killed on their soil, as we have with their casualties here."

"I don't care about any of that!" she said furiously. "I want my husband back! I want our little girl's daddy back!"

"I'm sorry, ma'am," he said yet again. How many times had he stayed calm when somebody who'd lost the person who mattered most to her went to pieces in front of him? The duty couldn't be easy. How did he stand it? Why didn't he take a service pistol and blow his brains out? He went on, "I understand it can't possibly make up for your loss, but his military insurance will assist you and your daughter in getting through this—"

Blind with grief and rage, she swung at him. She wanted to tear his head off. He caught her wrist before she connected. His palm was warm and dry and very strong.

"Ma'am, that won't do you any good," he said in tones suggesting he'd been swung on before. "I had nothing to do with it. I'm only the person who has to give you the news. I wish I didn't have to come here to do it."

*Then what do you do it for?* The thought flashed through her mind, but she didn't come out with it. What was the use? With Bill gone, what was the use of anything?

"What will we do without him?" she said again. Would Linda even remember her father? Maybe a little—she'd been four when he went away. But only bits and pieces, nothing that really meant anything.

That was when it hit her. She would have to tell Linda that Daddy was dead. Linda knew what the word meant. She was a smart girl. But she knew it the way a kid did. She knew a dead bug when she saw one. Did she understand that, when a person died, he stayed dead the same way? Did she understand that forever meant forever, and there were no exceptions, even for her father?

Chances were she didn't . . . yet, although maybe all the deaths at the camp had taught her. If she didn't, she'd learn, a day, a week, a month, a year, at a time. *Christ, so will I,* Marian thought. Things like this happened to other people, or in movies. They didn't happen to *you.*

Except when they did.

"The United States is grateful for your husband's courage, ma'am," the Air Force major said.

"Oh, *fuck* the United States!" Marian didn't remember ever using that word before. She used it now. Had she known a stronger one, she would have used that, too.

# 24

MAJOR JEFF WALPOLE GOT up on the firing step to look across the barbed wire at the Red Chinese positions. He got down again in a hurry. A good thing he did, too: a bullet aimed at him cracked past a couple of seconds later. It might have missed. Did you want to find out, though?

The battalion CO had a big grin on his face. Cade Curtis couldn't see why. The Chinks were too goddamn close and too goddamn aggressive. But Walpole said, "Those bastards have worries of their own."

"How's that, sir?" Cade was glad every day the Red Chinese didn't try to storm the American lines. He wasn't even slightly sure they wouldn't break through.

"They'll be the ones with supply problems for a while," Major Walpole said. "Didn't you hear Armed Forces Radio this morning?"

"No, sir," Cade said. "They were throwing mortars at us this morning."

"That's always fun." Walpole had the ribbon for his own Bronze Star with a V. Cade didn't know if he'd won it in this war or the last, but he'd be a man who knew something about mortars. He went on, "Anyway, we bombed a couple of the cities on the Trans-Siberian Railway. Blagoveshchensk and Khabarovsk."

Cade knew Khabarovsk lay north of Vladivostok, or what remained of Vladivostok. He wasn't so sure about the other place, or about how to pronounce it. Instead of trying, he found a different kind of question: "When you say bombed, do you mean *bombed*? Like with atoms?"

"With atoms, yeah," Major Walpole agreed. "So they

won't put Humpty-Dumpty together again in a few days, the way they would if they were fixing up ordinary bomb damage."

"Yes, sir," Cade said, but he wondered if Walpole was an optimist. Mao's men had driven new tracks through the ruins of Harbin way faster than American military intelligence guessed they could. He didn't care about laborers, only about the labor they did. Was Stalin likely to prove more merciful? When had he ever?

Staff Sergeant Klein ambled up the trench. A cigarette dangled from the corner of his mouth. Nodding to Walpole, he said, "Sir, I hear you tell the lieutenant we dropped some more A-bombs?"

"That's right, Sergeant. Khabarovsk and Blagoveshchensk." Walpole could say it.

"Yeah, I know where those are at. That'll slow the trains down some," Klein said. If he knew where Blagoveshchensk was, he was one up on Cade. After a meditative puff, he went on, "Any idea where the Russians'll clobber us for payback?"

"I haven't heard anything," Major Walpole answered. "It would be nice if we could keep them from hitting us anywhere."

"Yes, sir. It sure would." By the way Klein said that, he didn't believe it would happen no matter how nice it was. He pulled out his cigarettes. "You guys want a smoke? Look at me—I'm turning into a tobacco shop for officers."

"I'll take one. Thanks," Walpole said.

"Thank you, Sergeant. Me, too," Cade added. A private had given him the matches he used to light up. They advertised a bar on Hotel Street in Honolulu where you could probably buy the hostesses along with the drinks they served.

The smoke still burned as it went down the pipe and into his lungs. It didn't make him think he'd lose his last can of C-rats any more, though. And he did get the little jolt of relaxed alertness that made people start using cigarettes to begin with.

"See what you did?" he said to Lou Klein. "You turned me into a junkie."

Major Walpole laughed. "You mean you weren't before? I didn't think there was anybody over here who didn't smoke like a steel-mill chimney. Christ, even the North Koreans puff away every chance they get, and those sorry bastards don't have food half the time, let alone tobacco."

"I've never seen 'em short of small-arms ammo, though," Cade said.

"Uh-huh. The cartridges get through. I think they make their own in Pyongyang, too," Walpole said.

"Cartridges aren't hard. Anybody with some brass bar stock and a lathe can crank 'em out," Klein said. "The Red Chinese ain't makin' tanks, but they sure as hell turn out copies of Russian submachine guns and the rounds to shoot from 'em."

Cade looked down at his own PPSh. "By the maker's stamps, this one's from Russia," he said. "But I've seen those Chinese copies, too. They work just as well as Stalin's specials."

"Pretty soon, they will make their own tanks," Walpole said. "Then they'll make their own planes, and Katie bar the door after that."

"Unless we bomb the fuckers back to the Stone Age before they get that far," Klein said.

"If we're going to hang on to our half of Korea, we may need to," Walpole said. "We can screw the Russians' logistics, same way they did with us. But we can't screw up Mao's logistics, or not very much. Red China's right across the goddamn river, for Chrissake. We can make 'em work harder to haul the shit over here, but it's not like we can stop 'em."

Cade had had that same unhappy thought. "Mao's got I don't know how many hundred million people," he said. "However many we kill, how much difference will it make?"

"Gotta get ourselves more bombs. Bigger bombs. Sooner or later, we'll make the Chinks sit up and take notice." Lou Klein sounded like a man with all the angles figured.

He made a hell of a staff sergeant. He could have run the company better than Cade. They both knew it. So, no doubt, did Major Walpole. If Walpole and all the battalion officers suddenly bought a plot, Klein could probably handle that many men, too.

But, because he could do his part of the military job so well, he thought he could do even more. He reminded Cade of the poets and craftsmen in Socrates' *Apology*. They too knew their own business inside and out-, but thought they also knew everything else because they did.

And a fat lot of good explaining all that had done the ancient Greek. Socrates had paid the price then. The whole world was paying it now.

No sooner had that cheerful notion crossed Cade's mind than the Red Chinese started lobbing some more mortar bombs at the American trenches. Mortar rounds—and the nasty little tubes that fired them—were even easier to make than ordinary firearms and ammo. The tolerances were looser, and the tubes didn't have to be very strong. Home-made artillery, perfect for a country full of blacksmiths like Mao's so-called People's Republic of China.

Curtis threw himself flat. Lou Klein was diving for the mud as soon as he was. Jerry Walpole, who didn't get to the front as much as the two men of lower rank, stayed on his pins half a second longer. It cost him. When he went down, it was with a howl of pain. He clutched at his left thigh. Red started soaking his trouser leg and oozing out between his fingers.

"Corpsman!" Sergeant Klein yelled. "The major's down! We need a corpsman, God damn it to fucking hell!"

Cade lay closer to Major Walpole. The first thing he did was grab the morphine syrette out of the pouch on Walpole's belt and stick him with it. The next thing was to pull his own bayonet from the sheath on his belt and use it to cut away the wounded man's pants so he could see the wound.

It was a nasty, ragged gash. It was bleeding, but not gush-ing blood. Cade guessed the fragment hadn't torn the femo-ral artery—that could kill you in a couple of minutes. He wished for pins to close the cut. Since wishing didn't pro-duce them, he did the next best thing: he dusted the wound with sulfa, slapped on a bandage, and taped it down as tight as he could.

"You'll be okay, sir," he said, hoping he was right. While he was busy like that, the mortar bombs still coming in seemed more an annoyance than a danger.

Stretcher-bearers with Red Cross armbands that wouldn't do them any good carried the wounded major away. They also ignored the mortar fire. Cade wondered whether the bat-talion had any healthy officers senior to him. If it didn't, he'd just inherited it. Well, if Lou Klein might swing a battalion, so could he—again, he hoped.


It was getting close to the top of the hour. Harry Truman turned on the radio on his desk to WMAL to catch the NBC news. It would tell him a little of what was going on in the country and the world. And the way it told the stories would let him judge how big a son of a bitch the people who ran NBC thought he was.

He didn't care, or not enough to let what they thought of him change anything he did. For better or worse, he was his own man. He might make mistakes—he had made mistakes—but they were his, nobody else's. The buck *did* stop here. It had to.

*Bong! Bong! Bong!* The NBC chimes sounded. "In Washington today," the announcer said, "Republican Senator Joseph McCarthy of Wisconsin again lashed out at the Truman administration. Here is a recording of some of his remarks."

A momentary pause, and then Joe McCarthy's raspy voice poured out over the airwaves: "How much trouble have the Democrats landed us in because they're soft on Communism? All the Reds we uncovered in the State Department must have told Stalin we were weak. They must have pointed out where our defenses had holes. Otherwise, how could the Reds have hit us so hard? Treason and blindness to treason lurk in too many high places."

"That was Senator McCarthy," the newsman said. "He—"

"—has his head wedged," Truman finished for him, and turned off the radio with an angry twist of the wrist. McCarthy had started his Red-baiting witch hunt even before the Korean War broke out. He'd got shriller since the fighting started, and shriller yet after the A-bombs began to fall.

At first, Truman had figured McCarthy was a stalking horse for Robert Taft and the other Republicans who still wanted to be isolationists. Tail Gunner Joe said the things politer pols like Senator Taft only thought. And he didn't just say them—he bellowed them at the top of his lungs.

He'd succeeded in convincing Truman he was nobody's stalking horse. He was for nobody except Joe McCarthy. Did he aim to run for President in 1952? He'd be awfully young. Bob Taft had been waiting his turn for a long time. Or Eisenhower might get the nod, the way U. S. Grant had in 1868.

Truman wasn't thrilled about the idea of either of those men in the White House. Taft *did* want to pretend nothing existed beyond the borders of the United States. That was hard in the middle of World War III, but he might try anyhow. And Eisenhower struck the President as an amiable but lightweight executive, someone who might run an auto company but not a country.

Next to Joe McCarthy, though, they both looked like the second coming of Abraham Lincoln. They were reasonably honest. You might not fancy their principles, but they had some. McCarthy . . . The way it looked to Truman, McCarthy didn't just want to be President. He wanted to be *Führer,* and he didn't care whose toes he trampled on his way to the job.

Lie? Smear? Cheat? Invent? He used all those stunts, and wrapped himself in the American flag while he did it. That was part of what made him so dangerous: if you attacked him, you seemed to attack the country as well.

*I have to decide whether I'll run,* Truman thought once more. If it looked as if he would lose and drag the Democrats down with him, then he'd do best to bow out. With this war, he wondered whether he would have a chance against anybody the Republicans put up.

But if he didn't run, who would? The Democrats hadn't had a disputed nomination since 1932. He shrugged. If he decided he wouldn't run, he also wouldn't need to worry about that any more. No one would care what he thought thirty seconds after he announced he was through. He would turn into the lamest of lame ducks.

Stalin and Mao had no worries like that. They'd give orders till somebody carried them out feet-first. Truman had done his best to arrange that for Uncle Joe, but it hadn't quite worked out. A damn shame, really. How the Reds would have worked out who succeeded their longtime dictator would have been . . . interesting.

Muttering under his breath, he fired up the radio again. He did need to hear what was going on. The sound came on almost at once; the tubes were still warm. "Defense Secretary Marshall has declined to comment on Senator McCarthy's latest accusations," the newsman said. "McCarthy continues to charge that the war is not being fought hard enough, and that, while Marshall was Secretary of State, he permitted many Communists to join the State Department."

There had been some Reds in the State Department. A few of them *had* given Moscow a hand. More were people who'd been Communists in the 1930s, when, if you were young and you hated the Nazis, that was where you were liable to end up. Just about all of them had got over it.

There were also some Reds at Los Alamos and other places that worked on A-bombs. Without their help, Stalin might not have had any of his own yet. That was a crying shame, no two ways about it. Things there had also tightened up, though. Or Truman sure hoped they had.

He telephoned George Marshall. When the Secretary of Defense came on the line, Truman said, "Isn't it wonderful to be loved?"

"Excuse me, Mr. President?" Marshall said.

"Well, let me put it this way instead—when an SOB like Joe McCarthy comes after you with a meat-axe, you must be doing something right."

"Oh. Him." The patrician distaste in Marshall's voice could have belonged to a Roman senator eyeing a barbarian chieftain sightseeing in the imperial city during Hadrian's reign.

"Yeah, him," Truman said. "He's a snake, and a poisonous one at that."

"People like him are part of the price we pay for living in a free country." Marshall paused. "I keep telling myself so. Some days, I have more trouble believing it than others."

"I know what you mean, and this is one of *those* days," Truman said. "This is one of the days when I remember how many people in the Weimar Republic said the same thing about that beer-hall babbler in Munich. His stupid party would never amount to a hill of beans, not in a million years."

"Oh, yes. That's also crossed my mind, sir," Marshall said. "The Nazis *didn't* amount to much, not until the Depression gave them a boost. I can hope McCarthy won't, either."

"So can I. So do I." But Truman wasn't happy with his own answer. Marshall was right: the Depression had let Hitler take off. A national disaster had a way of discrediting the people who were in charge when it happened.

Well, what was World War III if it wasn't a national disaster? So far, only Maine and the western part of the United States had had bombs fall on them. But Truman knew *so far* meant just that and no further. The Russians weren't done. He'd just hit them again. Now they would try to hit back. American defenses would do their best to stop whatever Stalin came up with. And maybe their best would prove good enough, and maybe it wouldn't.

What would happen if, say, Detroit got it, and Chicago, and Boston, and Miami? Would that be enough of a catastrophe to make the citizens storm the White House and the

Capitol with torches and pitchforks and—very likely—nooses? If it wasn't, what would be?

And wouldn't that be the kind of tide a power-hungry, opportunistic bastard like Joe McCarthy could ride to power? Tail Gunner Joe was bound to hope it was. Not quite aware he was thinking out loud, Truman said, "That man ought to have himself an accident."

"Those are Stalin's rules, sir, and Hitler's, not ours," Marshall said.

The President sighed. "Uh-huh. I know. But if Hitler'd had an accident like that in, oh, 1928, the world'd be better off today."

"Maybe. Or maybe the Germans would have wound up with a dictator who knew what he was doing and didn't make the dumb mistakes Adolf did," Marshall replied. "It's all a crapshoot, and you don't know what the dice will do till you roll 'em."

"There's a cheerful thought!" Truman exclaimed. He'd had too many cheerful thoughts like that lately.


Vasili Yasevich walked through the pines toward the Amur. He hadn't seen many people lately. He didn't much want to see people right now. He was ragged and dirty and tired and hungry, but he preferred all of those to some friendly fool who'd start asking questions.

Snow crunched beneath his *valenki*. May or not, it lingered long here under the trees. Back in the day, people had said that tigers lived in these woods. His father had sold what he claimed to be tiger liver and gall bladder—and other, more intimate, parts—to Chinese customers. He'd charged through the nose for them, too, even though he didn't think they did anything. He knew the Chinese thought they did something, and that was what counted.

A tiger would get it over with quicker than either the Chinese police or the MGB. A tiger would also get it over with quicker than getting caught on the fringes of an atomic blast. He'd been far enough from Harbin not to get hurt when that A-bomb went off. He was traveling through the chilly night a few days before when a flash of light far, far away said another town got fed to that fire. He didn't know for sure which one, but Khabarovsk seemed the best guess.

Now people there were melted and burned and blinded

and going through the hell of radiation sickness. He'd already seen that once. Once was three times too many for a single lifetime.

But the Chinese character that meant *crisis* combined the ones for *danger* and *opportunity*. If he made it to the Soviet side of the Amur, he could claim he came from the outskirts of Khabarovsk and had got away with just the clothes on his back. Most of the time, the MGB would automatically snatch up anybody who couldn't show proper papers. Even the Chekists, though, had to realize plenty of refugees from cities that got A-bombed wouldn't have made a point of taking their documents with them.

Danger, yes. From everything his father and mother had said, danger was constant company in the USSR. But also opportunity. He had a chance to fit himself into Soviet life he never would have got if not for the American bombers.

One thing at a time. First he had to reach the far side of the Amur. That might not be so easy. He could already hear it gurgling past in front of him, so he was getting close. He knew it was broad and swift and cold. Trying to swim it was probably asking to freeze or to get swept downstream and drowned.

Half an hour later, he reached the river. He'd come this far. The Chinese hadn't caught him. That struck him as a miracle bigger than any the priests in the Orthodox church in Harbin blathered about when he was a kid. The pines on the far side of the river belonged to another country, one where his looks didn't brand him a foreign devil. All he had to do was cross.

The Amur held a few low, muddy islands. They were boat-shaped, with the long stretch paralleling the current. Vasili got the idea that the ones he saw might not be there five years from now, but that others could rise to take their places.

He wondered if he could make a raft and paddle or pole out to one of them. It would be a useful way station . . . if he could get to it. What he had for chopping down trees, unfortunately, were his straight razor and the little knife in the top of his right felt boot.

He bent down and scooped up a handful of water to drink. The river was bitterly cold, even worse than he'd guessed. No, he didn't want to swim in it. But how could he cross if he didn't? He wasn't Jesus, to walk across on top of the water in one of those priestly miracles.

That water was glassy clear. Fish swam in it—he could see

them. His stomach growled. He'd always thought the Japanese were disgusting for eating raw fish. If he could somehow pull one of these out of the water, he didn't think he'd bother cleaning it before he gulped it. Scales? Fins? Bones? Guts? Down the hatch!

Then he saw the most beautiful thing he'd ever seen. He was sure of it. When you wanted—when you had—to cross a river, what could be more gorgeous than a man with a fishing pole sitting in a rowboat?

Was the man Russian or Chinese? Vasili didn't know or care. He still had one trade dollar and a little of the opium he'd left Harbin with. What food he'd eaten on the way north, he'd bought with the other silver coin and the rest of the drug. When they already suspected you of peddling it, you stopped caring about what they'd do if they caught you.

Vasili cupped his hands in front of his mouth and yelled "Hey!" as loud as he could. The fellow in the boat kept right on fishing. "Hey!" Vasili yelled again, even louder this time—loud enough so something in his throat started to hurt. He waved his arms. He jumped up and down.

After what seemed forever and a day, the fisherman noticed he was there. The man waved back to him, as if to a friend.

"Hey!" Vasili screamed one more time. He almost added *Yob tvoyu mat', idiot!* Almost but not quite: a Russian would understand the obscenity, and even a Chinese on the border might. He did wave again, and beckon, and yell, "Come here!"

Slowly, languidly, the fisherman started rowing toward him. Just the way he did it made Vasili think he had to be a Russian. Chinese didn't act as if they had all the time in the world. They knew too well they didn't.

And, sure enough, when the man got close enough to hail Vasili without rupturing his lungs, he called, *"Zdrast'ye!"* By then, Vasili had seen that he wore a shaggy russet beard. It might help keep him warm through the winters in these parts. Vasili's whiskers were getting longer and thicker by the day, too.

"How are you?" Vasili answered, also in Russian. "How's the fishing?"

"Not too bad, not too bad," the fellow said. He picked up a bottle from the bottom of the boat and raised it to his mouth.

His throat worked. Russians ran on vodka the way tanks ran on diesel fuel. "Ah! That's the straight goods!"

"How about you take me over to the other side?" Vasili said.

"What?" The man stared at him. "You *want* to go over there?" He jerked a thumb back at the Soviet side of the river.

"*Da.* That's right," Vasili said.

A look of sozzled cunning spread across the fisherman's face. "How come? What did you do on your side?"

"I got a big shot sore at me. What else do you need to do?"

"Not fucking much. So it's the same down there as it is on our side, huh?"

"It's got to be the same all over the world," Vasili said sourly. "I can give you some silver. I can give you a little opium, too, if you let me have a couple of fish."

"Opium? I'd rather drink vodka."

*Fool,* Vasili thought. Aloud, he said, "I bet you can find somebody who wants it."

"Maybe." That shrewd look came back. "How do I know you ain't trying to get me into trouble?"

"How do I know you aren't a Chekist?" Vasili returned.

The fisherman guffawed. "Think I'd be out here dicking around if I belonged to the MGB? Those cunts make you *do* stuff. You can't just take off and go fishing every time you get a hard-on for it."

From everything Vasili'd heard, that was true. He said, "I'll give you a trade dollar for the trip, along with the opium for the fish."

"A dollar? From America? They'd slice my balls off if I tried to do anything with it." Now the Russian—the Soviet Russian—looked alarmed.

As patiently as he could, Vasili said, "They call them Mex dollars in China. It's still silver. It's still heavy. If you can't pass it, you can melt it down." He sounded as persuasive as he knew how, as if he were trying to get a girl into bed with him. "Come on, pal. Take me across and then forget you ever saw me."

"It's like that, huh?"

"Of course it's like that. What, you think I came to China for my fucking vacation? Come on, take me over. It'll be worthwhile for you, as long as you keep your yap shut."

If the fisherman decided it was too risky, all Vasili could do was wait till another boat came along. If another boat ever came along. He made himself remember that, and didn't cuss as hard as he might have. He tried to look friendly and harmless.

He must have managed, because the Russian rowed over. The boat's nose or prow or whatever you called it scraped on Chinese mud. "*Khorosho.* Hop in."

In Vasili hopped. He showed the fisherman the trade dollar and the opium. He also flipped open his straight razor. "I'll pay you when we get across."

Not much later, the boat grated on Soviet soil. It sounded the same as the Chinese mud had. Vasili left the coin and the glass jar. He took three trout.

"Thanks," he said, and got out. The fisherman, whose name he'd never learned, went back into the Amur as fast as he could.

*I've come home,* Vasili thought. Then he found out what raw fish tasted like.


Istvan Szolovits crouched in a foxhole that wasn't deep enough. Up ahead, a machine gun threw death in his direction. Along with the stream of reports from the gun, every so often a bullet would crack past not nearly far enough over his head. The team running that gun knew what they were doing with it. They traversed it so the rounds streamed back and forth. Anyone who got up and tried to advance on it asked to catch one with his teeth, or maybe with his navel. The gunners were shooting low.

Istvan wasn't sure whether the machine gun was in Bochum or Essen. For that matter, he wasn't sure whether he was in Bochum or Essen. The two German towns west of Dortmund blended seamlessly, one into the other. The only difference between them Istvan could see was that mail to them didn't go through the same post office.

He still had no idea why nobody'd killed him. He had to be luckier than he'd ever imagined. The Russians were determined to get as much use as they could from the Hungarian troops they'd brought forward. They thought using soldiers meant using them up, too. As far as the Russians were concerned, men were as disposable as bullets or boots.

That applied to their own troops. It applied even more to soldiers from Hungary or Poland or Czechoslovakia or Bulgaria or Romania. If getting killed advanced the sacred cause of socialism, or if the Russian marshals even suspected it might, they spent troops like kopeks.

*Foomp! Foomp!* Those were mortars going off. With the evil little beasts, the Hungarians didn't even have to stick their noses out of their holes to shoot back at the machine gun. Istvan approved of shooting back without running the risk of getting hurt.

The machine gun fell silent. Istvan wondered whether the mortar had killed the men who served it or they were bluffing and waiting to shoot down anybody naive enough to try to advance. Such questions were important. If you were a Hungarian soldier fighting in the Ruhr, they were life-and-death important.

In the lull, somebody from the other side shouted in Magyar: "What are you fools doing fighting for Stalin? Come over to the Americans! You'll be free, and no one will try to kill you or make you do anything you don't want to do!"

Hearing the man reminded Istvan how many Magyars had left their own country for the United States in the days before the First World War. It reminded him all kinds of ways, in fact. The American soldier who spoke the language had plainly learned from his folks as a child, not in school. He had a peasant accent from the back of beyond, and an old-fashioned peasant accent at that. Magyar in Hungary had moved on, while his was stuck in the past like a fly in amber.

None of which had anything to do with the price of beer. He might talk like a clodhopper from 1895, but his message was modern as tomorrow. He wasn't saying anything Istvan hadn't asked himself a hundred times. Istvan didn't care a filler about the solidarity of workers and peasants all over the world. He was here because Stalin and Stalin's followers, both Russian and Hungarian, would have killed him or tortured him or jailed him had he tried to refuse. That was the long and short of it.

*"Kibaszott szarházi!"* Those were Sergeant Gergely's dulcet tones. How did he know that the Magyar-speaking American was a fucking shithouse clown? Odds were he didn't, but that didn't stop him.

"God fuck your stinking, wrinkled whore of a mother!" the guy on the other side yelled back. Istvan giggled. Maybe he hadn't learned *all* his Magyar from his mommy and daddy.

"Yell all you want, dog's dick," Gergely said. "We didn't drop any A-bombs on your country."

"No, Stalin did. You just suck him off," the Hungarian-American replied.

Sergeant Gergely spoke to his own men: "You see how we're all friends together, right?"

Some of the Magyars answered to show him they agreed. Whether in fact they did or not was anybody's guess. Gergely had to know that. This was his second war fighting for a dubious cause. He had a different dubious cause now from the one he'd aided during World War II, but, as then, Hungary was doing what a great power required, not what it wanted to do itself.

Istvan Szolovits kept his mouth shut. He didn't think protestations of loyalty would give the sergeant any more confidence in him. For that matter, he had no confidence in himself. If he found a chance to surrender to the Americans without getting killed, he figured he would jump at it. The Magyar-speaking Yank had that much right.

In the meantime, though, he needed to keep fighting. Chances to surrender didn't come along every day. The Americans would cheerfully kill him most of the time. The best way to stay alive and wait for the moment he might not find involved shooting back at them when they fired at him.

Which they did, with rifles, machine guns, and artillery. Under cover of all that flying metal, some of them started moving forward through the wreckage of whichever German city this turned out to be. They aimed to flank out the Hungarians and drive them back.

Istvan was ready to retreat, if he could come out of his hole without getting killed. But half a dozen Soviet T-54s rumbled forward like dinosaurs squashing little mammals under their feet in some prehistoric swamp. Unlike those ancient little mammals, some of the Americans carried bazookas. But when two rockets in a row glanced off the tanks' turtle turrets without penetrating, the Yanks gave it up as a bad job and fell back to their old line.

An American who'd stopped a machine-gun bullet from one of the tanks with his face lay only fifty meters or so from Istvan's hole. Greed overcame caution. He crawled to the dead Yank, took his food and cigarettes and first-aid kit, and slithered back to cover.

After dark fell, he gave Sergeant Gergely two of the three

packs he'd looted. "Thanks, kid, but those Russian tankers deserve these more than I do," the veteran said.

"Could be, but I know you and I don't know them," Istvan said. "Boy, that American who spoke Magyar sure talked funny, didn't he?"

"Oh, just a little," Gergely answered. "Like he had cowshit on his boots and rode a donkey to church. I'll tell you something else, though—you think the Yanks won't fuck you over same as the krauts and the Ivans, you're nuts. They're big. You ain't. That's all it takes."

"Could be," Szolovits said again.

Gergely couldn't have seen the expression on his face. It was too dark. He chuckled anyhow, unpleasantly. "Don't do anything stupid—that's all I've got to tell you," he said. Istvan wished it weren't such good advice.

**25**

THE DOCTOR WHO EXAMINED Konstantin Moro-
zov's burned legs looked Jewish as Jewish could be: sallow
skin, dark eyes, hooked nose. But she also filled out her
white coat very nicely. "Sergeant, you look like you're fit to
go back on duty," she said. "Do you feel fit?"

His flesh remained tender—or, if you wanted to tell the
whole story, sore. He nodded anyway. "Yes, Comrade Doctor," he answered. He might have said no to a sawbones who
shaved and won another day or two on this cot. Telling a
woman no was harder. It felt like admitting he had a needle
dick.

"All right." She wrote something on the paper in the clipboard she carried. "The *rodina* needs every man who can
fight." He was going to say *I serve the Soviet Union!,* but
she'd already moved on to the next iron cot.

They handed him a fresh set of tankman's coveralls and a
new leather helmet with built-in earphones. They gave him
just enough time to put his sergeant's shoulder boards on the
coveralls. They they sent him over to the replacements' assignment depot.

"What was your last duty before you were wounded?"
asked the military clerk in charge of the depot. He wore a
patch over his right eye, so chances were he'd paid his dues
during the Great Patriotic War. He could still do a job like
this, and save a whole man for combat.

"Tank commander," Morozov replied proudly.

*"Ochen khorosho,"* the mutilated man said. "Have a seat
on one of the benches. I don't think you'll need to wait long."

Konstantin sat. The bench was too low. The building had

been a school till war washed over it. Now half the roof had burned away. On one wall was a poster of a bulldozer clearing away rubble from the last war. Konstantin couldn't read the words. It wasn't his language, or even his alphabet. If he'd had to guess, though, he would have figured it said something like *We're getting back on our feet.*

He scowled. *You're a bunch of fucking Fritzes,* he thought. *We flattened you once. Now we'll do it again.* After everything he'd seen in his own country during the last war, he wasn't about to waste sympathy on Germans.

"I'm just out of the aid station," he said to the corporal next to him. "Can you give me a smoke?"

"Sure thing, Comrade Sergeant." The other guy let him have a *papiros.* He smoked one himself, too. They started talking. The corporal's name was Igor Pechnikov. He added, "My father really did make brick stoves. How's that for a kick in the head?"

"Funny," Konstantin said. Pechnikov was a son of a stovemaker both by surname and for real. Names built from trades and the trades themselves hardly ever matched these days, but they did with him. Morozov asked, "What do you do in the army?"

"I'm an RPG man," the other guy answered. "A 155 took out most of my squad, so they're putting me in a new unit. How about you?"

"We probably shouldn't be friends. I'm in a tank, and you go around blowing them up," Morozov said.

"Not ours. The enemy's," the corporal said.

"I do understand that, yes." Konstantin was about to say more, but the one-eyed clerk chose that moment to shout his name. He thumped Pechnikov on the shoulder, shouted "I serve the Soviet Union!", and hurried over to the clerk's little table. His legs hurt more than he wished they did; he could have used those extra couple of days on his back.

A captain stood there. He eyed Morozov the way a hungry man would eye pork sausages in a butcher's shop. "A tank commander, are you?" he said.

"That's right, Comrade Captain," Morozov replied.

"Are you fit?"

"Sir, they wouldn't have let me leave the aid station if I wasn't." That was nonsense, and the captain had to know it as well as Konstantin did. Aid stations were for getting people back into the fight fast.

The officer didn't complain, though. He just said, "I'm Arkady Lapshin. Come along with me."

Konstantin came. A jeep waited outside: Lend-Lease from the last war or captured in this one. The lance-corporal behind the wheel saluted Lapshin, nodded to Konstantin, and zoomed away as soon as they got in.

Sometimes he stayed on the road, sometimes not. The going was often better away from it. Much of the toughest fighting had been along the highways, and they showed it. The jeep went wherever the driver wanted it to. For a vehicle with tires, not tracks, it got around.

Artillery began to fire as they neared the front. Lapshin took it in stride. Morozov tried not to fidget, there on the jeep's hard back seat. He was used to armor between himself and shell fragments. These were Soviet shells going out, but American shells were liable to start coming in to answer them.

He thought the driver would take him into a tank park, the way they'd done things the last time he needed a new machine. But he'd had three crewmen out of four then. Now he was the sole survivor. If he hadn't been head and shoulders out of the T-54 when it got hit, he'd be as dead as the rest of them. Luck. All luck. Or God, if you could take God seriously.

No tank park this time. A tank under some fruit trees. Three men were working on the engine: a corporal, a lance-corporal, and a private. The jeep stopped. Lapshin hopped out. "This way," he said, so Konstantin followed him.

The three soldiers—especially the corporal—eyed Morozov with what could only be disdain. He knew what that had to mean. Their old commander must have stopped one, maybe when he stood up in his cupola. The corporal had to be the gunner. He would have wanted command—and the promotion likely to go with it—for himself. How big a pain in the neck would he be now that he hadn't got them?

Captain Lapshin was, or affected to be, oblivious to the sour looks. "Here's your new commander, boys," he said cheerfully. "Sergeant Morozov did it in the last war, too. He's just over a wound. Morozov, here's your crew: Juris Eigims, Gennady Kalyakin, and Vazgen Sarkisyan." He introduced them in order of rank, and almost surely in the order gunner-driver-loader.

*Great,* Morozov thought. *Only one other Slav.* Sarkisyan

was squat and swarthy, with a beard he'd need to shave twice a day. He looked like the Armenian he was, in other words. Kalyakin had a Byelorussian accent. Eigims . . . Yes, Eigims would be trouble.

By his name, he was a Latvian, or maybe a Lithuanian. Either way, he would have been a kid when the USSR annexed his homeland. Some of the Balts were still pissy over that, not that they could do anything about it. Pissy or not, he'd have to shoot straight if he wanted to keep breathing. But how many other ways would he try to undercut his new superior? By the scowl on his blue-eyed face, as many as he could.

"What were you guys doing with the engine?" Morozov asked.

"Just trying to get it running smoother," Eigims answered. His Russian held a musical lilt. He seemed fluent enough, which was good. Sarkisyan didn't talk much, but a loader didn't need a whole lot of Russian. As long as he got the difference between AP and HE, they'd do fine. A gunner, though, had to be able to talk and to understand.

"How's the fuel? How much water in it? How are the filters?" Konstantin asked the basic questions. Water in the fuel was worse than in a gasoline engine. And diesel fuel, being thicker than gasoline, carried more dirt and impurities along with it. With bad filters, crud could mess up your machinery in nothing flat.

"All seem all right. Check for yourself if you care to, Comrade Sergeant." By the way Eigims said it, Konstantin realized they'd gummed up the engine on purpose somewhere. Where? That was for him to find.

And he did, too: clogged injectors on two of the engine's cylinders. He cleaned them out. "Fire it up now," he said. "You should be able to hear a difference." Juris Eigims kicked at the dirt. If he'd disliked Konstantin before, he hated him now.

As things went, Luisa Hozzel was lucky. The Russians who'd swept into Fulda hadn't raped her. They seemed to be behaving better than they had in the last war. The house had lost its windows, but it hadn't taken any direct shell hits. Now she had plywood or cardboard over all of them.

And she'd taken Gustav's Third *Reich* medals up into the

attic and out of sight before any Red Army soldiers came in. Most of the men around here had served in the *Wehrmacht* or the *Waffen*-SS, and most of the ones who had served fought on the Eastern Front. The Russians hadn't dragged anybody out of his house and shot him in the town square for what he'd done then. A couple of men on the block had gone missing, though, and their families with them. Maybe they'd died in the first hours of the invasion. Maybe they'd fled. Luisa didn't believe it, though.

She stayed indoors as much as she could. Almost all the women in Fulda seemed to do that. The Russians might show better manners than they'd had before, but how far could you trust them? People still whispered horror stories about everything they'd done in eastern Germany.

She couldn't stay in all the time, though. She had to get food. Whenever she headed for the grocer's, she put on her oldest, frumpiest clothes. She messed up her hair so it looked more like a stork's nest than anything else. She scrubbed her face with harsh laundry soap. She did her best to look as if she were in her late forties, not her late twenties.

So far, it had worked. The Americans who'd held Fulda before had whistled and howled at her when she walked by. She'd always ignored them, which made them laugh. They went no further than laughing and whistling and howling, though. Plenty of other German girls didn't ignore them. If you were out for what you could get, you could get plenty from the Amis.

By contrast, the Russians now in Fulda ignored her. Or they had so far, though every time she left the house her heart jumped into her mouth till she got inside again.

Another trip today. She stuck a stringbag inside her purse, fortified herself with a knock of straight schnapps, and stepped out into the big, dangerous world. Sunlight, even the watery sunlight Fulda usually got, made her blink and squint. She didn't mind. With her face screwed up, she'd look older and homelier yet.

Fulda had changed since the Russians drove the Americans out. Part of that was battle damage; the Amis and the German emergency militia had fought hard to hold the town, but they'd got overwhelmed. (She had no idea what had happened to Gustav after he and Max and some others went off to play soldiers again. She prayed he was all right. She didn't know what else she could do.)

And part of it was the different flavor of propaganda she had to put up with. When Fulda was part of the U.S. occupation zone, posters had said things like *It goes forward with the Marshall plan!* It had seemed to go forward, too. Now . . .

Now she stared at Joseph Stalin and his bushy mustache—more impressive than Hitler's, she had to admit—everywhere she went. *For a free, socialist Germany!* the message under his portrait said. Other posters showed the Russian hammer and sickle and the East German hammer and compass side by side. *Together to victory!* that one shouted. Still others showed Russian tanks and soldiers going forward. They declared *The proletariat on the march is invincible!*

Walls, fences, lampposts, telephone poles—they'd all got a thick layer of those posters. She hadn't yet seen a dog with one of them pasted to its side, but that had to be only a matter of time.

Three Russian soldiers came up the street toward her. They reeled instead of walking—they were drunk. Everything people said about how Russians poured it down seemed to be true. Luisa got out of their way and ducked into a shop that sold secondhand clothes. With Russians, as with her own people, drunks were dangerous. They didn't care about what they did, and they forgot rules they respected sober.

Ice ran up her back when one of the Ivans peered in after her. But then he staggered after his friends. She breathed again.

"Can I show you anything?" asked the shopkeeper, a woman—probably—too old to need to worry about Russian attentions.

"Thank you, no," Luisa said. "I'm sorry, but I just wanted to get away from those . . . people." She didn't know the woman wouldn't report her, so she used a neutral word.

"Oh." The shopkeeper nodded. "Well, it's not as if you're the first one. They've made me worry about them a couple of times. Me!" She laughed. She knew she was no spring chicken. Lowering her voice, she went on, "The *Führer* was right, you know. They really are *Untermenschen.*"

Didn't she remember anything from the Nazi days about keeping her mouth shut? She'd just put her life in Luisa's hands. "I think I'd better go," Luisa said. "I want to see what the grocery has left." She didn't say *I want to see if the grocery has anything left*. Whether this foolish woman did or not, she knew better than to come out with anything so suicidal.

*"Auf wiedersehen,"* the shopkeeper said wistfully as Luisa left. She couldn't have got much business even before the Russians came. She was bound to have even less now.

The grocer's was another two and a half blocks along the street. Several more Red Army men passed Luisa as she walked. They were all more or less sober, and none of them bothered her. Maybe her hideous disguise was working. Maybe they just had orders not to fraternize.

No, it couldn't be just that. The first couple of years after the last round of fighting stopped, the Amis had orders like those. Orders or not, they'd done their best to pick up anything in a skirt.

*"Guten Tag, Frau* Hozzel," the grocer said when she walked in.

*"Guten Tag,* Horst," Luisa answered. *"Wie geht's?"*

He shrugged and waved at the half-empty shelves. "It goes like this, that's how. Whatever I can get, I put out."

"It's not as bad as it was in '44 or '45," Luisa said. There'd been nothing on the shelves then. People got by with turnips and cabbages. And older folks, the ones from her parents' generation, claimed even those bad times were nothing next to 1917 and 1918.

She picked up a tin of pickled beets. The label was in German, but it was no brand she'd ever seen before. It was no brand at all, in fact: it said *Canned at State Canning Plant Number Fourteen.* "Where did this come from?" she asked.

"Somewhere in the east," the grocer answered. "It's not very good, but the Russians want to get rid of them, so I have lots."

"It's food." Luisa put three tins in the stringbag. She walked along till she came upon sardines in smaller, flatter tins. Their label said they'd come from State Canning Plant Number Three. "How about these?"

"I won't lie to you. They're pretty bad," Horst said.

"Well . . ." Luisa hadn't seen anything like them since the invasion. "How bad is pretty bad?"

"My cat wouldn't touch them—that's how bad," the grocer told her. "You might want to use them if you're fertilizing a garden in your yard. Otherwise? Not a chance."

"They're expensive for fertilizer. We'll see." She put one tin in the stringbag. She chose some potatoes that didn't seem too wretched. Horst's spinach actually looked good. Up and down the aisles, doing the best she could.

When she came to the counter to pay, he took a box out from under it. "Want some of these? I save them for my good customers." The box held strawberries.

"You bet I do! How much?" She winced when he told her, but nodded.

He wrapped them in brown paper and string so no one could see what they were. She paid him and walked out the door happier than she'd dreamt she would be. Strawberries! Something nice when you didn't expect it made even life under the Russians worth living.

When Marian Staley woke up, all she saw was fog. Sleeping in the Studebaker with Linda always made the windows steam up on the inside. She rolled one of them down and looked out. It was foggy on the outside, too. She couldn't see farther than fifty feet or so. Summer might be only three weeks away, but northern Washington hadn't got the news.

Linda was snoring in the front seat. She was getting over a cold she'd probably picked up from one of the other children in her class. Packs of kids produced swarms of germs. Marian remembered that from her own elementary-school days. When somebody came down with chicken pox or measles or mumps or scarlet fever, pretty soon the whole class— sometimes the whole school—did.

These days, penicillin flattened scarlet fever. The others kept turning up like the bad pennies they were. They were less common than Linda's ordinary cold, but not enough less.

Pretty soon, Marian would have to get Linda up, get her breakfast, and take her back to the infectious world of other children. If she thought about things like that, she wouldn't have to think about the A-bomb crater—and it was exactly that—in her own life.

She'd known going to war was dangerous. You couldn't help knowing that, in an intellectual way. When countries fought wars, some people didn't come home again. You built statues to commemorate them, you felt sorry for their widows and other loved ones, and you thought how lucky you were that such a horrible thing hadn't happened to you.

Only this time it had.

Bill wasn't coming home again. He'd never take them to a Rainiers game again (not that there'd be any Rainiers games for a while, either). He'd never teach Linda how to tie her shoes. He'd never change a flat tire or install new spark plugs with his usual matter-of-fact competence. He'd never turn off the bedroom light, put his face between her legs, and brazenly flutter his tongue right there, oh God *right* there. . . .

Marian shied away from that thought hard, like a skittish horse sidestepping and almost rearing when a piece of paper blew across the path in front of it. She was supposed to miss her dead husband because he'd been a good daddy and a good provider, dammit, not because he'd made her feel things she'd never imagined before the first time he got her girdle down and her panties off.

Well, wasn't she?

She'd been a good girl before she met Bill. Looking back, that felt like a lot of wasted time and wasted fun. It was what they told you to do, though, so you did it—till one day you got so horny, or somebody got you so horny, that you didn't any more. She'd never do that with him again. He'd never do that with her, do it to her. . . .

She puddled up at the same time as she wanted to touch herself. She missed her dead husband almost every conscious moment. She hadn't missed him quite like this before, though. Till she woke up this morning, she'd blotted out all thoughts about that part of their life together.

*Why?* she wondered. Making love, especially making love with somebody you really wanted to make love with *you,* was the best thing in the world you could do with your time. You couldn't do it all the time, but didn't that make the times you could all the sweeter?

When she looked down at her wristwatch, she let out a loud, long, this-is-the-world-and-I'm-stuck-with-it sigh. Then she leaned over the back of the front seat and shook her daughter. "Linda? Linda, honey? Time to get up, sweetie. It's a school day."

"I don't wanna," Linda muttered, still three-quarters asleep. Kindergarten had gone from exciting, different, new fun to boring routine in nothing flat. Linda was a human being, in other words—still on the small side, but unmistakably one of the tribe.

She eventually did stagger forth from the car. Marian took her to the stinking latrine tent and then to breakfast. The guy behind the counter gave each of them a bowl of cornflakes with reconstituted milk. "Yuck!" Linda said.

"You've got to eat it. So do I," Marian sad. She had instant coffee with it: a meal without a single natural ingredient anywhere in sight. No, that wasn't true—she did sweeten the coffee with sugar, not saccharine.

"Yuck!" Linda said again, but she emptied her little bowl. She wasn't fussy about food, for which Marian thanked heaven.

Marian had more trouble choking down her own cereal. As far as she was concerned, powdered milk was as much a chemical weapon as poison gas. It was cheap, and it was much easier to transport than whole milk. That made it ideal for feeding people in refugee camps. It tasted horrible? It was even worse than powdered mashed potatoes (a suppertime unfavorite)? So what? As long as the people stuck in refugee camps got fed at all, the government didn't care if they hated everything they ate.

She got Linda to the kindergarten on time. Then, without anybody to look after, she had no idea what to do with herself. Those bad thoughts that watching Linda kept her too busy to notice clamored for attention now. She mooched along with her head down, hardly caring where she was going. If not for her little girl, her gloom might have taken an even darker, more self-destructive turn. What really scared her was that it might anyhow.

"Good morning!"

That was so plainly aimed at her, she had to look up. From the guttural *r,* she already knew it was Fayvl Tabakman. "Hello," she said to the cobbler.

He studied her with narrowed, worried eyes. "How you are doing?" he asked. His English was quite good, especially since he'd had only a few years speaking it, but perfect it wasn't.

Marian started to say *Fine,* the way you did when anybody asked how you were. Only the note of genuine concern she heard in his voice made her answer honestly instead: "Not so hot, Mr. Tabakman. Not so hot."

He nodded. "I believe you. It is still very new for you, too new to take it all in. You have no notion how such a thing could have happened to *you.*"

*What do you know about it?* The angry thought fell to pieces as soon as it formed. He knew all about it. He'd known for years. His loved ones hadn't died in combat, the way Bill had. They'd been murdered, for no reason at all that anyone sane could find.

"How ... How did you get through it without going crazy?" she asked.

"Being at Auschwitz, that was almost a help," the Jew answered. "I had so much work to do, and I was so busy trying to stay alive my own self, when did I have time to grieve? And I was starving. Everything shuts down then—the feelings, too. So when I was freed and I could start thinking about what happened, time had gone by. Time is a blessing. Every day further away is a blessing."

"I—suppose so." It wasn't so much that Marian didn't believe as that she hadn't had enough days go by yet.

"It's true." He nodded again, and touched the brim of his cloth cap. "Well, I don't trouble you no more."

"You're not troubling me," she said quickly. "You know what I'm going through. You know better than I do—you've been through it yourself already."

"Today, tomorrow, the next day, the day after that, one at a time," Tabakman said. "It's all you can do. It's all anybody can do. You want somebody to talk to, I can maybe listen." He smiled with one side of his mouth. "Not a whole bunch of things to do in this place, you know?"

*I'm more interesting than twiddling his thumbs,* Marian thought. But she couldn't stay miffed. She didn't try very hard. Her wound was still fresh and raw. His might have scarred over, but, say what he would, how could it not still fester underneath?

Pain drew pain. Shared pain drew understanding. Or it might, anyhow. She could hope. A little while earlier, she hadn't been able to imagine even so much. You took what you could get, if you could get anything at all.


The mirror in the bathroom of the ground-floor flat Gustav Hozzel was defending hadn't broken. He couldn't guess why not; almost everything else in the place had. But he got his first good look at himself for a couple of weeks.

He looked like an Ami, but that was the uniform's fault. It was filthy and badly worn. So was he. Aside from looking like an American, he looked like hell. His whiskers were at that haven't-shaved-in-five-days stumblebum stage. More of the ones on his chin were coming in white.

His eyes . . . It wasn't that the bags under them would hold enough to take him to Brazil. That just meant he was desperately short on sleep. No *Frontschwein* ever got enough or, too often, any. The look in them worried him more. They were the eyes of a man who'd seen too much, done too much, and knew he had too much more to see and do.

A lot of *Landsers* on the Eastern Front had had eyes like that from the end of 1943 on. They knew they wouldn't whip the Ivans. And they knew they had to keep fighting anyway. It wasn't despair. Damnation came a lot closer.

No doubt he'd had that look himself in the old days. Now he had it again. He'd been a kid then. He'd seen all the hideous things that could happen, but somehow he'd been sure they would always happen to someone else. He wasn't sure of that any more. He knew too well anything could happen to anybody.

"Surrender!" a Red Army soldier shouted in German. "We'll treat you well if you do!"

All the emergency militiamen in the block of flats burst out laughing. They wouldn't have believed that *Quatsch* in the last war, let alone this one. *"Yob tvoyu mat'!"* one of them shouted back. As some of the Ivans could *Deutsch sprechen,* so a good many Germans had picked up bits of filthy Russian. What other kind was worth learning?

Of course, yelling *Fuck your mother!* at people with guns had a price. The Russians started hosing down the building with four heavy machine guns on the same mount. They hadn't played with that kind of toy the last time. The Germans had; the Americans, too. It made a dandy light flak weapon to chase off low-flying raiders or maybe even shoot them down.

And, if you pointed it at a ground target, it also did a grand job of chewing that to pieces, along with anyone unlucky enough to be inside. When the mechanized death rattle started outside, Gustav threw himself flat. That was all he could do, that and pray. Hiding behind something wouldn't help. What could you hide behind to keep off a slug as big as your thumb?

The one drawback to the monster was that it gobbled ammo at a rate even industrial giants like the Russians and Americans found ridiculous. A minute went through a cou-

ple of thousand cartridges. On the other hand, the bullets
from those cartridges went through anything this side of a
tank out to a kilometer and a half.

They were shooting a little high. Part of the upper stories
of the block of flats collapsed with a rending crash—luckily,
not the part right above Gustav. And he'd never look in *that*
mirror again. The Russians must have bought themselves
about seven hundred years of bad luck.

He hoped like anything they had. As soon as the quad gun
stopped, he started shooting. He wasn't the only one, but the
return fire was thinner than it would have been before the
Russians turned their creature loose. Unless your men were
all hiding down in the cellar, they'd take casualties.

He got a glimpse of somebody with fancy shoulder boards
sending soldiers forward. A burst snarled from his PPSh.
The Russian officer clutched at himself as he fell over. Dead
or wounded, Gustav didn't care. The bastard was out of the
fight. With luck, whoever took over for him wouldn't know
what the plan was. Russians without plans panicked at any
little thing. With plans, they would trample you and mash
you flat.

They kept coming without missing a beat, so evidently the
plan was to clear out the blocks of flats right around here.
Gustav smelled smoke, fresh and strong. Red Army heavy
machine guns could fire incendiary rounds. Or any ordinary
hot slug might have set something on fire above his head.

Time to leave, then. Burning a building down was one of
the oldest ways to clear it of foes, and still one of the best.
Time to leave, before he couldn't get away. He fed the PPSh
a fresh magazine, then bade that bathroom a none too fond
farewell. Small sparkling pieces of the mirror crunched
under the soles of his boots.

The rest of the flat was in even worse shape. When he got
out into the hallway, he almost bumped into Rolf. They both
started to raise their weapons, then stopped when they realized they were on the same side. "Sorry about that," Gustav
said with a sickly grin.

"It's all right. That shit happens." The ex-LAH man's grin
seemed more wolfish than sickly. "Don't want to stay in the
oven till you bake all golden brown?"

"Fuck golden brown. Fuck you, too," Gustav said. "Let's
get the hell out of here."

Rolf started whistling something as they hurried down the

stairs to the cellar. Gustav didn't recognize it at first. Then he did, and almost tripped and broke his neck. It was "Heigh Ho! Heigh Ho! It's off to work we go," the dwarfs' song from *Snow White*. Where the devil did that come from?

After another second or two, it made ... some sense, anyhow. In German lore and legend, dwarfs were mostly underground beings, miners and tunnelers and the like. The German militiamen in Bochum and Essen and now Duisburg used the same skills. The cellars on this block and the next one over all had tunnels running from one to the next. You could move through them, as the two Germans were doing now, or, if you had to, you could fight in them.

"I haven't had so much fun in I can't remember when," Gustav said as they tramped through the darkness toward the next block farther west.

"You want fun, go play with yourself," Rolf answered. "We've got to stop the Russians. They've trampled almost the whole *Vaterland* now."

"I never would have noticed if you hadn't told me," Gustav said. "Why the hell do you think we're in goddamn Duisburg when we started out in Fulda?"

"But if Stalin conquers the whole *Reich,* he'll Bolshevize it," Rolf said, as if that were the worst thing he could imagine.

Gustav could think of worse ones. "If Stalin takes the whole *Reich,* odds are he'll kill both of us by the time he does."

"If all the *Vaterland* bows down to the hammer and sickle, I don't want to live." Rolf still sounded like a *Waffen*-SS man, all right.

"*I* want to live," Gustav said. "I want to throw him out of my country. I want to kill Russians. I'm not so very interested in dying myself, thank you very much."

"Sometimes death in battle is necessary for the higher good." Rolf couldn't strike a pose here in the gloom, but he sounded as if he wanted to.

It wasn't that he was wrong: more that an asshole who was right remained an asshole. "If you want to get killed, don't let me stop you," Gustav said. Then he froze as a flashlight beam speared him and Rolf from out of the black ahead.

"Come on, chuckleheads!" said a German voice behind the beam. "We're going to blow this tunnel in a couple of minutes, to keep the Ivans from following you guys."

That got Gustav and Rolf moving, as the soldier with the flashlight no doubt meant it to. Gustav wondered what kind of fieldworks they had on the next block, how long they could hold them, and how many Russians would die attacking them. He lit a smoke. He was starting to like Luckies. And he was still in there fighting.

# 26

IT WAS PAST CLOSING time. Gently but firmly, Daisy Baxter had herded RAF and USAF men out of the Owl and Unicorn into the blacked-out streets of Fakenham. Some of them were liable to fall off their bicycles on the way back to the base at Sculthorpe. They might get knots on their noggins and scrapes on their knees. They were unlikely to smash themselves up the way they could driving drunk in motorcars.

Surveying the mess, she let out a long sigh. The more they drank, the worse the slobs they became. Empty and almost empty pints everywhere, ashtrays overflowing with butts, cigarettes stubbed out on tabletops, potato-crisp and meat-pie wrappers tossed to the floor . . . At least no one tonight had thrown up before he could get to the toilets. She hated that.

Daisy sighed again. She wanted to go to bed herself. It had been another long day. But she had to clean up first. That was one of the rules. You couldn't sleep till things were tidy. If you didn't take care of it, the elves wouldn't, either. You just couldn't get good elves these days.

She lit a cigarette. After she'd done it, she wondered why she'd bothered. The smoke already in the pub left the air as thick and gray and curdled as a bad London fog. Just breathing had to give her as much nicotine as the Navy Cut between her index and middle fingers. But there it was, so she finished it.

Then she got to work. First she emptied the ashtrays and wiped the tables and the long bars clean. Then she swept the garbage off the floor. After she put away the broom and the dustpan, she got the carpet sweeper out of the closet to pick up what they couldn't. She'd deal with the squadrons of mugs after she took care of that.

Someone knocked on the door.

"Oh, bloody hell!" Daisy exclaimed. She could swear if she felt like it—who was going to hear her and be shocked? And feel like it she did. Every so often, one of the flyers, Yank or British, would decide he had to have one more pint no matter what, and bugger the laws that said he couldn't till tomorrow. That she'd lose her license for drawing him the pint never bothered him a farthing's worth. Why should it? It wasn't *his* license.

Sometimes, if she quietly went about her business and pretended the tipsy fool outside wasn't there, he would give up and go away. Sometimes he wouldn't, and then she'd have to deal with him. That was almost as much fun as visiting the dentist.

The one tonight wasn't going away, damn him. He knocked, paused, knocked some more. Another pause. Some more knocks. He was as regular and persistent as a woodpecker. He had to have a head just as hard as a woodpecker's, too.

Daisy muttered something she'd heard once from a liquored-up, belligerent ordnance sergeant. It should have made the tables and chairs catch fire. Muttering some more, she pushed out through the blackout curtains to the door.

She didn't open it. Through the wood and the tiny windows—useless now, with no lights on the street—she said, "It's past closing time. I can't serve you." She didn't say *So sod off!,* but her voice was full of the suggestion.

She waited for the angry, beery insistence. She'd been down this road too many times. She was sick of it. Right this second, she was sick of everything that had to do with running a pub.

But the American voice on the other side of the door didn't sound beery at all: "I don't want a pint. I just want to talk to you."

She still had to finish cleaning the floor. She had to wash and dry the glass mugs. She found herself opening the door anyhow. "Well, then, you'd better come in, hadn't you?"

"Thanks." Bruce McNulty stepped over the threshold. A little light leaked under the bottom of the blackout curtains: enough to make him seem to have suddenly materialized there. It was also enough to make Daisy shut the door behind him before the wandering air-raid warden walked by and started shouting at her.

When she pulled the curtains back to let him into the smoky snug, she saw that he was carrying a bouquet of roses. "What in blazes are those?" she demanded, pointing.

"They're something to help me say I'm sorry," McNulty answered. "I was out of line when I stomped out of here the last time I came. I was a jerk, but at least I know I was a jerk."

"You didn't have to do that," Daisy said. No one had brought her flowers since Tom, just before he had to go back to the Continent from leave, before he went off on the attack he didn't come back from. It hadn't been like him to do such a thing; he'd surprised her—startled her, really. Maybe he'd guessed something. Or maybe all the talk like that was just moonshine.

"I didn't do it because I had to. I did it because I wanted to." McNulty shifted from foot to foot like a nervous schoolboy. "Now I'd better get back to base, huh? I know you've got work to do here. You don't need me hanging around wasting your time."

"You're not wasting my time," Daisy said. "And thank you very much! I didn't say that before, did I? They're—they're lovely. There was no need—I *did* say that." She couldn't remember the last time she'd felt so flustered.

"My pleasure, believe me. Anyway, I'm gone. But is it okay if I come back as long as the Russians let me?"

"Of course it is! D'you think I want to see a good customer get away?" But Daisy realized flipness wouldn't do. When he joked about the Russians, he was trying not to think about flying through the valley of the shadow of death. She had no excuse like that. Quickly, she added, "I didn't want you to leave to begin with. I lost my temper, that's all. Believe me, I'm sorry."

"You don't have anything to be sorry about," he said, which didn't come within miles of being true. Had he tried to kiss her then, she would have let him. She might have let him do more than that, too, which she hadn't come close to doing in all the years since Tom's tank brewed up.

He didn't, though. He only touched the patent-leather brim of his cap in that way he had, nodded, and walked back out into the quiet night. The door closed. He was gone. Daisy stared at the place where he'd been, then at the roses in her arms. They were sweet. She could smell them through the clouds of tobacco smoke.

She took them upstairs, to the rooms where she'd never invited any of the men who drank at the Owl and Unicorn. If she left them down in the pub, everybody would wonder who'd given them to her and what she'd done to make him give them to her. Or rather, they wouldn't wonder what she'd done. They'd be sure. What else could she have done?

And then they'd start talking. Somebody would start lying. And her reputation would wind up as flat as the center of Norwich.

That wouldn't happen now, anyway. Out of sight, out of mind. A lot of the flyers might well have been out of their minds. Considering what they did to earn what their countries paid them, who could blame them?

Daisy'd seen only the outskirts of Norwich before the soldiers chased her home. She was no saint even if she didn't sleep with pilots. She wanted revenge for the city close to home. The men flying out of Sculthorpe were the ones who gave it to her. Good for them, too!

In the meantime, she still had the mugs to deal with. She set about that, then cleaned out the toilets. Afterwards, she scrubbed her hands with the strongest soap and the hottest water she could stand. They still felt filthy afterwards. They always felt that way after the toilets, no matter how clean she got them. She knew it was in her mind. Knowing didn't help her change.

At last, she went upstairs again. Her nose twitched—the roses perfumed her rooms. She smiled. Bruce McNulty knew how to do an apology up brown: no doubt of that. How much that meant, what she ought to do about it . . . She'd worry about such things some other time. She set the alarm clock, snuggled under the covers, and slept.

Whenever a motorcar came to the collective farm, Ihor Shevchenko worried. Motorcars meant the authorities. The authorities meant trouble. Ihor's ancestors—serfs for generations uncounted—would have understood exactly how he felt. The symbols that panicked them might have been different from that black Gaz, but the panic would have been the same.

Two men got out and clumped toward the dining hall. It was early in the morning. People were still spooning up kasha, drinking glasses of tea, and smoking their first cigarettes. Like Ihor, the rest of the *kolkhozniks* eyed one another in apprehension when the badly tuned engine stopped so close by.

As soon as Ihor saw the men, he knew they had to belong to the MGB. The Chekists didn't just mean trouble. They meant disaster for whomever their gaze fell upon. These fellows wore gray suits that fit their lumpy bodies none too well. One had a red tie, the other a black. Fedoras sat at a challenging angle on their bullet heads.

They eyed the *kolkhozniks* in the dining hall the way Ihor would have eyed a chicken he was about to take to the chopping block. "We're here to bring two men into the service of the glorious, ever-victorious Red Army of the Soviet Union," the one with the red tie announced. He spoke Russian, of course. To expect a Chekist, even a Chekist born in Kiev, to use Ukrainian would have been to expect the sun to rise in the west. He figured the nervous people in front of him would be able to understand . . . and he was right. Nodding to his partner, he said, "Read the names, Vanya."

"I'll do it," the one with the black tie—Vanya—said. He fumbled in an inside pocket that held the paper with those names. The fumbling showed he had a shoulder holster, though the bulge under his left arm, and under his boss', had already warned of that. He unfolded the paper. "First name is Gavrysh, Bogdan Stepanovich." In his mouth, too, Ukrainian *h*'s turned to Russian *g*'s.

Bohdan stared in horror. He always made noises that marked him as a patriotic man. He'd fought against the Nazis, and must have thought the government would keep leaving him alone this time around.

"Come on," said the MGB man with the red tie—the one who wasn't Vanya. "Do you serve the Soviet Union or don't you?"

"I serve the Soviet Union!" Bohdan choked out. Any other answer would have sent him to the gulags instead of the Red Army, or maybe into the Red Army after a beating that should have earned him a medical exemption.

His wife put her head down and covered her face with her hands. Elizaveta was shocked, and well she might be. Ihor guessed it wouldn't be more than a couple of weeks before she decided she was at least as well off without him. Ihor didn't *know* Bohdan was as big a gasbag in private as in public, but it sure seemed likely to him.

Miserably, the *kolkhoznik* got up and walked over to the two MGB men. The one with the red tie nodded to Vanya. "The other whore, and then we'll be on our way." He sounded as if getting out of here was his fondest wish. He also sounded like a *zek,* dropping *mat'* into his talk without noticing he was doing it.

"The other one. Right." Vanya peered down at the paper again. "Shevchenko, Igor Semyonovich."

Anya shrieked, then clapped both hands to her mouth. Ihor felt as if someone had slapped him in the face with a meter-long salmon. "You can't do that!" he said automatically.

*Tovarishch* Red Tie glowered at him. With the Chekist's ugly, badly shaved mug, it was a good glower. "No, huh?" he growled. His voice wasn't deep enough for a truly scary growl, but he did his best with what he had. "You want to find out what we can do and what we can't, prick?"

"But . . . But . . . But . . ." Ihor unstuck himself. He got to his feet, stepped away from the table—and from his wife—and pulled up his trouser leg to show his scars. "One of your people was here not too long ago. He looked at the leg, and he said the wound was too bad for the Army to take me back."

"Well, I'm here now, and I'm telling you something fucking else," the MGB man said. "Get over here with What's-his-face if you know what's good for you. You want to get cute, we'll teach you more about cute than you ever wanted to find out."

They would, too. And they'd enjoy themselves while they were doing it. Nobody here would lift a finger to save him. If the collective farm rebelled, the Chekists would take a couple of T-34s out of storage—maybe not even the new ones, but the originals with the two-man turret and the smaller gun—and level the place to the ground. They'd shoot the men right away. They'd have their fun with the women, then shoot them, too. All the *kolkhozniks* knew as much. Ihor could see the sick certainty in their eyes. He was sure they could also see it in his.

He limped over to the Chekists. "Cut the playacting, cunt-face," the one with the red tie said. "Won't do you no good."

"It isn't playacting. It's how I walk. But . . ." Ihor drew

himself to stiff attention. It wasn't as if he'd forgotten how. "I serve the Soviet Union!" *As well as I can,* he added, but only to himself.

"Let's go," Red Tie said. Go they did. Ihor looked back over his shoulder once, but only once. Seeing Anya wailing like that made him feel worse, not better.

He and Bohdan got into the Gaz's back seat. Vanya slammed the door closed behind them. That was when Ihor discovered the rear doors had no latches on the inside. He also discovered that a grill of steel mesh separated the passengers in the back seat from the ones up front.

Vanya drove. *Tovarishch* Red Tie—Ihor still didn't know his name—sat on the passenger side and took it easy. "We drop off these dingleberries, then head out to the next worthless fucking dump," he said.

"That's about the size of it," Vanya agreed. "Shitty goddamn job, but somebody's gotta do it."

"Hey, we serve the Soviet Union, too," the other Chekist said. "How are we gonna whip the imperialists without soldiers, huh? Gotta find 'em somewhere. These cunts ain't much, but they're better'n nothin'."

They drove down to Vasilkov, south of Kiev. It had been a small, sleepy town. Now it was bustling: it had taken over many of the functions Kiev had performed till it was visited by hell on earth. The place put Ihor in mind of a four-year-old in a two-year-old's clothes—it was too big for its britches.

The Gaz stopped in front of a Red Army recruiting station. "We'll take you inside," Red Tie told Ihor and Bohdan. "Don't want anything getting fucked up, the way it could if we just leave you on the sidewalk." *Don't want you bugging out*—Ihor had no trouble reading between the lines.

A sergeant with a patch where his left eye should have been and scars all over that side of his face waved to the MGB men as if they were old friends. They probably were. "Well, what kind of ravens' meat have you got for me this time?" he called.

"Ravens' meat? These are veterans! Good, solid men." Red Tie sounded insulted.

"They're veterans, are they?" The sergeant's glower put the Chekist's to shame, but he had unfair advantages in frightfulness. "You pussies fought the Hitlerites?"

"Yes, Comrade Sergeant," Ihor and Bohdan said together.

"Then we don't even have to waste time with the oath. You

swore it the last time, and it still holds." The cyclops sergeant jabbed a thumb at a doorway behind him. "Go through there. They'll do your paperwork and kit you out. This time tomorrow, you'll be on a train heading west. Something to look forward to, hey?"

Ihor looked forward only to going home to Anya. All he wanted to do was stay alive. Now if only the state cared a kopek for what he wanted!

When Aaron Finch came to the door, Ruth opened it with the oddest expression on her face. After he kissed her, he asked, "Okay, what's Leon gone and done?" That was the likeliest thing he could think of to make her wear such a bemused look.

"Leon didn't do anything," Ruth said. As if to contradict her, Aaron got attacked by a toddling tornado in a cowboy outfit. Leon hadn't seen him all day. When you'd just turned two, that was a decent chunk of your lifespan.

Once the tickling and rough-housing and other greetings were out of the way, Aaron asked, "*Nu?* What *is* going on then?" He was positive something had to be.

By way of reply, his wife took an envelope out of a cut-glass bowl on a little table near the door and handed it to him. "This is for you," she said.

"Oh," he said: a little breath of a word. His was not the sort of household that got a letter from the White House, a letter whose envelope was embossed with the Presidential seal, every day. He eyed it in mock alarm. "They must be drafting me."

Ruth poked him in the ribs. He wriggled to make her happy, even though he wasn't ticklish. "Open it, you—you *bulvan,* you," she said.

*"Bulvan!"* Leon said happily. He collected new words the way FDR had collected stamps. He had no idea that one was Yiddish, not English. He didn't know the difference, or care. He didn't know it meant *ox* or *jerk.* He just liked the sound of it.

Open it Aaron did: carefully, so he could keep the envelope for a souvenir along with whatever it held. The stationery had the Presidential emblem at the top of the sheet, too.

"Read!" Ruth said, as if she were Leon demanding a story. Aaron read: "'Dear Mr. Finch: It is with great pleasure that I congratulate you for the brave action you took in capturing the Soviet aviator who had bailed out of his bomber after attacking Los Angeles. What you did showed courage, quick wits, and patriotism. Americans can and should take you for an example. Your country owes you a debt of gratitude.'"

It wasn't one of those printed letters made to look as if they were typewritten, with a machine signature likewise impersonating the real McCoy. He could feel the way the typewriter's strokes indented the paper in the back. The President's signature, sloppy and smeary, was also the genuine article. The typed-by/author line at the bottom left read rc/HST.

Ruth stared at the letter. "Wow!" she said. "That's something! Well, so are you." She kissed him.

He wagged a finger at her. "Don't tell Roxane about it. She'll think I'm selling out the workers again."

"She's not that bad," Ruth said.

"Like heck she's not," Aaron replied. "But if you hadn't gone to Marvin's with her that one afternoon, we never would've run into each other. I'll cut her some slack on account of that."

"I guess we wouldn't," Ruth said. "I hadn't thought of it that way."

"There ought to be stories where some little thing happens differently and everything that comes afterwards gets changed from the way it really was," Aaron said thoughtfully. "They might be fun, make you think a little while you're reading. You know, like if the South won the Civil War."

"Or if the Nazis won World War II." Ruth showed she got what he was talking about.

He shook his head anyway. "Nobody's ever gonna want to read about that, not in a million years. What else could a story like that be about except them killing everybody they didn't like—everybody who wasn't German, I mean?"

His father and mother had come to America from a little Romanian town. After the war, his older brother up in Oregon (who had lived through the bomb that fell on Portland) had got a couple of letters from a relative on their mother's side. He'd sent money once. Then the Iron Curtain thudded down, and letters stopped getting through.

Ruth's family sprang from a village right on the border between Byelorussia and the Ukraine. No one on this side of the Atlantic had heard a word from the ones who didn't emigrate, not after Hitler invaded the USSR. Those people had to be dead now.

He didn't want to think about things like that, especially not when he was holding a letter from Harry Truman. Evidently, Ruth didn't want to think about things like that, either, because she pointed at the letter and said, "You ought to frame it and hang it in the living room. The envelope, too."

"Maybe I will," he answered. He was handy with tools; he could make the frame and cut the glass himself. It would be cheap. That notion led to another, one which made him chuckle.

"What's so funny?" his wife asked.

"I was just thinking about Roxane and Howard again. They'll be thrilled when they come over and see it, won't they?"

"They probably will. They *aren't* that bad, Aaron. They want America to be better, that's all."

"Huh." Aaron had heard Marvin say the same thing. Saying it, though, didn't necessarily make it so. But Aaron didn't push it to a quarrel. Fighting with your wife struck him as a losing proposition. To Marvin, it was something more like sport, though Aaron didn't believe for a minute that poor Sarah felt the same way. Instead of going on about Roxane and Howard Bauman, Aaron asked, "What smells good?"

"Short ribs," Ruth answered. "They should be ready any minute. I've got 'em stewing with potatoes and carrots and onions and mushrooms."

"Sounds wonderful," Aaron said. One of the reasons it sounded wonderful was that it meant some short ribs had made it to the store. They'd eaten a lot of spaghetti with tomato sauce and macaroni and cheese lately. You didn't need refrigerated railroad cars to ship that kind of stuff into town. For meat, you did.

He splashed Tabasco sauce on his short ribs. Ruth eyed him, but didn't say anything about it. He splashed Tabasco or horseradish on everything this side of oranges and lemon-meringue pie. He poured hot sauce onto eggs. When he drank beer from a glass and not from the bottle or can, he sprinkled salt into it. Leon loved that because of the way it made the bubbles rise so spectacularly. Like Tabasco, the salt added flavor. He hadn't had his taste buds shot off in the war, but all those packs of cigarettes had scorched them into submission.

After supper, Ruth washed and he dried. As she used steel wool on the aluminum pot the ribs had stewed in, she remarked, "I wonder how you got that letter."

"Beats me," Aaron said. "It's pretty nice, though, isn't it?"

"I mean," Ruth went on as if he hadn't spoken, "it was in the local news and everything, but how did it get all the way back to Washington?"

"Well, Truman *did* come out here to inspect the damage, and—" Aaron broke off. He snapped his fingers as an answer glowed like a shooting star inside his head.

"What?" his wife asked.

"I bet Herschel fixed it," Aaron said. "He gives the Democrats money all the time. I know he's met Truman. And his business has been rotten since the bombs fell. So maybe he thought this would make me feel good even if it didn't put any money in my pocket."

"If he did, he was right," Ruth said.

"Yeah. I know." Aaron smiled cynically. "Roxane would say he was just tricking me so I'd go on working for Blue Front without that extra money. She'd be right, too, I guess. But whether she is or whether she ain't, I'm still gonna frame that letter!"

"Down below five hundred meters, Comrade Pilot," Vladimir Zorin said from the Tu-4's right-hand seat.

"Thanks. I know. *Bozhemoi,* but I hate night landings!" Boris Gribkov was keeping an eye on the altimeter, too. At the same time, he was peering out through the bomber's crappy Plexiglas windshield, looking for the landing lights that would let him put the big plane down.

They wouldn't be much—he knew that. He'd be landing on a stretch of *Autobahn* northeast of Munich. The Bavarian city lay in Red Army hands. He was still nervous, not only about the makeshift runway but also about the chance of American marauders. Deliberately, he made himself forget about those. If they jumped him now, he was dead. It was that simple. So he didn't need to worry about them.

From the bombardier's position, which had the best view in the plane, Alexander Lavrov called, "I see them, Comrade Pilot! Almost dead ahead—a cunt-hair's worth to starboard."

"Good job, Sasha! I see 'em, too—now." The lights were provided by a bunch of soldiers shining flashlights up into the air. It wouldn't have worked on a cloudy night, but it did here. Even as things were, the lights seemed mighty faint to Boris. Well, it wasn't as if they wanted their presence so far forward advertised—just the opposite, in fact.

"I'm going to land it," he told Zorin, and then turned the intercom to the all-hands setting. "Crew, strap in and prepare for landing!"

He'd already lowered the flaps to slow the hulking airplane. While he changed course ever so slightly, he watched the altimeter, the airspeed indicator, and—as always—the engine temperatures. As he did on takeoffs, he opened the engine cowlings that let heat escape but spoiled the bomber's aerodynamics.

*Bump!* He was down, more smoothly than he'd expected. He hit the brakes hard, steering as straight as he could. The Tu-4 needed more than two and a half kilometers of runway to take off fully laden, but a good bit less than that to land with tanks close to dry.

When he came to a stop, a man with a flashlight guided him forward and then off the edge of the paved highway to a waiting revetment with steel mesh on the ground to keep the plane from sinking in. "You did that just right," Zorin said admiringly.

"*Spasibo,* Volodya," Boris answered. "If they're smart, they'll have fixed several, depending on where we landed and how far we had to taxi." He chuckled dryly. "I wouldn't want to have to back her up."

"Well," the copilot said, "no."

They got out as soon as the props stopped spinning. Groundcrew men were already draping the Tu-4 with camouflage netting. They'd be here only a day or two. No one wanted to give the Americans any excuse to visit.

"Welcome! Welcome!" That well-educated, self-satisfied voice had to belong to a senior officer. Sure enough, the man who owned it went on, "I'm Colonel Madinov. I run this madhouse. We're going to give the decadent imperialists a kick in the balls they'll never forget."

"We serve the Soviet Union, Comrade Colonel," Gribkov said. He couldn't see Leonid Tsederbaum's eyes on him; the navigator stood several meters to the rear. He felt them all the same.

"Well, come on. We'll get you fed and we'll get you settled for now," Madinov said. "When the sun comes up, we'll review what you're going to do to Paris."

Tsederbaum coughed softly, as if one of the little bushes growing by the side of the *Autobahn* bothered him. Gribkov wasn't happy, either. He didn't want to tear the heart out of a world-famous city. But that hadn't stopped the Americans who hit Moscow and Leningrad and Kiev. It also wouldn't stop him. And he didn't believe it would stop his navigator.

After shchi and sausages, the Tu-4 crew met Colonel Madinov in what had been a Catholic church. Blackout curtains shielded windows and doorway. Kerosene lamps gave enough light to use. With Madinov was a very pink young man in Soviet flying togs. "This is Klement Gottwald," Madinov said. "He speaks Russian with an accent and English almost without one. He's trained up on the B-29's radio. He'll take your man's seat there on the attack run."

Leonid Tsederbaum said something in German—or maybe it was Yiddish. Gottwald looked surprised, then smiled. In that accented Russian the colonel had mentioned, he said, "I serve the Soviet Union! I do, and I was born a Sudeten German. That's funny, if you like." Since the Germans in the Sudetenland had given Hitler his excuse to swallow Czechoslovakia, it was at least curious to find one of them helping the USSR along.

Andrei Aksakov, the regular radioman, spoke excellent Russian but no English—Boris wasn't sure about German. If he was disappointed to get bumped from this mission, he didn't show it.

"Comrade Colonel, we'll also need new American IFF codes, if you have them," Vladimir Zorin said. He didn't add *This will be suicidal without them,* but he might as well have.

Madinov nodded. "A technician is entering them into your set right now."

"From what they told us before we flew here, sir, this will be a low-level mission," Gribkov said. "We won't have the long parachute delay till the bomb goes off. How do we escape before the blast knocks us down?"

"It will still have a parachute, of course," Madinov said, and Boris nodded back. The colonel went on, "There will be a thirty-second wait once it touches down. That will buy you several kilometers."

Boris thought about it. Could anyone in Paris disarm the

bomb in half a minute, even if he started trying right away? It seemed unlikely. "Fair enough, Comrade Colonel," the pilot said.

"I don't like this myself, but we have to do it," Madinov said. "Paris is as big a transportation hub for France as Moscow is for us. Smashing it will keep the Americans from resupplying their forces farther east."

"Yes, sir," Boris said. The colonel was taking a chance to tell the bomber crew he didn't care for his orders. His courage deserved respect.

Madinov pointed to a couple of bottles of vodka that sat on the altar instead of sacramental wine. "We'll drink to the success you'll have tomorrow." Drink they did. Everyone had a good knock; nobody got enough to get smashed.

Boris and his crewmen devoted the next day to checking the Tu-4 from nose to tail, making as sure as they could that it was ready to do its part. "We'll paint another city on the nose." Leonid Tsederbaum sounded almost gay at the prospect.

That he was, Boris didn't believe for a minute. "Right," he said tightly. He didn't like this, either. But what could you do?

Part of the plan involved jamming enemy radio and radar, starting well before the bomber (and how many others with it, from different stretches of highway?) took off. That might help. It might not. The Soviet techs had been doing it on and off for a week, to confuse the Americans and French.

After dark, armorers loaded the A-bomb into the Tu-4. They were not quite seven hundred kilometers from Paris: between an hour and an hour and a half, plus the same time back. A short mission, as these things went. Usually, they had to sweat out getting shot down for most of a day.

A track made from more steel mesh led them back to the *Autobahn,* from which they'd take off. The bomb was heavy, but the fuel load was pretty light. They got airborne more easily than they had, say, on the way to Bordeaux.

As soon as they crossed the front, the IFF claimed they were a B-29 on the way home. Gottwald spoke in whistling English once, then switched to Russian to use the intercom: "So much static, we could hardly understand each other. That's good. It helps."

Tsederbaum also spoke over the intercom: "Hitler wanted Paris burning, too. He didn't get his wish. We will."

*I don't like the way he said that,* Boris thought. Who would like getting compared to the Nazi *Führer*?

After the one challenge, no Yank or Frenchman wondered about the Tu-4 or what it was doing. The short flight went as smoothly as a training run. Guided by radar, Lavrov dropped the bomb near the Arc de Triomphe.

As soon as it was gone, Boris pushed the throttles to the red line. Even so, the flash almost blinded him and the blast wave nearly swatted him from the sky. A mushroom cloud, full of fire and lightning, mounted to the stratosphere. Behind the bomber, Paris burned.

Read on for an excerpt from

# FALLOUT
## THE HOT WAR

# By Harry Turtledove

Published by Del Rey

**1**

IT WAS A BRIGHT, warm, sticky day in Washington, D.C. Summer wasn't here yet, but it was less than two weeks away. President Harry Truman turned his swivel chair away from the desk in the Oval Office. For the moment, all the urgent papers demanding his attention could damn well shut up and wait. The green of the White House lawn seemed far more appealing.

Three or four robins hopped across the neatly mown grass. Every so often, one would pause and cock its head to one side, as if listening. Maybe the birds were doing just that. Pretty soon, one of them pecked at something. It straightened with a fat earthworm wrapped around its beak. The worm didn't want to get eaten. It wiggled and clung. The robin swallowed it anyway, then went back to hunting.

"Go get 'em, boy," Truman said softly. "Maybe you'll catch Joe McCarthy next. I can hope, anyhow."

The robins didn't know when they were well off. Here in Washington, they didn't need to worry—too much—about getting blown to hell and gone by an atom bomb. Lord only knew how many robins the Russians had just incinerated in Paris.

Of course, robins in Europe weren't the same birds as the ones here. Truman had seen that as an artillery officer in the First World War and then again when he met with Stalin and Attlee at Potsdam, outside of Berlin. Robins over there were smaller than the American ones, and had redder breasts. He supposed the local ones had got their name by reminding colonists of the birds back home.

But, when you got right down do it, what the French robins

looked like didn't matter. The A-bomb didn't care. It blew them up any which way. It blew up a hell of a lot of French people, too.

When the telephone rang, Truman spun the chair back toward his desk. He picked up the handset. "Yes?"

"Mr. President . . ." Rose Conway, his private secretary, needed a moment before she could go on: "Mr. President, I have a call for you from Charles de Gaulle."

"Jumping Jehosaphat!" Truman said, and meant it most sincerely. He couldn't stand de Gaulle, and was sure it was mutual. At the end of the last war, French and American troops had almost started shooting at each other when the French tried to occupy northwestern Italy. De Gaulle had been running France then, and Truman had cut off American aid to him.

These days, de Gaulle was out of French politics—or he had been. *Damn shame,* Truman thought unkindly. If he'd been in politics, he'd likely have been in Paris, and the bomb could have fried him along with all the poor, harmless little robins.

Here he was, though, unfried and on the telephone. And since he was . . . "Go ahead and put him through, Rose. I'd better find out what he's got to say."

"Yes, Mr. President. One moment," she said. Truman heard some clicks and pops. Then Rose Conway told someone, "The President is on the line, sir."

"Thank you." Charles de Gaulle spoke fluent if nasal English. But he sounded as if he were calling from the Cave of the Winds. The connection was terrible. Well, most of France's phone service would have been centered in or routed through Paris. De Gaulle might have been lucky to get through at all. The Frenchman said, "Are you there, President Truman?"

"I am, General, yes," Truman answered. "Where exactly are you, sir?"

"I am in Colombey-les-Deux-Eglises, about two hundred kilometers southeast of martyred Paris." Or maybe de Gaulle said *murdered Paris.* Both were true enough—all too true, in fact.

Two hundred kilometers was just over a hundred twenty miles. Truman remembered that from his days as a battery commander. He'd hardly had to worry about the metric system since. "Glad to hear you're safe," he said, thinking what a liar politics had turned him into.

"I am safe, yes, but my beloved country has had the heart torn out of her." De Gaulle seemed matter-of-fact, which made what he said all the more melodramatic.

"That is tragic, General, but it's not as if America hasn't taken plenty of hard knocks, too," Truman said.

"Seattle. Denver. *Hollywood.* Such places." Charles de Gaulle's scorn was palpable. "This is *Paris,* Mr. President!"

In lieu of *Screw you, buddy, and the horse you rode in on,* which was the first thing that sprang to mind, Truman said, "Well, the United States is hitting the goddamn Russians harder than they're hitting the Free World."

"All the Russian hovels added together do not approach equaling Paris." De Gaulle's contempt was plenty big enough to enfold the USSR as well as the USA.

Instead of calling him on it, Truman tried a different tack: "Why exactly are *you* calling me, General? You haven't been part of the French government for five years now. Or are you again?"

"In a manner of speaking, I am, yes," de Gaulle replied. "You will understand that the explosion eliminated large portions of the country's administration. Certain individuals have approached me to head a Committee of National Salvation. I could not refuse *la belle France* in her hour of need, and so I have assumed that position for the purpose of restoring order."

"I . . . see," Truman said slowly. It made a certain amount of sense. De Gaulle was a national hero for leading the Free French during the war and for putting France back on her feet once England and the USA chased the Nazis out of the country (with, yes, some help from those Free French).

But both Churchill and FDR had despised him (by all accounts, that was mutual). Harry Truman didn't agree with all of Roosevelt's opinions, but about de Gaulle he thought his predecessor had got it spot on. He hadn't been a bit sorry when the tall, proud, touchy Frenchman left politics for his little village in the middle of nowhere to write his memoirs.

If de Gaulle was back, though, Truman would have to deal with him. The Red Army wasn't far from the French border. In spite of everything America and Britain (and the French, and the West Germans) could do, it was getting closer by the day. If de Gaulle cut his own deal with Stalin, a free Western

Europe would be just a memory, even if American A-bombs flattened most of the Soviet Union.

And so he needed to keep the new boss of this French committee at least partway happy. De Gaulle understood he needed to do that, of course, understood it and exploited it. Trying to hide a sigh, Truman asked, "What do you need from the United States, General? Whatever it is, if we can get it to you, it's yours."

"For this I thank you, Mr. President. I have always known how generous a people Americans are." De Gaulle could be gracious when he felt like it. The one drawback to that was, he didn't feel like it very often. "Medical supplies of all sorts are urgently needed, naturally. And if you have experts on the effects of what you call fallout and how to mitigate those effects, that, too, would be of great value to us."

"I'll see what I can do," Truman promised. Both sides had fused most of their A-bombs to burst high in the air. That spread destruction more widely and also cut down on the amount of radioactive crud that blew downwind after the blast. But the Paris strike was a low-altitude, hit-and-run raid. The A-bomb had gone off at ground level or very close to it. And now the French would have to clean up the mess . . . if they could.

"Has the fallout reached, uh, Colombey-les-Deux-Eglises?" Truman asked, with a certain amount of pride that he'd remembered the name of the place and brought it out pretty well for a Yank.

"The Geiger counters say it has, yes, but not to any serious degree. This place lies in the direction of the prevailing winds," de Gaulle said. "Closer to Paris, you will understand, the situation is more dire. We have many cases of radiation sickness."

"That's nasty stuff. Horrible stuff. We'll send you doctors who have some experience with it, yes." Truman didn't tell de Gaulle that nothing the doctors tried seemed to do much good. You watched and you waited and you kept people as clean and comfortable as you could, and either they got better or they didn't. But then, de Gaulle might well already know that. Paris wasn't the first French city to have had hellfire visited on it, just the biggest. And the war still showed no signs of ending.

* * *

Boris Gribkov, Vladimir Zorin, and Leonid Tsederbaum joined the queue in front of the field kitchen near Munich. The bomber pilot, copilot, and navigator carried tin mess kits the Red Army men holding this part of what had been West Germany gave them.

Nose twitching, Zorin said, "I smell shchi."

"That'll fill us up," Gribkov said. With shchi, you started with cabbage, as you did with beets for borscht. Then you threw anything else you happened to have into the pot along with it. You let it simmer till it all got done, and then you ate it.

That was how Red Army—and Red Air Force—field kitchens turned it out, anyway, in enormous sheet-metal tureens. No doubt fancy cooks fixed it with more subtlety. Gribkov cared not a kopek for subtlety. Filling his belly was the only thing he worried about.

A Red Army noncom saw his blues and his officer's shoulder boards and started to step out of line. "Go ahead, Comrade," he said.

"No, no, no," Boris answered. "We won't starve to death before we get up there. Keep your place."

"You're the guys who gave it to the froggies, aren't you?" the sergeant said.

"Well, some of them," Gribkov told him. The Tu-4 that he flew had a crew of eleven.

"Good," the noncom said. "You ought to drop a bomb on these German pussies, too. Blast 'em all to the devil so nobody has to worry about 'em any more. You ask me, every one of 'em's still a Nazi under the skin."

"I wouldn't be surprised," Zorin said. Gribkov wouldn't have, either. By everything he'd heard, German troops still fought the Red Army as fanatically as they had when Hitler called the shots.

He glanced over at Leonid Tsederbaum. The *Zhid* looked back, his handsome, swarthy face showing nothing. If anybody hated Germans and Nazis even worse than a Russian, you had to figure a Jew would. But Tsederbaum didn't say anything that would show he did.

As a matter of fact, Tsederbaum hadn't said one whole hell of a lot since he guided the Tu-4 back from the attack on Paris. He'd already made it plain that he didn't like dropping atom bombs on famous, important cities. Boris Gribkov didn't like it worth a damn, either. Liking it had nothing to do with the price of vodka.

Your superior told you to do something. You saluted. You said *I serve the Soviet Union!* And you went out and did it or you died trying. If you screwed it up, your superior gave it to you in the neck. If he didn't, somebody would give it to *him*. How else could anyone run a military? The Germans, the enemy whose example the Russians knew best, had the same kind of rules.

All the same, Boris kept sneaking glances at Tsederbaum as men with mess kits shuffled toward those bubbling, fragrant cauldrons. The navigator had never been one of your talky guys. When he did open his yap, what came out of it was dryly ironic more often than not. But yeah, he'd been even quieter than usual lately.

When Gribkov reached the shchi, the chubby-cheeked corporal with the ladle—who ever heard of a skinny cook?—beamed at him. "Here you go, sir!" he said, and dug deep into the pot for the good stuff at the bottom. He did the same for Zorin and Tsederbaum. Gribkov didn't think he *was* a hero, but he didn't mind getting treated like one.

That sergeant who wanted to bomb the Germans waved the flyers to a commandeered bus bench. Then he and the rest of the Red Army men politely left them alone. They were heroes to the ground-pounders, enough so that Gribkov wished he felt more like a hero to himself.

He dug into the shchi. "Not half bad," he said. "I do wonder what the meat is, though."

"You mean whether it'd neigh or bark or meow?" Zorin chuckled for all the world as if he were joking.

"As long as I don't see the critter it came from, I'm not going to worry about it," Boris said. "I just wonder, that's all."

"Curiosity killed the cat—which is why it's in the shchi." By the way Zorin shoveled in the soup, he didn't worry about it, either.

The crack, though, was more one Gribkov would have expected from Tsederbaum. When he stole another look at the Jew, Tsederbaum caught him doing it. Raising his spoon in mock salute, the navigator said, "The condemned man ate a hearty meal."

Nobody'd condemned them. They'd won medals for bombing America and then making it back to the *rodina*. Boris pulled a small metal flask off his belt. "Here," he said. "I've got some vodka. That's good for whatever's bothering you."

Leonid Tsederbaum's smile called him a Russian, or possibly a small, stupid child. As if humoring such a child, the *Zhid* took a knock. But he said, "There's not enough vodka in the world to fix what ails me."

"How do you know? How much have you drunk?" Zorin asked. Tsederbaum's chuckle was on the dutiful side. Boris Gribkov, who drank himself before passing the flask to Zorin, thought it was a good question. Sometimes if you got smashed out of your skull, whatever you'd been chewing on didn't seem so bad in the light of the morning-after hangover.

In a day or two, the crew would fly the Tu-4 back to the Soviet Union. Chances were they'd pick up another gong for their tunic fronts. And then somebody would tell them what to do next, and they'd do it—or die trying.

They slept on pews in a gutted church. With enough blankets cocooning you, it wasn't so bad. At least you had room to stretch out. At some point in the middle of the night, Tsederbaum got up and headed outside. "Sorry to bother you," he whispered to Gribkov, who sleepily raised his head.

*Heading for the latrine,* Boris thought. He wondered if he ought to do the same. Instead, he yawned and submerged in slumber again.

Then somebody shook him awake. It was predawn twilight. Even in the gray gloom, he could see how pale Vladimir Zorin looked. "What is it?" Gribkov asked. Whatever it was, it wouldn't be good.

But it was worse than he'd dreamt. "That stupid fucking kike!" Zorin sounded furious. "He went and blew his goddamn head off!"

*"Bozhemoi!"* Gribkov untangled himself and scrambled to his feet. "I knew something was eating him, but I never imagined—"

"Who would? Who in his right mind would, I mean?" the copilot said.

Boris pulled on his boots. "Take me to him."

"Come on." Zorin led him out just past the stinking trenches where Soviet fighting men eased themselves. There lay Leonid Abramovich Tsederbaum. He'd put the business end of his Tokarev automatic in his mouth and pulled the trigger. The back of his once-so-clever head was a red, ru-ined mess. Flies had already started buzzing around it.

Going through his pockets, Gribkov found a note. He rec-ognized Tsederbaum's precise script at once. All it said was *Men a hundred years from now will know what I have done. Let them also know I did not do it willingly. Maybe then they will not spit whenever they say my name.*

He showed Zorin the note. Then he fumbled in his own pockets till he found a matchbook. He lit a match and touched it to the edge of the paper. He held it till it scorched his fingers, then dropped it and let it burn itself out. Once it did, he kicked at the ashes till nothing discernible was left.

"Good job," the copilot said. "Now they won't be able to go after his family."

"Right," Gribkov said tightly. The world would never know just why Leonid Tsederbaum had killed himself. Boris wished *he* didn't know. Better not to start thinking about things like that. You only got into trouble when you did. He had to keep flying. He wondered how he'd manage.